Barn Notes

MARINA SKYE

Barn Notes — Backcountry Series Book 1
by Marina Skye

Copyright © 2023 Marina Skye

CHAPTER 1

The Moment the World Stopped Spinning

Marina tucked the wheelbarrow up along the fence and hung the pitchfork on the wall hook. She was making her way back to the front entrance gate when she saw him. This tall, ripped cowboy talking with the stable manager of the nonprofit rescue. Marina didn't want to interrupt their conversation so she removed her gloves and waited behind the gate. Danielle, the stable manager, called her on over to join them.

"This is Marina. She's been a volunteer here for several years. Marina, this is Sawyer. He helps us out with details about the horse breeds and is a generous donor."

"Good morning." He tipped his hat. The look on his face was that of someone whose world had just stopped spinning.

"Good morning, pleasure to meet you." Her eyes shied away.

"Likewise." His eyes remained fixed on her.

"Um, so I have the chores finished. Is there anything else you need from me today, Danielle?"

"No, sweety, but thank you. I appreciate ya."

"No problem."

"Actually, if you have a second to spare, I'd like to ask you something." Sawyer took his hat off and waved at Danielle as she walked back to the barn. He ran his fingers through his light wavy hair, which fell almost to his distinct jawline.

"What can I do for you?" Marina asked.

"So, you volunteer here every day?" He had a charming southern accent.

"No. Just one or two Sundays a month. I try, anyways. Sometimes more, sometimes less." Her accent wasn't as strong as his.

"I'm looking to hire somebody to help out around my stables in the mornings. I'm trying to avoid getting up so early to do morning chores and I've been traveling a little more often than I'm entirely comfortable with. Would you be interested?"

She smiled, "What's it pay?" She asked, although she would accept the offer no matter the pay.

"Whatever you think is fair."

"I think I'll let you decide."

"Deal. How about twenty bucks an hour and you don't have to be there early. Whenever you get there in the mornings is fine by me. I enjoy doing the evening chores myself. Once in a while I have to go out of town on a Saturday. Would you be willing to work the occasional Saturday?"

"Sure. Yeah, absolutely."

"Let me put your number in my phone and I'll text you the address. Then you'll have my number too."

He got her number and shook her hand. "Pleasure. Enjoy the rest of your day." He walked back to his big white truck wearing a smile. He was dressed well too, wearing bootcut jeans and a plaid button up shirt and nice boots with rounded toes.

Her morning had just gone from good to great. She was ecstatic. She loved being around the horses. It was calming and brought her a sense of peace. It was quiet out in the country amongst the fields and the fresh air made her feel alive. Having an actual paying job doing what she loved would be ideal.

She received a text from him as she was leaving the stables. It read, "It was a pleasure meeting you this morning. I look forward to meeting up to show you around. When are you able to start and when could you come out to the stables?"

She was excited to hear from him so quickly. She wrote back, "I can come out today if you're free. I can start tomorrow if that works for you."

"Absolutely. I'll meet you out there shortly. The address is 2300 Foxtrot Lane."

She was one who often looked for subtle clues throughout daily life, messages from the universe telling her she was where she should be when she was meant to be there. Her favorite number was twenty-three and she had a horse figurine as a kid named Foxtrot. He was white with tan speckles and sported a beige mane and tail.

As she pulled up, it was clear Sawyer had gotten there just before her. She walked up to the wooden oak-stained barn, which looked more like a rustic wedding venue, and took in the beautiful modern-yet-country home and the emerald pastures that stretched as far as she could see. There was beautiful landscaping all around the property. It all looked very well kept.

He opened the barn door that faced the drive for her, "Come on in, I'll show ya around."

Dear Lord, he was a good-looking guy...okay, gorgeous actually. If she would have dreamt up the perfect man, he would've been it. If looking up "perfect man" in the dictionary was a thing, his picture would've been right there beside the definition. He had just the right amount of scruff on his face and light brownish-blonde wavy hair sticking out from beneath his hat. How did those jeans fit so perfectly? She didn't usually check guys out like that because she had a boyfriend who she had been with for a long time. Lately their relationship had been quite rocky; he'd just been so distant. Normally, she would've felt guilty for checking out someone else, but for some reason, she didn't this time. She couldn't help it. He took her breath away. She found it almost difficult to swallow when talking to him.

"I don't want to be rude so I'll introduce you to my friends first." He led her to the horses, who were in their stables. "This here is Foxtrot, hence the name of the road. He was my first horse that I bought before I moved here to town from Tennessee. I built the house and the barn then went back up for him. He stayed at my parents' farm until I had this place ready." He bent down to pet his dog, an Australian Shepherd, Collie mix. "This here is Huck,"

"He's beautiful!" She petted Foxtrot's freckled face while thinking he looks exactly like her figurine, then petted Huck.

"This is Legend. He's my calm guy. More of a trail riding horse."

"That's my kind of pace," Marina chuckled, admiring the shiny brown coat and black mane. He was a dark dun.

"Yeah? You're not a runner?"

"No. Actually, I'm comfortable around and on a horse until they start running. I don't know, I guess I don't feel in control or that I'd be able to hang on well enough."

"We might have to work together on that."

"I'd be open to learning for sure."

"This young lady is Athena. She's a palomino Appaloosa. She thinks she's in charge around here. This gray and black guy down here is Smokie. He isn't mine; I'm just boarding him for a buddy while he's out of town for work for a few weeks. Training him too."

"They're all beautiful. You have great taste."

"Thanks. I like to think so."

He walked her through the barn and it was beautiful. There was a cabinet that looked to be hand-built, which held supplies such as fly spray, mane detangler, and brushes. The bridles and lead ropes were hung on the wall in an organized fashion just inside the back door and the saddles all rested on stands. The counter along the wall opposite the stalls was also hand-built and clean, not dusty or dirty like you'd think a barn would be. There was also a hand-built table with chairs in the corner and a separate large stall for hay and feed at the end of the barn.

Everything was organized, but not as if he were obsessive-compulsive. It didn't seem as though a busy guy would have time to take such meticulous care of a horse barn. He showed her where to put them out to pasture, where to put out the hay in the mornings, where the wheelbarrow and pitchforks were, and all the other essentials like the hose for filling the water troughs.

"If you get real muddy, there's an outdoor shower out on this end of the barn. Its sides are enclosed and on a cement pad. Technically, it's for the horses but I use it too."

"Sounds good. So, what do you do for work, if you don't mind me asking? I didn't see farming equipment or anything."

"Yeah, I'm actually not a farmer. I specialize in horse breeding, I guess you could say. I own a company that organizes horse breeding for other companies and farms and such. I determine horse breeds as well, which is important for registering a horse and for bloodline tracing. Pedigree Analyst, I guess is the technical term. I do train horses for people too."

"That's interesting. Sounds like a fun job. I can see why you'd travel a lot and work some Saturdays."

"I actually need to work with Smokie a bit while he's here, so maybe you can be a spectator."

"Yeah, I'd love that." She raked her hair out of her face with her finger tips.

"Well, that's pretty much it. There's really nothing to it. Pretty much the same stuff you do out at the rescue center. Oh, um, if you have time in the mornings, could you just keep an eye out for any fence issues? There's a four-wheeler parked outside by the shower you can use. There's always gas in it. Or you can walk it...whatever you wanna do. If you don't get to it, I can do it that evening. Just leave me a note or shoot me a text. The pasture is separated into three because of having to separate the genders and the horses I'm training sometimes, but each is only 2 acres."

"Sure, I can do that, no problem. How many acres are here total?"

"Let's see, each pasture is right close to two, then the barn and house make up another three or four. So, I guess ten or close to it. That wooded trail behind the house there separates another twenty acres that I own but it's field and wooded with muddy four-wheeler trails. It's fun. I'll have to take ya out there sometime."

"That does sound fun. Okay, well, I'll be here in the morning. Probably around seven or eight-ish if that's okay?"

"Yeah, absolutely. I usually leave for work shortly before eight. I'm going to enjoy not having to be up before six though, not gonna lie."

"I don't blame you there," she laughed. "Although, not to be nosey, but I'm surprised you don't work from home."

"Sometimes I do, especially if I'm under the weather or need half the day off for something or I just can't pull myself together on a particular morning. But honestly, if I don't leave the house, I'll find too much else to do around here. I wouldn't get much work accomplished. I prefer to work with my hands so I end up building stuff. I own the business but I have a bookkeeper who doubles as my assistant because I'm not good with financial business-related stuff. So, he and I set up shop in a small rental space next to the flower shop in town. There's a coffee shop across the street. It's perfect."

"That does sound perfect. I love the little bakery in town. They have the best donuts. You seem to have a perfect set-up here. This place is great, I think I'm going to really like it here. I appreciate the opportunity."

"Oh, I appreciate the help! I think this is going to work out great for both you and I."

"Most likely. Well, if I don't see you in the morning, I hope you have a wonderful day. Thanks for showing me the ropes." She shook his hand then headed to her car as he walked to the house. On her way home, she called her best friend. She was too excited to not tell her about the new job but also about Sawyer.

"Hey, what's up?" Becka, Marina's best friend, answered.

"I was just shown around at my new job. I have to say, I am *so* excited."

"Wait, new job? Really? What kind of job?" Becka sounded excited for her.

"Barn chores. I mean, I have fun doing them at the rescue and this guy was there today and asked me if I wanted to come work for him at his stables."

"Awesome! You'll love that."

"What I'm going to love even more is that this guy is smoking hot. I mean like...so hot!"

"Oooh, that's even more awesome! I wanna see. You have a pic?"

"Unfortunately, no. I'll get one someday but he doesn't expect to be there whenever I am. Total bummer."

"Right! Well, I can't wait to see this dude. Maybe I'll have to join you for chores some morning."

"That would be fun! You can do that anytime. The stables are beautiful and the horses are too. He's going to pay better than my part-time job that I hate so I'll probably quit that altogether, even though it's only for a couple hours each morning during the week. I might have to work a Saturday morning here and there but I'm okay with that."

"Yeah, that definitely sounds like a good gig."

"It'll get me out of the house more too. That's never a bad thing."

"True. More time away from that boyfriend of yours would be a good thing."

"Exactly. Well, I'm home now and have my own house chores to do so I'll talk to you later. I start the new job tomorrow. I'll let you know how it goes."

"Yes, please do! Later, girl."

CHAPTER 2

Smokie's Lesson

Marina's first day on the job was a warm, muggy summer Monday morning. Sawyer had already left for work by the time she entered the stables. The horses perked up their ears and began to fuss, hungry. She greeted each one of them with a forehead pet.

She started the coffee; he leaves a coffee pot on the counter in the barn and stores coffee grounds in a handmade bread box. The coffee pot played country music as it brewed. She found it amusing. There was a small box of fresh donuts from her favorite donut shop and a note folded out of horse stationery that stood on top of the box. It read "Thank you again for taking care of my hooved furballs, I appreciate you. Hope you have a wonderful day. Call if you need anything."

She smiled reading the note. *He seems like a sweet guy.*

She wasn't naïve though; she'd thought that about other people in her life too and ended up disappointed. She reminded herself to not get her hopes up too high. After all, why on Earth was this guy single? *Was* he single? It didn't matter anyways because she was in a relationship, however complicated and unhappy it might be.

There was also an envelope with cash. It read "Today's pay."

She left it there for the time being, poured some coffee and quickly ate a donut, then carried on with chores. She led the horses out to pasture and gave them hay, shoveled out the paddock stalls, took the four-wheeler out to check the fence perimeter, and filled the water troughs. She groomed them and put the brush and lead ropes away then documented her hours on the pay envelope and took out only what she was supposed to be paid for the two hours she'd been there. She tucked the rest back into the envelope then poured more coffee and ate the other donut as she shut off the coffee pot and cleaned it out. She left for the day, already looking forward to the next.

Dishes, laundry, lunch, sweeping. The day went by quickly and the entire time she couldn't help but think of him. She's a taken woman for crying out loud, she shouldn't be thinking of someone else this way. Whether it be lust or love, she didn't need it. Not either one. She already had a man complicating her life.

It had rained during the night and stayed warm so a heavy fog had settled in, the sun trying hard to burn it off as it came up. It was Saturday and Sawyer was out of town, needing Marina to do the chores over the weekend. The note said, "All that cash is yours. Don't be leaving it behind now."

Monday morning, Sawyer's truck was still at the house when Marina got to the barn. The note on the counter read, "I'll be right out." She was confused, but it only took a few minutes for him to come strolling out of the house.

"Good morning." He finished buttoning up his shirt.

"Good morning." She propped the big door open. "What are you doing home?"

"Well, I got ahead over the weekend so I thought I'd stick around for a bit this morning and help you out."

She was thinking he could've just let her know she wasn't needed but she was good with seeing him anyways.

"Okay. Sounds good."

"I'll go ahead and check the fence." He walked over to the four-wheeler, Huck close on his heels.

"Perfect," she said, staring at how well his jeans fit his rear as he sat on the four-wheeler and revved it up. Huck barked excitedly. She didn't let him see that she was staring at him.

She carried on doing the other chores and had them finished by the time he and Huck returned. The two horses she had turned out already ran along the fence as he came tearing up. She was leading Legend out to pasture, so after he parked the four-wheeler, he grabbed a rope to lead Smokie.

"I was thinking I'd work Smokie for a short bit this morning. Wanna help?"

"Yeah, sure!"

"Great." He led Smokie into the round pen. "There are apples and carrots in the barn fridge if you wouldn't mind putting a couple in a bucket. It can be left just outside of the gate." He grabbed a whip off the wall.

"That's for the horse though, right?" she joked. That caught him off guard and he stopped in his tracks and laughed. "Wow, I did not expect that from you."

"I'm sorry, that was completely inappropriate." She laughed but was a little embarrassed.

"Actually, it was hilarious. Don't threaten me with a good time," he laughed.

They both chuckled as she entered the gate and closed it behind her, leaving the bucket outside the gate with Huck.

"I'm assuming you haven't used a whip before...on a horse, anyway..." He hesitated and smiled as she laughed. "You just whip the ground and it makes them run. You want them running in a circle. It teaches them discipline but lets them know who should be in control." He whipped the ground and Smokie started running, "It wears them out a bit too so they're easier to teach when you're on their backs. He's barely green broke so directionality is what we're doing today."

"Gotcha," she replied as he handed her the whip. She whipped it just as he had been but was certain she didn't look half as good doing it as he had.

"You're a natural. Look at you!" He leaned back against the wooden fence, palms on the rails. Smokie exhaled a sigh.

"How long have you been working with him?"

"He's only been here a few days. I've only had him in here once before now. Mainly starting from scratch in case he had any bad habits. Walked him on the lead rope, making him stop when I did, simple stuff like that."

"Have you been training a long time? Horses in general, I mean."

"I think it's been about twelve years now. My dad taught me when I lived in Tennessee still. I'd go to auctions and fairs with him. Dad is an equestrian vet. Well, was; he's retired now. Sort of. He claims to be retired but he won't actually ever retire, I'm sure. He still does freelance sub-contracting work for farmers and stuff. He loves it. He just always wants a foot in the door, ya know?"

"I get it. It's been his life for so long, it has to be hard to change his ways."

"He's still young. I think he'll be fifty-two this year. He gets bored."

"He must have done well to be able to retire so young."

"Yeah, he's done well for himself. He's the one that got me into pedigree stuff. He said, as an equine vet, he encountered *so* many people wanting to know their horse's genetics and get their horses registered. Especially if they were showing or racing them. He said there's money in the Pedigree route and Dad gives the best advice so that's what I do. I love it."

"That's wonderful. It's great that you love what you do. That's more important than the money, I think."

"Well, the way I see it is ya might as well love what ya do or life would be miserable."

"That's true, absolutely."

"Sounds like you're close with your dad. Y'all have a great relationship?"

"We do. I do with both my parents. Mom is a nurse. She'll probably never retire either." He chuckled and joined Marina at the center of the pen. He walked with such swagger. She handed him the whip as Smokie calmed to a trot. He put a hand straight out, signaling to stop, and Smokey did just that. Dust rolled then began to settle as Marina admired the horse's beauty, his black and silver tail relaxed and his stance at ease.

"I think we'll let him have a break for a couple hours. Wanna grab the treats from the bucket for him?"

"Sure." She bent down, grabbing an apple and carrot. When she turned back toward them, Sawyer darted his eyes back to Smokie while petting him. Was her boss just checking her out? Nah! She was wearing cut-off jean shorts but there's no way he'd be checking her out. She gave Smokie the apple and he ate it in about three crunches and his lips reached for the carrot, which she let him have. She tightened the knot at the front of her plaid button-up tank top and petted down Smokie's face then gave his jaw a scratchin' before letting out a sigh.

"If you don't need anything else from me today, I'll get going. I have some errands to run in town."

"Oh, yeah. Yeah, go ahead. Thanks for doing the chores and hanging out."

"Of course, silly, it's my job." She smirked.

"I still appreciate it. The company too." He tipped his hat to her just before she turned away. Smokie started to rear up and nay. Marina turned back around to see Sawyer resting his forehead on Smokie's, shushing him. He stretched out his arms and glided his hands back and forth on Smokie's neck. Smokie calmed immediately. He led Smokie out to pasture as she headed to her car.

She turned back a few more times, just to watch him. She was sure thankful for his genetics. That man wore the rugged modern cowboy thing very well.

CHAPTER 3

Appreciation

S he made her way into town one Saturday morning to run an errand to the bakery for Danielle and, as she went back out to her car, she heard a loud whistle. Her attention was oriented toward the coffee shop across the street. Sawyer waved her over to him and she approached, smiling.

"Care to join me?" He pulled out the patio chair next to him for her to sit.

"I'd love to, actually. Thanks. Let me run inside for a coffee real quick. I love this place."

He walked in with her and paid for her iced vanilla latte with almond milk.

"Oh, Sawyer, no. I got this."

He smiled at her but it was too late, he had already paid. She sat with him outside at the table.

"Thank you for the coffee. You didn't have to do that."

"Yeah, but I wanted to. It's the gentlemanly thing to do." He took a drink of his coffee, steam clouding upon his face.

"It's sweet. I thought chivalry was dead until I met you." She grinned, taking a sip of coffee, the ice sloshing in her plastic cup. "What are you doing over here on a Saturday?"

"I came for a fancy coffee since they make it way better than I can at home." He chuckled as he took a sip. "I actually had to come into work for a bit. Just wanted to get ahead on some stuff. I have an order of hay to put in too. Honestly, I think I was just motivated to get something done today."

"Did you already do the barn chores or do you want me to go do them?"

"That's sweet of you to offer but I did it already. I woke up early, unfortunately, and couldn't get back to sleep, hence the extra coffee. What are you doing over here this way? I saw you went into the bakery but didn't leave with anything. I can never do that."

She laughed. "Ah, yeah, I actually had to place an order for Danielle for tomorrow morning. It's Volunteer Appreciation Day at the rescue center so we're having a gathering after chores."

"Aww, that's nice. You don't really get a day off this week, do you?"

"Well, I mean, today was just an errand, I'm not really working."

"Your errand kind of turned into a casual coffee date. You probably didn't expect that this morning. Hope you didn't have to be somewhere else I'm keeping you from." He took another sip while staring at her, waiting to hear the response he was hoping for.

She cleared her throat after almost choking on her coffee. "I guess it did. I'm completely okay with that. I don't have anywhere I need to be."

"I'm glad you came into town today. We never get to hang out and chat. I'm always gone for work already by the time you come in to do chores."

"Yeah, me too. This is nice," she agreed.

After about another half hour of chatting at Chillax-a-latte Café and getting coffee refills to-go, he walked over to his office and she left to go home.

She prepared a charcuterie platter to take. The event was just supposed to be a few hours and wasn't so much an event as it was an early luncheon. Just a casual gathering for the volunteers as a thank you. Danielle had Marina order a mixed pastry box but Marina wanted to bring the charcuterie platter just to help take pressure off Danielle. Danielle was indecisive about what food to order.

Sunday morning, Marina went to the rescue center for chores. She had put the charcuterie platter in the kitchen fridge to keep it cold until everyone got there. It was quite a drive for Marina, so she stayed after chores and helped Danielle set up tables and dressed them with tablecloths, set out folding chairs, and filled a large cooler with ice. She dumped drinks into the cooler and hung up the "Thank You, Volunteers" banner that Danielle used every year.

"I think that about does it. Looks like we're ready. Thanks for staying to help." Danielle looked up at Marina as Marina climbed down the ladder.

"You know I like to help in any way I can."

As she reached the ground, she saw Sawyer's truck pulling in.

"Well, what on Earth?" Danielle wondered aloud with her hands in her pockets.

"You weren't expecting him?" Marina asked.

"No, but it's sweet that he came by."

Sawyer carried a small giftbag and waved in a huge truck with a flatbed trailer full of hay. The trailer backed in as Sawyer guided it.

Others started pulling into the drive.

"Good morning, ladies." He nodded, walking up to the pavilion.

"Good morning," they greeted, a bit confused.

Marina had an uncontrollable smile on her face. She always did when she laid eyes on him. It was instantaneous. He probably noticed too but it seemed as though he did the same when he saw her. She was just now realizing this. The thought of that only widened her smile.

"What's this I'm seeing, Sawyer? I didn't order hay," Danielle asked.

"Well, I know a guy. He gave me a great deal when I placed my order yesterday and I knew y'all could use some. It's a donation."

"Oh my God. You're just the best, Sawyer. What would we do without you and your generosity?" She gave Sawyer a big hug.

"I'm just glad I can help." He handed her the gift bag and she pulled out a five-hundred-dollar gift card. Poor Danielle started to cry.

"Hey now, this is a party. No crying allowed," he said as she bear-hugged him again. "We all appreciate what you do here. You're a wonderful lady with a big heart and these horses appreciate it too. You can see it in their eyes. Every single one of them."

"This is just too much. I can't believe you did this." Danielle wiped her tears off her cheeks.

"Well, I heard it's Volunteer Appreciation Day but, as the head of this facility, you need to be shown appreciation too. All the volunteers and horses appreciate you so this is from all of us."

He sat a gift bag down on the table next to his hat and proceeded to take out gift cards, handing them out to all the volunteers. They were all so thankful.

Marina handed him a bottled water then sat backwards at the picnic table.

"Thanks." He sat next to her.

"You want help unloading that hay? It's the least I could do after what you just did."

"Nah. I appreciate it but the guys who hauled it here will get it. They've been hired to unload it too."

"That's really awesome of you to do all of this. Thank you for doing what we can't."

"I'm just thankful for what this place does. I don't have the room at my place to do something like this, let alone the knowledge Danielle has. I've known her for years and she works so hard. It kills me to see her struggle with bringing in donations. I saw her social media post about needing hay. Since I got a great deal ordering mine and I was financially able, I wanted to help her out."

"You're an amazing, selfless person. I hope you know that."

"Maybe it's how I was raised but it makes me feel good, helping others."

"That's a great quality to have. Generosity like that makes a person a hero in my eyes." She shyly looked away.

"Thanks, that's very kind of you to say." He smirked and patted her shoulder as others gathered at the picnic table. "Let's eat!"

CHAPTER 4

Equine Fantasy

B ecka answered Marina's call, "Hey, what's up?"
"So, the rescue is having a benefit trail ride and equine
fantasy day. Danielle is gathering volunteers. You interested? You
can hang out with me for the day. Bonus!"

"Yeah, sure! Sounds like fun. This weekend? Text me the
details."

"Yes, this weekend. Sorry for the short notice. I'll text you.
Thanks, I appreciate it."

Marina called a couple more girlfriends who also agreed to
volunteer, for which she was grateful. They needed help saddling
up horses and running the pony rides for the children and the
regular volunteers just weren't enough. Marina was also setting up
a booth for her children's book that she wrote based on the rescue
facility. She told Danielle she would recruit help and the volunteers could be placed wherever help was needed.

The last couple of days that week went by quickly. Sawyer was
out of town through Friday evening so she did the morning and
evening chores, which she didn't mind. She liked helping him out
any way she could and working with the horses was always
satisfying.

Saturday morning was warm and muggy. The girls all met at

the entrance of the local fairgrounds and Danielle had them unloading and setting up tables within minutes. There was a face painting station where Becka would set up, Marina and Raquel's book station and a raffle drawing station, along with a few others. Tents were staked down and the sudden scent of popcorn and funnel cakes filled the air. Game stations, mainly horseshoes and cornhole, were set up as trucks with trailers began pulling into the stables. Marina spotted Sawyer leading Foxtrot out of the trailer and didn't even try to fight the smile that spread across her face.

"Hey, girls!" Marina waved them over to her from the other booths. They gathered under her book tent. "So, I just saw my boss leading one of his horses into the stables."

"Oooh, the hot boss?" Becka asked excitedly.

"Yeah, that's the one." Marina breathed deeply.

"Can't wait to see this guy," Andrea agreed.

"It'll suddenly feel much hotter outside, I can tell you that much. This man makes me melt. I feel like I'm having a solid hot flash whenever I'm around him. I feel flushed every time he speaks to me." Marina fanned her face with one of her books.

"Not sure about your boss, but the guy walking this way looks like he belongs on a stripper stage." Raquel stared beyond Marina.

Curiously Marina turned around to see that it was, indeed, Sawyer approaching. He smiled and tipped his hat at all the ladies standing there gaping at him. He patted Marina on the back and said, "I thought I recognized this beautiful lady over here."

"Hey, Sawyer! I didn't realize you would be here this weekend."

"Yeah, Foxtrot is the unicorn."

"Nice!" Marina laughed a polite, cute laugh. "I heard there's jousting horses too."

"There are. Also, a winged Pegasus." Sawyer pointed over at a black horse with large, realistic feathered wings. "I've always wanted a black Friesian horse named that," he laughed.

"Oh wow! They pulled out all the stops, didn't they?"

"They really did. The kids are going to love this."

"Yeah, they will," she agreed. The other girls just stared at him, looking him up and down then at each other with gaping mouths.

"So what part are you playing for the day?" Marina asked.

"I guess cowboy. I think. I'm just saddling up horses and trading them in and out at the stables when they need breaks." He flipped through a copy of Marina's book that was displayed on the table called *Forever Home*. "This is you! You wrote this?"

"I did. I chose a random pen name but yeah, that's me. Amanda means worthy of love, that's why I chose it."

"These illustrations are great. Very colorful."

"Thank you. I enjoyed creating it. I'm hoping to sell a few copies. I donate a portion of every sale back to the rescue center."

"That's amazing. I'll help you promote."

"Great, thanks!"

"Absolutely." He stared at her a moment and smiled. She paused and realized how rude she had been. "Oh, I'm sorry. These gals are my friends. I'm horrible at introductions, I apologize. This is Becka, Raquel, and Andrea."

"No worries. Nice to meet you, ladies."

"So nice to meet you." Raquel shyly smiled, holding back a squeal.

"Well, I better get Foxtrot over to Rainbow Land. He's hitched for the time being." Sawyer laughed and rolled the sleeves of his plaid button-up shirt, which wasn't buttoned at the top.

"Yeah, stop back over later when you get time." Marina sat in the chair at the table.

"Will do." He waved at all the ladies and walked away.

He got half way back to Foxtrot, who was hitched to a post, before any of the girls spoke. They all just watched him walk til that point.

"OH...MY...GOD!" Becka stood in front of Marina at the table, leaning on it.

"I know, right?"

"Ok, yeah. You're blushing now, but I'm sure I am too. Holy cow, he's smokin' hot!" Raquel was still staring in his direction.

"You are quite the lucky lady." Andrea wiped her face with water from her water bottle, trying to cool down her hot flash.

"I am, huh? Yeah, I *so* am." Marina agreed with a grin, twirling her hair.

Marina sold several books during the festival, which helped raise money for the rescue center. Any station Sawyer was working, raked in quite a profit. Young ladies donated just to be around him, even though his attention remained on Marina, the horses, and the job at hand. The jousting was a big hit and the unicorn drew much attention from the little girls. Adorable photo shoots were available for both events, thanks to Andrea's photography skills. It was a long day in the heat and humidity but the festival was a success.

The booths had been packed up and horses were being loaded in trailers as Sawyer helped Marina pack up and take tents down before she aided in loading Foxtrot.

CHAPTER 5

Four-Wheeling

Sawyer had Marina do chores the following Saturday morning because he had an errand to run. She was finishing up at the barn, turning the last of the horses out to pasture when Sawyer pulled in. He was hauling a trailer with a four-wheeler on it. She hung up the lead rope and headed out to his truck. He stepped up onto the trailer.

"So, is this the errand you had to run?" She tucked her hands into the back pockets of her jeans.

"Yes, ma'am, it is. The dealer finally got it in. I ordered it a couple of weeks ago." He unstrapped it and kicked the blocks out from behind the tires.

"It's nice! It matches your blue Jeep even. I love the lime green accents too."

"Thanks. Yeah, I like that they match. You busy today?"

"No. Whatchya have in mind?"

"I was thinkin' we should take both four-wheelers out on the trail. Just ride around, maybe get a little muddy." He blocked the sun from his eyes with his forearm.

"That sounds fun, sure!" She shrugged a shoulder as if she wasn't screaming with excitement on the inside. "Should we pack a cooler?"

"Yeah, sounds good. There's a small one in the storage area in the barn. It'll fit right on the back of this. Just pack us each a few bottles of water from the fridge. There are electrolyte juices and beer in there too. Pack whatever you want."

"Will do." She went to the barn and packed the cooler while he filled both four-wheelers with gas just outside the barn doors. She strapped the cooler onto the four-wheeler rack and he grabbed his sunglasses from his truck, tossing her the keys to the new four-wheeler.

"Wait. These are to the new one."

He nodded. "Hop on it."

"You sure? I don't mind riding the other one."

"Don't worry, you're not gonna hurt it. Test it out."

"Okay." She hopped on it and started it up. He revved his up and nodded for her to follow him. They headed downline from the pasture, across the field, and onto the wooded trail. The trail was cleared into a two-track, oaks lining both sides. The sun would peek through the live oaks canopied over the trail, Spanish moss hanging from their branches. She hadn't been down the trail before and he noticed she was slowing down. She was taking in the scenery. He stopped and shut his four-wheeler off so she did too.

"Sorry, I got caught up gawking at the trees."

"Don't be sorry. It's my favorite part of the trail. It's beautiful."

"It really is. There's a lot of green moss on the ground and rocks here too. This area stay pretty damp?"

"Yeah. It's pretty shaded so it doesn't dry up well."

"It makes it even more beautiful."

"I love that you're a nature person."

"Yeah? Why?"

"I just do. It means you appreciate the important stuff. I'm a nature person myself." He started his four-wheeler back up and she followed him farther down the trail. The ground became wet just before they dipped lower down a small hill into the mud, which splattered up a couple of feet on either side of them. She laughed as they wore mud all over their clothes. They approached a fence line that sectioned off his property but took a few sharp turns on the trail that kept them on his side of it.

"Who owns that?" she hollered.

"Some lady that turned it into conservation land. Has endangered toxic plants I've heard."

She gave a thumbs up and they sped fast, back around through more mud where he did a donut and began following her. She'd rather follow him because she enjoyed that view too. She let him follow her for a bit before she did a donut to put herself back behind him. He clapped his hands, proud of her for making a bold move when she had seemed nervous about the new machine. She laughed and they came into a more open space, stopping near a huge magnolia tree.

"What a pretty magnolia!"

"It's a hidden treasure." He picked a big white magnolia bloom off the tree and placed it in her hair above her ear. They shared a brief moment, smiles exchanged and eyes connected.

"Do you want water?" she interrupted their moment.

He cleared his throat, "Sure. Yeah, thanks. She handed him a water bottle from the cooler. He hiked the thighs of his jeans up and sat on the grass against the old magnolia. She sat next to him and cracked open her water.

"It's been a while since I got this dirty," she laughed.

"Really? You're not livin' then." He chuckled and smeared some dirt on her face.

"Oh, that's how you wanna play?" She scooped up mud from the knee of her jeans and flung it onto his shirt. He playfully tackled her, carefully holding his body weight barely above hers. She suddenly felt relaxed, feeling the grass tickle against her skin. His eyes gazed into hers for a moment before he sat up and took her by the hand, pulling her up to sit next to him.

"You don't make work feel like work." She shoved him and he leaned to the side.

"Work shouldn't be boring. Everyone should like their job."

"Working with and caring for horses is great but you make it even more rewarding."

"Good. I try. Actually, this is just how I am. I was hoping you'd be cool with it."

"Absolutely. I'm always saying no two work days should be the same. Having an awesome boss helps."

"I'm just a humble guy. I like to relax and enjoy life. It gets harder to do as an adult but we need to now and then; just relax and enjoy everything the best we can."

"It does get harder to do as an adult." She laid back again with her arms up and behind her head. "You know, when I was a kid, I'd find a patch of thick lush grass and lie on my back. I'd watch the clouds move and it would make me feel like I was moving. I'd take the time to watch them change shape and imagine how high they really were, like if I were amongst the clouds, how far above the ground I'd be, and how soft and cozy the clouds would feel. When I'd have trouble falling asleep at night, I'd close my eyes and imagine floating on a cloud, sinking into it, light as a feather."

"I love that." He laid back next to her.

They watched the clouds for a while as if the white balls of cotton were a puppet show, shared a beer while chatting, then enjoyed the muddy ride back to the barn.

CHAPTER 6

Sis Visits

M arina's sister, Savannah, was visiting from central Florida for the weekend. She stayed at Marina's house even though she didn't get along with Marina's boyfriend very well. They found things outside the house to do so Savannah didn't stress as much.

Marina had hoisted kayaks into the back of Savannah's truck and the two of them were headed to the store to load up on drinks and snacks for the river. They were picking out fresh fruit when a familiar guy's voice over to the right said "How do you tell if melons are ripe?" Sawyer held two cantaloupe melons to his chest, representing breasts. The girls laughed as he approached them smiling.

"Honestly, I have no idea. Knocking on them has never worked for me so I smell them." Marina took one of his melons and sniffed it.

"Well, that's odd," he laughed.

"This one's good." She handed it back and took the other one. He put the first in his basket as she sniffed the other, then put it in his basket.

"I'm assuming you wanted the set?" Marina laughed, remembering Savannah was clueless as to who this guy was.

"What are you up to today?" he asked as he put a lemon in his basket.

"My sister and I are going kayaking so we're just loading up on stuff to fill the cooler with. Oh, I'm sorry, where are my manners? This is my sister Savannah. Savannah, this is Sawyer."

Sawyer reached to shake Savannah's hand but she hesitated for a second before taking it. "*The* Sawyer? Okay, wow. It's a pleasure. I've heard a lot about you."

"Uh oh."

"Oh, it's all been good."

"That's a relief. So...what exactly have you heard?" Sawyer was curious. His smirk showed confidence.

"That...you're the best boss ever." Savannah didn't want to embarrass Marina or give Sawyer any hint that Marina was really into him. Marina looked suddenly relieved.

"Is that so?" He smiled a crooked smile at Marina.

"Yep. Best boss ever," Marina agreed.

"Well, I'm glad to hear it. You're easy to be good to." He winked. "I'll let you ladies get your shopping done." He turned to walk away but stopped. "Oh, I wanted to let you know I won't be going to work in the morning. I have a hay shipment coming in early so I'll help you with chores if you still want to come in."

"Okay, I'll be there. I can help you with unloading hay too if you'd like."

"Sure, if you want to. Don't feel obligated though. The truck should be there by seven. They usually come early on Mondays."

"I'll be there. We can do the chores beforehand. I am your employee, ya know. You pay me to do things like unload hay."

"I wouldn't make you do that, it's a lot of work."

"Well, I look forward to helping. See, Savannah? Best boss ever."

"Oh, I see alright." Savannah bumped Marina's elbow with hers.

"Pleasure to meet you, Savannah." Sawyer tipped his hat and

turned away as he added, "Marina, bring your swimsuit. We might have to jump in the pool after getting all sweaty in the morning."

The girls were crushing on him behind his back, "Will do, Boss!"

Once Sawyer had walked out of sight the girls were squealing like a couple of teenagers at a boy band concert.

"Oh my God! I can't believe that's your boss!"

"I know! How lucky am I?"

"Extremely! Seriously. Good Lord. I'm officially totally jealous."

"He's hard to not think about. I seriously think about him all the time."

"Well, yeah! No shit! I would too. Now you get to see him sweaty *and* in the pool tomorrow."

"You have no idea how excited I am to unload hay." They laughed and put grapes and apples in their basket. Little did they know Sawyer was in the next aisle and heard pretty much their entire conversation. They would've been horrified to know he overheard, so he quietly made his way to the checkout before they did. He was gone by the time they got back out to the truck.

Dumping the items into the cooler on the tailgate Savannah asked, "So, why haven't you broken up with Derrick yet? I mean, you have a super-hot boss who seems to have the hots for you and—"

"You think so?" Marina interrupted.

"Uh, yeah! He winked at you even. He couldn't stop smiling and smirking. Then he tells you to bring your suit. Come on, he totally likes you."

"I hope so. That would be amazing," Marina said excitedly. "But would that make me a hussy if I dropped one guy in hopes of another?"

"Not in your case! Your boyfriend treats you like crap. Your ridiculously hot boss treats you better. I think it's time you worry about yourself. Besides, you haven't been happy with Derrick for so long. Even if you are single for a while, I honestly think dumping him would be the best thing to do."

"I just need to save some money. Sawyer pays me well but I don't work many hours."

"Think he would give you a raise or more hours if you asked?"

"I don't want to ask. I haven't even been there long. I'll get a night job a few nights a week bartending or something. When I save up enough money, I am going to leave Derrick." Marina shut the tailgate.

"Paddle therapy, here we come." They climbed into the truck.

It was a calm day out on the water with only a slight breeze and herons stalked fish along the water's edge as flapping pelicans flew overhead. Not far downriver, the girls took their tank tops off, donning suit tops to ease their tans. They stopped along a sandbar to take a dip. Sawyer was, once again, the topic of conversation.

"See, you can't get him out of your head."

"I know, I'm sorry. I'll shut up."

"No, I don't mean I want you to shut up, I'm just simply pointing out that you've got a huge crush on your boss."

"I do, don't I?"

"Absolutely. Why shouldn't you? I mean, he's sweet and generous from what you've told me, he's eye candy for sure, he has similar interests as you and has morals. Manners and a sense of humor too. What's not to like?"

"Not a single damn thing. There's nothing I don't like about that guy. Seriously, I can't think of anything. Then again, I'm not around him much at all. Definitely not as much as I'd like to be."

"Don't blame ya there." Savannah swished the water around with her hand along the water's surface.

"I feel pathetic."

"Why?"

"Because I'm thinking this way about a guy when I'm with a different guy."

"So? Ok, normally that wouldn't be cool but, in your situation, I'm definitely not judging you. I think you need to trade up. It's no loss, honestly, if you dump Derrick and things don't work with Sawyer."

"True. Except I'd have my heart broken and be completely crushed if Sawyer and I didn't work out. I'd have to either face him at work or find a different job. That's assuming he's even into me. What if he's just one of those overconfident, egotistical guys who loves attention from the ladies? I can't imagine that being the case but maybe I should ask around."

"If that'll make you feel better, sure. The worst that could happen would be he finds out you're asking about him. Then, if he mentions it to you, just say you wanted to know who you work for, just to keep yourself safe."

"True..." Marina stepped out of the water, drying her hair with a towel, sand sticking to her feet. Savannah followed and toweled off. They returned to their kayaks, pushed them into the water, and jumped in them. The lack of a decent breeze made the air thick and muggy. That was summertime in Northwest Florida though. It was either unbearably muggy and hot, which Marina didn't mind, or storming so the outdoors couldn't be enjoyed. Summer was Marina's favorite season. Even more so now that Sawyer was around. She'd love to see that man sweat.

"I couldn't bear to have my heart broken though, especially by him. I like him too much."

"Why do you think he'd break your heart?"

"I don't, I'm just saying what if. After the relationship I'm currently in, I'd be setting some strong boundaries and the wall I've been building around my heart is tall. I would definitely have my guard up, ya know? Even with him, I'd want to take things slow and get to know him. Even though I fantasize about ripping his clothes off." Marina turned that serious note into one less serious.

Savannah busted out laughing. "I would too! I wish I didn't have to leave tonight. I'd go help you unload hay in the morning. Then again, I wouldn't wanna get in the way, just in case."

"You wouldn't be in the way. It's not like anything will happen. No matter how he does feel about me, he knows I have a boyfriend and I can't see him being one to disrespect that. Not on his terms anyway."

"Makes sense. Still wish I could tag along."

"Me too. Oh, did I tell you he leaves a note for me in the barn every morning?"

"Really? Like, what kind of note?"

"A sweet one. Sometimes he leaves me donuts from my favorite shop. When I turn the coffee pot on in the barn it plays music."

"Geez, what kind of barn is this?"

"Right! You should see this place. It's beautiful. But anyways, the notes say cute things like 'I hope you enjoy your day' and 'Thank you for everything you do'."

"Aww, that's sweet."

"I know. I love it. It's adorable."

"I don't know any guys that do that kind of thing."

"Me neither. I'm glad he does though. It's nice to be around a compassionate guy who isn't too macho to show he cares and has a soft side."

"Seems like he has a humorous side too."

"Yeah, I hadn't really seen too much of that side of him yet. I like it."

"Has Derrick seen your boss yet?"

"No..." Marina grimaced with furrowed eyebrows.

"Uh oh! Boy is he gonna be pissed!" Savannah laughed. "Serves him right, though. If he treated you better, he wouldn't have anything to worry about."

"I know. I'm the only one trying and I'm just tired. I'm mentally and emotionally drained. I'm giving up and he just doesn't care enough. It's like he doesn't want to be with me but doesn't want me to be with anyone else either, so we're just stuck in this toxic, insidious relationship. I feel like life is trying to redirect me, like I'm disconnecting from the boring, abusive daily

life I currently live and branching into something better, something more freeing and exciting, where I'm in control of myself.
He does what he wants to, I'm going to as well. He's a manipulative narcissist."

"That's how it should be. You worry about you."

CHAPTER 7

Hay Day

Her tank top strap hung down off her shoulder, complimenting her distressed cut-off jean shorts and slip-on sneakers, and her hair was a messy ponytail.

He put on his gloves and tossed her a pair.

"I thought you hired a crew to unload hay when they brought it?"

"Nah, just when they deliver it to the rescue. I like to do the work myself here at home. I don't mind a hard day's work." He stepped up onto the trailer then took her hand to help her up.

"I like that."

"What? That I like to work?" He tossed a bale off, then another.

"Yeah. That you don't just hire people to do everything for you. You do what you can yourself." She tossed down a bale. "Although, you did hire me, I suppose. You're a humble guy and I admire that."

"Thanks, that means a lot. I didn't necessarily *need* to hire you but I wanted to." He unbuttoned his short-sleeved button-up plaid shirt and his skin glistened in the bright morning sun. She caught herself staring and regrettably dropped a bale of hay off the trailer. The twine had loosened and the bale broke apart.

"Sorry, I'll clean it up." She acted timidly, as if he would scold her for dropping the bale, but was actually trying to hide the fact that she was checking him out. He laughed and wiped his forehead with the back of his gloved hand.

"Nah, don't worry about it. The horses don't care about a little dirt. If you're getting tired, you can take a break. Hell, I don't expect you to do all of this anyways." He tossed a bale off the trailer and onto the growing pile.

"Oh, no. I'm not tired. I just got a little distracted, that's all." She threw another bale down. He wrinkled his forehead in confusion, but only briefly. He realized she had been distracted by him unbuttoning his shirt. That put a smile on his face.

"I appreciate your help, ya know? I really do."

"It's no problem. I like helping you out. You're an easy guy to work for." She swiped a fallen strand of hair out of her face.

"Glad to hear it, thanks." He jumped down and got three bottles of water out of the fridge just inside the barn. He handed her one as she climbed down off the trailer, put one under his arm, and drank from the third.

She chugged, then sarcastically asked, "Who's the other one for?"

"Us." He cracked it open and poured some over his head, soaking himself. She witnessed this in what seemed like a slow-motion scene in a movie. His wet hair dripped onto his wet skin and ran down to his jeans. He shook his head, his hair whipping back and forth, and she realized she was gawking with her mouth open. He reached over her, pouring water onto her. She squealed from the surprise of the cold. At least it *seemed* frigid compared to the suffocating heat and humidity. She didn't really care either way, she was too occupied watching his every move.

"Okay, you're a fun boss too," she laughed.

He laughed then bit his bottom lip. "You have no idea."

Him saying that put a pleased smile upon her drenched face.

"What do ya say we go hop in the pool?" He kicked his boots off right there in the driveway.

"You're serious?"

"Yeah. How 'bout it?" He stripped his shirt the rest of the way off and she swallowed hard, trying to clear her throat.

"You make it hard to say no."

"You're wearing your suit. Strip down."

She hesitated. "You noticed?"

"Maybe. Maybe I assumed that strap around your neck was for dippin'. Maybe I was kind of hoping you'd forget your suit."

"Why? You don't wanna swim?" She took her shorts off and kicked her shoes toward where his boots had been discarded.

"Oh, I wanna swim. Doesn't mean we actually need suits though." He took his jeans off, leaving only his boxer briefs.

Oh, dear God! She thought to herself. "You did tell me to bring it though, remember?"

"Yeah, well, I didn't wanna make it weird." He snickered and she laughed, loving that he would throw out random flirtations. She was a bit surprised by his bold flirting attempts, but she was also definitely enjoying them.

She walked with him to the backyard and Huck followed. There was a gray stone patio complete with matching built-in grill and firepit. The pool was like something you'd find at a tropical resort, surrounded by palms and crowned with a rock waterfall. There weren't any steps into the pool, it was a walk-in that resembled sand, like a shore. The water was an aqua lagoon. It was paradise.

"Wow, Sawyer! This is...amazing!"

"You like?"

"Absolutely! It's perfect. It's like a resort."

"Thanks. I designed it. I didn't create it, just designed it."

"You have exquisite taste."

He walked into the water and reached for her hand. She dropped her shorts onto a lounge chair and pulled her shirt up over her head, also ditching that, before walking to him. Shyly, she took his hand and walked into the water with him.

"That's a...pretty suit." He was distracted by her bikini, how it fit her just right in all the right places. The bottoms were cheeky and tied on the side, the top revealing a whole lot of cleavage. It was yellow, which complimented her light hair and tanning skin. He tried to not stare but would glance frequently.

"You're just swimming in your briefs?"

"That okay?"

"Sure." She tried to resist a smile.

"Swim shorts wouldn't feel cozy under jeans while unloading hay in this heat. I'm too lazy to go in and change."

"Makes sense," she playfully agreed.

He sank further into the water so she followed. He dove under then came up, shaking his hair.

"It's refreshing." He convinced her to go under too.

She sank down as he swam over to the shallow to sit. She surfaced, swam toward him and came walking out of the shallow water. To him it seemed like she moved in slow-motion, water dripping from her body as she raised her hands and pushed her wet hair back from her face. The sun danced on her glowing skin, shimmering with every move. She sat next to him, the water calm and lower than waist deep. She pulled her knees up and wrapped her arms around them. He stared at her, those blue eyes twinkling with the reflection of the matching water.

"What?" She smiled.

"You're beautiful, you know that?"

She looked away and inhaled deeply. "Am I?"

He gently laid his hand upon her arm. "Yes, yes you are."

She looked back at him and rested her chin on her shoulder. She didn't say anything.

"You deserve someone that will tell you that every day." He looked forward, watching the waterfall.

"I appreciate that. That's sweet."

"It's true." He dragged his gaze back to hers. They paused a few seconds, their fixed stares saying all the things their mouths couldn't. She could get lost in those eyes for eternity. Maybe she should tell him that.

She really shouldn't though.

"Those eyes of yours..." She stopped when she realized she had just started to say it out loud.

"What about them?" He didn't stray from eye contact with her.

"They're captivating." She couldn't look away either.

"Really? Because I was thinking the same about yours."

Her eyes were a tealish-green with gold flecks.

She swallowed the nervous lump in her throat. "So, your tattoo..." She touched his bicep.

"It's pretty much a tribute to my playing music as a hobby." The partial sleeve tattoo that covered his right bicep and shoulder was an acoustic guitar wrapped in music staves. There was a realistic-looking horseshoe on the guitar.

"It's creative. You design it?"

"I did, thanks. You design yours? It looks familiar."

"You saw it?"

"Of course I did."

"I did. It's an illustration I did for the dedication of the book I wrote for the rescue. It's the horseshoe from the interior title page." It was small and on the front of her left hip.

"We both have horseshoe tattoos. What are the chances?"

"Maybe it means we're lucky." She smiled.

"I know I am, I found you."

She looked at him with apprehension.

"Anyways, you hungry?" He stood from the water and offered a hand.

She took it and rose to her feet. "Actually, I told Becka I'd meet her for lunch if I was done with hay by then. I completely forgot. What time is it?"

"Oh, um...I'm not sure. Just so you know, you're welcome to use the pool whenever." He handed her a towel from a hook.

"Thanks, I appreciate that. You never know, I might be hanging out back here someday when you get home," she joked as she dried off.

"I'd be more than okay with that. In fact, I'd probably join you."

She smiled. "Thanks for today."

"Are you kidding? No, thank you! We unloaded almost that entire trailer so I appreciate the help. I know it was a small load but still. I'll walk you out."

She gathered her clothes from the lounge chair and headed back toward the barn to retrieve her shoes.

"You wanna get changed in the house first? You're welcome to."

"Oh, nah. I'll just drive home like this. Thanks though." She rushed around to the front yard, not knowing how long she could suppress the feeling of wanting to throw herself at him after sharing that moment in the pool and him being in just his underwear. He followed close behind her.

"Anytime." He shut her car door for her and headed back to the house.

CHAPTER 8

Lunch with Becka

Marina suggested the Mexican restaurant in town. She arrived before Becka and decided to wait outside on a brightly painted bench.

"Hey, sorry, traffic was crazy." Becka adjusted her purse strap on her shoulder.

"It's all good. You hungry?" Marina stood from the bench.

"That's a silly question. You know who you just asked, right?"

"True." Marina laughed, holding the door open for Becka to enter first. They were seated and the waitress took their drink order.

"It's only one o'clock. You're having a daiquiri already?" Becka questioned. "That's not like you."

"I need one." Marina seemed anxious.

"You okay? Something happen with the asshole boyfriend?"

"No, it's not anything negative."

"Okay. Now I'm intrigued. Spill."

"So, I helped Sawyer unload hay today."

"'Kay?"

"The way he looked, all sweaty."

"Oooh, go on..." Becka leaned forward.

"He had told me yesterday to wear my swimsuit, so I did. He invited me to strip and join him in the pool."

"Oh my God! No way!"

"Yes way. So, we got in the pool but I didn't stay long."

"Why not?"

"Because we shared a moment. I'm not certain but I think he wanted to kiss me."

"Seriously?"

"Yeah. The tension was strong and I think if I wouldn't have left something might have happened." Marina leaned forward.

"Like what?" Becka leaned in further.

"I don't know. If he didn't kiss me, I probably would've kissed him. He was swimming in his boxer briefs for crying out loud."

"Oh, dear Lord. I can only imagine..." Becka sat back in the booth set, slouching.

"Sometimes he gives these hints or does something that makes me think he has feelings for me. I do really want to tell him how I feel."

"He's throwing you hints on purpose; he's trying to get a sense of where you stand. You might want to flirt back or he might think you aren't interested. Then what if he ends up dating someone else?"

"That would destroy me. I can't stand the thought. He isn't mine to claim though and I can't claim him while with someone else."

"Well, say something to him. Or flirt to keep him interested.

"Play hard to get you mean?"

"If you have to. Just don't give him the impression that you're not into him."

"He knows I have a boyfriend."

"I'm sure Sawyer's a respectful guy but if the tension is that strong already, he may make a move anyways. Don't be surprised if he does." Becka crunched on chips and salsa.

"I realized today we have matching tattoos. How weird is that?"

"What?"

"My little horseshoe. He has one on the guitar on his arm."

"That's crazy. What a coincidence."

"He's the most Heavenly creature I've ever laid eyes on. I don't think it's a coincidence. I feel like, I don't know, like he was sent to me. Like we were supposed to meet and be together. Is that crazy?"

"Nope. Even if only to make you realize you deserve better than the jerk you're currently with. I seriously don't like your boyfriend."

Marina laughed. "I love that you're so blunt. Nobody likes him."

"Don't sacrifice your happiness, he's not worth it. You have a better man right in front of you."

"You're right."

"I know."

They both laughed.

CHAPTER 9

Gardening

T he barn note read, "Do you have time to hoe around today?"

She laughed but was confused as to what he meant. He pulled in the drive a while later hauling a trailer loaded down with plants and soil bags. She was leading the last horse out to pasture from the barn, Huck in tow, who then ran to the truck and barked. She busted out laughing. He asked why she was cracking up when he exited the truck. She could barely get the words out when she replied "Oh my gosh, the barn note."

Then he laughed, adjusting his black cowboy hat.

"It was a good one, wasn't it? I'm glad you're laughing, I took a chance on that one."

He started unloading plants, handing her the small stuff. He'd drag the bigger plants, the tropical cannas and palms, to the edge of the trailer then hop off to carry them to the side of the house.

"You want me to grab the wheelbarrow, make it easier?"

"Nah, I got this." He tossed a couple of bags of soil over his shoulder and hefted a palm in the other hand. He was so strong. She didn't know if he was stubborn or just showing off but the look worked on him. His boots were dusted with rust-colored clay and he had dirt smudged up his forearms and across his gray t-shirt. Wiping his hands on the thighs and rear of his jeans, he was filthy but she loved it.

"Rough morning at the nursery? Or do you like it dirty in the mornings?"

He tipped his head back laughing, "There it is! That dirty sarcasm that I like. I knew you had it in ya."

She laughed and grabbed a shovel he had leaning against the house. She started digging where he set the plants, each in their own particular spot.

"I think you need to get dirtier though." He smudged dirt down her arm.

"Well, I guess we match now," she chuckled.

Huck lay in the shade near the house watching Marina as Sawyer unreeled the hose. It had a sprayer nozzle. She placed a hibiscus bush down into the hole she dug and wiped her forehead with her arm, the dirty one. Her forehead had dirt all across it.

"I could make another inappropriate comment but I'll show you instead. Let me help you with that." He lightly sprayed her with the hose. She jumped up, yelling his name, and chased him through the yard while he playfully threatened her with the hose. Huck was running and barking, biting at the hose water. She had a handful of dirt ready to throw at him.

"I'm already dirty. What's that gonna do?"

"You're right. I don't know." She shrugged and dropped the dirt, laughing.

He laughed and stood, relaxed, hose sprayer loose in his hand.

"I'll let you have this hose. After we get these planted, I need to clean out the horse trailer. It could use a good hosin' down."

"You need help?"

"Nah, you don't wanna be out here with that. That's a real dirty job."

"I'm not scared of horse poop, ya know..."

"I know you're not, and I appreciate it. I'll take care of it though."

He dug holes and she filled them with plants after removing them from the temporary plastic pots.

"We'll save the pots and start veggie seeds in them just before spring. If you just wanna stack 'em, I'll take them out to the barn when we're done."

"I'll do that. What veggies you planting?"

"I don't know. Anything you want, I'll plant."

"Okay. I'll think about it."

"I'll plant out in the same spot I usually do." He pointed at a corner area between the pasture and the backyard.

"Room for vines too?"

"Absolutely. Seriously. Anything you want."

She smiled and nodded then placed the last palm in the hole. He helped pack the soil around it.

"I can spread the mulch later, after I clean out the trailer. You don't have to feel obligated to stay if you have other plans."

"You trying to get rid of me?" She stood and brushed dirt off her knees.

"Never."

"Good. Because I'll spread the mulch while you clean the trailer."

"If you want to, I'm fine with that. Just let me take it out there for you."

"That, I won't argue with."

He grabbed a few bags of mulch off the trailer and plopped them up by the house.

"Thanks. That was half the work right there."

"I do believe it was, yeah." He brushed his hands together.

She ripped open bags of mulch as he went out to the trailer next to the barn. There wasn't much to spread out and she finished quickly. Sweaty and dirty, she followed the harsh sound of the hose spraying against metal out to the trailer to let him know she was leaving.

She nearly tripped over her own feet when she spotted his t-shirt lying on the ground. She wrapped her hair up in a hair tie as she came around the backside of the trailer. He was standing in it spraying the hose, wet straw and mud flying out onto the ground even though he had shoveled out the big mess first.

His black hat tipped down shadowing his eyes, his boots wet and muddy, his low-rise bootcut jeans a little dirty; the sight of him had her mouth watering.

He looked up as if he could feel her eyes on him and stopped spraying.

"I'm going to head home unless you need anything else."

"No ma'am, I'm good. Thanks for your help today."

"Of course. I enjoyed it."

"Me too. Enjoy the rest of your day, Marina."

"You too." She flashed him a flirty smile.

She couldn't wait to call Becka on her way home to talk about him.

CHAPTER 10

Huck

I t was late when Marina got back to the barn with the four-wheeler. She had seen tracks that morning in the pasture mud that looked to belong to a big cat. She texted Sawyer to let him know then did the evening chores early so she could follow the tracks and get back before dark. The dog had gone out with her because he loved running alongside the four-wheeler. She noticed halfway back that Huck wasn't behind her so she'd stopped and whistled and called for him. He liked to wander off and chase stuff but he'd always come right back. She continued back to the barn without him.

Sawyer had made it back just before she did. He had a late night at work.

"You're still here?" Sawyer locked his truck.

"Yeah, I thought I'd go ahead and research the tracks I texted you about this morning."

"Alone? That's not safe." He gassed up the four-wheeler for her as she climbed off the machine and stretched.

"Well, I wanted to check it out before dark. I'd hate for the horses to get hurt. Oh, and Huck went out with me but halfway back he wandered off. I tried to get him to come back to me."

"How long has he been out alone?"

46

"Maybe ten minutes or so."

"I think I'll take this out to look for him really quick."

"Probably a good idea. He's usually back by now?"

"Yeah, unless he's on the trail of something. You wanna come with?" He sat on the four-wheeler.

"Yeah, sure." She climbed on behind him, wrapping her arms around his tight abs. She could easily feel them through his t-shirt. The wind blew her hair as they drove off to the woods on the two-track trail. They'd stop a few times, whistling and calling for him, but ended up driving almost a half mile into the woods before they noticed two sets of tracks.

He stopped and shut off the four-wheeler, listening.

They heard the dog barking and snarling then yipping. Sawyer told Marina, "Stay there!" then ran toward the sounds of a wounded dog. He found Huck laying in the mud, bleeding, but he couldn't tell from where through the thick coat of fur. He carried Huck back to the four-wheeler.

"Oh my God!" Marina gasped.

"Can you drive back while I hold him?"

"Of course." She started it up and they headed full speed to the barn.

Sawyer laid Huck down in a stall on the hay and fumbled for his phone in his back pocket. His hands were covered in blood so Marina dialed the vet for him. She put it on speakerphone so Sawyer could talk to the vet easier. It was the vet he'd used for the horses since he moved there. Doctor Summit was a kind man in his sixties.

Sawyer was trying not to panic but he was extremely worried about the dog. While on the phone, he was applying pressure to a deep wound on Huck's side as Huck was whimpering and crying. Marina handed him gauze from the barn's first-aid kit and he wrapped it around Huck tightly. He knew the wound was serious and Huck may not survive even after seeing the vet.

"Doc, it's Sawyer. I need your help." Sawyer's voice was almost cracking.

"What's going on, Cowboy?"

"Huck was attacked just now. It's bad, he's losing a lot of blood and I can't tell where it's all coming from. I'm freakin' out here." Sawyer combed his shaky, bloody fingers through the soaked fur coat in search of open wounds.

"Okay, okay, I'll meet you at the barn. I'm putting my boots on now."

Marina sat the phone down behind her and looked up at Sawyer who's eyes were glossy. She helped apply pressure to Huck's side. The surrounding straw was tainted red.

Doctor Summit was on his way in a rush and Sawyer eagerly awaited his arrival, holding onto Huck while sitting on the straw.

"Sawyer, I am so sorry. I should've looked for him sooner," Marina apologized with tears in her eyes but Sawyer was shaking his head.

"No, please don't. Don't blame yourself. He does this. He gets on the trail of something and he takes off and won't come back. This isn't my first rodeo with having to track him down. He does usually come back eventually but if there's something out there nearby, he gets stupid and won't listen. He's just doing his job, ya know? Being protective. He's been impossible to train on returning. I should've come home as soon as you texted me this morning. I could've shut him in the barn. I should've taken care of the issue before he or you went out there. This could've been you. I can't stand the thought of that. This is on me. You did great letting me know you saw tracks but I should've come home, or at least had you put him in the barn." He paused, swiping his fallen hair from his face with the backside of his bloody hand. "I'm so sorry, Huck. Poor boy, just trying to run that cat off and got yourself hurt." Sawyer hugged Huck. Marina sat down next to Sawyer and laid a hand on his shoulder while petting Huck with the other.

"I still should've turned back for him right away. I'm so sorry."

Sawyer hugged her, trying not to touch her with his bloody

hands. "Accidents happen. Huck shouldn't be so stubborn either. He wasn't out there long enough for you to have to worry, really."

The vet pulled in and came running into the barn with his medical bag.

"Hey there, Sawyer. I'm so sorry your pooch got injured. Let's take a look-see." He sat his bag down next to the dog and opened it, crouching down on his knee. "Well, Huck, what did you get yourself into? You're lookin' mighty rough, boy."

"It's bad, isn't it?" Sawyer asked, already knowing the answer. He let out a depressed sigh.

"Yeah, it's bad alright. These wounds are really deep. I can't tell if there's damage to organs through all the blood. I'm giving him painkillers and a light sedative to help him feel a little more comfortable. I can either take him with me to the clinic and see if there's internal damage or I can stitch him up and bandage him here and hope for the best. Of course, I'll give him an antibiotic too." He wiped his hand on the hanky he pulled out of his back pocket.

"I'll do whatever you think is best, Doc."

"It was a cat, wasn't it?"

"Yeah, we think so, based on the tracks and sounds. I heard him fighting but didn't see what it was. He was already on the ground by the time I got to him."

"I don't mind taking him in. Hell, y'all can come too," the doc offered as he packed his bag.

"You can go home, Marina. I'll take him."

"I'd rather come with you if that's ok." She was worried. "Even if only for emotional support."

"Of course. Thank you."

Sawyer carried Huck out to Doc's truck and laid him in the truck bed on a thick blanket. Huck had stopped whimpering, thanks to the meds.

Once they arrived at the clinic, Sawyer carried Huck inside after Doc unlocked the door and flipped the light on. It was after hours and the place was empty.

"Follow me on back." Doc led the way to an exam room, walking with a slight limp. Sawyer laid Huck up on the table. Huck seemed to be calm and almost sleeping. Doc changed from his normal driving glasses to binocular-type goggles to better examine the wound. He pulled a big overhead light overtop of Huck then put on a set of disposable gloves and proceeded to take off the blood-soaked bandage.

"I think I'll start with an x-ray then we'll go from there. Wanna carry him on in here?"

Sawyer did as he was told and Doc took an x-ray before sending them back to the exam room. Marina watched, helpless, as Sawyer washed his hands at the sink before anxiously pacing across the small space. Doc came in with the x-ray film and hung it up on the light board. Flipping on the light and switching glasses again, he rubbed his rough whiskery chin.

"Looks like he has two broken ribs. See here?" He pointed out the cracks.

"Shit," Sawyer wiped his tired face and sat in a chair. "There's nothin' we can do for that, is there?"

"No, no but I think I might need to open him up and make sure it's just...well, we don't wanna just stitch him up I don't think. I wanna make sure there's no major internal bleeding that needs to be stopped. There's been a lot of blood loss."

"I know. I have a feeling we'll be leaving here without him tonight." Sawyer adjusted his hat nervously.

"You mean...you don't think he'll make it?" Marina stood from the chair, her guilt finally getting the best of her. She felt responsible, irresponsible even, and hated that she'd let this happen. Doc wheeled an ultrasound machine into the room.

"Oh, Sawyer, I really hope that's not the case." She stepped closer to him and put a hand on his shoulder and Sawyer wrapped an arm around her.

"I hope not too. I'm glad he was out there with you because that cat could've attacked you if Huck wasn't out there to keep it distracted."

"It's not fair to Huck though." She started to cry, subtle tears rolling down her cheeks.

"He felt it was his duty to protect you, as well as the horses, the property...that's his home. He didn't want that cat there. He knew it was trouble."

"I just feel horrible he was hurt. So badly too."

"I know, me too." He stood and scooped her up into his arms, her face pressed against his chest, his bloody shirt dampened by her tears. He stroked her hair and rested his chin upon her head. He felt a lump in his throat that made it difficult to swallow.

Only seconds after Doc began the ultrasound, he shook his head. "Well, Cowboy, I hate to tell ya this, but this boy is pretty messed up. He's all sliced, a few organs are torn up but I can't tell how badly. It just all looks a mess on this screen. To be honest, I'm not sure how he's still alive."

Sawyer sighed deeply and his eyes wandered around the room as he tried not to tear up.

"What would you do, Doc?"

"To be honest, if he did survive, he would have a long, painful recovery. I can't even tell where the blood is coming from. I can call a tech in to do an exploratory surgery and try to fix him up, but to tell you the truth...I would choose the humane thing and put him down as the hero he is. He's just really bad off, Sawyer."

Marina looked up at Sawyer, who was having a hard time making the decision. She took his hand.

"I don't want him to suffer. That's if he could even be saved. If that's what you recommend, Doc...I trust you."

"Okay, I'll go get the injections. You folks take a minute to say goodbye. We'll need to do this soon before the sedative wears off. I didn't give him much."

"We'll make it quick, Doc."

Marina said goodbye to Huck and apologized to him, thanking him for keeping her safe. She petted his soft ears then stepped back. "I'll step out so you can have a minute."

"I want you to stay with me," he squeezed her hand and she

nodded. Sawyer said his heartbroken goodbyes, petting Huck, telling him he was a good boy and he was proud of him. Marina couldn't fight the lump in her throat anymore. She quietly cried, standing behind Sawyer. She felt nauseous, she couldn't believe this was happening. Doc came into the room to lay Huck to rest, one injection, then the other. Sawyer's long, labored inhales and exhales came with nasal flaring. He was resisting the urge to let it all out, his hand upon Huck the whole time. Marina took a gentle hold of Sawyer's arm. When Huck was at peace, Sawyer let out a long exhale and turned to Marina, wrapping his arms around her tightly. Doc left the room to give them a minute. No words were exchanged. He let tears escape as he squeezed his eyes shut. His jaw clenched, not releasing any sound. She consoled him, rubbing his back. When they came out of the room a few minutes later, Sawyer was holding his hat against his chest and holding Marina's hand. His eyes revealed he had been crying; they were red and glassy.

He paid Doc and thanked him, shaking the older man's hand before Marina joined him in walking out to the truck. He opened her door for her and just stood there a few moments after she climbed in.

"Thank you for coming with me tonight."

"Of course. I'm so sorry this all happened the way it did."

"Me too. That's life, ya know? I think I did the right thing. Do you?"

"It's a hard decision but I think you did right by him."

"I hope so." He shut her door.

It was a quiet ride back and she went home after a long, heartbroken hug.

CHAPTER 11

Confessions to Raquel

M arina stopped in town the next afternoon to get "fancy coffee" and meet Raquel at the coffee shop. Sawyer spotted her from his office window across the street and waited for her to enter before he darted two doors down to the flower shop.

There were fresh-cut flowers for sale at a stand just outside the shop window. Sawyer picked out several of the most beautiful and had the young girl quickly arrange them into a bouquet. He paid her, waited for a car to drive by, then walked across the street to the café.

She was coming out of the coffee shop with her iced vanilla latte and Raquel's coffee when Sawyer met her on the sidewalk. Raquel was approaching but slowed to watch without interrupting.

Marina noticed the flowers and smiled before greeting him, "Hey!"

"Hey. I saw you over here and was hoping I'd catch you before you left." He handed her the bouquet.

"You bought these for me?" She set their coffees down on one of the patio tables before taking the flowers and smelling the bouquet.

"I did. I wanted to thank you for being supportive last night."

"That's so sweet. I actually read your note this morning that thanked me as well." She smiled at him.

"Yeah, well...I had an excuse to buy you flowers."

"You needed an excuse?"

"Not really. You deserve to be spoiled every day."

"You're so good to me, you know that?"

"It's easy to be good to you." He looked over and saw Raquel leaning against the corner of the building, flipping through her phone as if she wasn't spying.

"I'll let you get back to your day. Enjoy." He tipped his hat to her and waved at Raquel before walking back across the street.

"Thank you, Sawyer!"

"Oooh, he's buying you flowers now?" Raquel waved back at Sawyer and nudged elbows with Marina.

"Isn't he just the sweetest? He said I deserve to be spoiled every day."

"Aww, he has a crush on you."

"He had a rough night last night. I guess he appreciated that I stayed to comfort him, but I feel like it was all my fault. I feel horrible." Marina sat at the patio table.

"What happened?" Raquel pulled out a chair and sat.

"I saw big cat tracks and texted Sawyer to let him know. He said he'd check it out when he got home but I took the four-wheeler out later to check for myself. The dog followed me and wouldn't come back. I called for him but came in without him when he didn't obey. Then Sawyer got home and we went back out to search for the dog."

"You find him?"

"Yeah, right after he'd been attacked by the big cat."

"Oh no!"

"It was horrible. I drove back so he could carry the dog on the back of the four-wheeler. They were both covered in blood. The vet came to the barn but we had to take the dog to the clinic. He had internal damage and was bleeding badly. Sawyer decided to put the dog down and was completely heartbroken. He even cried and held me in his arms. It made me cry. I feel so bad."

"Wow, I'm so sorry. It doesn't look as though he blames you though."

"He doesn't, but that's just who he is. He's so kind. He told me it's not my fault and accidents happen. The dog was stubborn and protective, he was doing his job. It still makes me feel like crap though."

"I understand that. It's not your fault though, really. I'm sorry you both had to deal with that."

"Thanks. Poor guy. Poor Huck too. Neither of them deserved that. Huck was a sweetheart. Always greeted me with his tail wagging."

"I'm so sorry. It's so sweet he bought you flowers. He's showing you he doesn't hold you accountable."

"I do feel that way though, at least partially. If I had waited and not gone out there, he wouldn't have followed me."

"He might have run after it later though. Or it could've attacked you or Sawyer or all the horses in the pasture. He was doing his job keeping the cat away."

"I hope Sawyer shoots that cat, but I doubt he will. He's a lover not a fighter."

"You never know. He probably will shoot it so the dog didn't die in vain. I would."

"Me too," Marina agreed.

CHAPTER 12

Backcountry Bar

F riday morning, her barn note read, "Hope you don't have plans for tonight. I want to take you to my usual Friday night hangout. We can relax and have some fun!"

She was excited because she didn't know where he hung out and thought it would be exciting to be seen with him in public around people he knew. They didn't get to hang out much, but when they did it was explosive chemistry and sexual tension. At least, that was her point of view.

Oh, what to wear? She didn't want to dress too sexy and look desperate, but not too modest either. That afternoon, she tried on most of her wardrobe and finally settled on bootcut jeans and wedge sandals with a cute, low-cut, dressy tank top. She wore small earrings and her hair down and wavy.

The day seemed to drag on, perhaps because her excitement was making her nervous.

When the time finally came, she was anxiously waiting near a window at home, watching for him to pull up. She felt clammy the moment she spotted his truck. He got out and opened her door for her. She didn't have to worry about her boyfriend since he was drinking at his buddy's house. She didn't even bother telling him she was going out and she went as far as to shut her phone off as she climbed into the truck. He got in and they drove off.

My God, he smells good and looks even better. she thought to herself.

"You look great," he mentioned. "I mean, you always do but... you look really great."

"Thanks. So do you." He had jeans on, a bootcut style as well, and they fit so tightly on his thighs and rear. His black cowboy hat looked sharp with the aqua t-shirt matching his eyes. His casual cowboy look was so sexy, she almost didn't notice the guitar case in the back seat.

"You play?" she asked.

"I do. Do you sing?"

"You mean, like, in the shower or car?" She laughed. "I've done karaoke a couple of times. I don't think I sucked."

"Maybe we'll find out tonight."

"That might depend on the crowd. Where are we going, anyways?"

"I go to a little dive bar every Friday night to play music and hang out. Pretty much the same usual crowd. They'd be bitchin' if I didn't bring that guitar. We play card games, darts and drink. Just relax and bullshit and have a good time kickin' back. Often times, I play with my buddies. If they don't show up, I'll just play a couple of acoustic songs. We do cover band country."

"That's awesome! I'm excited!"

"So, if I can get you up there to sing with me, or even solo, what would you wanna sing?"

"Are you a Miranda Lambert fan? I could do some Miranda."

"Let's do it! How about the Keith Urban, Miranda duet? You like that one?"

"*We Were Us?* Sure do. I'm in the mood for some *It All Comes Out in the Wash*, too."

"We can do that."

"I have a feeling this will be a fun night."

"It already is." He winked at her. "I have a few songs planned that I'm hoping you like."

He had made sure his bandmates would be there that night and for such a quiet little bar, the parking lot was busy. It's usually hopping pretty good for a couple of hours Friday evenings then dwindles down to just the regulars before the end of the night.

"So, the owners of this joint are a married couple. Great people. There aren't normally any trouble makers around here but we regulars look out for them. They call us whenever they need anything, whether it be bouncers for an event or to help throw someone out or to fix stuff that breaks. They pay us with a free bar tab for the night and we like helping out."

"That's sweet of you." She smiled. "You're a great person, you know that?"

"Thanks, I try."

"I think it comes easy for you. I can tell. You have a big heart naturally. It radiates from you every day. You've been good to me too. I appreciate our relationship."

"Me too. I feel like we're more like friends than boss and employee by now. You?"

"Absolutely. You're helping me through a tough time. Your friendship means a lot to me," she agreed.

"The way I see it is, you're a great person with a big heart as well and you deserve to smile and be happy. If I can help with that, the pleasure is all mine."

He let her out of the truck and they walked into the bar side by side. She was surprised it wasn't smoke-filled and extremely loud. Everyone definitely noticed Sawyer walk in and they all shouted in welcoming excitement. She smiled, realizing how popular he was there.

"Good evening, everybody! We have a newby tonight. Her name is Marina. Let's show her what our Friday nights are made of."

Everyone was cheering and welcoming her. It made her feel at home and comfortable right away.

"Hey, Bob. Anything this young lady orders tonight goes on my tab. Cool?"

"Absolutely, Sawyer. You got it." Old Man Bob nodded and smiled.

"You want a drink?" Sawyer asked her.

"Yeah. Any kind of fruity vodka."

"I'll fix ya right up." Bob pulled a glass out from behind the bar and mixed her a drink. He even put fresh fruit in it.

"The usual beer for you, Sawyer?"

"To start, yeah. Thank you, sir."

They took their drinks to a table where some regulars were playing poker. Sawyer pulled out a chair for her and took the only other open chair, which happened to be directly across from her. He made his way around the table, flipped his chair around, and straddled the backwards chair.

He even sits on a chair in the sexiest way. Nothing this man does isn't sexy.

"You bring that guitar?" one of the locals asked.

"I sure did. It's in the truck."

"What the hell is it doing out there?"

"I wanted to see if the others showed up first before I lugged it on in."

"You know we like your acoustic solos anyways. Get your ass out there and get it."

Sawyer laughed. "Yes, sir." He looked at her and said, "I'll be right back. Don't trust any one of them." He pointed at all the people at the table as he stood then laughed on his way out.

"Hi there, I'm Gladys, Bob's wife. So, where ya from, sweetheart?" Bob's wife came out from the back room, wiping her hands on a dish towel then shook Marina's hand.

"I'm from here. About an hour or so away, originally, but have lived here the last several years."

"Why ain't we never seen ya in here before?"

"I don't know. Good question. I'm glad I'm here now though. Thank you all for the warm welcome."

"Oh, absolutely, honey. Come on over here for a second." Gladys waved her over to the bar. She followed and Bob joined their conversation at the end of the bar.

"So, Sawyer is the best guy. I mean, really the *best*! He's got a heart of gold. He's only ever brought two dates in here before but neither of them made it back for a second visit. He said he could tell they weren't the one for him. He's got great intuition, like a woman," Gladys went on.

Bob laughed. "So we'll know by the end of the night if you'll be coming around with him again. I don't mean this in a negative way at all either. We can tell just by the way he interacts with you if y'all will hit it off. We hope you have good intentions with him. He doesn't need his heart broken again."

"I really like him. I have only good intentions; I promise you that. What do you mean, again?"

"A few years back he was in love. They never came in here together but he told us all about it once he became a regular. She cheated on him after a year or two together. I forget how long he said exactly, so he has trust issues. It sounded like she emotionally abused him too. Bless his heart." She spoke softly because Sawyer was walking back in.

"That's horrible. He hadn't told me. We don't get to spend much time together. I work at his barn in the mornings while he's at work. Occasionally, I work a Saturday or do evening chores if he's working late. He sometimes gets home before I leave so I see him briefly then but, unfortunately, we've only got a chance to hang out a few times."

"Well, he already sees something in you if he's bringing you in here because he said he wasn't doing that again."

"This here tonight might just be a trial date," Bob said as he wiped off the countertop.

"Noted." She smiled and tapped her hand on the bar. "Thank you, both."

She didn't think she should bring up her messy relationship

with her boyfriend or that she has reservations about a new relationship. Not this soon anyways.

She joined Sawyer back at the table.

"I can only imagine what *that* conversation was about." Sawyer smiled and nodded at Gladys, who waved at him.

"What are you doin', boy? Get up there and play us somethin'," one of the locals said before chugging his beer and belching.

"Any requests?" He took his guitar out of the case as the other band members began hauling their equipment in.

"Told ya we'd show up!" One of them slapped Sawyer on the shoulder.

"I would've played without ya," he laughed.

"Who's this new hottie?"

"Jake, this is Marina. Marina, this is Jake. He thinks he's a lady's man."

Jake reached out and shook her hand.

"Pleasure," she smiled.

"She your date?" Jake asked Sawyer.

Sawyer looked up at him from the bar stool on stage then at her. "If she wants to be." He smiled.

"But you're claiming her? Like...?"

"Yeah, Jake. She came with me tonight."

She was thrilled to hear he was putting a claim on her. She bit her lip and grinned, then took a sip to try to hide it.

"So, this first song is one by Morgan Wallen. Y'all know that I'm a huge fan. It's recently become a favorite of mine," Sawyer announced as he adjusted himself on the barstool and the other guys finished situating. He propped his guitar on one leg and placed his fingers on the strings, ready to play.

She was instantly amazed at his smooth voice and recognized the song. It was *Somebody's Problem*. Gladys and Bob nudged each other, smiling. Marina looked back at them in time to see it and Gladys gave her a thumbs up. The next song they played was *Singles You Up* by Jordan Davis.

Marina went up to the bar to order another drink for herself and a beer for Sawyer. She took it up to him and said, "I'm picking up what you're putting down." She walked away with a playful glance back at him. He just stared at her with a sideways smile.

The band had half the place up dancing and singing along while standing to play *Neon Eyes*. They finally took a break to refill drinks and spend some time chatting with the crowd.

Sawyer got up close behind Marina, his hand on her shoulder, and asked, "You ready to sing with me?"

"I think I've had enough liquid courage to. Can't promise I'm any good though."

"I've heard you singing while doin' chores. You've got a beautiful voice." He bumped her elbow with his own. She felt almost horrified. He took her by the hand and brought her up onto the small stage area and set a barstool next to his, placing the microphone in the center.

"Duet?" he asked.

"Let's do it," she agreed. They sang *We Were Us* and the band was so talented to just be able to play whatever they were sprung with, including Sawyer. They sounded great together, like they had been performing together for years.

"You're amazing!" He whispered to her when the song was finished.

"Really? Thanks. Maybe because you were singing too."

"Nah, it's you. How about *I Run to You* by Lady A? Together."

"Let's do it!" They sang the duet together and the crowd loved it.

"How about you take the next one solo? Show 'em whatcha got."

She looked nervous, looking around the room with uncertainty glistening in her eyes. Her heart was beating at a quick pace. She briefly chewed her lip then cleared her throat then slowly stood and adjusted the microphone height. They started playing

It All Comes Out in the Wash and she sang it almost as good as Miranda herself. She earned a standing ovation for that one.

"Girl! You got it goin' on!" Gladys cheered loudly over the sound of clapping.

She took a seat on the stool for her next number, *The House That Built Me*. Sitting made her feel less vulnerable in the unfamiliar crowd. That song hit home for her.

The guys went on to play a few more, just the guys. They played *You Can Have Your Way With Me* by Brady Seals, *Down to the Honkytonk* by Jake Owen, and then Sawyer and Jake sang *Only One That's Gone* by Morgan Wallen and Chris Stapleton.

After they had finished their set and the room was mostly empty, Sawyer headed up to the bar. "Bob, let me get a Jack 'n Coke to finish off my tab for the night. Marina, you want another?"

"Oh, no. I'm good, thank you. Any more you'll have to carry me out."

"In that case..." he joked. She laughed.

"How did you know I love that song by Brady Seals?" she asked.

"I didn't. I only play songs I really like though so I guess we have that one in common."

"We hope to see you back again soon, Marina," Bob winked at her then nodded to Sawyer who nodded his head yes.

"I believe you will. Thank you all so much for everything. I haven't had fun like this in a really long time."

"Everyone, have a good night." Sawyer threw his guitar case over his shoulder as they left out the door.

"This was a lot of fun. Thank you for bringing me here with you tonight."

"I'm glad you agreed to come along. We make one hell of a team up on that stage."

"I think everyone would agree with that. I was nervous at first but I had a blast."

"It's a comfortable crowd."

He walked her to the porch when he took her home and Derrick met them at the door.

"Where have you been?" He sounded angry so Sawyer told her to have a good night and thanks for filling in, as a cover story for her to work with if need be. He walked slowly back to the truck just in case he needed to step in.

"I filled in as a singer for his band tonight. You weren't home when I was asked. You were out getting drunk with your friends." She shoved her way into the house as Derrick gave Sawyer the stink eye from the doorway, which he was too stubborn to move from.

Sawyer just tipped his hat and smiled, rolled up his window, and drove off.

CHAPTER 13

Field Ride

The barn note read, "Let's go for a ride."

He had asked her to come to work on Saturday but this time his truck was there. She assumed he would've been out of town. The troughs had been freshly filled and there was hay in the feed bags already but the horses weren't out. She was about to open Athena's stall door when Sawyer entered the barn.

"Mornin', beautiful." He tipped his hat to her. Did he really just compliment her out loud? And did he mean it?

"Morning, handsome," she returned the compliment and, of course, she meant it too. He smiled a big smile and strapped on a pair of work gloves. He grabbed a bale of hay that was in the walkway and stacked it at the other end of the barn in the feed room. She watched him walk the whole way. Nobody else on Earth could pull off a simple t-shirt and jeans as sumptuously as he could.

"Are you riding today? I can saddle one up for you."

"You're sweet, but I thought maybe we'd go for a ride together if you want to." He flopped the gloves onto the counter and grabbed a water bottle out of the fridge for each of them.

"Sure! Where are we riding?" She took the water he handed her.

"Maybe here. Just follow the tree line all around the field. It'd give us a chance to chat."

"Uh oh. Is that a good thing or should I be worried?" She leaned her back against the stall.

He stepped close to her, really close, and took a halter off Athena's stall hook as he said in a deep tone, "It's always a good thing."

She hoped he couldn't hear her heart thumping. The closer he got to her, the harder it pounded. She yearned for that voice of his, and when his tone dove deep it plunged her into a spine-tingling bottomless euphoria.

She realized she hadn't opened the stall yet when Athena started lipping her hair. "I'll ride Athena. It looks like she's itching for attention. You can ride Legend, he's calm and gentle."

"Okay." She snapped back to reality and opened the stall door. He draped the halter over Athena's face and buckled it while Marina let Legend out. They saddled up just outside the big barn doors. Legend let out a whuffling breath as Marina hoisted herself into the saddle. Athena reared her head upward in a jolt when Sawyer mounted onto her back.

"Maybe she doesn't wanna be ridden after all." Marina laughed.

"Nah, she needs it whether she wants to or not. Mares have attitudes, that's why I only have one," he explained with a laugh. "She's gotten lazy so I'll walk the attitude right outta her today. She likes to try eating on walks even."

"Well shoot, I have days like that," Marina defended the mare as she circled Legend around.

"You definitely don't look it though."

"I appreciate that." She flicked her hair behind her shoulder before he settled up next to her. He gave her a flirty smile, more like a sly smirk. She couldn't help but return one herself, it was physically unavoidable.

The tall grass of the field brushed over the horse's lower legs as they trekked along the tree line side by side. He couldn't help but watch Marina reposition her rear in the saddle. She noticed his eyes trailing to her saddle.

He cleared his throat and asked, "So, did you grow up here?"

"I did. Well, here in Northwest Florida anyways. I was out of high school when I moved over this way though. Had met my boyfriend and moved in together a couple years later." Sawyer hung his head then looked off into the distance across the field.

"I lost my dad soon after that. I went through a rough time, pretty much by myself too. My mom and sister I'm close with of course but they lived hours from me."

He looked back at her with saddened eyes, "What about your boyfriend? Wasn't he supportive?"

Marina swallowed hard and shook her head no.

"Are you kidding? He wasn't there for you when you needed him the most?"

"Not really. Not like he should've been. Not like I would've been for him, anyways."

"I'm so sorry. I didn't know about your dad. Hopefully, I haven't ever been insensitive about family talk."

"Thanks, and no, not at all. I've learned to be tough anyways. I'm there for myself, rely on myself. I mean, I try anyways. I really miss my dad. I could use his advice these days."

"I'm sure it's not even close to the same but I'll always listen and be there for you if you need anyone. I care about you, you know?"

"Thank you, Sawyer. That means the world to me." She looked at him with appreciation in her eyes.

"I can see the hurt in your eyes when you talk about your boyfriend."

"I'm sorry." She shamefully put her head down.

"No, hey, don't be sorry. I'm sorry. I was just making an observation. I can tell he's hurting you."

"Yeah, that's what I could use Dad's advice on. I know what Dad would say but it would be easier to hear it from him." She squinted and pointed. "Is that a rose bush?"

"Well, I'll be damned! I never planted one out here." He halted Athena to a stop, flopped the reins onto the saddle horn, and dismounted. He walked over to the blooming red rose bush and snapped off a stem. He popped off the thorns and handed it to Marina, who was still on Legend's back. "Ma'am."

She blushed and gladly accepted the rose. Her smile lit up her face. The sunlight beamed across her bare tank-top-strapped shoulders. He tapped her on the knee then got back up onto Athena.

Marina put her nose into the rose. "Every Valentine's Day my dad would buy us girls a single long-stem red rose. I haven't much liked Valentine's Day since he passed. Derrick doesn't apparently care to celebrate it either."

"That's really sweet, a great memory. You know he would carry on that tradition if he were still here."

"Yeah, I know he would. Red roses are bittersweet. I love them for the sweet memories but they've made me sad since he's been gone."

"I'm so sorry you lost him. Maybe the roses are a sign he's thinking of you right now too."

"Maybe. I'd like to think so. Well, now I can love roses again because I'll think of you and this sweet gesture. Thank you for that."

"Yes, ma'am. You're welcome." They exchanged sweet smiles.

"As far as Derrick goes, well, a real man would know how a lady should be treated. No offense."

"No offense taken. I agree."

"What does your mom do?" He rubbed the scruff of his chin.

"She's a teacher, about to retire soon."

"Nice. That's a noble career with a lot of patience involved."

"She's a wonderful woman with a big heart."

"Well, I know she has a daughter who takes after her."

She looked over at him smiling.

"It's true. You're a kind soul."

"Thanks, Sawyer. You are too, ya know."

"Well thank ya."

"I actually asked around about you after I started working here."

"Did ya now?"

"Yes, and everyone in town who knows you had nothing but great things to say. You're popular with the ladies in their discussions too. I've overheard a few that I wasn't a part of.

"Really?" He seemed genuinely surprised and snapped a tall reed of grass off to chew on.

"You can't tell me you're surprised."

"Why not? What do they say? I really don't get out much so not sure what there is to talk about."

"Oh, come on, Sawyer. For real? It's all compliments, of course, that you're a nice guy, a gentleman, how totally and insanely attractive you are, things they wish they could do with you."

He wrinkled his eyebrows with the stiff blade of grass sticking out of the corner of his mouth. "Seriously? I had no idea. I honestly pay no attention."

"I like that about you. That you aren't cocky and arrogant, don't give all the girls in town your attention. You're a stand-up guy who's focused on his everyday life."

"Wow, that's quite the compliment. I appreciate that. I think you're the same way, ya know. You're oblivious to how guys look at you. You're a simple woman but create stares and smiles wherever you go."

"I guess so. Not sure what they'd see, I guess."

"I know exactly what they see, Marina." There was that deep tone again as he looked at her. She had a bright-eyed delicate look on her face. Her lips parted as she inadvertently batted her eyes.

"I hope someday you can see in yourself what I see in you; your beauty, personality, and strength. You're right about it being a turn-on, that you aren't over-confident, but it makes me wanna show you why you should be. It breaks my heart that you don't see yourself the way I see you. You will one day though, Miss

Marina, I promise you that." He flicked away the reed he had been chewing on. She didn't know how to react. She wanted to fall into his arms romantically but also wanted to tackle him off that saddle and onto the ground. She was surprised by his boldness.

"I'm not sure why you're single, Sawyer. Any girl would be *so* lucky to have you."

"That's sweet of you to say. I don't just want any girl though."

"I can't believe I just said it out loud, honestly," she joked with a giggle.

"Why's that? I wanna know how you feel. It's important to be open and honest with each other."

"You're absolutely right. So, if I may ask, why didn't your last relationship work out?"

"I asked her to move in. She brought over a few things but wouldn't fully move in. I found out she didn't want to give up her place because she was still inviting other guys over."

Marina's eyes grew huge, "What? Who would need more than just you?"

"Thanks. I couldn't be with someone that wasn't committed completely to me. It broke my heart and I've had some trust issues. I went on a couple dates since but it never got past the first date. I didn't feel a connection, didn't click with them. They weren't anyone I'd care to get to know better. I decided to focus on work and stay busy with the guys and playing music, riding and training horses. Love would happen when it was supposed to. I'm good with things turning out the way they did."

"Until you needed barn help. You must have been getting burned out doing everything yourself."

"Nah, I enjoy chores actually."

She looked at him, confused, with a raised brow. He looked at her and smiled that sly, crooked smile. They were coming up to the barn and Sawyer dismounted before Athena was fully still. He hustled over to Marina and helped her down, even though she's dismounted plenty of horses on her own before. She swung a leg over as he took her by her waist and slowly lowered her down close to him. His arm strength proved capable with ease. She realized her hands were still on his forearms and his on her waist once her feet were on solid ground. There was a divine tension before she slid her hands softly off his arms. He considerately removed his hands from her waist and tenderly swiped her hair out of her face.

"Thank you for riding with me today. I enjoyed our chat."

"Me too. Thanks." She still had the rose in one hand.

"I didn't try to trick you, although I'm sure it seems like I did."

"What do you mean?"

"I mean, having you come over today, a Saturday, just to spend time together."

"I don't care if it was a trick or not, I like spending time with you. You already know that though."

"I was hoping so."

There was a pause as they were captured within the paint of their own canvas, eye-to-eye.

"We should remove their tack." Marina snapped out of the near-hypnosis.

"Oh, right. Yeah, you probably need to head home soon, don't you?" He walked around the other side of Athena and unbuckled the saddle strap.

"Yeah, I should. Although he's not working today and thinks you're out of town."

"So, you saying we can take our time putting this tack away?" He lifted the saddle off Athena and walked it into the barn. Athena's coat was a darker shade from the sweat beneath the saddle.

"I don't see why not." Marina unstrapped Legend's saddle.

"Here, I'll take it." He came out of the barn and took the saddle from her. She took off Legend's halter and bit then rinsed it with the hose before hanging it up. He took Athena's off and rinsed it then they led the horses to pasture. They stood along the

MARINA SKYE

fence, watching the horses graze for a moment after Sawyer shut the gate.

"I just want to let you know that I see that wall you're building to protect your pretty little heart. You don't have to be courageous. If you want saving, I'll gladly save you." His elbow leaned against the wooden rail.

She turned to him, feeling dainty and fragile, "I have no doubt you will. Until then, I'll enjoy getting to know you. Thank you for being understanding. You're a good friend and easy to talk to."

"Anytime." He walked her to her car and opened the door for her.

"You know..." She paused before sitting in the seat. "You treat a lady the way she ought to be treated. Thanks for continuously showing me the difference." She sat and he shut her door.

He gave a smile and a nod as he tipped his hat to her again.

CHAPTER 14

New Horse Scouting

S awyer was on the phone, the few words of his conversation that she caught sounded like a possible horse purchase. He asked when he could come to look at it and excitedly thanked the person before he hung up and came back into the barn.

"What are you doing Saturday?" he asked as he got a bottle of water from the fridge.

She locked the stall and replied, "I don't think I have plans. Why do you ask?"

"So...a friend just told me he has a mare that just had a foal. It's a draft. I'm going to look at it Saturday at his farm about two hours from here. Wanna go? I mean, you'll be helping take care of it, so..."

"Well, I don't think cleaning its stall gives me the right to decide if you should get it or not." She raised a brow at him in a mock challenge, but he just stared with puppy dog eyes, waiting for her to say yes.

"Sure, I'd actually love to go." She chuckled because he was like a kid anxious for Christmas morning, all antsy.

"I'll swing by and pick you up. Nine in the morning sound okay? I told him it would be close to noon."

"I'll be ready."She smiled excitedly.

He nodded and yelled, "Yee haw!" as he kicked up some straw on his way out of the barn.

She was secretly just as excited as he was, of course, about seeing the adorable foal, but more so to spend time with him. To be that close to him for half the day or more was nerve-racking but exciting at the same time. Perhaps spending time with her was the reason he was so excited. Nah, probably just excited about the foal. She knew that was wishful thinking on her part. Time was going to drag on til then.

Friday came and went. She didn't see him because he had left before she got there. She likes the days he's running late leaving the house because he will make it a point to run out to say good morning, but that has only happened a couple times. He always leaves a barn note though, even if he quickly says good morning before running to his truck. He must have put the notes out there early, perhaps even the night before. It was sweet that he never failed to remember a note. It made her feel special. She simply wasn't accustomed to that.

She had told Derrick she was going on a day trip for work with her boss but knew he would be jealous; he always was. She wasn't sure why since she always behaved herself. She didn't even bother looking at other men until her new boss came along. She was one of those loyal women who was beautiful and intelligent with a great personality, so he knew what he had and knew others would want it too. But he had been acting distant lately and cold toward her. His reasoning was simple, he had been flirting with other women right in front of her for a while. Who knows what he did behind her back? He was interested in someone else but didn't want to let her go either. She had her suspicions for a long time and asked him to his face but he would repeatedly deny it. He didn't look at her the same as he used to anymore.

What would be the perfect way to get his attention onto the fact that she could have any other man she wanted? That she could be swept away into the arms of a guy more worthy? Was

Derrick worth the effort? At this point, she'd rather have Sawyer's attention.

She took a little extra time on her makeup that morning. Nine o'clock exactly she heard his huge dually truck pull in the drive. She grabbed her purse and trotted to the door. Stepping out onto the porch behind her, Derrick leaned against the doorway with his arms folded while Sawyer got out of the truck and came around to open the passenger door for her. She waved back to Derrick, who just nodded with a scowl on his face, as she climbed into the truck. That excited her even more, her boyfriend was so jealous, it made her smile to the point of biting her lip. Sawyer tipped his hat and smiled at Derrick while walking back around to the driver's side and got in.

"You seem happy this morning. More so than usual, even." Sawyer drank his coffee and pulled away from the house.

"Yeah, well..." She paused, not sure if she should admit it out loud. "I can't lie. I could tell he was jealous as soon as you stepped out of the truck. Then when you opened my door he crossed his arms. He hasn't opened my door for me in years. I pump my own gas when we drive anywhere together too."

"You're kidding..."

"Unfortunately, no. He isn't just not chivalrous, he's a complete manipulative liar. I don't want to bore you with my drama." She chuckled slightly.

"We've got a two-hour drive, Marina. I'm here to listen if you wanna unload. No judgment, no advice or suggestions unless you ask. I'd like to get to know you better anyways." He took his hat off and laid it up on the dash, then ran his fingers through his hair, which made her salivate to the point of having to swallow several times before she could speak. She tried to not make it obvious that she was watching his every move. She wanted his hair between her fingers. She needed to keep herself occupied.

She went on to talk about the little and not-so-little ways her boyfriend manipulates and how, lately, she takes stabs back just to mess with him. She's tired of feeling belittled and betrayed and like she just isn't good enough. It's embarrassing to be treated the way he treats her if they go out into public. He acts as though he's embarrassed of her, interrupting when she talks like he didn't hear her voice and what she has to say doesn't matter. He sits on his phone instead of spending time with her. He doesn't help her carry in groceries...all the little things that add up. She was frustrated with him and the relationship altogether.

She's been trying to build a life with someone who isn't helping to carry the bricks and she's burned out and he wonders why she gets irritated with him. She has checked out of the relationship completely. She's even been told by people around town that he's messing around behind her back. She was talking herself into leaving the relationship but was scared of change and of being on her own. She had relied on Derrick for too much and for too long.

Sawyer listened without saying anything, just letting her vent until she looked as though she was about to get emotional.

"Do you want to know what I think?"

"As a friend, yes. I'd like a man's point of view, definitely. I want to know if I'm just being pathetic."

"Dump him."

"What?" She was surprised at his bluntness.

"Dump him. No, you're not being pathetic. You have every right to feel that way. I know we've only known each other a short time but you definitely deserve better. I'm not sure how you deal with that but I see you as a strong woman who shouldn't, and doesn't want to, take that kind of shit from a man. In my opinion he's not a man. A real man would open doors for a lady, stop in the middle of a sentence to let her speak, never lie to her..." He paused, as if thinking carefully about his next words. "I don't want you to be treated that way. It breaks my heart, especially to see you tear up."

A single tear rolled down her cheek. She was hoping he didn't see it but he reached over and gently wiped it off her face. The lump in her throat felt lodged. He was so sweet it made her want to cry but, at the same time, it was relieving to know she wasn't exaggerating when she described her drowning emotions out loud.

"If it's destroying you, darlin', it's not love. It's a man's job to restore his lady's faith in true love. To never break promises and always show compassion. You'll know the difference one day. Honey, when a strong woman loves a man, only the man himself can screw it up for both of them."

"I can tell you're one of those real men."

"Absolutely. Thank you."

"How is it you aren't taken then? I know I've asked before but I'm serious."

"Because I got tired of women much like your boyfriend: lying, manipulating, you name it. I'm a pretty good judge of character nowadays. That's why I usually don't make it beyond the first date or two. I'm not married because I take vows and promises seriously."

"It's okay to have specific standards. Sounds like I need to raise mine to more like what your idea of a man is."

He smiled a sly smile and nodded, "Sounds like we both could enjoy each other's company."

"I like the sound of that." She looked out her window for a moment before looking over at him.

They smiled at each other.

"Thank you, Sawyer."

"For what?"

"Listening. Bosses don't usually get vented to by their employees, do they? I mean, typically."

"We aren't the typical boss and employee either though. I'm here to listen anytime. Seriously, I don't mind. Day or night. You call if you need me, or just knock on my door. In fact, if you want a key—"

"Oh, no, you don't have to do that but I appreciate it," she interrupted. "I don't want to be one of those needy, taking-advantage-type chicks."

"You aren't that at all. I'm serious about being here for you. I honestly already cherish our relationship. The best decision I've made in a long time was asking you to come work for me. I've been thankful every day since."

"Oh, Sawyer, that's so sweet. I'm extremely thankful too, but before I start to tear up, we better play some music up in here. Hope we can agree on some. Country okay?"

"I work in a barn, of course it's okay."

After playing *name that song title and artist* first for a while, they rolled up onto the horse ranch.

"I'm so excited!" Sawyer hopped out of the truck and ran around to open her door.

The rancher came out a few seconds later. "Hey there, Sawyer. Who's this pretty lady you got with ya?"

Sawyer smiled proudly and replied, "This is Marina. My new ranch sidekick."

"Pleasure to meet you, young lady." He shook her hand.

"The pleasure is all mine."

"I've done pedigree work for ol' Dave here. Bought one of my horses from him too. Legend."

"Well, we had the vet out here this morning for one of the mare's checkups. Turns out, ya won't believe this, she's pregnant too."

"That's great! Another draft?"

"Yeah, yeah, another draft. I'm gonna have to build a bigger damn barn."

They all laughed in agreement.

"Well, let's go see this youngin'. She's a spunky little thing. Won't be little for long though."

"You have the sire here too?"

"Sure do. I'll show ya him first." The old man led them out to a pasture where the tall sire stood near the fence. "That there is Drummer." He was a dark dun color, much like a Clydesdale, but was a Gypsy Vanner.

"He's beautiful." Marina was in awe at how huge the horse

was. All that muscular horsepower grazing so gracefully. They headed to the barn to see the mare and foal. The mare was lighter than the sire and skewbald. The fluffy foot foal came trotting around from behind her and Marina's jaw dropped. "Oh my God, she's absolutely stunning!" She reached her hand out and the foal came right to her. She was a light buckskin color with black mane and tail, and white hoof fluff. Her muzzle twitched around on her hand before she petted her. "Ugh I think I'm in love." Marina scratched the foal down her head and neck.

"Me too." Sawyer looked at Marina when he said it and the rancher noticed, raised his eyebrows at Sawyer, and gave the elbow knock.

"She's really a great looking foal. I'll take her when she's ready. Just give me a call."

"Okay, sounds good. She'll be ready by Christmas." Dave patted Sawyer's shoulder.

"Perfect. Can I see the other while we're here? The pregnant one?"

"Oh, yeah. Absolutely. She's on the other end of the barn down here."

They walked down and the old man opened the stall. She, too, was huge. She was solid black.

"What color is the sire?"

"He's black too. He's got some gray on his nose and in his mane and tail, which is weird for a Friesian, but it looks more silver. Real beauty he is. He isn't here but I have a picture of him. He was boarded here a month or so ago. Had to pasture them together for a few hours to prep his stall since he arrived early. I guess that's what happens when ya aren't better prepared." He chuckled and wiped his face with a hanky.

"Well if you don't have any buyers lined up by the time that one is ready, let me know."

"Well alright. I don't so far."

"I appreciate it. I'm really excited to get this one home. Oh, hey, you don't happen to know where I can get a Belgian do ya?"

79

Dave nodded his head to the side for them to follow him. "Well, I have one but you aren't gonna want her."

"Whatcha got, Dave?"

"I went to the farmer's auction last week up in Alabama. Bought a young Brabant Belgian, only about a year or so old." Dave limped alongside Sawyer and Marina until they reached the fence of a round pen behind the barn. "She's in rough shape. Was on her way to a kill pen if nobody bought her and you know me, I can't let that happen. She looks so rough that nobody was bidding. I snagged her for $200. Figured I'd give her a fighting chance, anyways." He stopped at the gate and pointed.

"Oh, Jesus!" Sawyer was astonished at what he saw.

"Oh, my!" Marina covered her mouth in shock.

"She looks better now than she did last week, if you can believe it."

"Seriously?" Marina was about to tear up at the site of the poor horse.

"Oh, yeah. She's gained eighteen pounds already."

The glassy eyed beauty stood solid. Her dapple gray, almost snowflake color pattern was beautiful, but she was dangerously thin for a draft horse.

"Her hooves were way too long and her coat looked rough. The farrier came out the day after I brought her home. Wasn't sure if she could even stand in the trailer that far. She laid down the whole ride."

"That's not good." Sawyer's hands were on his hips, his brow furrowed.

"The vet will do an evaluation on her too when he comes out tomorrow. The farrier will be back out around the same time to give her another trim. She could only take so much that first day. I think I can fatten her up. I'll get her looking and feeling her best in no time."

"I have no doubt you will. You always do, Dave." Sawyer gave Dave a pat on the back. "I'll give you eight hundred for her and pay for her care while she's here."

"You want her?" Dave asked, perplexed.

"I do. My parents just retired theirs and need a younger one. They run carriage rides in the winter up in Tennessee. If I had the trailer with me, I'd take her today. She may not be in the best shape for traveling that far right now though."

"Well, ok. If you want her, we can work that out. She's not worth that much right now. You can get her when you get the foal in December."

"Perfect. Thank you, and she will be worth it by the time I get her from ya."

"Pleasure doin' business with ya, as always, Sawyer. I'll call ya when the youngin is ready and weaned." They shook hands.

Back on the road there was talk of adding on a new stall and shopping for new supplies. They were both excited. He adored the way she was with the foal. He caught himself staring more at her than the foal he had been so excited to meet.

CHAPTER 15

Horse Creek

Т he barn note read, "Saddle Up!"

It confused her seeing as Sawyer wasn't even home. She finished chores and led the horses to pasture, except Legend, who she started saddling. She was cinching the saddle belt when Sawyer pulled in. Dust settled as he entered the barn.

"Good morning." He tipped his hat.

"Good morning. Did you want two saddled up?"

"Yes, ma'am. They out in the pasture?"

"Yeah, I was confused since you weren't here. I can go get another."

"Oh, no, it's all good. I'm going to take Smokie. He needs a few lessons today."

"Oh, okay. What lessons are you working on with him?"

"Trail riding and water. He's scared of water." Sawyer shrugged with a wrinkled nose.

"That's not good," Marina shook her head.

"I was hoping to make it back in time to help you out this morning. I'm sorry."

"Oh, don't be sorry. I appreciate the gesture though."

"We might get wet and muddy today. You okay with that?"

"Always. Sounds like a good time." Marina placed the halter

gently around Legend's ear and pulled his hair through.

"You chose the perfect horse, by the way," Sawyer said, walking away, his jeans stretched tightly across his rear and thighs. They almost didn't move when he walked.

"Why's that?" she asked as he turned and took a few steps backwards.

"He's the best trail rider I've got. Maybe Smokie can learn a few things." He turned back around, walking to the pasture.

Lord, that man can wear the Hell out of those jeans. She couldn't stop staring. She buckled the halter and led Legend outside as Sawyer whistled at Smokie. The horse walked right over to him like he's known him for years. He walked right alongside Sawyer back to the barn.

"It's amazing how well he listens to you."

"Yeah, he's really come a long way since he got here. He's full of potential, just needs repetition. Next, we'll be teaching his owner to do what I do so Smokie doesn't revert back to his stubborn ways." He threw the blanket onto Smokie's back.

"Well, he's doing great. Hopefully today goes just as smoothly."

"I hope so but something tells me the water might be problematic." He tossed the saddle onto Smokie's back and started cinching the buckle. Sawyer slapped Smokie's side and Smokie let out a huff.

Marina just looked at him as she stood with Legend just outside the barn doors.

"He likes to bloat his belly when ya put the saddle on so it's not too tight. I don't wanna slide off the side when we start riding. He does it every time."

Marina giggled. He reads the horses so well. He was born to work with them.

"My mom had a horse that did that. She acted more like a mule."

"Stubborn?"

"Most definitely. She was a dominant mare. Major attitude."

"They're the most challenging to train too."

"Worse than stallions?"

"Definitely. A wild stallion would be easier." He put the halter on Smokie's face gently and buckled it. "Ready? It could be an adventure." Sawyer stepped into the stirrup and hoisted himself onto Smokie's back with ease.

"I look forward to adventures," Marina replied, stepping into the stirrup. She swung a leg over the saddle and adjusted herself straight. Sawyer made a clicking sound out the side of his mouth, holding the reins over to the right, spinning Smokie around.

"Want me to follow you?" Marina and Legend walked behind Sawyer and Smokie.

"Actually, when we get up here to the edge of the woods, I'll have you pass me and you lead. Smokie hasn't been down a wooded trail before. He'll need to follow Legend to be more comfortable. Then once you're ahead of us I'll have you stay more to the right of the trail so if Smokie decides to act like an ass, there's room to pass if need be."

"Sounds like a plan." Marina swatted at a fly buzzing near Legend's ear. Poor guy kept twitching his ear, it was driving him crazy. Tiny clouds of dust poofed up behind each hoof that clunked the dirt. Marina stayed about ten feet or so behind Sawyer as to not put too much pressure on Smokie. She could tell Sawyer had trained Legend because she hadn't ever ridden a horse with such grace, even as he simply walked through the grassy field and dirt paths. Sawyer rode like a natural with complete confidence. His rear matched that saddle perfectly. She couldn't help noticing. Enjoying the view while following behind him, she soaked it all in while she could.

"Doing okay back there?" he asked.

"Perfectly," she answered.

His body didn't sway much, but instead flowed fluently with each step Smokie took.

"I don't wanna teach him to stop just before the woods. I want him to not hesitate, so if you would go ahead and get in front of us but stay to the right in case he freaks out. Not too fast now, just real easy."

"Yes, sir." She made a clicking sound and gently clunked a heel into Legend's side. He boosted his walk fast enough to catch up and go around, gradually crossing over in front of Smokie. She stayed over to the right side like Sawyer asked. Smokie jerked his head up and slowed to almost a stop but Sawyer clunked his heel and gave him a pat on the neck.

"Let's go. It's alright." The reins were loose to show trust instead of total control. Smokie lowered his head as if he were ducking under a low-lying limb. He was slow with caution so Marina tried to match their speed until they got into the wood's edge. She entered the shade beneath the trees and looked back. Smokie looked like a scared horse out of a cartoon, nostrils flared and ears back. His eyes were darting around and huge.

"Good boy," Sawyer patted him again, an enthusiastic voice.

"Look at you, Smokie!" Marina encouraged.

"Go ahead and pick up pace a bit. Maybe he'll follow."

"Okay," she clicked and clunked. Legend picked up pace to a fast walk.

"It's okay, buddy. Let's catch up. Follow Legend."

Smokie picked up pace and his head was fully raised now and ears up on point.

"He's doing well," Marina pointed out.

"He is. He's really young, not even two. Not sure what his colthood was like but he was definitely deprived. He couldn't even be ridden 'til he was brought here."

"You haven't had him here long at all."

"Nah. I'm guessing he witnessed other horses being ridden so he wasn't that scared. He didn't like the feel of the blanket on his back the first time but I just kept flopping it up there when I'd move him from stall to pasture and back or when I'd saddle another up. Even when I was cleaning stalls. It spooked him the first time and he reared up in the stall. Thought he was gonna bust right through the wall. He got them all a bit stirred up. The first time I put a saddle on him I did it in the circle pen so he had room to throw a fit but I could still wrangle him if I had to."

"Good thinking." She laughed at the image in her head. Smokie tried to walk alongside Legend so Sawyer allowed it for a few minutes then pulled back gently on the reins, just enough to slow him. He led him to walk directly behind Legend.

"I want him to learn to follow in a single file line so if he's on a trail with several horses he doesn't get too pushy.

"I rode a horse like that once. I had scrapes and bruises after that ride." She laughed at the memory. "It's funny now but it wasn't then."

"I bet." He laughed along with her as he redirected Smokie to ride beside Legend and keep pace.

"It's amazing how far he's come with you working him. It's like he senses the trust and patience.

"Thanks. Horses don't usually use both halves of their brain at once. They use their senses differently on each side of their brain so I kinda see it as like they've got a split personality. That's why they're unpredictable. It took a while for me to learn patterns and predict their actions. This one is skittish. He's pretty jumpy. Can't let your guard down around him."

"Poor thing. He must have been living a sheltered life before your buddy bought him."

"I think so. You've met Chris actually."

"Oh, the buddy that bought Smokie?"

"Yep. He's not as savvy with horses but wants to ride. He takes good care of them."

"Why didn't he buy a broken horse then?"

"Well, funny story. He told the auctioneer he wanted a broken horse. The auctioneer took that as mentally or physically broken, I think." Sawyer chuckled.

"Oh no!"

"Yeah, but Smokie's young and he's getting trained right away. He's doing great already so I think it was a smart buy, after all."

"That's great. I'm impressed at how well he's doing. He seems more relaxed now."

"He sure is. Until we get to the creek." Sawyer smirked then dodged a rogue branch near his head. It almost took his hat off. She giggled. "I think I'll take lead, the water is getting close but you'll lead once we get closer. Maybe he'll just calmly follow. Probably wishful thinking."

"Hope you prepare just in case."

"Definitely." Sawyer led Smokie ahead a bit and Legend fell in line to follow. Marina didn't even have to move the reins. The horses' tails swooshed side to side, whipping themselves to fend off flies.

"He seems to be comfortable both leading and following so I'll let you go ahead of us again. The water is coming up soon."

"Sounds good." She passed them again as the ground turned damp, then to mush. The faint sound of water trickling grew louder just before the creek came into sight. Marina directed Legend down the slight embankment and into the water. Water rippled around Legend's knees as he high-stepped through the creek. It was only six feet or so across. Smokie followed and lowered his head. His hair from his mane fell down into his eyes, his ears pinned back and nostrils flared. He huffed loudly. That was his typical 'I don't want to' noise.

"It's okay, Smokie. You got this." Sawyer patted his neck, reaching further this time, then pulled on the reins a bit to lift his head. Smokie gnawed on the bit and pawed the ground with his left front hoof as Marina and Legend made it across the creek and waited along the water's edge.

"Come on, Smokie!" Marina coaxed. A hoof stepped in then right back out.

"Something tells me we're gonna be here a while."

"Looks that way," Marina agreed. A hoof went in again but this time to splash. Smokie stomped at the water and seemed to enjoy the cooling effect. His lips nipped at the water and slurped it.

"He sure is taking his time." Sawyer laughed, sitting back in the saddle, relaxed and barely holding onto the reins. Smokie took another step into the water, two hooves now under the surface. A back leg closed in on a front, then the other leg. He looked as if he were about to...yep. There he went. Smokie lowered himself down like a dog and laid in the water. Marina was laughing as Sawyer's legs were now all wet. Then Smokie started to roll so Sawyer bailed, holding his hat on his head.

"Damn it, Smokie!" he hollered. "Damn horse," he muttered as he waded through the water that came up to nearly his knees, then chuckled. As he approached Smokie at the front, Marina dismounted and dropped the reins. She trusted Legend would stay put. Legend sipped a drink at the water's edge, paying no attention to Smokie rolling around and grunting. He'd roll to one side then roll to the other, keeping his head out of the water. Marina stepped into the water, put her hands under the surface then playfully showered Sawyer with a splash.

Sawyer paused and hung his head then laughed and splashed her back. She squealed and shielded her face but enjoyed every second of it. They were enjoying the cool water on their skin until Smokie stood up and shook himself off. He snorted just before Sawyer calmly took hold of his reins. "I might as well walk him on out now."

Marina stepped up onto the shallow bank next to Legend, who was too lazy to play in the water. Sawyer led Smokie across then hopped back up onto his back, dripping wet. That dripping-wet look fit him perfectly. Sun rays shone through branches and lit up his upper chest. His button-up shirt wasn't buttoned all the way up.

"Good thing you wore shorts today," he observed with a crooked grin.

"No doubt." She grinned at him in return, gripping the saddle horn and hoisting herself up into the seat.

"Not sure why you bothered to wear a shirt." She giggled as Legend stepped around in a circle.

"I didn't expect to get this wet," he joked.

"Obviously."

"Next time I'll be better prepared." He unbuttoned his shirt the rest of the way to allow the breeze to better dry his shirt. She glanced back at him briefly and thought to herself, *he did not just do that.* She glanced back again a moment later. Oh, but he did. He did just release his chest to the open air, the flashes of light dancing upon his distinguished pecks, dampened with creek water. She tried to keep from staring.

She cleared her throat and bit her lip, clenching her eyes shut for just a moment. When she opened them again, he was riding next to her, trying not to look over at his chest. He sat taller than her in the saddle so it was difficult not to.

"This could've been a complete disaster, you know..." Sawyer was looking at her, she could feel it.

"Well, he's not afraid of water anymore. I'm sure it helped being a hot day."

"Maybe so. He could've reared up or bucked me off, hurt somebody. We all got lucky."

"Yeah, we did. He had a great instructor though." Marina looked over at him but struggled to keep eye contact and quickly turned her eyes back to the path in front of them.

"I didn't teach him to roll in the creek." Sawyer chuckled.

"No, but you taught him patience and had Legend take the lead. You gave him a sense of security. He feels safe with you."

"Thanks," he accepted the compliment.

"Of course. But ya know, it would've been much funnier if you would've taught him to roll." She laughed.

"He encouraged you to splash, didn't he?"

"Actually, yeah, he did. I was hoping you'd laugh about it."

"Why wouldn't I laugh?" Sawyer realized her situation at home must be the walk-on-eggshells type.

"I'm just glad you have a sense of humor." She was relieved to know she could have fun with him.

"I'm glad we can have fun like this. That's all." She smiled up at him, his blue eyes gazing back at her.

Smokie's tail was more like a whip now that it was wet. Every time he'd whip it, Sawyer would feel droplets all over his back.

"Always." His smile just about melted her out of the saddle. "You know you can be completely yourself around me, right? Like, just open up and never worry about a negative reaction. I want to get to know you for who you really are. If it's any consolation, I already like everything about you; that I've seen anyways. Personality, work ethic...everything."

She could tell he tried to cover the fact that he was talking about physically too.

"I appreciate that, Sawyer. You've given me no reason to hide anything. I do feel I can be myself around you. You make me feel comfortable."

"Good. Glad to hear it." He dodged another branch and some hanging moss almost confiscated his hat. They continued a short distance to a split in the trail.

"So, if we were to go straight it would lead around the back-side of the property. It narrows to just a tree line and the trail just stops at a pond. We can go back this way to the left and it comes out at the field's edge but not through water again."

"Okay, I'll follow you." She gently pulled the reins to the left, changing Legend's direction. He followed closely behind Smokie at first, then backed off, giving room for Smokie's tail to whip. Once they reached the open field, they rode at a canter side by side all the way back to the barn.

They dismounted up by the barn and led the horses around the corner to the wash station. Sawyer removed the tack and Marina turned on the faucet. She gently started spraying Legend. Mud ran from the horse's lower legs and down the drain. Sawyer hung his hat on the hook to keep it from getting wet. Their boots stood together against the wall as Sawyer sprayed down Smokie with the second hose. Legend didn't get really dirty but his lower legs were a mess. Sawyer, with a straight face, sprayed Marina quickly then pretended he didn't mean to. She stood, surprised for a moment, looking down at her wet clothes.

"Sorry 'bout that." Sawyer smirked.

"I don't think you are." Marina sprayed him back.

"Yeah, you're right." He returned the spray.

They weren't even dodging the water, just having fun. The water running down his chest made the heated air feel even hotter. It felt as though the cold water spraying at her wasn't cooling her off at all.

"Okay, okay, truce." She stopped spraying.

"You're calling a truce already?" He released the hose handle, then sprayed her once more really quick. She just stared at him and laughed.

"Don't happen to have dry clothes in your car, do you?"

"Nope. Sure don't." She rang out the bottom of her shirt.

"That's a bummer." He grinned.

"Sure is. I might have a towel or something. I'll go look."

"If you want to put these guys out to pasture, I'll go in and grab you a t-shirt of mine to wear. I'll make sure it's a longer one." He turned the water faucet off at the wall.

"Okay. I mean, if it's no trouble."

"Not at all." He walked off barefoot with his wet button-up shirt clinging to his skin. She clicked for the horses to follow her as she walked them out. Her hair was sopping wet, same as his. The horses joined the others in the pasture and she locked the gate behind her as she exited. He walked back out shirtless, his wet jeans riding low on his hips. He was holding a blue t-shirt.

"Here you go. I hope it's long enough in case you ride home without your shorts. The only other one I had was white."

"Yeah, blue is probably better, thanks. I'll bring it back Monday morning."

"No rush. Want a beer?" He went into the barn and opened the fridge.

"Maybe a water, thanks." She went into a stall and took her wet clothes off, flopping them over the stall door. It grabbed his attention as he shut the fridge door and popped the top off his beer with a horseshoe bottle opener that was mounted onto the edge of the counter next to the fridge. She slipped the t-shirt on. When she opened the stall door, he was leaning against the fridge, facing her, taking a chug of beer. The shirt barely covered her rear so she walked carefully, tugging at the bottom in the front.

"It's a little short but it will do." She held her wet clothes in her hand, out away from the dry shirt.

He nearly choked on his beer and had to turn away. "It'll get ya home dry."

"Thank you, again."

"Absolutely." He had a difficult time not looking below her face level.

"I'll walk you to the car." He grabbed the bottle of water he had set on the counter for her and walked beside her to the car. She opened the door and tossed her wet clothes across and onto the floor on the passenger side. She pulled the shirt down in the back as she leaned over. She heard him take a deep breath.

"I had a lot of fun today. Thanks for taking me out with you."

"Oh, I had a blast. Thanks for tagging along. Sorry about the wet clothes." He handed her the water.

She laughed. "I'm not sorry. That was half the fun. I'll take a real shower when I get home."

"I'm about to. A cold one. I'm sure I'll see you this week sometime." He gave her a hug and his skin was already hot from the sun.

"I look forward to it. Enjoy your evening."

"You too." He held on to the top corner of her car door as she got in, careful to keep her legs together. He smiled and shut her door. She waved then he walked up the driveway, hands in his pockets, as she drove out.

The barn note Monday morning read, "You make me look forward to tomorrow." He was so sweet. She touched her fingertips to her lips with an excited smile and laid the neatly folded blue t-shirt on the countertop by the coffee pot. The sun shone a bit brighter that day and the coffee tasted richer.

CHAPTER 16

Fishing the Pond

"Happy Birthday, Beauty! Let me take you fishin'." Is what the barn note read. She was surprised.

She was thinking it had been a while since she'd gone fishing. She texted him right away. "Aww, thank you! Not sure how you knew it was my birthday, but I'd love to go fishing with you. When?"

He promptly replied, saying, "This afternoon if you aren't busy" and added a wink emoji.

"I'll be there when you get home from work." While she did chores, Justin questioned Sawyer about why he doesn't get asked to go fishing. Sawyer told him he'd have him over soon to go.

That afternoon came quickly after Marina ran grocery errands in town. She returned to Sawyer's shortly after four but he was already home.

"I thought for sure I'd beat you here." She exited her car and walked up to the porch. He had all the fishing gear sitting there ready. He looked great in those plaid cargo shorts, a gray t-shirt, and his HEYDUDE shoes.

"I might have gotten bored at work and...maybe excited to hang out with you."

"Really?" She tossed her hair out of her face.

"Yeah, really." He picked up the poles and tackle box. "You wanna grab that little cooler?"

"Sure. So, I was surprised that you wanted to take me fishing." She followed him to the four-wheelers.

"Why?"

"Isn't that something you normally do with your guy friends?"

"Once in a while. Justin actually told me today he'd like to go soon."

"Why didn't you invite him along? I don't mind meeting your friends."

"I just wanted to hang with you, get to know each other better. I like being around you. Plus, it's your birthday." He strapped the poles to the four-wheeler then put the tackle box on the back as she set the cooler on hers.

"That's nice that you want to get to know me, but there's not much to tell that you don't already know." She hopped onto the four-wheeler. "I'm a simple girl."

"I like that about you." He hiked his shorts up on his thighs then sat on his. "I know that's not true though...about there not being much to tell."

She laughed. "I have no life except hanging out with you or my girlfriends every now and then."

"What else do you like to do though? Doesn't your boyfriend go do stuff with you?"

"*Pfft*, no. It's like he's embarrassed to be seen with me or something. He's a homebody and expects me to be as well. He has a problem with me going to do stuff I enjoy, even on my birthday."

"I find it hard to believe he'd be embarrassed to be seen with you. I definitely wouldn't be. I'd wanna take you out to show you off. Spin you 'round a dance floor, cookouts with friends, out to dinner, the whole bit."

"That's kind of you to say."

"I mean it. He's a dumbass."

"Well, that's because you're a gentleman."

"Thanks. I meant every word."

They revved up the four-wheelers and she followed him through the field.

"So, where are we fishing?" She caught up to him, riding alongside.

"The pond at the end of the creek. It's not huge but I've caught some decent fish in it. There's plenty of fish in the pond but I'm fishing for one in particular." His sly sideways smile was so sexy.

She just smiled. She loved spending time with him and loved that he wanted to spend time with her, even just as friends.

When they reached the pond, they unloaded the equipment.

"So, what do we have for bait?" She opened the tackle box but didn't find bait.

"Over here under this tree there's dark soil where the earthworms are really abundant. They make perfect bait."

"Convenient. Cheap too."

"Exactly. Just gotta dig around for 'em. If you don't want to get your hands dirty, I can grab some for ya," he joked, looking up at her as he squatted under the tree.

Her tongue in her cheek, she replied, "Actually, I don't mind getting dirty." She squatted next to him. Together, they dug out several earthworms and baited their hooks.

"Not gonne lie, it's pretty hot you're a dirty girl." He lowered his sunglasses down onto his face.

She laughed and shook her head. "So, do you hunt too?"

"Yeah. Jake, the lady's man from the bar the other night, and I usually hunt together."

"What do y'all hunt for?"

"Whatever we'll eat; deer mainly. If we catch keepers today, I'll clean them and grill them if you wanna stay and eat 'em with me."

"Do you not want them to go to waste, or are you trying to spend more time with me?" She wiped her dirty hands on her jean shorts.

"Maybe both." He shrugged a shoulder then cast his line into the water, letting the bobber float.

"Good. I accept the offer."

"Yeah?" He sounded excited and tipped his glasses up when he looked at her. "Your boyfriend won't be pissed?"

She shrugged. "I don't care anymore, honestly. He's probably going to be out scoping out other women. He thinks I don't know he does that after work. That's probably the reason he doesn't take me out. I hear things, I know people, it's not a very big town."

Sawyer's expression looked concerned.

"He does that? Seriously?"

"Oh yeah. I can't even mention your name though."

"That's ridiculous. Why would he need to scope out other women when he has you? Makes no sense." Sawyer shook his head in disbelief.

"Thanks, that's sweet."

"Seriously though. He's a dick."

"You have no idea, Sawyer."

"Why are you still with him? If I may ask."

"You can ask me anything. I guess I tolerate him, but as a roommate more than anything. I own the house. I bought it with inheritance money after my dad passed. I had been renting it when he moved in with me. I'd love to kick him out but can't afford to. I guess I could post an ad for a new roommate and *then* kick him out though."

"A good man doesn't choose many girls, instead he loves one girl in so many different ways." He took a chug of beer. "Have you thought about selling or renting it out?"

"First of all, that's deep and I agree completely. Second of all, I have thought about it, I just don't know what to do."

"You always have somewhere to go so don't you worry about that. You do what you need to do for yourself."

She nodded her head in agreement then paused. "Am I asking for too much?"

Sawyer shook his head no.

"I mean, to stay faithful and loyal and treat me with respect? That should be a given in a relationship, right?"

"Absolutely. You're not asking for too much. In fact, you're asking for the bare minimum."

"I think so too. I refuse to keep fighting tears every time I'm treated poorly. I won't take it anymore, not from him. I deserve more than the bare minimum."

"You absolutely do. Don't let him dim the sparkle in your eyes."

She sweetly smiled at him.

"My heart breaks for you. I don't want you crying in bed at night, wondering if you're good enough. That's no way to live."

"I'm quite tired of it myself. It's been longer than I can remember since his actions matched his words. He can't seem to keep a promise, either. I'm too good of a person for that situation. I'm unapologetic about it too. I need to start protecting my emotional health. I feel stressed and always worried about what he will say when I come home later than I should or when I'm not constantly up doing house chores. I feel like I'm not allowed to sit and relax. He does though, of course. I started leaving some chores for him to do."

"Good. You need to put yourself first and not care what he thinks anymore. He obviously doesn't care about your feelings." He reeled in his line after feeling a nibble but had nothing on the line.

"I'm sorry," she sighed. "I must sound so negative and here you wanted to come out here to have a good time."

"Absolutely not. It's perfectly acceptable to not be positive all the time. It does sound like you're starting to see that you deserve better though, so that's positive. Look, we're human. We have a wide range of emotions. Trust me, I've been there. If whomever you're talking with doesn't understand that, they shouldn't be the one you're venting to. Everyone needs someone safe. I'll always be that for you." He re-cast again after baiting his hook with a fresh worm.

"Your kindness reminds me that there are still good people in the world. Even though I should be venting to my girlfriends. Thank you, Sawyer."

"Anytime, no matter what. I got you." Just then he had a bite on his pole so he reeled it in. She was excited for him.

"Hey look at that! It's a keeper." He took it off the hook and put it in the cooler of ice.

"Nice! Is that a bass?"

"Yep. He needs a friend to join him on the grill."

She laughed and re-cast after baiting her hook.

The birds sang and frogs hopped. The clouds rolled over and the sun began to set just enough to dim their lighting. She pointed out how the leaves on the trees were starting to turn color. She had a bite on her line and waited until the fish tugged again before she gave it a yank.

"I think I got one!" She started reeling and pulling back.

"Looks like it might be a keeper." He propped his sunglasses up on his head atop his flowing hair. The sun bounced off his eyes, making them shine.

"Sure feels like it." She kept reeling.

"Need help?" He dropped his pole.

"Maybe..." she flirted, knowing she didn't need help at all.

He walked up behind her eagerly and wrapped his arms around her, placing his hands over hers. They reeled it in together and it was, indeed, a keeper.

"Nice! Good work." He fist bumped her.

"Thanks for the help." She held the pole steady as Sawyer chased the flopping fish at the end of the line with his hands.

"It's bigger than mine. Nice."

"Looks like I *have* to stay for dinner now." She smirked.

"I mean, I won't hold you hostage."

"Oh, no, it's ok. I'd rather have dinner here with you. Hostage or not."

"Good. That's what I want too. What do ya think? Wanna fish anymore or just take a short walk around the pond before heading back?"

"Let's walk." She hooked her line onto the pole to keep the hook from dangling and set it on the four-wheeler. He put her fish in the cooler and wiped his hands on his shorts. "Slimy bastards."

She laughed.

He snapped off a cattail as they began walking, peeling it. The sunlight was dimming now.

"It's been a while since I've been fishing. Thanks." She pointed out a turtle walking along a log.

"Thank you for fishing with me. Hope you don't end up in trouble when you go home." The turtle dove into the water.

"It'll be okay. I feel relaxed and happy when I'm around you."

"Good, I'm glad to hear that." He looked over at her. "I'm happy around you too. I'm glad we got to do this today."

"Me too. I think talking to you gave me better clarity."

"Oh? How so?"

"You helped me realize I need to put myself first and do whatever needs to be done to make myself happy again."

"Glad I could help." He paused, then pointed over the water, leaning toward her. "Look. Fireflies."

"I've always thought fireflies over water were romantic. Maybe it's because of fairytale movies I watched as a kid."

"Maybe. I've always thought that too, though. I hear that seeing them is good luck." He dropped the cattail.

"I could use some good luck."

They smiled sweet smiles at each other. The crickets started chirping as they finished the loop around the pond.

"Let's go grill these guys," he said.

"I'm hungry."

"I'm always hungry," he said with a laugh as they loaded up.

He taught her how to clean fish, then they grilled them on the back patio and ate outside, talking about the little things, like what they loved to do as kids. The conversation was happy and revolved around memories they cherished. It was exactly what she needed and the best birthday she'd had in a long time.

CHAPTER 17

Greasin' Up Feelings

M arina pulled into the drive by the barn a little earlier than usual. Sawyer was bent over, working under the hood of his blue Jeep.

"What are you doing home?" She leaned on the Jeep across from him.

"Well, I was gonna take the Jeep to work today but it made a weird noise so I decided to stay home and fix it. I guess I should drive it more often."

"Need help? I don't know anything about fixing cars but I could hand you tools or something."

"If you want to. Or you can just stand there lookin' pretty." He smiled at her as if maybe he was glad she offered.

"Actually, can you hand me this wrench I dropped?"

"Sure." She walked over to him and bent over, picking up the wrench. Upon straightening and handing it to him, her tank top strap fell. He took a double look at her and paused. She looked at him, noticing his stare. He had a look on his face as if something had just taken his breath away. He bit his bottom lip and got back under the hood. It was an awkward pause, but awkward in a good way. It seemed like it was in slow-motion yet happened too quickly at the same time. That stare made her heart skip a beat. She pulled her strap back up onto her shoulder. It was slightly breezy that morning, so once in a while her hair would cross her face. She stood next to him, watching him twist the wrench. He swept her hair to the side but left a grease mark on her cheek and laughed. "I'm sorry."

"For what?"

"You, um..." He cleared his throat. "You have grease on your cheek now."

"That's ok, I match you then."

He looked in the side mirror but had none on his face.

"What do you m—"

She quickly smeared a greasy finger across his face.

"Oh, I see!"

She laughed, which made him laugh.

"What are you gonna do about it? Fire me?" she teased.

"I don't think I could ever do that." He looked at her ever so softly, his glacier-blue eyes sparkling. She slapped him on the arm with the shop rag to break the undeniable tension.

"Wanna crank it up? Let's see if she's fixed."

Marina started up the Jeep and there were no strange noises.

"Perfect!" He let the hood slam shut. He wiped his hands with the dirty rag.

"What was wrong with it?"

"I just tightened up a few things. These damned dirt roads are rough, it probably rattled stuff loose. I guess I better clean up and go to work."

"I'll get busy on chores."

"I'll help you real quick." He put the tools back into the toolbox.

"I can do it. Go ahead and go."

"It's okay, really, my boss is a cool guy. He won't mind," Sawyer sarcastically replied with a smirk.

"If you insist." Marina shrugged and turned, walking toward the barn with her hands in the back pockets of her cut-off denim shorts. She could feel his eyes on her and debated on turning around to see. He was...he was totally watching her walk. The reflection in the barn window gave him away. She fought a smile. He caught up and walked next to her.

Upon entering the barn, she poured a cup of coffee, since he had already brewed a pot. She saw there was a note but didn't read it right away. He filled the water troughs as she took hay out to the pasture to fill the feed bags. They both turned horses out and pitched the stalls.

"Tonight's Friday...wanna hang?" That's what the barn note read. She read it as he gassed up the four-wheelers. He entered the barn just after she set the note down and picked her coffee up in a rush.

"I checked the fence already this morning but it's gassed up for tomorrow."

"Okay, great. Thanks."

"I'm going to go to work for a bit. I have some breeding stuff I need to do for a farmer and my computer is at the office, but that's all I need to do today. You have plans tonight?"

"I don't, actually. What do you have in mind?"

"Gladys is trying out her new brick oven today. Feel like pizza and drinks?"

"Sure. Sounds fun."

"I don't plan to play music tonight, just thought we could hang out."

"Sounds good to me. So just dress casual?"

"What you have on is perfect."

She smiled. "Okay, you need me to do any evening chores?"

"Nah, I'll do them before we go eat. Then I'll shower and pick you up, if that's okay. No need for you to be driving that late going home."

"Perfect." She knew her boyfriend would be furious but she didn't care. In fact, she looked forward to rubbing a good time in his face. The more he drank the worse it got for her. It was to the point where she didn't want to go home anymore anyways.

"Have a good day at work." She headed to her car and he waved on his way to his Jeep.

She was in the shower at home when Derrick got home from work. When she shut the water off, he quickly hung up his phone.

"Who was that?" she asked in a calm, nonchalant tone as she toweled off in the bathroom, the door cracked slightly.

"Why the hell does it matter? It was work related so don't worry about it," he shouted defensively.

"Whoa. Okay fine. You don't have to get nasty about me asking."

"Apparently, I do. It's none of your business."

"I see. Okay. Well, I don't need to be around here with your attitude tonight so I'm leaving." She shut the door the rest of the way and got dressed into clean cut-off shorts and a clean tank top. He entered back into the bedroom as she re-entered the bathroom.

"Where are you goin'?"

"Don't worry about it. It's none of your business." She smiled, feeling vindicated. She put her makeup on, did her hair, slipped her wedge sandals on, and grabbed her purse on her way out the door. Sawyer pulled up out front in the Jeep just as she stepped out. She was thinking to herself that was perfect timing. The screen door didn't slam, Derrick caught it with his foot.

Derrick had followed her out and was instantly angry seeing it was Sawyer she was going out with. He yelled at her, "Seriously? This guy again?"

"He's my boss. We're just friends." She rolled her eyes, awaiting the wrath.

"I don't believe that. Not at all. He wants more from you and you know it. You just teasing him or are you giving him what he wants?"

"You're crazy!" She started down the steps but he grabbed her arm harshly. Sawyer quickly stepped out of the Jeep, ready to defend her.

"Let go!" She jerked her arm away, freeing herself.

"I forbid you to leave with him," he growled at her.

"Forbid me? Wow! And if I were to say that to you—"

He stuck his finger in her face as he grabbed her arm again. Sawyer was opening the passenger door for her and hollered, "Hey! Let her go!"

"Or what, tough guy?"

Sawyer started marching toward the porch but Derrick let her go with a slight shove.

"Get in the Jeep," Sawyer instructed Marina. She got into the jeep and shut the door but left the window down. Sawyer told Derrick, "Lay a hand on her again and you'll find out exactly how tough I am." Then he walked back to the Jeep.

"Is that a threat? I heard a threat."

"Nah, it's a warning. I promise I'll come for you if you don't respect her. I don't break my promises." Sawyer got in the Jeep and they flung dirt up behind the tires as they sped off.

"I'm so sorry," Marina apologized, embarrassed about the entire scene.

"No. Don't you apologize. Not for his behavior."

"I'm sorry you had to stick up for me. Thank you."

"Please, you know I have your back. You know that, right?"

"I do. You proved that just now. That was kind of you. I don't want him coming after you though."

"I can hold my own. You don't worry about me." He patted her thigh and she was quiet the rest of the ride. Only a few minutes up the next dirt road was the Backcountry Bar. They didn't exit the Jeep right away when they pulled in but he did shut the engine off.

"Hey..." Sawyer wanted her attention. "I'm sorry you had to deal with him treating you that way. Just know I'm always here for you. Whether it's as someone to vent to, or escape to, or for protection. I seriously mean that. I don't want you around him."

"I know you mean it and you have no idea how much I appreciate it. It's just sad that my boss has to step in."

"Hey, I'm more than your boss." He gently turned her chin so she would look into his eyes. "I'm your friend."

"Yes, you are."

"I want you to have fun tonight. If that means drinking til I have to carry you out, I'm okay with that. We'll eat pizza and dance, chat with folks, whatever you want to do. It's all you tonight."

"Thank you. I hope to forget about him for tonight and just cut loose and have fun with you. I'm starving, let's go eat." She playfully tapped his arm with the back of her hand and exited the Jeep. He followed her, smiling, then caught up to her. He opened the bar door for her and excited shouts of greeting met them.

"It's been a few weeks," Gladys pointed out.

"I've been busy and working out of town or at the office the last few weekends. Sorry, y'all."

"I see you brought Marina with ya." Gladys winked at Sawyer. "Glad to see you back, sweety." She leaned forward over the bar and handed Marina a menu.

"Thanks, it's good to be back. I'm starving. Your pizza oven ready for use?"

"It always is for you and Sawyer. You haven't had a pizza from my new oven yet, have you?"

"I have not. We're excited to try one though."

"Y'all let me know what you want on it and I'll make it quick."

"Sounds good, thanks." Marina walked back down to Sawyer who was chatting with Bob at the end of the bar. "What kind of pizza do you want?"

"I'll eat anything. Honestly. You go ahead and decide. Surprise me."

"Okay." She walked back down to Gladys at the computer to put the order in.

A local patted Sawyer on the shoulder and told him, "You brought in a real pretty lady tonight. Is it serious or can I take a shot?" He was a scruffy guy, the burly type.

He was joking, apparently, because Sawyer chuckled when he answered, "She sure is pretty but she's taken."

"By you?" the man asked.

Sawyer hesitated and returned the shoulder pat. "Maybe. Hopefully someday."

She pretended not to overhear but she couldn't believe what she had just heard. The thought seemed too good to be true. Him saying it aloud was exciting. She would want to take it slow after the hellacious relationship she was in currently. She couldn't wait to be done with the jerk, just to be financially stable enough to pack her stuff and leave. She was saving though, adding her extra barn hours from weekends to an account Derrick didn't know about. Sawyer paid her well but she would need an extra part-time gig. That got her thinking.

"Hey, Gladys? You wouldn't happen to be hiring, would you?" Marina leaned her elbows against the bar in an attempt to keep her words hidden from Sawyer.

"Well, is it you that's askin'?"

"Yes, ma'am. Just even one night a week. I've tended bar before, served as a waitress too."

"I think we could come up with something. When ya looking?"

"Right away."

"Well, I can't have ya working Friday nights because we want ya to be able to come in with Sawyer and have fun..." She winked and nudged Marina's elbow. "But Monday nights do well because, let's face it, everybody hates Mondays. So those are options, oh and Saturday nights once a month we have a biker night. With it just being my old man and I, we get tired out quickly by Saturday. You could do a little of everything, just help out wherever needed. You can keep all your tips too."

"Sounds great. Thank you."

"Sure, Hun. If you wanna come in tomorrow night to try it out and see if it's what you want to do that'll be fine by me." She spoke softly so she didn't draw Sawyer's attention but at this point, Sawyer was next to Marina at the bar.

"I appreciate it. I'll be in tomorrow." She turned to Sawyer to find him looking confused.

"It may not be my business, but are you inquiring about a job?"

"Yeah. Just a night each week maybe."

"I can pay you more if..."

"No, no no. That's sweet of you to offer. Really. I need to stash money away and I'm not afraid to work for it."

"I know. I know you're a hard worker. I admire your work ethic, but I don't want you stressing yourself out either. You could've just asked me."

"No, sir. I need more time out of the house too. If that makes sense."

"After what I witnessed tonight, yeah, it makes perfect sense."

"So, you understand?"

"Hey, you don't have to explain anything to anyone, including me. I have a feeling I'll have to come up here and jack a few jaws if dudes start messing with you."

"Look at you, all macho and protective."

He chuckled and side-hugged her.

"You should be able to do what you want to do. I'm just letting you know I'm willing to accommodate any way I can to make life easier for you so you don't have to bust your ass at another job."

"You're too good to me already. I keep telling you that." She turned her attention to Gladys who was delivering their pizza.

"Come and get it!" She sat it on a nearby table and Bob slid their drinks across the bar to them.

"Thanks, man." Sawyer held his glass up in a cheers-type fashion then set them on their table and pulled Marina's chair out for her.

"This pizza looks amazing!" He sat backwards on the chair next to Marina.

"It really does. Thanks, Gladys."

Gladys waved her dish towel at them before flopping it over her shoulder on her way back to the kitchen.

"So, what's on this?" Sawyer dished her up a slice.

"It's my favorite. Ham, green peppers, extra cheese with cajun crust."

Sawyer took a bite. "It's amazing."

She nodded in agreement as she took a bite.

They laughed and chatted and ended up eating the whole pizza between the two of them. He motioned for a second round of drinks, which Bob happily poured, and Sawyer went up to the bar to get them.

There were three young ladies who had just arrived. They were asking Gladys about Sawyer down at the other end. Marina noticed them checking him out as if they were stray dogs at a meat market. Gladys handed one of them a menu, trying to distract them into ordering, but one asked fairly loudly, "Is he on the menu?" The young lady's eyes were fixed on Sawyer.

Marina heard her so she knew Sawyer had to have heard as well. She was worried Sawyer's attention would turn to them. They were pretty but acted like a group of high school popular girls. Marina wasn't sure why she was worried. After all, he wasn't even her man to put a claim on. But logic be damned, she instantly felt possessive. She looked at Sawyer then peered back at the girls.

Sawyer, though, didn't even acknowledge them. He got the drinks from Bob and made his way back to the table. Marina couldn't help but smile at him, knowing the girls would be jealous, but proud that he didn't stray his attention away from her. She wasn't trying to be spiteful but those girls were being too forward. She was curious as to how Sawyer would react to being hit on but he went on about his business, not interested in any of them. Why would he not be looking for a little flirtation? All men do, don't they? Most like the attention. This piqued her curiosity.

Should she ask him? Probably not. She was going to anyways though. She couldn't wait to see how it played out.

"Did you not notice those girls checking you out?"

"I heard one ask if I was on the menu..." He laughed and sipped his beer.

"Yeah, I heard that too. Pretty sure she meant for you to hear."

"Most likely." He brushed crumbs off the table. "I'm not interested in them." He looked straight into Marina's eyes. She stared back into his for a moment before Gladys leaned a hand on Sawyer's strong shoulder.

"Listen. These girls up here are probably going to be a handful so if they bother you, I'll kick 'em out."

"Oh, it's ok. Thank you, Gladys."

"Well, I'm cutting them off after two drinks. I don't need them causing a scene. Damn college kids, anyways."

Sawyer laughed. "I'm not paying them any attention. No need to."

"I know. Your attention is on the prettiest girl in the room already."

"Sure is," he agreed, looking at Marina.

"You're single. It's not like we're on a date or anything. Really, it's okay." Marina hoped he would still pass.

He wrinkled his brows.

"You don't get it, do you?" Gladys whispered in her ragged voice.

"Get what?" Marina asked as Gladys walked away.

"He's into you, sweetie," Gladys said loudly. Sawyer took a drink of his beer as Marina adjusted herself nervously in her chair then looked up at him.

He was looking at her with a sultry grin.

"She's not wrong," he said, taking another drink.

Marina was about to say something when one of the girls approached their table.

"Excuse me? Hi. I'm Tamara."

"Nice to meet you, Tamara. I'm Sawyer. This beautiful young lady is Marina."

"I was just wondering if you're here together, like, together as a couple. Or a date or whatever?"

Marina just smiled and took a drink of her fruity vodka.

"Yeah, we're here together."

"Oh, okay. So, I'm guessing you wouldn't want to dance with me?"

Marina almost choked on her drink at the audacity of this chick.

"Sorry." Sawyer apparently wasn't impressed with her audacity either. "I'm with her."

"Like just for this evening, or...?"

Sawyer turned to the girl, not wanting to be rude to a female, but he had had enough. "With all due respect, ma'am, I'm not interested in anyone else."

"Well, with all due respect, sir, that's because you haven't gotten to know me yet." She had a hand rested upon her hip.

"He's not interested and he told you that so now you're harassing him. Maybe just let us be," Marina spoke up.

"Fine. If you change your mind, Cowboy, I'll be at the bar." She walked away, slowly swinging her hips, almost as if she were putting on a catwalk show.

Sawyer didn't look at her. Instead, he took a drink and kept his eyes locked on Marina.

"Thanks. She was starting to piss me off."

"I could tell. You had an irked look on your face," Marina chuckled.

"Some people, I tell ya."

"She really wanted you. Can't say I blame her."

"Doesn't matter. I'm not interested."

"Because I'm here?"

He smiled and tilted his head as if she should know the answer to that question. "I have all I need right here at this table."

"Beer?" Marina teased.

"You're a smartass." Sawyer laughed anyway.

"Really though, you didn't have to do that on my account."

"I didn't. I'm not interested in her or anyone else. I don't have eyes for anybody but you. But you're taken. So, I'll have to be patient and accept our relationship for what it is. I'm hopeful for what it could be." He stood up and held out his hand to her. "Care to dance?"

"I'd love to." She took his hand and they slow danced right there by their table as the jukebox played. Her arms were up around his neck, his around her waist. Their eyes would catch and she'd tip her head against his solid chest. She may have glanced over at the jealous girls a couple of times incognito style. Of course, they were staring and gossiping. One had her arms folded, another her hand on her hip.

Marina loved that he felt this way. He had finally admitted his feelings for her out loud to her directly. She knew for sure now that all those flirtations meant something to him. He softly ran his fingers through her hair around her face and she laid a hand upon his chest. Being this close to him was comforting, like a warm cup of coffee between her hands on a cold morning. His hand ran down the small of her back. It was difficult to be this close to him without kissing him. She was hoping he would kiss her. She didn't want the song playing to end, but it did and Bob hollered last call. They both seemed saddened by the dance ending.

"Would you like another drink?"

"No thanks, I'm good." Marina got her purse from their table after letting go of Sawyer's hand and he went up to the bar and paid their tab. They said goodnight to Bob and Gladys. He held out his arm for her to entangle hers with and they strutted past the girls and out the door, elbows locked.

CHAPTER 18

Crying in the Barn

S awyer woke a little earlier than his alarm was set for. He stretched and rubbed his eyes with his fingertips, swung his legs off the bed, and sat on the edge. He relieved a scratch on his lower back then got up. His bare feet thumped the floor as he made his way to the kitchen.

He made coffee and leaned on the kitchen counter, looking out the window as he drank it. He got a granola bar out of the pantry and put it on the counter then went back to the window, realizing something was off. He narrowed his brows, peering toward the barn.

There was a light on in the barn. He knew he had shut it off the night prior because he remembered walking from the barn to the house in the dark. He set his coffee mug down and got dressed in the bedroom, buttoning his jeans as he slipped on his boots by the door. He didn't bother buttoning his shirt. He snatched his hat off the hook by the door and flipped it onto his head.

He quietly pulled the door shut behind him and went out to the barn, cautiously opening the smaller barn door. Foxtrot let out a huff and offered his face to be touched over his stall door. The others were sleeping, their body weight on just three hooves. Sawyer patted Foxtrot's nose and snuck down to the storage room where the hay bales were. That door was cracked open and the light was on. He stood to the side of the door with a fist ready and pushed it open with his foot.

He instantly relaxed, confused by what he found. Why wouldn't she have come to the house? Maybe she did but he didn't hear her? Marina was curled up with a blanket on the lower stacked hay bales, sleeping. She had dried mascara down her cheeks and she was wearing her clothes from the day before. He covered her up better and watched her sleep for a few minutes, debating on whether or not he should wake her. He went back to the house to finish getting himself ready for work and to get the coffee he had poured and his breakfast. He left the door unlocked when he went back to the barn.

He did the chores as quietly as possible then leaned against the counter in the barn, drinking his coffee, waiting on her to wake. He started the barn coffee pot, knowing the aroma would wake her. The radio turned on but he kept the volume low. *Quittin' Time* played and the lyrics were ironic. It was near her normal waking time anyways. He was a patient man so didn't mind waiting.

She came out of the room rubbing her face, trying to get her eyes to wake up. She was surprised and embarrassed to see him since he usually went straight to work.

"Good morning." He tipped his hat and sipped his coffee.

"Morning. I am so sorry."

"Sorry for what? Having a sleepover with the horses?"

She pulled out a chair and sat at the table, still trying to gather herself.

"I didn't know where else to go. Becka was working and I didn't want to wake Raquel's kids. I guess I just went where I felt safe."

"Safe?" He asked with piqued interest as he pulled out a chair and sat.

"Derrick and I had an argument. I told him I was done, just tired of being the only one trying in the relationship. I didn't appreciate the way he treats me and how he constantly lies. He's so controlling. Then I made the mistake of bringing you up. He didn't believe me that there's nothing going on between us. I feel defeated." She rubbed her arm, which drew his attention to the bruises. The distinct outline of fingerprints ringed her bicep.

He set his coffee down so hard that it splashed out of the cup, then he gently touched her arm. She would've trembled if it were anyone but Sawyer.

"He did this?"

"I'm okay."

"No! No...this! This is not okay! This won't be happening again." He stood up and took his hat off, pacing, his fingers aggressively raking through his hair, "You are always safe here. Always. Day or night, you're always welcome." He scooched his chair closer to her and sat again, his knee touching hers.

"Thank you."

"Did you knock? I'm so sorry I didn't hear it." He took her hand in his.

"No. I didn't want to wake you."

He touched her face. "Wake me if you need me. Any time. Throw rocks at the window if you have to."

She nodded with her head down, ashamed. He tipped her chin up with his finger. "I'm serious." His eyes were so bright and saddened.

"I know. You're so kind. Thank you."

"These bruises piss me off."

"I'm okay, really."

"You know this is wrong, right?"

"Of course I do. I told him I want him out before supper time today. He didn't respect my feelings or boundaries so he is the problem. His leaving is the only solution. This has never happened before; I just want you to know that. Him leaving a mark was the last straw." She paused then, her brow quirking and head tipping to the side in thought. "I left the light on. That's how you knew I was out here, huh?"

"Yeah, I saw the light from the kitchen. I didn't expect it to be you this early though. I didn't see your car."

"I parked on the other side of the barn so it didn't worry you. Sorry."

"Don't be sorry. I'm glad you know you can come here whenever." He gave her a comforting embrace that made her instantly feel safe, sheltered by this rugged soft-hearted man whom she had grown so fond of. He could tell she had survived enormous pain and he could see it once in a while, like that morning when the gleam left her bright eyes. He hated that she endured so much.

"I'm glad you kicked him out but I am sorry about your breakup." He sipped his coffee, trying to hide his almost-smile.

"Are you smiling?" she asked.

"What? Nah, I don't like seeing you hurting. But I'm glad you aren't willing to deal with everything he puts you through anymore. You deserve so much more."

"Do I? I felt guilty spending so much time with you lately."

"It was for work." He shrugged. "Besides, hanging out together doesn't compare to what he was doing behind your back." Again, he sipped to avoid smiling. He was relieved she was a free woman, not attached to a relationship.

"Was it though? I'm not complaining either way. Absolutely not. I just feel a little guilty because I like spending time with you. In fact, I look forward to having the chance to see you every day, even for a brief minute," she bravely admitted.

He openly smiled this time. "I enjoy seeing you too. Too much, probably."

She smiled back. "These were tears of relief by the way. I must look like a total pathetic mess." She fiddled with her hair and he picked a piece of hay out of it.

"I don't think that's possible."

"You're sweet." She shied away, looking down. "So, why aren't you at work? You usually leave before now." She looked at the horseshoe clock on the barn wall.

"I had to make sure you were okay. I would've worried all day."

"You could've woken me so you weren't late."

"I'm my own boss, remember? So, I have the coolest boss ever." He got up and refilled his coffee mug and grabbed a clean cup from the metal horseshoe mug stand, pouring her one as well. He brought it to her at the table then sat.

She thanked him, wrapping her hands around it.

"I have the coolest boss ever too." She smiled.

"You sure you're okay?"

"Yeah. I think I'm actually more relieved now. Thank you, Sawyer, for everything. I like that we can chat."

"That's what friends are for. Was he home when you left?"

"Yeah. Hopefully he's packing all of his shit. I don't care to see him again."

"I don't blame you." Sawyer's fist tightened up and his knuckles cracked.

"Don't even think about it, Sawyer."

"What?"

"Don't retaliate. Please."

"Listen. I'm going to go to work for a while, unless you want me to stay..." He paused because she was shaking her head no.

"I'm fine."

"I left the front door unlocked. Go in and take a shower, get something to eat. Just chill and watch tv or go riding or whatever. Do whatever you want but don't go back home until we know he's gone. Okay?"

"Okay."

"Promise?" His eyebrows rose in question.

"I promise." Her lips tightened.

"Make yourself at home. Take a nap in my bed if you're tired. I don't mind."

"Okay, thanks. I might do that, actually."

"Go for it. Consider the chores done, I'm gonna turn the horses loose then head out." He stood and scooched the chair in.

"I can do that."

"Nope, you go on to the house. I'll see you in a while."

"Okay, have a good day at work." She stood, pushing her chair in.

"I'll try. Call me if you need anything."

"Will do." She smiled sweetly.

He kissed her forehead as he briefly wrapped his arms around her again. He opened the stalls and made a clicking noise as he put his hat on. All the horses followed him as a herd. She picked up her coffee mug and headed for the house. He waited for Foxtrot to go through the gate into the pasture and shut the gate behind him.

It happened to cross his mind that she had never been inside his house before and she may want to know where things are. He stomped dirt off his boots up the steps to the front porch of the house and opened the door. When he stepped inside, he noticed she had taken her shoes off.

She peered out of the bathroom wrapped in only a gray towel.

"Is this bathroom okay?" she asked shyly.

"Yeah, of course." He cleared his throat, thrown off by her near nakedness. "Make yourself at home. I just wanted to ask if you needed anything before I head out."

"I'm sure I can manage. Thank you." She smiled at him, assuring herself her towel was tucked well at her chest.

He paused, staring at her for a moment, then snapped out of his trance. "Sorry, um, would you like a tour? Get to know where things are real quick before I leave? I suppose that would be the polite thing to do...give you a tour."

"Sure, if you have time." She felt behind her to make sure her rear was covered completely. She followed him, her bare feet barely making a sound on the hardwood floor.

"That was my room and master bath, obviously. Sorry, I didn't make my bed. It's not very presentable."

"I don't care about things like that. You'll just get in it again later so why waste the time?"

"Right! I usually at least flip the covers up though but nobody ever goes in there but me. Living room." They passed through and entered the dining room, her following close behind him.

"Your home is absolutely beautiful. Did you design it yourself?"

"I did, actually. Thank you."

The wooden beams across the ceiling made the room look bigger and rustic and they matched the hardwood floor. The fireplace had a matching beam for the mantle with flat gray stone lining the fireplace. The area rug in the center of the living room was white and shades of gray. There was a black-framed grayscale painting on the wall of horses and a few small potted plants sitting around. A huge tv was mounted on the wall in front of the couch. Dark gray furniture and the coffee table looked rustic, matching the rest of the wood in the house. A black cast iron horse statue was placed in the center of the coffee table.

"Hand-built?" she asked as she ran her dainty hand across the dining room table.

"It is. Dad and I built that, the coffee table, and end-tables. The end-tables in all the bedrooms too. Oh, and my headboard. The sliding barn doors to the rooms as well. They do lock shut though."

"It's all so beautiful. Looks like a magazine."

"Thanks. I figured if I was building the house, I'd design and decorate it the way I wanted because I don't ever plan to leave it. I left the walls white out here and light gray in the bedrooms so I can just change décor later without having to repaint."

"Brilliant. It works, all of it. You have exquisite taste. Country but modern. Fits you well."

He rubbed her shoulder with a smile. It didn't make her uncomfortable in the slightest. She felt an intensity that she forced herself to ignore and nearly dropped her towel but didn't let him notice.

"This is the kitchen. Help yourself to anything. The coffee pot is still on. Make yourself something to eat."

She smiled and nodded.

The cabinets were wooden and almost looked like miniature barn doors, right down to the black hardware. The faucet over the sink was also black with a huge white farmhouse-style basin, black appliances, and countertops. Somehow, he made rustic look elegant. Everything was so immaculate too, especially for a bachelor horse guy.

"It's impressive you did so much of this yourself. That's something to be proud of."

"Thanks. My dad and I did most of it ourselves. It was a process for sure. I love it though."

"It's cozy. Gives a comfortable charming presence."

"I agree. Feels like home should."

He showed her through the rest of the house, including the home gym, office, and spare bedroom, then brought her back to the bedroom doorway.

"I'm gonna head off to work but I don't plan to work all day. Feel free to stay here as long as you want to. I have a spare room, as you saw. It's yours if you want it. There's the workout room too if you feel like taking out some frustration."

"Thanks, Sawyer."

"Anytime. Come here." He wrapped his arms around her again, brushed her hair out of her face, and looked her in the eyes. She could've just melted. She could tell she was starting to breathe heavily and swallowed hard.

"Maybe I'll see you later after work." He headed to the door.

"Maybe." She smiled a devilish smile, completely planning to stay until he returned.

He nodded and left, gently closing the door behind him.

She watched him out the window as she held her towel shut. His hands were in his pockets until he got into his truck. She showered then poured a bowl of cereal. She felt it was less invasive than actually cooking something. She chilled on the couch, watching tv, allowing her hair to air dry before snuggling in his bed for a nap.

Meanwhile, Sawyer fumed all the way to Marina's house. That's right. He detoured. He parked out front and marched to the front door, pounding his fist on it. Derrick opened the door and was alarmed to see Sawyer. His eyes widened. Sawyer pushed the door open and stepped inside, uninvited.

"What the hell?" Derrick shouted in protest.

"You left bruises." Sawyer got in his face, which was lower in height than his.

"What?"

"You heard me. You left bruises on Marina's arm. Now I'm gonna have to leave a few on you."

"I just grabbed her arm. She's fine." He turned to walk away but Sawyer grabbed his shoulder.

"It's not fine. I've seen you grab her arm and not leave bruises so you really screwed up." Sawyer kept a strong hold on him.

"Dude, back the hell off. It's none of your business." Derrick jerked away from Sawyer.

"What did you just say to me?" Sawyer was about to come unhinged with rage. He was absolutely furious at this guy's derogatory behavior.

"Why do you care so much? Huh? You screwing her?" He puffed up at Sawyer, being dramatic and now pending self-destruction. Sawyer threw a solid right hook and hit him right in the nose. Blood crept through Derrick's fingers as he covered his face and gasped but didn't say a word.

"Since you wanna screw around on her, that's none of your damn business. I don't see any boxes for packing. You better be gone before I get out of work. I'll be back to make sure."

"Screw you. Get the hell out!" He shoved Sawyer—tried to, anyway—but Sawyer didn't budge. Sawyer's jaw tightened up so much the tension could be seen. His nostrils flared and the deepening brow crease was intimidating.

"The audacity. You're an unstable asshole. Don't speak to her, don't look at her, don't talk to her. I warned you once before so you might want to take me seriously this time."

"Or what?" He wiped blood off his face and wiped his hands on his shorts.

"I'm gonna break more than your nose."

Derrick just *hmph*ed.

Sawyer stepped closer, getting in his face again and grabbed the front of his shirt.

"I'm a reasonable and kind man but I don't take kindly to men disrespecting women. Especially one I'm quite fond of. Like I said, you better be gone before I get back. Pack quick, I won't be working long. I'm not opposed to killin' ya when I return if it means protecting her." Sawyer's eyes were cold and sharp. He shoved Derrick aside and walked out.

Sawyer got to the office and Justin had his feet propped up on his desk.

"Mornin', boss man." Justin looked up, then down, then quickly back up again, "Dude! What happened to your hand?"

Sawyer's hand was red and swollen with blood dried on his knuckles.

"Had to put an asshole in his place."

"That's why you came in late?"

"Yep." Sawyer sat and leaned back in his chair.

"Who pissed in your Cheerios already this morning?" Justin chuckled.

"Marina was dealing with an unkind situation last night. I found her asleep in the barn this morning, bruises on her arm."

"No shit?"

"No shit."

"How badly did you mess the dude up?"

"Just broke his nose. For now."

"You threatened him though, didn't you?"

"Damn right I did. Told him if he's still there when I check after work, I'm not opposed to killin' him." He was getting all worked up again, his brows turned in.

"Damn. You mean it though?"

"Yeah. Absolutely. He lays another hand on her and I'm gonna lose it." He sat up in his chair.

Justin got some ice from their mini fridge in the back and put it in a hand towel. He tossed it at Sawyer, who caught it with his beaten hand. He growled, clenching his teeth, and carefully put the ice on it.

"Gonna wash the dude's blood off your hand?"

"Eventually." Sawyer tipped his head back with his eyes closed. "Got any Advil in your desk?"

Justin got a bottle out of his lower desk drawer and tossed it to him. Sawyer awkwardly caught it with his less-dominant hand.

"You ass."

Justin laughed. "So you just barged in and punched him?"

"Kinda. I did knock first. He asked if I was screwing her and it was disrespectful so I decked him."

"Awesome." Justin laughed. "Wish I could've been there. You should've picked me up first."

"Then I threatened him. I won't be surprised if the cops show up here today." Sawyer shrugged. He couldn't care less.

"Where's she at? Was she there?"

"Nope. I told her to stay at my house today. I'd make sure he was gone before she returned home. I offered for her just to stay with me."

"Good. Poor girl."

"I'll stop and make her a house key before going home. It was disheartening to see her like that this morning. Broke my heart."

"You're a good man, Sawyer. She's lucky to have you as a friend."

"Thanks, man." He tossed the Advil bottle back to Justin as he got up to wash his hand. He found gauze in a first aid kit and a steri-strip. His knuckle was busted open a crack.

On Sawyer's way home a few hours later, he did, in fact, stop at the hardware store to have a key made. Then he drove by Marina's house. Derrick wasn't there. The truck wasn't there but Sawyer wanted to be sure so he knocked and looked in a few windows. A neighbor loudly wheeling her trash out to the road hollered, "Nobody's home! That jerk packed some boxes and left less than an hour ago."

"Perfect, thanks. Hey, will you do me a big favor?" Sawyer approached the older lady. "Will you give me a call if you see him come back? No matter the time of day or night. Please?" He handed her his business card from his wallet.

"Why?" She asked with caution, looking at his wrapped hand.

"Because he hurt Marina. She kicked him out after he left some bruises on her. I told him to never come back. I'll send the cops if he returns so that call isn't on you. I'm her boss by the way, a good friend too."

"Her boss?" she asked, not convinced.

"I'm really concerned about her safety. Please..." He held out his hand and, after a few moments, she shook it and nodded.

"Thank you." He tipped his hat and left.

Marina was still there at Sawyer's house when he got home. She heard his truck door and opened the door for him, meeting him on the porch.

"How was work? Oh my God, your hand!"

"Oh, I'm fine." He kicked his boots off by the door.

"Sawyer, you didn't. Please tell me you didn't go over there."

"Well, then I'd be lyin'."

"Oh my God!" She held her hands over her face.

"He was disrespectful so I broke his nose." Sawyer acted like it was no big deal. He took his keys and wallet out of his pockets and put them on his dresser.

"Is that blood on your shirt?" She grabbed his shirt to look closer.

"Huh? I guess it is."

"Who's?"

"Not sure." He looked his hand over while unwrapping it.

"You need ice?" She took hold of his hand to inspect.

"Nah, already put ice on it at work. It'll heal up in a day or two."

"I can do the chores for you before I leave then."

"No, no you won't." He gently placed his hands on her shoulders. "I don't want you stressing today, that means no working either." He noticed she was wearing a shirt of his but her same shorts.

"I hope you don't mind." She had a timid air about her.

"Never. I admit I like you in my shirts. They look good on ya."

There it was, that sultry stare into her eyes. She couldn't let him think he was a rebound though. She slipped her flip flops on, ready to leave. "I did the dishes then just chilled. Oh, and I took a nap in your bed, which was extremely comfortable, by the way. Soak your shirt in ice so the blood comes out. I'm so sorry about your hand."

"You didn't have to do dishes. My hand will be fine. It was worth the pain. I'm sure he's hurting way worse." That smug look on his face was attractive. Any face he made was though.

"I made sure he was gone before you went home. I wanted to know he wouldn't be there when you left here."

"Thank you." She heaved a sigh of relief.

"Oh..." He reached into his other front pocket and pulled out the key he had made. "Here, I want you to have this."

"Is this key to your house? Oh, I can't accept this."

"Yes, you can. Please. You always have a place here." He folded her hand with the key inside.

"Are you sure? I don't want to have to use it."

"I trust you completely. Besides, I like having you around so I want you to use this key."

She embraced him and held him tight for a few moments. Lifting up onto her toes, she kissed his cheek and grabbed her shirt from the arm of the couch. No more words were needed and she left with a smile.

From that night on, he vowed he would always leave the porch light on for her.

The next morning, she was exhausted. She didn't sleep a wink.

She laid awake most of the night, worried he would come back and be more furious than normal after having had his nose broken. He didn't return though. Sawyer's message was received loud and clear.

She got herself around quickly and headed to Sawyer's for chore duty. Sawyer was gone to work already but he left a note as usual, a longer one. It read "You've slayed the dragon. I know you're a warrior but you can take that armor off around me. Put your dented shield down and lay your insecurities to rest. You're safe in my castle, Princess, and you have the key...to my heart."

She was astonished. She had to have read the note a dozen times, the last line even more. He flirts with innocence and she revels in it. She definitely felt attracted to him as well. He's all she thought about anymore. Day and night. Now she knew he felt the same way. It was going to be a good day.

CHAPTER 19

Girl Talk

Marina met her girlfriends at Chillax-A-Latte after picking up a box of donuts across the street. They sat outside at a patio table. Raquel sat and scooched her chair in as Andrea opened the umbrella. Marina set the box of assorted donuts on the table and opened it.

"I've got coffee!" Becka came out of the shop and placed the coffees beside the box.

"Perfect! Thank you. Dig in, ladies."

"It's been a couple of weeks since we all got to hang out. What's everyone been up to?" Andrea grabbed a donut and napkin from the stack.

"I finished my novel, finally. It's ready for submission." Raquel seemed excited.

"That's wonderful! I can't wait to read it." Marina was excited for her.

"I love a good escape from reality," Becka agreed.

"Is it a romance?" Andrea asked.

"It is. You'll love it."

"Maybe you could write one about Marina and that hot boss of hers someday," Andrea added, looking over at Marina as she sipped her coffee.

"Oh, my goodness, Andrea!" Marina laughed but loved the notion.

"Is it really wishful thinking though? I mean, y'all seem friendly...and flirty." Andrea raised her brows.

Marina paused for a minute, looking around at all the girls. "Okay a girl can dream."

She sighed.

"Hey, don't miss out on the truly wonderful things in life because you're scared. Let go of control and live. Welcome him, let whatever happens just happen. He's totally crushing on you!" Raquel stated, bobbing her head back and forth.

"I mean, he did just bust Derrick's nose and threatened him," Marina leaned in and whispered as folks were approaching to enter the shop. "I'm crushing on him too."

"What? Are you serious?" Becka inquired with a mouthful of donut.

"Oh, my goodness!" Andrea was shocked.

The girls wanted to hear more.

"Derrick left bruises on my arm and Sawyer saw him one night before that...the way Derrick treated me."

"So, Sawyer broke his nose?" Raquel snickered.

"Yeah. I was at Sawyer's house. It's an embarrassing story."

"Uh-uh. Spill it," Becka interrupted.

"Derrick and I had a fight so I left and went to Sawyer's but I didn't want to wake him. He found me asleep in the barn the next morning. I was completely appalled. We had a nice conversation. He was patient and understanding, he was even really late for work but didn't care. He wanted to make sure I was okay. He told me to stay at his house while he was working but, apparently, made a pit stop on his way there. He had a few busted knuckles when he got home. I had a feeling he was going to do something; he was not happy when he noticed my bruises. He actually gave me a house key, which I don't want to have to use."

"Screw that, girl! Use it!" Becka shouted. The girls all laughed.

"You know, a man saying he wants you and showing you

that he wants to keep you are two totally different things." Raquel patted Marina's shoulder. "If Derrick thinks the grass is greener anywhere else, he's crazy. He deserves to lose you."

"That sounds like something an author would say and thank you." Marina chuckled.

"That's hot though, that he'd bust a dude up for you. I bet he looked so hot doing it too." Andrea sat back with her arms folded. She must have been envisioning it because she was surprisingly less loquacious.

"I'm sure he did." Marina laughed as she rearranged her messy hair bun, feeling the sun's warmth upon her neck.

"When we plant seeds of positivity and hope in someone's mind, they germinate, gathering strength and courage, then bloom into something magnificent and they believe the hope too. He's doing that for you, I can tell. It sounds like Sawyer is a guy with genuine intentions. I'm sure he realizes the depths of sacrifice it took for you to work for him while in a different relationship. That's gotta be difficult for you." Raquel snagged a second donut.

"I think it's made it easier for me, to be honest. It's made me realize that what I had was all wrong and what I need is better and right in front of me. The thought of breaking up with Derrick was tough at first because it's all I knew and I didn't have the confidence to move on alone but Sawyer is changing the way I see myself."

"Honey, we've been telling you this all along. You've got this. You don't need a man who treats you like crap. You have us too for support," Andrea comforted her.

"Sawyer too." Becka added.

"Thanks, girls. I didn't wish for life to get easier no matter what I was going through, I wished to become stronger so I could deal with whatever came my way," Marina explained.

"You are strong. You've dealt with a lot of crap for too long. I'm glad you've outgrown that dick of a boyfriend and see your worth. We saw your worth all along. I'm proud of you, boo." Becka leaned over and gave Marina a hug.

"I love you girls. I'm sorry for all the drama and complaining over the last couple years. Hopefully moving forward I'll have nothing but drama-free personal growth stuff to chat about."

"Girl, that's what friends are for—to vent to, get advice from —and there better be a lot of hot guy chat in there too." Andrea proposed a toast with her coffee.

"Cheers!" They tapped their cardboard cups.

CHAPTER 20

SOS

Marina was checking out at the grocery store when she received a text. It was an SOS text from Sawyer's phone. She rushed out of the store and sped to his house, calling him back the whole way but he didn't answer. She rushed to the barn and found a sparse blood trail leading from the barn to the front porch and a bloody partial handprint on the doorway and knob. She busted through the door to see his dirty boots flung on the floor and him standing in just his jeans, leaning against the washroom doorway, trying to rip gauze off the roll with his teeth. His side was bleeding as well as the side of his head and face. His jeans had blood and dirt on them. He was covered in dirt and struggling to take a deep breath.

"Smokie's still in the corral but I don't know if I shut the gate."

"Smokie can deal, I'm worried about you. What happened?" She panicked and ripped the gauze for him. "Can you walk?"

"I think I crawled to the house." He was dizzy so she ducked under his arm and slowly helped him to the couch. There was a blanket on the back of the couch so she spread it out for him to lay on. He sat and laid back slowly, obviously in pain.

"I was running him. Then started to ride him but he got bit

on the head by a huge horsefly so he reared and bucked me off. I had seen the fly so I swatted at it but it bit him and he flung me across the corral. It happened too fast to hang on."

"Oh my God! You must have hit the corral or he trampled or kicked you or something. You're bleeding everywhere."

"He kicked me when he was playing bronco and knocked me out. Not sure after that."

She quickly assessed the damage. "I think you should go to the hospital." She moved around his hair.

"Nah. This isn't the first time I've been hurt by horsepower." He tried to laugh but the pain was too much.

"Seriously, Sawyer. You're really hurt. I'm glad you let me know."

"Thank you for coming."

"Of course. I got really worried when you weren't answering and had a horrible gut feeling." She turned on the flashlight on her phone and checked his pupils for dilation. "You probably have a concussion."

"Probably broken ribs too."

"Your side is torn open, Sawyer. Let me take you to the hospital. Please."

"I should probably shower first."

"No, you're not. You can barely walk, you got kicked hard and were knocked out. You don't need to fall in the shower too."

"You could hold me up in there."

"Okay, now I know you got kicked in the head," she joked with a laugh.

"Sorry, that was inappropriate."

"I don't mind jokes, you should know that by now." She helped him sit up after bandaging his side. He put his arm around her shoulder and she helped him up.

"Actually, let me go pull my car up here to the porch. Sit for a minute and promise you'll wait on me. Don't get up."

"Yes, ma'am." He swiped his hair out of his face.

She ran to her car and drove it to the porch, opened the

passenger door, grabbed her bag of groceries, and ran it inside. She tossed it into the fridge then grabbed his wallet and flip-flops and helped him to the car.

"Feels weird, you opening my door."

She laughed and handed him his ripped and dirty t-shirt. He put it on as she got in and drove off. He tipped his seat back so he was more comfortable. It hurt to sit up.

"Don't fall asleep."

"I won't, I'm not tired, just in pain. I'm sorry." He held his side.

"For what?"

"Making you drop what you were doing to come to my aid. I didn't mean to panic you but I'm glad you came."

"I'm glad I did too."

"I'm happy I can rely on you. Thank you." He padded her leg weakly, yet she still felt his strength.

"I'll always be here for you. Just like you're always here for me." She smiled and looked over at him.

She was careful taking turns around corners so he didn't feel more discomfort. They pulled up at the emergency room doors and she ran around to open his door. He slowly sat up and she helped him out and through the automatic doors.

"Can we get help?" Marina hollered. A nurse quickly wheeled a wheelchair over to him. The receptionist stood up behind her desk in the center of the room and paged an E.R. doctor.

"What happened?" the nurse asked, checking his pupils with a light.

"Horse bucked me off and kicked me." Sawyer squinted to shield his eyes from the light.

"I'm guessing you have a concussion. Go ahead and check in at the desk and we'll get ya back ASAP."

"Thank you." Marina wheeled him to the desk where he strained to get his wallet out of his back pocket to hand over his ID and insurance card. The receptionist checked him in just as a male nurse called him back to a room.

"Ooh, you're bleeding through your shirt. Go ahead and remove it and I'll get your vitals," the nurse said, holding a blood pressure cuff, waiting for Sawyer to pull his shirt up over his head. It took a minute, he was in pain.

Marina noticed the nurse was checking Sawyer out.

"So, you're a cowboy, huh?" The nurse asked, strapping the cuff on Sawyer's bicep.

"That's right. Well, sorta."

"Sorta?"

"I train horses sometimes and have a few of my own. I don't like... herd cattle or anything." Sawyer handed Marina his shirt.

"That's a pretty deep gash there on your side." The nurse was jotting down notes.

"I'm not sure how that happened. After the apparent kick to the head, it was lights out."

"Oh, you poor thing. Your sister here must have been scared."

"She's not my sister." Sawyer grunted as the nurse removed the bandage.

"Oh, she's not? Girlfriend?"

"Nah, she's a really good friend."

Marina smiled at Sawyer. He didn't say employee this time.

"So, are you seeing anyone?" The nurse flirted.

"Not at the moment, no." Sawyer smiled back at Marina.

"If I may be so bold..."

The nurse paused but Sawyer interrupted by saying, "I'm flattered, but my saloon doors don't swing that way."

"Ah, gotcha. Well, if you ever change your mind, you know where to find me." The nurse took the blood pressure cuff off Sawyer's bicep.

Sawyer politely smiled and nodded at the nurse before the nurse left the room.

Sawyer looked at Marina and whispered, "Don't even."

She waved her hand up and turned to giggle quietly.

"I swear, everywhere I go." He shook his head.

"You get hit on by cute guy nurses? He was attractive." She laughed.

"Well, hit on anyways..." He adjusted in the chair.

"Well, you're hot. Who wouldn't try to flirt with you?" She looked around the room, avoiding eye contact. He shook his head, assuming she was just joking. The doctor came in and quickly read over his chart.

"So, kicked by a horse? I bet that wasn't cozy." The doctor pulled the stool over to Sawyer and sat.

"Not exactly."

More light was directed at Sawyer's eyes. Again, he squinted.

"Sensitive to light, aren't ya?"

"Yep."

"Big headache?"

"Yep, wouldn't you?"

"Yeah, looks like a concussion. Let me check your head out." The doctor parted Sawyer's hair repeatedly, looking for where the blood, which was now dried now in his hair, had come from "I see a partial hoof scuff or what looks to be. I don't think it's deep enough for stitches but we'll clean it up. Let's see these ribs."

Sawyer bit his lip out of pain as the doctor poked and prodded.

"This will need stitches. I'll get an x-ray really quick of your head and abdomen. Are these the only areas that hurt or are bleeding?"

"I think so. Maybe muscles or bruises, but yeah those are the main areas of concern."

"Okay, I'll wheel you down to x-ray."

Marina stayed in the exam room while Sawyer was being x-rayed. He wasn't gone long but meanwhile, the nurse set a suture tray up.

"That was quick." She held the door open for Sawyer to be wheeled back in.

The doctor put the x-rays up on the light board, "No broken

skull but you have a concussion. There's one cracked rib but the rest is stitchable. You got lucky."

"I did. Although, I don't feel as lucky as I should at the moment."

"I can understand that. You're about to feel less lucky." The doctor pulled the tray over. "You'll have to move your arm out of the way for me." He tilted the patient chair back and Sawyer raised his arm up over his head.

"I can give you a local first." The doctor picked a syringe of lidocaine up from the tray.

"I don't need it, Doc."

"You sure?"

"Yeah, I'm sure." He held his hand out to Marina so she stood next to him and held it. He smiled as though he didn't need the comfort but wanted it from her anyways.

He wrinkled his nose a few times as the doctor did his work, but he was tough. She thought it was sexy that he was a tough guy. He really was in rough shape and she was proud of him for having endured so much pain. She was relieved he was okay.

On the ride home, it was quiet for a few minutes before she spoke up and said, "You really gave me a scare today. You have no idea how worried I was."

"I'm sorry I scared you. I'm glad you were around to help."

"Me too." She was starting to tear up.

He turned to her, again with his hand on her leg, "Hey. I'm okay. You don't have to worry anymore. The doctor said I'm fine too."

She nodded without saying a word, afraid she would cry. She didn't want him to see her cry over him.

"You're a kind soul. You know that?" He leaned back in the seat.

"I care about you."

"Good, because I care about you too," he winked when she looked over at him.

She helped him inside the house. The soreness didn't seem as bad now so he was pretty efficient at getting inside and to the bathroom.

"Man, my head is pounding. You mind closing the blinds while I'm in the shower?"

"Sure." She slid his flip-flops over closer to the door since he just flung them off upon entering. He took his dirty shirt off and tossed it in the hamper across the room then unbuttoned his jeans. She watched from the living room as she was leaning over the couch to close the window blinds. Down went his jeans. He wasn't shy about it. His black boxer briefs clung to his sculpted body so perfectly like always. She knew she should look away but she couldn't force herself to. What if he caught her looking? She almost didn't care. It's not like she hadn't seen them before in the pool.

"Do you want me to hang out here on the couch in case you holler?"

"Sure. That's probably a good idea. Thanks." He stepped into the bathroom and turned the shower on. She could see into the bedroom from the couch but was talking herself into looking the other way. Maybe she should turn the tv on to distract herself. But then she might not be able to hear him if he needed her. Could keep the volume off. It still wouldn't distract her. She heard his dresser drawer shut then a few seconds later the glass shower door. She checked her email on her phone as well as social media, attempting to focus on something besides his godly body.

It was impossible.

She was failing. He didn't shut the doors. Either of them. They were wide open; the bedroom and bathroom doors. The ten minutes he was showering seemed like an eternity. It was so inappropriate of her to be wishing he would step out from the bathroom completely naked......

Stop. Just stop. This man was her boss, for crying out loud. Friend too, for sure, but how dare she? Was he signaling for her to join by leaving the doors open and stripping his jeans off before her eyes? The shower turned off and the sound of the water quickly subsided.

"Marina! Can you help?"

Her eyes widened and she froze for a second, "Okay, I'm coming." She entered the bedroom and stood next to the bathroom with her back against the wall like an FBI agent about to bust down a door.

"What can I help with? You okay?"

"Yeah, but I forgot my towel. It's on the hook just inside the door."

She was thinking surely, he could've stepped out and got it himself, but she reached around the corner, feeling for the towel, unhooked it, and tossed it to him. He caught it laughing.

"What's so funny?" she asked from the bedroom, still up against the wall.

"It's sweet you think I'm modest."

"Is that your ego talking or the painkillers?"

"Perhaps both."

She could hear him toweling his hair dry. She should backtrack to the living room now but her feet weren't wanting to move. Did he have briefs in there with him? He did forget his towel.

Oh, right, the dresser drawer that she heard was probably him getting a pair to take in with him. But then he made the modest comment, so...she was slowly tiptoeing toward the bedroom door when he stepped out of the bathroom holding a hand against his stitches.

"Where you goin'?"

She stopped dead in her tracks. "Um, I thought I'd give you privacy to get dressed."

"I'm dressed enough."

She turned around. He wore only navy boxer briefs. Only those. Her heart pounded as fast as a racehorse's. Dear God, he looked amazing. She realized she was probably staring and breathing heavier so quickly looked up at his eyes and didn't let them wander.

"Will you redress my bandage?"

Knowing full well he was capable of doing it himself with the use of a mirror she, of course, said yes anyways. He sat on the edge of the bed while she got the bag of bandage supplies the doctor gave him from the living room.

"Is it throbbing? I can feel your pulse all around it."

"Yeah, it is. It hurts."

"Is your script ready at the pharmacy?"

"I don't know. I'll look at my phone in a minute."

She put his new bandage on then threw the wrappers in the bathroom trash.

"I'll go get your phone for you. You should stay in bed."

"Yes, ma'am."

She returned with his phone and he checked for messages.

"My script is ready." He started to get up from the bed but she stopped him, her hand on his shoulder.

"Whoa, where do you think you're going?"

"To get my script."

"The Hell you are. You aren't driving."

"Why not?"

"You have a concussion. Two hours ago, you were knocked out and could barely walk. I'll go get your script after you get back in bed."

"Seriously, you don't need—" he started to argue but she interrupted.

"You don't have a choice, sir." She flopped the blanket up over him and walked out. She brought him a glass of water and set it on the nightstand. "Can I get you anything else before I go or while in town?"

"I'm good now, thanks."

"Call me if you need me but I'll hustle."

"Take your time, I'm fine. I kinda like you being bossy, by the way."

"I'll be right back." She shook her head, snickering, and she grabbed her purse from the end-table by the couch before leaving.

Upon her return, she anticipated a stubborn, manly cowboy disobeying her stay-in-bed order but much to her surprise he was still lying in bed. She brought his meds into the bedroom and took the pill bottle out of the bag, checked the label, then set it on the nightstand next to his water.

"You weren't gone long." His hands folded behind his head and his feet crossed out in front of him.

"I told you I'd hustle."

"You're surprised I'm still in bed, aren't you?"

She laughed. "Actually, yes, I am. You can take a pain pill in about two hours. Might want to set alarms on your phone unless you plan to take a nap."

"I might actually. I never put Smokie away!" He remembered suddenly and panicked.

"I did. He stayed right in the corral the whole time it looked like. He's all locked up."

"Thank God." Sawyer sighed with relief.

"No need to worry about anything. You just need to take care of yourself."

"You're already doing that for me. And doing a great job too, I might add."

"Oh yeah?"

"Yeah, absolutely. Thank you for taking care of me."

"You're welcome. It's my pleasure."

"Really though. You're amazing." He held her hand but was getting drowsy.

"Go ahead and rest. I'll still be here when you wake up."

He closed his blue eyes and within a few seconds, had fallen asleep. She gently gave back his hand and took a spare pillow from his bed out to the couch where she too fell asleep.

A while later, she felt her hair move, which woke her up. Sawyer had run his fingers through her hair and was standing next to her.

"Sorry, I didn't mean to wake you."

"Are you okay? You need something?" She rubbed her eyes.

"No, just was watching you sleep for a minute. I got up to get more water."

"I would've gotten it for you. Just holler." She sat up.

"I didn't know you were still here honestly."

"I wasn't about to leave you alone."

"I'm sure you have better things to do. Besides, I'm feeling better after that little nap. It's kind of you to stay but I'm good. Really."

"What time is it?" She looked around for a clock.

"It's almost seven."

"Oh, jeez. I guess I slept a couple of hours. I didn't realize I was even that tired. You hungry? I can make you something." She stood up, pulling her wrinkled shirt down.

"Why don't I just order a pizza and have it delivered? Is that okay with you?"

"Yeah, but you don't have to, I can—" she started but he interrupted.

"You've done so much already. You don't need to make me dinner too. Let's do pizza and a movie. If you don't have plans."

"No, no I don't. That sounds great actually."

"I thought it would be nice. Your usual is good with me."

"Deal." She folded the blanket and put it back on the couch.

He used his phone to place the order, then he sat on the couch next to Marina and reached for the remote on the coffee table, but she had to intervene when he was taken back with rib pain. She handed it to him and he thanked her. At least he had put pants on before joining her on the couch. That would've been awkward for her at least. The way these light gray joggers fit though...barefoot and shirtless. It was going to drive her nuts. There would be no movie concentration whatsoever.

"Can I get you a shirt?" she asked, staring at the tv and clearing her throat.

"Oh, sorry. I guess I probably should put one on. I'm not

used to having to dress for a lady. There's a clean one folded on my dresser, if you don't mind." Before he could finish the sentence, she was already in the bedroom. She brought the shirt back and handed it to him.

"Me being shirtless makes you uncomfortable? Sorry, I didn't realize."

She hesitated answering for a moment, trying to choose her words wisely.

"Let's just say I should focus on the movie that we choose." She rubbed the back of her neck nervously.

He grinned at her squirminess.

She could feel him staring at her so she looked at him trying to keep eye contact as he put his white t-shirt on. Oh, God. It was a fitted t-shirt. As in, it was tight enough to distinguish his pecks. This wasn't much easier than him being shirtless.

"You're trying to make this awkward, aren't you?" She laughed, shaking her head.

"What do you mean?" He snickered. He was loving the fact that she was obviously attracted to him. At least he hoped that's what she meant. He wanted her to say it out loud.

"Nevermind. Let's pick a movie. What genre are you thinking?"

"You're totally avoiding the question." He turned to her.

"What? No." She snatched the remote from him.

"Yes. Yes, you are. Come on, tell me what you meant."

"It doesn't matter." She tried to get him to drop it, regretting having said anything out loud.

"It does to me."

Were they going to start arguing like a couple? She was desperate to change the subject.

"What type of movie are you in the mood for?" she asked again.

"Let's not do comedy. I don't wanna laugh."

"Good point."

She flipped through streaming options as he stared at her, waiting on an answer.

The doorbell rang.

"Oh, thank God!" She jumped up. Relieved that the pizza delivery guy had impeccable timing. Sawyer wasn't thrilled with the interruption. He bit the inside of his cheek.

"Look! Pizza's here!" She shut the door with her bare foot while holding the pizza flat with both hands.

"You may have avoided this conversation for now but it'll come up again."

"I don't doubt that it will." She laughed and put the pizza box on the coffee table. "You care if I grab plates and napkins from the kitchen?"

"Not at all. Thanks." He watched her walk into the other room before opening the box.

"What do you want to drink?" she hollered.

"I'll take a Pepsi."

She came back in and sat down, plating their pizza. She handed him his drink so he didn't have to reach for it. He stared at her, smiling. Again, she felt the stare and looked over.

"What?" she asked, smirking before taking a bite.

"I just appreciate you. More than you know."

"Aww, you're so sweet. I appreciate you too."

"We're a great team, you know that?"

"We really are." She wiped her lips with her napkin, "I'm always up for action."

"Yeah? Oh, you mean movies? Like shooting and fighting and blood and stuff?" he asked excitedly.

"The bloodier the better."

He chuckled. "This is great."

He was thankful she didn't choose a romance drama. That might have been awkward. He was a romantic but not a huge fan of that movie genre. He was thrilled that she was an action fan. Everything about her was intriguing to him.

"Here, I'll let you choose." She handed him back the remote.

"Why don't we trade spots? You should sit on the end so I can put up the footstool for you. That way you can lean back more comfortably." She stood and motioned for him to move over. It took a minute for him to scooch over then she raised the footrest. She sat back down next to him, a little closer this time. He reached around her and grabbed the blanket that she had refolded and laid on the back of the couch. He unfolded it and spread it over both of them. It was white fleece with horses on it.

"My mom bought me this. She said it reminded her of a baby blanket I had that I dragged everywhere."

"Aww, that's adorable. It's a pretty blanket. Cozy too." She held it to her face to feel the softness against her skin. He looked at her with admiration. She clicked on a movie. Halfway through it, she was leaning over against his shoulder. He found himself paying more attention to her than the movie. She hadn't moved in a while, so when the movie was over, he noticed she had fallen asleep. He put his footrest down as quietly as he could so as not to disturb her and carefully cupped her head in his hand, scooched forward, and laid her over. He lifted her legs onto the couch and put a pillow under her head. He covered her with the cozy blanket and turned off the tv then made sure the front door was locked, stripped down to his boxer briefs in the bedroom, and went to bed with his door left open.

Her alarm went off on her phone at seven the next morning. She shut it off and jumped up, startled and a little disoriented. Realizing where she was, she folded the blanket and returned it to the back of the couch.

He got out of bed and stood in the bedroom doorway as she put her shoes on.

"I'm so sorry I woke you." She looked up while tying her shoe to see him leaning against the doorframe in his underwear. *The perfect site to wake up to* is what she thought to herself.

"You didn't wake me."

"Do you need help changing your bandage or making breakfast before I do chores?"

"No thanks, I'm good. I think I'll take a pill for this headache and go back to bed."

"Okay, I'll do the chores this evening. You don't need to be out there ripping your stitches."

"Yeah. Actually, that would be great. Thanks."

She stood and looked in his eyes, trying so hard to keep her eyes focused on his and not elsewhere. She swore he did this purposefully. "Okay then. Thank you for a nice evening. It was really nice getting to hang out with you like that."

"No, thank you. We should do that more often. Not the almost-killed-by-a-horse part but the rest, definitely."

"We will. I promise. Sorry that I crashed here, I didn't plan to."

"Don't be sorry. I left the bedroom door open in case you weren't comfortable enough."

Her eyebrows raised, surprised at his invitation.

"Oh! Um, I was good apparently. Thanks, though. Okay, well, I'll go do chores. Oh, I better grab my bag of groceries. I'll just put them in the barn fridge until I go." She rushed to the kitchen then back to the front door with her grocery bag. She pushed her hair back behind her ear and he gave her a big hug, it felt like every upper body muscle of his was wrapped around her. She could've suffocated in his bicep. She could feel her heart racing.

"I'll check on you tonight when I come back." She opened the door and stepped out. He stopped in the doorway as she walked to the barn.

"Thank you again, Marina. I owe you."

"No, you don't." She smiled a flirty smile, which made him smile sideways. She was going to have to take a cold shower when she got home from the barn.

Marina went back to the barn that evening. She was surprised to see a note since he shouldn't have been out there. It read, "You're amazing." His notes always made her smile.

After she finished chores and walked the horses to their stalls, she went up to the house to check on Sawyer. She knocked and he hollered, "It's open."

Upon entering she informed him, "Ya know, it's not safe to leave your door unlocked."

"I knew you'd be here to check on me."

"What if it wasn't me who entered? I have a key too, remember?"

"I guess I'd have to kick some ass." He laughed, putting on a t-shirt.

"In your condition?" She laughed. "Okay, you still could kick some ass. At least you're wearing pants so it wouldn't be a weird ass kickin'."

"I know you're uncomfortable with me not wearing a shirt." He pulled it down over the top of his sweatpants.

"So, the conversation arises again...it's just extremely distracting. That's all."

"Oh, so uncomfortable in a good way?"

She bit her bottom lip, smiling. "How are you feeling?"

"My head doesn't hurt as bad today. Ribs are still really sore, of course. I'm sure they will be for a while."

"They're bruised pretty good."

"Yeah. Too bad I don't have a tough guy story to back it up."

"You were training a horse, that's pretty tough-guy to me."

"Your opinion is all that matters."

"Good to know. Did you tell Justin why you weren't at work today?"

"I called him this morning. He told me I'm a sucky cowboy."

"So that's why only my opinion matters?" She grinned.

"Pretty much." He ran his fingers through his wavy hair. It made her want to run her fingers through his hair too, every time.

"You want dinner?" she asked.

"Nah, I'm not really hungry. Thank you, though."

"Sure. You'll call me if you need anything, right?"

"Absolutely. You don't have to knock ya know. Just come on in."

"I wouldn't want to intrude or interrupt anything."

"What would you be interrupting?"

"Um, in case you had company or weren't dressed."

"I never have company."

"You're never dressed either," she said sarcastically.

"Touché."

"I don't wanna have to use the key. It's not my house."

"I was serious when I said I want you to. Surprise me anytime."

She nodded, not really sure what to say. "I'll see you in the morning, Sawyer. Call if you need me. Don't overdo it please."

"Yes ma'am."

She loved it when he called her that.

CHAPTER 21

Confessions to Justin

S awyer rested his feet upon his desk in his office and paused from typing on the laptop, grabbing his coffee, taking sip after sip. He clearly had something on his mind.

"Hey, Justin."

"Yeah?" Justin was calculating numbers so he didn't look up at Sawyer.

"Can you take a quick break for a sec? I need to pick your brain about something."

"Okay. Would it happen to be about that beautiful young lady you bought flowers for?" Justin spun around in this chair, facing Sawyer.

"Yeah, actually, it is."

"Ahhh, you have a crush."

"You could say that. Yeah, I definitely have strong feelings for her. I can't help it. She's amazing. She's smart, funny, fun to be around, and absolutely beautiful. Great work ethic, kind...I'm so attracted to her that it's hard to be around her without making a move but I'm her boss, ya know? I mean, we're friends too, and have been hanging out."

"Tough predicament you're in. She feel the same way about you?"

"I mean, I think so. I hope so." Sawyer placed a pencil behind his ear. "She's always all smiles when we're around each other. I've been trying to fight my feelings but I crave being around her. She's addicting."

"Why don't you ask her out?"

"She's been through a tough breakup. She needs time to heal. I'm just wondering how much time. I don't want to rush her by any means but we just fit well together."

"That's great, man. Really. It's great. My advice...if you're asking for it?"

"By all means."

"Flirt a little. Let her know you're interested but make sure she's ready to pursue a relationship before making a move. You both will know when to make that move. The sexual tension and attraction will be too strong to resist. Then just let it flow." Justin got up and poured another cup of coffee.

"Yeah. Good advice. I have been flirting though, I think she flirts back. Not as much as I'd like her to, though. She just seems shy about it, or maybe she's playing hard to get. That tension is there for sure. I'll roll with it. Thanks."

"You better give me daily reports."

"Will do." Sawyer chuckled and got back to work but every now and then he would watch out the window, hoping Marina would be visiting the coffee shop or bakery nearby.

"Look at you, watching for her to stroll by. You expecting her to or you just got it bad for her?"

"Well, I'm not expecting her to stroll by." Sawyer scratched his chin scruff and tried not to smile.

"Yep. You got it bad. So, when do I get to meet this girl that's got you so distracted?"

"Why? So you can flirt with her?"

"That sounds like jealousy to me."

"Okay, okay. I guess it does, huh?"

"Yep. Now you and I both know how ya really feel." Justin sat back down at his desk, scooching his chair in.

"Maybe I'll ask her to lunch soon. You can meet her then."

"I can't wait."

"I've never denied my feelings for her. I kinda enjoy just flirting with her and proving I'm someone she can trust though. I don't want to screw this up."

"Of course she can trust you. You're the most honest guy I know. You're kind and generous. True integrity."

"Thanks, Justin. That means a lot."

"It's the truth. In fact, I have no idea why you're still single."

"I'm picky." Sawyer shrugged before filling his empty coffee mug with water from the standing water machine.

"Well, I don't blame you there. You're a hot dude." He paused as Sawyer whipped his head around and scowled at him. Justin laughed. "Come on, man. If I were a chick, I'd be all over you."

"No! No, you wouldn't." Sawyer looked terrified but then they both laughed."

"Look, I have to protect myself too. I don't want another broken heart. It's finally healed, ya know? I don't wanna be the rebound guy either. Although, I can't see her being that way."

"Well, maybe not purposefully." Justin tossed a wad of paper into the trash can.

"I don't want to overstep her boundaries so I need to find out what those are, I suppose. She seems to be avoiding flirting back too much. Maybe she's being polite at my flirting attempts and not flirting at all. If she *is* flirting, I want her to just cut loose."

"She's probably trying not to move too fast, no matter how she feels about you."

"Yeah. I hope she isn't worried about a relationship affecting her job..." He paused then sighed.

"That her?" Justin looked out the window beyond Sawyer and Sawyer whipped around in his chair. There was no one there. Justin busted out laughing as Sawyer slowly turned his chair back, biting his inner cheek, and glared at Justin.

"Dude, you about gave yourself whiplash. You're almost healed up from your pony ride, you better take it easy."

"Not cool, man!" Sawyer shook his head. "Get back to work," he joked.

CHAPTER 22

Testing the Waters

"It's going to be hot today, you're welcome to take a dip" is what the barn note read.

She was sweating only a quarter of the way through chores and tied her hair up. She had brought her suit with her that day and left it in her car. She debated using the pool, even though he gave permission. She felt awkward using his amenities without him there. The temperature was already in the nineties with high humidity and the sun was beating on her skin, burning it. It was unusually hot for early fall.

She finished chores and sprayed each horse down with the hose before putting them out to pasture. That pool sounded too tempting to ignore so she fetched her suit from the car and changed in the barn. The palms planted at the pool's edge barely had a flutter to their fanned leaves. It would've been ideal to have a slight breeze. She laid her towel and bottled water on a lounge chair and took a swim to cool herself off.

She let her hair down, placing her hair tie on her wrist. She laid in the sun on her back and eventually rolled over to her stomach. Having laid out a while, she could feel a burn upon her skin and realized she hadn't put sunscreen on. She had forgotten to bring it. She took a dip again to cool off, planning to leave soon so she didn't burn too badly, but she was enjoying the quiet peace-fulness poolside. The sound of the small waterfall and the view of the beautiful tropical landscaping was paradise.

As she was swimming, Sawyer had come home early. Surpris-ingly, she didn't hear him pull into the drive. He saw her car was there but she wasn't in the barn so he went inside the house. He spotted her in the pool from the kitchen window and went to the French doors to watch her. He stood shirtless, wearing only jeans, arms propped up against the window above his head, his bare feet crossed. She walked out of the pool, ringing water from her hair, and as she bent down for her towel, she saw him at the door but pretended not to. She wouldn't have been able to stop staring at him. She laid on the lounge chair to air dry after towel drying, that way she didn't have to change clothes before going home.

He came out of the house, quietly, while she was facing the opposite direction. He slid the other lounge chair close to hers, which prompted her to finally lift her head. He sat on the chair, facing her, his shins against her chair. He smiled a crooked smile, shaking a bottle of lotion.

"You're getting pink." He squirted some lotion into his hand and dropped the bottle onto his chair as he rubbed his hands together. Her heart started racing.

"I can feel it, I forgot lotion."

"I see you brought your suit though. You mind?"

"Not at all. Thanks." She had been anticipating a moment like this. She pulled her hair over to one side. His hands were about to be all over her. She held her breath as he smeared lotion all over her back, lifting the strap to her bikini. She closed her eyes and pressed her lips together, fighting the urges running through her mind.

"I respect and value you in every way, so if you're uncomfort-able, just say the word." He paused as he put more lotion in his hands.

She turned and looked at him, "I know you do. I'm not uncomfortable at all." She laid her head on her arms.

He took a moment to look into her eyes before moving to the backs of her legs. His hands were soft and he had a tender touch, which grew stronger the higher he rubbed up her legs. He stopped at her bikini line, which was fairly cheeky.

Her heart started beating faster as he moved to her shoulders and the back of her neck and she stretched one arm out at a time for him.

"Flip over." She liked the command in his deep voice.

"Yes, sir." She flipped onto her back. "I can finish if you'd rather," she offered.

"No sense in getting your hands all lotioned up and greasy too." He winked as he rubbed down her legs. There was no way she could tell him she was about to leave. Not now. She didn't want to leave now. She was definitely fighting a smile and held her breath again when he reached her upper thigh. She sat up on her elbows.

"Wanna spread 'em?"

"Huh?"

"Your legs."

She just stared at him.

"You don't want to be burned on the inside of your thighs."

"Oh, right." She swallowed and watched his hands glide up to her groin.

"Lay back and relax," he instructed softly.

She laid back and took a deep breath. The adrenaline rush was real; she started to feel shaky. He lotioned her stomach, then her chest, even her cleavage. She felt the urge to squirm but closed her eyes, biting her lip.

"I think you're good. Unless you need some on your face." He ran his fingers across her forehead and down her cheeks.

"Thank you. This was really thoughtful of you."

"Sure, we'll call it that." He chuckled.

"Are you saying you wanted to get your hands on me?"

"It worked, didn't it?" He stood up and stripped his jeans off, leaving only his boxer briefs on.

"Do you own swim shorts?" She laughed and adjusted her sunglasses on her face so he couldn't see that she was checking him out.

"Yeah, of course. This is more convenient. Practically the same thing." He sat in the lounge chair and put his feet up.

"These fit better anyways, I imagine. What time is it? Have I been out here all day?"

"Nah, it's only noonish. The A.C. went out at the office so I thought I might join you in the pool...if you were still here."

"So, you were hoping I would be?"

"Maybe." He rested his head back onto his crossed arms, smirking.

"Mr. Sawyer, what will I ever do with you?"

"Is that an actual question? Because I have many answers."

She laughed.

Without each other noticing, they kept glancing over at each other. Once in a while, he'd squirm like he was about to give in and come over to her. She'd tense up every time.

"Your lotion should be soaked in by now. Wanna dip?"

"Sure." She followed him into the pool. They swam for a short bit. He went under and popped up right in front of her. The site of water dripping off him was intoxicating. He shook his hair and then pushed it out of his face. She could tell he was wanting to kiss her and as much as she wanted that to happen, she panicked. They already barely had any clothes on, it would've easily turned into more than a kiss, which made her nervous.

She said, "I probably should get going."

"Errands to run?"

"Um, yeah, and phone calls to make."

He looked at her and smiled, knowing she was avoiding him getting too close. "Too soon?"

She looked at him, not sure what to admit.

"It's okay, Marina, I get it. I apologize for being pushy or too forward."

"Oh, you weren't being pushy at all. I'm just...I don't want you to feel like a rebound. Ya know?"

"I don't feel that way. Just so you know. I like spending time with you, especially at the pool."

She laughed. "I definitely enjoy spending time with you too. I guess I'm just nervous. You're so much more than I'm used to." She got out and toweled off.

He nodded. "I want you to be comfortable around me. There's nothing to be nervous about. I guess I did come on a bit strong, huh?"

"Noted." She chugged some water as he walked out of the pool. "And I kinda liked the strong approach. I don't want you to think I'm taking advantage of you in any way either."

"Oh, you don't have to worry about that. I know better. You don't have it in your pretty little heart to be that way."

"You're right, I don't." She smiled shyly.

"You can change in the house if you want."

"Okay. I'll go get my clothes."

"I'll see ya inside." He went to the house and had already put dry, distressed jeans on when she came in, still soaking wet. He was holding a green apple in his teeth as he came out of the kitchen, pulling down his white t-shirt. She was thinking *oh Lord!* and her lips parted as she stared.

"Want an apple?"

"Oh, no thanks. That's a great look on you by the way." She continued on her way to the bathroom to change, her towel wrapped around her lower half. She didn't see him fist-punch the air in excitement then bite his fist. When she came out of the bathroom after changing, he threw his apple core away and walked her to the door.

"I enjoyed our afternoon." She had one foot out the door.

"Me too. Glad my A.C. broke." He stepped out onto the porch behind her and watched her walk to her car. He waved as she looked back at him and smiled before getting in.

The barn note the next morning read, "I can't stop thinking about you. Nor do I want to".

CHAPTER 23

Man-to-Man

T he beginning of the week was chilly in the morning then
warmed later on. Tuesday, Marina even wore a light jacket
to do chores. "Do you have plans for Thanksgiving dinner?" Is
what the barn note read. It's sweet he would want to include her
in his holiday plans. She texted him right away.

"I do not have plans for Thanksgiving dinner."

His phone vibrated on his desk, which he excitedly picked up,
hoping it was her.

Justin stopped typing on his keyboard and commented with a
smirk, "It's her, isn't it? You're smiling."

"Yeah, it's her. She doesn't have plans."

"You asking her over?"

"I sure am," Sawyer wrote her back with "I'd love for you to
join me. I'm cooking at home."

"I'd love to! Thanks for the invite." She replied with a heart
emoji.

"Yes!" Sawyer fisted the air in excitement.

"You having family over too?" Justin asked.

"I'm not sure yet. My parents mentioned visiting. I should
probably find out for sure so I can let her know."

"You might want to mention it to her now that it's a possibility; In case it makes her nervous." Justin shrugged and began typing again.

"I should, yeah. Thanks. I'll do that." Sawyer picked his phone back up to start texting.

"I've invited my parents but not sure if they're attending yet."

"Aww, you want me to meet your parents?" She replied, feeling honored.

"Absolutely! I don't want you to feel pressured though, by any means."

"I would be honored to meet your parents. I'm sure they're wonderful people. Let me know if there's anything you'd like me to bring or if I can help you in the kitchen."

"Actually...I think it would be more fun to cook with you. If you're up for it."

"I wouldn't want it any other way."

Sawyer set his phone down on his desk and walked across the office to Justin's desk. He leaned his hip against it, arms folded. "She wants to cook with me," he said in a low voice.

"That could get steamy." Justin laughed.

"I hope so. I'm looking forward to spending quality time with her like that. So I wanna cook with her before mom gets there to help cook, ya know what I'm sayin'?"

"You're wanting her to meet your parents then?"

"Yeah. I'm telling you, Justin, she's the one."

"Wow! At the beginning of summer, you said you weren't interested in dating or anything. You weren't even checking chicks out when we'd be out anywhere."

"I know, and I meant all of it then. But then she came along. The very second I saw her I didn't ever wanna look at anyone else like that again. I didn't believe in love at first sight 'til I saw her. I knew that day we met that I wanted to know everything about her, I wanted to spend time with her, make memories. Ya know?" He paused. "Marina is everything I've ever wanted in a woman."

"You're really serious about her."

"I absolutely am. She just doesn't realize how much. My mom

is extremely critical of my relationships. Typical I suppose. So, I want to get a feel for how my mom feels. She usually has great instincts about personalities. She's been right on the money about the last few."

"No wonder you gave up, dude. It's your relationship though, not your mom's."

"I get that. I do. It's important to me that my parents get along with whomever I am serious with. Especially with Marina. I hope to be with her for a really long time."

"That's great, man. I'm happy for you. I'm sure all this is really exciting. It's been a while since I've felt that way about someone new but I remember. It would be a nightmare for your parents to not get along with your future wife. I mean...if you're that serious."

"I am."

"That was quick, you didn't hesitate just now. You realize that?"

Sawyer smiled from ear to ear. "Yeah."

"I wish I had your eager energy today, man." Justin leaned back in his chair.

"I can solve that. Coffee run." Sawyer headed out the door after grabbing his phone off his desk.

Justin laughed and shook his head. His buddy was head over heels in love, it was obvious. Sawyer didn't care that it was obvious, either. He wasn't ashamed. He was gushing with invisible hearts floating around him, just like comic book bubbles. He was like a teenager with a serious crush.

Marina texted Sawyer while he was leaving the coffee shop, asking if he wanted to do lunch. Sawyer rushed back to the office and set the coffee carrier on Justin's desk to text her back.

"She's asking me to do lunch today."

"Let me guess, you're saying yes?" Justin laughed as he took his coffee from the carrier.

"Of course! I should tell her here though, right? So, you can meet her."

"Yeah!"

"Do you want to join us?"

"Oh, no. No, no I wanna meet her, yeah. You two crazy kids go eat together though."

"Ok." Sawyer texted back for her to meet him at his office then told Justin, "It's going to be a really long next hour."

"We better get to work then. I have a feeling you're going to take an extra long lunch today," Justin joked.

"That's probably true." Sawyer nodded, sitting at his desk, sipping the warmth from his coffee. He must have looked at the clock on the wall a thousand times within that hour. He barely worked but instead thought of how he would introduce her to Justin and what Justin would think of her.

Sawyer hung up from a phone call and checked the time on his phone. His back was to the front windows but Justin faced them. Justin looked up just in time for something to catch his eye. It was Marina about to walk in but of course he wasn't aware of her identity.

"Holy sh..." He dropped his pen onto his desk as Sawyer turned around. Sawyer quickly stood and stepped over to open the door.

"Hey, Marina," Sawyer greeted her as she entered.

Justin's eyes grew huge. He stepped out from behind his desk and toward her.

"Justin, this is Marina. Marina, my partner in crime, Justin."

"Nice to meet you, Justin." Marina shook his hand.

"The pleasure's all mine. I've heard a lot about you. Sawyer might have mentioned having a beautiful employee."

Sawyer looked horrified but just smiled shyly when Marina turned to him and said, "Really?"

Sawyer shrugged then replied, "Okay, Justin, you've met her now so we're going to lunch. Be back in a while."

Justin smiled mischievously and said, "Uh huh." He waved at Marina as Sawyer politely ushered her out the door, his hand on the small of her back. That drove her crazy, something about a man's touch in that particular spot gave her butterflies.

She looked back and waved to Justin but Sawyer was giving him the 'I hate you' look. He opened the Jeep door for her, which was parked right out front of the office windows. The whole front of the space was window, as a matter of fact. As Sawyer walked around to the driver's side, he flipped Justin off on the down-low. Justin laughed and waved.

"Where are we eating lunch?" Marina asked.

"What are you in the mood for? There are a few places up the street that are good."

"I'm up for anything."

"There's a fresh deli café, a little Mexican place that has awesome tacos, and a burger place."

"How about the fresh deli today? I feel like eating light. Mexican next time?"

"Absolutely," Sawyer agreed, turning into the deli parking lot.

"These were totally within walking distance," she observed.

"I figured it's a little chilly out today so we could just drive."

"You're sweet."

"Hang on, I'll get your door." He shut off the Jeep.

They stepped into the deli café. Pepperoni was being sliced and the aroma filled the air. All the different selections of meats, cheeses, and veggies were presented so beautifully and small bowls of fresh fruit lined the countertop. Racks of bread loaves and bagels were fully stacked behind the counter.

"I didn't even know this place was here." Marina was looking at all the choices.

"It's a great place. Great food, great owners, I eat here often. A few times a week. There are so many options you can try something different every day of the year. They do catering too."

"Oh wow, that's great! I think I'm going to have a big chef salad and get creative with it."

"That sounds good. I think I need some carbs today though. Rye, maybe."

"I love rye. I'm trying to cut carbs though, actually."

"Why?"

"Just trying to keep my shape, stay healthy, ya know? It's harder for a gal." She was browsing through the glass.

"No, no I don't know. Seriously, you don't need to worry about that at all."

"Why do you say that?"

"Trust me. You have nothing to be self-conscious about. You're perfect the way you are. At least I think so."

She just smiled at him. "Thank you. That's kind of you to say."

"I mean it. That's my personal opinion but I'm sure it's everyone else's too."

She looked up at him as he stood next to her. She complimented him in her thoughts constantly, perhaps she should aloud though. It would let him know she found him attractive at least.

"You're in amazing shape for having a desk job, by the way."

"Thanks. The horses whip me into shape as much as I do them." He laughed and she ordered before him but he wouldn't let her pay. He handed the cashier his card as she was ordering.

"Why do you do that?" she asked, tucking her wallet back into her purse.

"Because that's what a gentleman does. Plus, I like to treat you."

"That's sweet but you don't need to." She tapped his arm in a friendly gesture.

"I absolutely do." He patted her back in return and smiled. They got their food and sat at a window booth. She had noticed he wasn't wearing his cowboy hat. His light waves had volume and, once in a while, he'd toss his head just slightly to get them out of his face and she couldn't help but stare. It was sexy.

"I noticed you aren't wearing your hat." She took a bite of salad.

"Yeah, usually while I'm at work I leave it in my Jeep. It's not as comfortable while using the computer. Don't need it for shade, either. My head needs to breathe."

She laughed. "Well for the record you look great without it. I mean you look great either way. I just don't see you much without it. It's a refreshing look on you." She glanced up at him and he was smiling at her. She smirked and took another bite.

"I do have something to ask you." He sat back on the seat.

"Ok." She put her fork down and took a drink.

"So, my parents are thinking about coming for Thanksgiving and they'd stay with me."

"Okay. Well, I don't want to intrude."

"No, no," he interrupted. "I was hoping you'd be okay with still coming. I'd like you to meet them. They'd like to meet you as well. They said they won't come if you're uncomfortable with it."

"They'd not come just for me? They don't need to do that. I'd love to meet them. I'm actually honored that you asked."

"You're surprised?"

"Honestly, yeah. I know we've grown closer but I'm surprised you want me to meet them. I'm excited, thank you."

"I didn't want to blindside you. I really do want you to meet them but only when you're ready. "

"Honestly, Sawyer, I'd love to. If they're anything like you I know they'll be wonderful." She took hold of his hand on the tabletop. He cupped her hands with his, looking into her eyes. After a brief moment, she slowly pulled her hand back and cleared her throat before thanking him.

"No, thank you. I admit I was a little nervous about asking you but Justin convinced me that I needed to do it today. My mom has been blowing up my phone for the last few days."

"You've been ignoring your mom?"

"I text her back vaguely, making excuses like being busy at work."

"Why were you nervous to ask me?"

"I wasn't sure if you'd want guests, especially when those guests are my parents. It's a lot of pressure on you."

"Pressure? Will it be that bad?"

"No," he laughed, "but my mom is critical. She's kinda tough at first, might ask questions and I don't want you to feel uncomfortable."

"It'll be fine. I'll be okay. Really. I'm an open book. Is there anything I shouldn't ask or talk about?"

"Not that I can think of. They're pretty much open books too. I think we all have a lot in common. Please don't be offended or freaked out if mom brings up past relationships. She means well, just protective of me. I'm her only child."

"Makes total sense. Let me know what I can bring and what time you plan to start cooking and I can help."

"I'll get everything. I'll let you know what time after I talk with Mom."

"Perfect. I'm glad we had this chat today."

"Me too," he agreed with a sigh of relief. "Thank you."

"For what?" she asked as they got up from the table.

"For being generous enough to spend the holiday with judgmental strangers."

"As long as I can spend it with you, I don't care who else is or isn't there." She smiled over her shoulder as she walked ahead of him.

"Good to know." He bit his lip, following her out of the deli.

They played a cat and mouse game with flirting. Played coy, if you will. The flirting and teasing were fun for both of them. They were testing the waters after each had been through tough relationships but it was obvious that they were attracted to each other. They both had caught feelings but were afraid of heartbreak. She couldn't imagine he could break her heart, but just the thought of him making her cry almost choked her up. If he felt the same way, they might have a chance. She assumed it was too early to ask.

Perhaps after meeting his parents, she would have a better idea of what she would be getting herself into. For now, she was enjoying spending a little quality time with him. It was interesting though, that he hadn't been dating, so maybe he wasn't healed. Maybe he was waiting patiently for her to heal. She craved him even though her heart was damaged.

They drove back to his office. She waved to Justin through the window and Sawyer chivalrously opened her car door. He gave her a hug before she got in. It was brief but she didn't want it to end. He smelled so good and his muscular back felt like Heaven beneath her hands, through his shirt. He waved at her and went inside as she drove off.

"So....? I saw that embrace so I'm assuming it went well?"

"It did, thankfully. I'm anxious now. I can call my mom back and warn her to be nice." He hiked the thighs of his jeans up and sat in his cozy office chair behind his desk.

"That's great! I want to know how Thanksgiving dinner goes."

"I'm thinking I'll have her over the night before to make pies with me. That way we get some alone time."

"Yes! Do that! Baking together is sexy." Justin bit the end of his pen. Sawyer laughed, blushing, then threw a wad of paper at Justin.

"Maybe she'll wear an apron. Only an apron," Justin joked.

"You're horrible, you know that?"

"What?" Justin shrugged.

"You joke but I know you're serious. I mean, that wouldn't be a bad thing but I don't wanna push it. Maybe another time later on."

"What will you do if she makes a move on you? Or do you plan to make a move on her?" Justin wiggled the pen around between two fingers.

"I don't know. I mean, if she made a move, I'd definitely roll with it. I'd make her glad she did. If I made the move, it would be smooth and subtle so it doesn't scare her off. It would be sad making pies the rest of the night by myself. I just don't want to ruin our friendship if she doesn't want a relationship right now. It's probably too soon for her, ya know?"

"Nah. Who wouldn't want to be your lady? I saw the way she looked at you. You deserve a great woman and if you see that in her don't lose your chance. I say once those pies are in the oven, if she hasn't made a move, you should."

"Thanks, man. I'm glad you and I are tight. I think I'll take that advice."

"Yeah?"

"Yeah. It's a deal. If she doesn't make a move but lays down some flirting I'll go ahead and make a move. I don't want to waste time. I definitely don't want her to think that I'm not interested and have her start dating someone else. That would kill me."

"You get jealous thinking about her with another dude?"

"Actually..." Sawyer hesitated then nodded. "Yeah, I do. It would break my heart."

"Then you gotta make a move. Just go for it."

"It's time I show her how I feel about her."

"You've only got two weeks before she meets your parents. Make it count. Maybe make a small move before then even."

"Not a bad idea."

CHAPTER 24

Full Moon

"You. Me. Jeep. Tonight, we ride." She chuckled when she read the barn note. She was already looking forward to it. She texted him so he wasn't waiting on a reply.

"Normally I don't like being bossed around but when you do it, it makes me smile."

He wrote back "Haha" with a laughing emoji.

She returned to his place when he got home from work. She stepped up onto the porch but before she could ring the doorbell he came out and left the door open behind him. He was barefoot, his low-rise bootcut jeans exposing his pelvic muscles as he rolled up the sleeves of his button-up shirt which was all undone, showing his smooth, bare chest and abs.

"Oh, Jesus!" she whispered to herself.

"What's that? You okay?"

"Yeah, yep. All good."

He reached inside for his boots then shut the door behind him.

"You like tacos?"

"Yeah, of course."

"Good, I know a place." He buttoned up his shirt after putting on his boots. He hadn't mentioned getting food but she was down for it. They got in the Jeep and she noticed the top was off.

"Hope you don't mind losing those curls in your hair." He put the Jeep into drive.

"It'll be fine." He told her to hang on and spun that Jeep around, flinging dirt everywhere. They drove through the cloud out of the driveway.

"So, there's this taco truck in town that makes the best tacos I've ever had. And I've had a lot of tacos. Hope you're hungry."

"I could eat."

"Good, I'm starving. I skipped lunch today."

"Why? That busy?"

"Yeah, it was a busy day so I just pushed through it. Looking forward to tacos."

"Aww, so you could still take me out in the Jeep?"

"Well, yeah. Plus, these tacos are amazing."

She laughed at his honesty, her loosely curled hair flowing behind her. He kept looking over at her. She was wearing a cute strapless sundress, floral, and her cowgirl boots went perfectly with it. Her tan legs soaked up the sun and he wanted so badly to put his hand on her leg.

They pulled up to the food truck and he ordered six tacos for himself and a drink. She ordered only two. They ate in the Jeep, laughing and listening to country music. They talked about songs and artists they enjoyed listening to. He talked about playing football in his high school and college days. She was on the swim team. Innocent, general conversations, getting to know each other better.

He drove her back to his place before climbing onto the hood of the Jeep and tapping the warm metal for her to sit next to him. She climbed up next to him, her palms resting on the hood on either side of her.

"Thanks for getting me out of the house tonight."

"I thought you might be having a hard time with the breakup and all."

She stared at the ground for a minute.

"I had to choose myself. He was never going to change so I wasn't going to put in any more effort. I want to be loved loudly, proudly, publicly, privately, and behind my back."

She looked at him with transient healing pain in her eyes.

"And you deserve to be loved that way."

"Thank you. I've learned to love and appreciate the person in the mirror. She's been through so much but still stands and smiles despite it all."

"This breakup allowed you to transform and gain wisdom. You chose that. You should be proud of yourself."

"I am now. Thanks."

"Insecurities and irrational fears that he forced upon you kept you controlled. It's time to heal and break away from all of that. Start doing what makes you happy."

"That's my plan. I kept giving chance after chance so I was valued less and less. He never expected me to walk away. He got comfortable with disrespecting me until I was too uncomfortable. I think his actions helped me with closure before I even broke up with him. I needed your voice of reason."

"He had many chances that he chose not to take. Take those chances back and give them to someone who wants just one. They'll only need one because they'll treat you right the first time." He stared into her eyes.

"I'm convinced, you give better advice than my girlfriends."

"What can I say? I'm a simple guy with an understanding soul." He laid his hand on his chest.

"That you are. You have wonderful character. I'm so lucky to have you as a good friend." She bumped her shoulder into his arm.

"It's okay to let me in whenever you're ready to. You can let your guard down with me. You're safe here in my arms." He wrapped his arms around her. It made her feel excited but nervous at the same time. She loved that he was so in touch with his feelings and hers and not afraid to express them. He was perfect in every way. A gentleman, so caring and attentive, generous, and hard-working. Then there was his sexiness and those eyes that could melt the sun. She got lost every time she looked deep into them. She believed there was no woman on Earth that could resist him, so he must have been holding out for someone really special. He was everything she had dreamt of and more.

"I've lost my footing before and I have yet to fall too far." She smiled at him.

"I'll make sure you fly. By the way, you know what fly stands for?"

"I didn't know it stood for anything."

"Yep, it means First Love Yourself and I think you've accomplished that." His one arm was still around her and the moon was full and bright enough to light the night sky.

"I think so too. I'm going to gravitate bravely toward things that are right for me from now on. I've apologized too much when I wasn't wrong. I won't do it anymore." She sat up straight and put her brave face on.

"I don't know why anyone would risk losing you. Some would say a girl with a great sense of humor, shy but has a dirty mind and a beautiful heart with good intentions is a deadly combination but I happen to think it's a perfect combination. Absolutely perfect. Sometimes your soulmate finds you and cherishes you from that day forward, never making you question your worth." He looked at her like she was more fragile than ceramic. He gently moved her hair out of her eyes. "A deep and powerful connection has been made between us and we've become an intrinsic part of each other's lives."

"I agree. Look! Shooting stars!" She pointed and they both watched the stars shoot across the sky.

"They were so bright!" She was excited. "Make a wish!"

He stared at her, smiling. "Your brightness can light up the darkest sky." He looked at her with admiration. He loved that she had the spirit to enjoy the simple, miraculous things in life. He turned her chin toward him and those eyes...those eyes of his...

"You make a wish?" she whispered.

"I did."

"It's so quiet out here. It's nice."

"If you listen with your eyes, you'll see the way I look at you reflects how I feel about you." He slowly moved in closer. She didn't lean away, she moved in closer to him. She could feel the way he felt about her and the butterflies flittered. While their eyes were still fixed on each other, his lips connected with hers, kissing her softly. Their eyes closed as they floated to somewhere higher— cloud nine. He cradled her face in his hands as she placed her hands on his arms. The kiss was delicate. She wanted to melt right there in his arms. They parted sweetly, still staring into each other's eyes.

"I got my wish," he whispered and smiled.

She giggled. "That's what I wished for too." She slid off the hood and stood in front of him, her hands on his thighs.

"Is this too soon for you?"

"No. Truthfully, I've wanted this for a really long time," she smiled then took his hand in hers. His lips were even softer than they looked. She reached up and kissed him softly again then gradually let his hand go as she backed away. Her eyes teased and batted as she smiled and walked over to her car.

His elbows rested on his knees and his hands were folded together, his head dropped for just a brief moment. He smiled and shook his head, watching her leave. He received the hint to take it slowly, loud and clear. She thought she'd end the night with a tease rather than indulging in what her heart truly desired. She wanted this feeling to last longer than just briefly. He was too important to rush.

CHAPTER 25

Backcountry Brawl

T he barn note read "Bar tonight?"
    She was already looking forward to that evening. There was nothing she looked forward to more than spending time with Sawyer. He nourished her soul. She did the chores with the horses out to pasture first. Legend followed her everywhere, nudging her with his nose every time she would stop the wheelbarrow. Smokie splashed water out of the trough as she attempted to fill it. He made Marina laugh. He had a hoof right in the trough. He definitely wasn't scared of water anymore. Foxtrot flirted with Athena over at the separation fence, which was adorable. She hung up the lead ropes and finished cleaning the barn stalls.

    She wasn't sure if Sawyer had planned to play music that night at the bar but she came up with a plan. She called Gladys and asked if she could get a message to Jake, since he played guitar with Sawyer's band. Gladys gave Marina his number so she texted him. She let Gladys know her plan once Jake responded to make sure there wouldn't be any conflicts. Gladys was excited and told Marina she would record the whole thing, which made Marina slightly nervous.

    She showered and had lunch.

    Later, she curled her hair and put on a cute, short, country-style pink dress and perfected her makeup, finishing the look with a matching light-pink lipstick. She saw Sawyer pull into the drive and her stomach grumbled, reminding her that she was starving. She pulled on her boots at the door and opened it as he was walking up the steps. He looked up when the door opened and stopped. He was breathless.

"Hey." She grabbed her skirt and fluttered it back and forth with her hands.

"Hey." He blinked a couple of times, looking her up and down.

"Is there anything you need to do before we leave?" she asked.

"I suddenly feel underdressed in this t-shirt. Let me grab a different shirt real quick." He finished walking up the steps then lifted her by the waist and twirled her around, her hands on his arms. She giggled as he put her down close to him.

"How'd I get so lucky?" he asked.

"I'm the lucky one." She wrapped her arms around his neck and stood on her toes as their lips connected. It was as if sparks flew. Their kiss was a little more daring than their last. Taking in more of each other each time. He wasn't sure how slow he should take the kissing. He hadn't slipped her much tongue yet. She thought it was sweet and knew if they kissed more passionately it would be difficult to hold back. He was being a gentleman and she thought it was the most romantic thing in the world.

"I'll hustle." He went in and was back out quickly. He was carrying a plaid button-up short-sleeved shirt that matched the teal t-shirt he had on. It looked great with those jeans. He looked great in any color but the blues on him made his eyes pop even more. He put it on while walking to the truck. He folded his collar down before opening her door for her. He never buttoned his shirt, just left it open. She loved that.

He smelled great too. He only wore cologne when they went out. She thought that was a sexy gesture. She actually did the same. Her perfume smelled like star jasmine and sweet olive blossoms. She concocted the blend herself and labeled it "Summer Intoxication."

He got in and started the truck.

"You look beautiful. You must be hungry, you're ready to roll."

"Thank you and I am, yeah. That ok?"

"Absolutely. I'm hungry too but whatever my cowgirl wants is what's happening," he promised.

She grinned, excited to spring a little surprise on him. Oh, he had no idea she was about to bust out of her comfort zone for him. Her hands were getting clammy when he took one of them in his truck, resting them on the center console. She didn't talk much on the ride there.

"You okay?"

"Yeah, I'm perfectly fine. Why?"

"You seem nervous. Is holding your hand okay?"

"Oh, yes, of course! Don't be silly. I'm good, really."

"Okay. You'd tell me, right?"

"Of course. I'm good, Sawyer, really."

"Okay..." He paused, then asked, "We ordering our usual?"

"Yeah, sounds great. I love that we have a usual."

"Me too. It's cute," he agreed, wrinkling his nose.

She laughed. He actually noticed she was quiet and nervous. Derrick wouldn't have. He had never paid any attention to her. Hopefully, Sawyer would always be this way, she appreciated it.

He opened her door for her when they got to the bar, then he opened the entrance door for her as well as they entered, his arm around her, everyone shouted their usual welcome. They waved briefly at the patrons as if they were in a parade.

Bob pulled a bottle, popped the lid off with an opener, and slid it across the bar. Sawyer pressed the bottle rim to his slips, tipping it back for a swallow.

"Wanna sit up here tonight instead of a table?" Marina asked.

"We can sit wherever you'd like."

"Well don't you look cute?" Gladys commented as she approached Marina with the fruity vodka Bob mixed for her.

"Aww, thanks."

"You always clean up nicely too, Sawyer." Gladys winked at Sawyer and he nodded. Gladys whispered in Marina's ear as Sawyer pulled out their barstools. Sawyer's eyebrows wrinkled in curiosity. Marina nodded to Gladys and sat on the stool. She took a few chugs of her vodka as Sawyer watched her with a one-sided smirk.

"Liquid courage," she said as she set her drink back down.

"Am I missing something?"

"Yep." Marina smiled as Jake walked in carrying his guitar case.

"Oh, shit! Were we playing tonight?" Sawyer about choked on his beer, turning around looking toward the door.

"Were you supposed to?" Marina asked, taking another chug.

"I didn't think so. Maybe he's doing a solo thing." He shrugged.

Marina got up and winked at Gladys, who waved her dish towel at her.

Jake plugged in his acoustic guitar to the speaker and sat on a stool he had drug up on the stage. There was already one stool up there with a microphone in front of it. Gladys had set it up shortly after Marina called her that morning.

Marina stood and took a deep breath.

"Pizza will have to wait a little bit," Gladys told Sawyer. "Ya might wanna turn your stool toward the stage," she said as Marina made her way up to the stage.

Sawyer turned his stool around, hiked the thighs of his jeans and sat on the stool, leaning back against the bar, one elbow resting on it. He was curious and anxious as Marina sat on the stool and crossed one leg over the other. She adjusted the microphone and nodded at Jake.

"What is she doing?" Sawyer smiled.

Bob leaned on the counter by Sawyer and Gladys stood

behind the bar. She pressed record on her phone and signaled to the two of them on the stage. Jake began to play and Marina joined in singing *Love Is A Cowboy* by Kelsea Ballerini. She sang it perfectly, looking at Sawyer the whole time. He smiled through the whole song, holding his beer. He didn't take a drink the whole time. She shook Jake's hand after the song ended and joined Sawyer back at the bar.

"So that's why you were nervous on the drive here," he said, relieved, as he gave her a big hug. She laughed and wrapped her arms around him between his shirt layers. He held her face under her flowing hair and kissed her right in front of everyone. It was a bigger kiss, bold, more tongue even. He wasn't shy about it and she was completely fine with that. People were still clapping for her. He pulled away slowly, looking into her teal-ish eyes. Their foreheads touched gently.

"You're amazing. That was the best surprise. Thank you."

"You're welcome. I meant it too."

"You're the best." He kissed her softly again as everyone settled down.

Gladys informed Sawyer she had recorded the whole thing, including their sweet embrace afterward.

"You're awesome, Gladys. So, you knew about this?"

"I sure did! Bob did too. You kids ready for that pizza now?"

"Yes, please!" Marina relaxed on the stool next to Sawyer.

Jake packed up his guitar and joined them up at the bar. A couple of patrons stood at the jukebox debating between songs and finally chose a playlist.

"Thanks, Jake. That was cool of you." Sawyer shook Jake's hand.

"Hey, no problem. Who can say no to that pretty face?" He patted Sawyer on the back.

"I understand that." Sawyer smiled at her.

"Y'all were great up there. Maybe Marina should sing with us more often." Sawyer put a hand on her knee.

"Hell yeah! I'll drink to that." Jake took a beer from Bob and clunked it against Sawyer's.

"Y'all would really let me sometime?"

"Absolutely." Sawyer agreed with Jake, who was nodding his head.

"That's so sweet. That would be fun."

"We practice some Sundays. You should come with Sawyer next week."

"Okay. I'll do that. As long as he's cool with it."

"Absolutely, Babe." He smiled and kissed her. She loved that he called her that.

"Aww. You two are too cute together." Gladys brought their pizza out and set it on the bar in front of them.

"It looks so good, Gladys, as always." Marina reached across the bar for napkins.

"Enjoy." She stepped over to Jake and he ordered a small pizza for himself.

"Is that cajun crust?" he leaned over, asking Sawyer.

"It is and it's awesome."

"Okay, cool. I'll try it on mine." He had Gladys add it to his pizza order.

As Marina was eating, Sawyer excused himself to the restroom and a couple of guys came in, eyeing Marina. Jake noticed but was having Bob pour him another beer, asking what he had on draft. One of the guys approached Marina. She was the best-looking gal in the joint, one of the only gals in fact.

"You with him?" The guy asked, talking about Jake.

"No," she answered politely, wiping her mouth with a napkin then turning to listen to Jake and Bob's conversation about beer tasting. Sawyer's empty stool remained empty for only a moment but the guy was close to Marina. Sawyer came out of the restroom and yelled "Hey!" and ran to Marina. Jake was clueless as to what was going on.

Sawyer yelled "Don't drink that!" to Marina and pointed at her drink. He grabbed the front of the guy's shirt and slammed him up against the bar. The guy was leaning back and scowling. Sawyer decked him right in the face with his fist. Marina and Jake jumped off the stools and both yelled, "Sawyer, stop!"

The crowd gasped and chairs scraped across the floor as they watched. At one point, the only sound was Sawyer punching the guy and the jukebox playing.

Jake took Marina by the arm and pulled her over by him.

"What the Hell, Sawyer?" Jake stepped in and tried to get Sawyer off the guy but Sawyer's grip was too strong. Marina didn't know what was going on or what to do but she wasn't about to get in between the brawlers. Jake almost got elbowed. Gladys whipped her dish towel at the guys.

"He just roofied her drink!" Sawyer was only inches from the guy's face.

"What?" Marina was shocked. How did she not notice?

"Are you sure?" Jake asked.

"I saw him do it." Sawyer slammed the guy again against the counter for resisting.

"I just wanted to take her home with me, have a little fun," the guy bravely admitted with a smug smirk, wiping blood off his mouth with the back of his hand.

Sawyer's eyes grew huge. "She's mine! You son of a bitch!" Sawyer kneed the guy in the groin. Marina liked the primal side she was witnessing.

Bob reached under the bar and brought out a vial. He put a droplet of thick liquid in Marina's drink and it turned color, confirming Sawyer's side of the story. Her eyes grew huge and Sawyer was even more furious. His eyes turned sharp. The guy apologized but Sawyer decked him again before dragging him to the door by the shirt and literally throwing him out. Sawyer stepped outside the door behind the guy, Jake right behind him.

"You ever come back here again, I'll kill you!"

"Sawyer." Jake grabbed Sawyer's arm.

The guy stumbled up from the pavement and got into his car.

"You okay, man?" Jake let go of Sawyer's arm.

Sawyer blew out a huge huff and ran his hands through his hair, pacing. At some point his hat had fallen off, he didn't even notice.

"No! No, I'm not okay. I could've killed that asshole."

Sawyer straightened his shirt out and walked back inside with Jake, who told him to breathe.

"My God, Sawyer, I've never seen you like that before." Gladys looked horrified, her hand on her chest.

"Sorry, ma'am."

"It's ok. Maybe we should've called the cops."

"I handled it."

"We saw that." Jake laughed sarcastically, drinking his beer.

"Are you okay, Babe?" He pulled Marina close to him. She was still in shock. "I'm sorry I went crazy on that guy. I didn't want you drinking that."

"I'm glad you saw him. I had no idea."

"Did he say anything to you?"

"Just asked if I was with Jake. I said no and kept eating."

"I was ordering beer. Sorry, bro, I didn't see him do it. Sorry, Marina."

"It's okay, Jake." Marina touched his arm.

"It's not your fault. He's the one in the wrong, not y'all." Sawyer's hands firmly pressed against the edge of the bar.

"Think he'll be back?" Bob laughed.

Everyone else laughed too. The bar crowd settled back down. Sawyer sat so Jake and Marina sat too, slowly.

Gladys brought out Jake's pizza and he took a bite while staring at Sawyer.

"I'm good." Sawyer reassured Jake.

"Okay...good." He continued to chew.

If Sawyer would've been a wild animal, the hair on the back of his neck would've still been standing straight up as he was coming down off his adrenaline high. Marina tried to calm him down.

"Let's not let him ruin our night. okay? Thank you for sticking up for me. He deserved to be biffed in the face, no doubt.

You're my knight in shining armor, Baby." She put her hand on his thigh.

He looked at her, still with fire and rage in his eyes. "Well I do have a white horse." He seemed to be calming a bit.

Jake picked up Sawyer's hat off the floor and placed it up on the bar. "Found your hat," he said timidly, chewing.

"Thanks." Sawyer slid it over to the other side of him.

"Dude, I didn't know you had it in ya," Jake said with a mouth full.

Sawyer just looked over at him. "Thanks for having my back."

"Always."

"You gonna throw me out for fighting?" Sawyer asked Gladys.

"Hell nah, that jerk deserved every deckin' he got."

"What was that vial of stuff, Bob?" Marina asked.

"It's a special nail polish."

"Nail polish?" Marine looked puzzled.

"Yep. Gals wear it when they go out. Before they take a drink, they dip a finger in their drink to make sure it doesn't change color. If it does, it's been roofied."

"Wow! That's brilliant. Maybe I should get some, huh?"

"I'll buy you some tomorrow." Sawyer chugged the rest of his beer.

Bob made Marina another drink in a new glass then poured Sawyer a whiskey on the rocks. Sawyer turned to Marina, his legs on either side of hers. He held her hands and told her "I'm so sorry you saw me like that. That never happens. Well, I did deck your ex too but that wasn't as crazy as this tonight."

"It's okay. You were justifiably upset. I wasn't scared of you, just of what was going on, I guess. I thought you might almost kill the guy. I'm not gonna lie though, that primal side of you screaming "She's mine!" was pretty sexy."

"Oh yeah?" He laughed, swirling his glass before taking a sip.

"Yeah. I like you being possessive and protective of me."

"It was more like saving you." He winked with a smirk.

"Sure. Of course. It was still sexy." She grabbed the front of his shirt with both hands and pulled him in for a kiss.

Jake was snickering at them.

"How about one more round before we call it an early night?" Sawyer grabbed a slice of pizza from the pan.

"I think you should get trashed tonight, dude." Jake smacked Sawyer on the shoulder.

"I might pour me a tall whiskey when I get home."

They didn't stay much longer and the three of them walked out together. Sawyer and Marina gave Jake a hug and thanked him, then got in the truck.

"Wanna have a drink with me on the porch?" he asked as he started the truck.

"Absolutely. The third drink is usually the charm for me."

"What do you mean?"

"I'm a lightweight. It'll knock me out. Don't even need a roofie." She laughed and Sawyer bit his lip then laughed.

Her barn note the following morning read "I'm proud to call you mine. You're the rhyme to my reason."

CHAPTER 26

Pie Prepping

T he barn note Wednesday morning read "You and I, tonight we bake pies. 4 pm".

Marina smiled, excited. She hadn't seen him in a few days and she rushed with chores that morning so she could plan her wardrobe for that afternoon. She still had errands to run in town yet. Of course, she would need to shower and shave as well.

She brainstormed what she could make and bring in addition to what they would bake. She wanted to add her own touch and bring something unexpected. After all, he was buying everything needed for the entire holiday dinner. She stopped at the store and bought ingredients for bruschetta. It was her favorite appetizer and, so far, they seem to have similar tastes in foods. Or maybe he just wasn't a picky eater. She took the ingredients to Sawyer's house still in the bag. She would make it fresh tomorrow.

Since it was just going to be her and Sawyer tonight, she didn't dress up. He'd be in sweat joggers or jeans anyways. She kept it cute yet simple: black leggings with black wedge booties and a pale pink sweater that hung down off one shoulder. She threw her hair up in a messy bun so it wasn't in the way of cooking. She put her kitchen hand mixer in the car just in case he didn't have one for whipping up the pies. He was a guy and lived alone, what were the chances he'd have one?

Around four pm, she knocked then cautiously walked in. "Sawyer?" she announced her arrival as she removed her jacket. It was chilly that afternoon and windy.

"In the kitchen," he replied before peeking around the wall. "Hey, you need help?" he asked, walking over to her and drying his hands on a towel he threw over his shoulder.

"I just have the one bag." She took her booties off by the door and followed him into the kitchen.

"You look cute." He put the bag on the countertop.

"Thanks. I figured I'd just dress comfortably."

"Well, it works for you." They took the items out of the shopping bag.

"Thank you. You like bruschetta? I thought I'd bring an appetizer for tomorrow if that's okay." She put the cold items in the fridge.

"Of course, it's okay. I actually love bruschetta." He stared at her rear as she was bent over. He quickly looked away when she shut the fridge door. "Thanks for the menu addition. That'll be great."

"The basil is from my garden. With it getting colder this week it will probably die so I wanted to get it harvested."

"Oh, nice. What else did you grow?" He clunked around in the bottom cabinet, getting out glass pie-baking dishes.

"Peppers, tomatoes, and okra, the basil pretty much takes over everything in that small raised garden. The damn squirrels ate my zucchini." She took a large bag of sliced okra out of the shopping bag, "I brought okra in case we needed a vegetable but I'm sure you have the whole menu covered."

"Fried okra is happenin'." He fist-bumped her. "I had no idea squirrels ate zucchini. Am I forgetting something?" He looked at the pie ingredients he had sitting on the counter. She joined in the pondering but it didn't take her long.

"Cinnamon," she pointed out.

He clapped his hands and darted back to the spice cabinet. "It was right in front of my face too."

"Looks like we have everything we need to get started," he said, his hands on his hips.

"Do you have a mixer?"

"We need one?"

"The pies turn out better with one."

"Oh, um..."

"I brought mine. It's in the car." Smiling, she went to the front door.

"Glad you thought of everything. This is why we make a great team," he hollered as she put on her boots. While she was getting the mixer from her car, Sawyer turned the Bluetooth speaker on. It was playing country music when she came back in.

"Okay, so it's been forever since I helped my mom make pies."

"That's okay. We'll do it together." She attached the beaters to the mixer and they combined ingredients in a bowl then she mixed it while he pressed the crust edges against the dish.

"Are we making pies besides pumpkin?" She shut the mixer off.

"I thought maybe a chocolate pie with crushed Oreo crust and a vanilla ice cream topping."

"Oooh, that sounds delicious! Chocolate chips on top too?"

"Even better."

She poured the pumpkin pie mixture into the two pie dishes and they carefully placed them in the oven so as to not spill over. He set the timer and got a bag of chocolate chips out of the cabinet as she pulled out a clean bowl.

"I'm glad you brought that mixer. We'll need it for this chocolate pie too. It's supposed to be whipped.

"All things are better whipped." She snickered, which made him laugh. It still surprised him that she joked in that manner with him.

They sang along to songs as they baked. Once she whipped up the chocolate pie and he finished spreading the Oreo crumb crust into the pan, she ejected the beaters from the mixer and handed him one. She licked hers from bottom to top, slowly, as she glanced up at him. He stared, jaw loose, and swallowed with his nostrils flared. She was hoping that drove him crazy. He then licked his. She watched, chin up and tongue against her teeth.

A song came on that she loved. Turned out he did too. He took her beater and put both of them in the sink then turned the volume up. The song was *Memory I Don't Mess With* by Lee Brice. Simultaneously, they said, "I love this song." He started singing along loudly and danced his way over to her. He took her by the hand and spun her around, her black socks sliding on the floor with ease. This song had a romantic and sexy rhythm. Holding his hand dancing, her almost-salsa style turned into a closer, more intimate form as he pulled her in closer by the small of her back. Her pelvis was pressed up against his low-rise jeans, her thigh between his. Her hands ran up his chest, wrinkling his t-shirt. She gripped his strong shoulder then ran her fingertips over his biceps. They moved their hips as one to the rhythm. The song was nearing the end but she didn't want it to. She wanted this to go on all night.

His hand was upon the side of her face and his eyes stared into hers. She wanted to dive into his deep lagoon-blue eyes and stay there for eternity. Her heart raced, she thought for sure he could hear it. She felt his chest and his was racing too. He sat her up on the countertop, close to the edge. He stepped in close, between her legs, with one hand on her thigh and the other on her cheek.

He leaned in and his phone rang loudly. He paused and looked over to see his phone vibrating on the edge of the counter. He grabbed it as it was about to fall onto the floor.

"Do you have to answer it?"

"I definitely don't want to...it's my mom."

"You should get it then."

He looked at her, not sure what to do. He set it in the center of the countertop and they picked up where they left off.

He kissed her so passionately, so fiercely. He had wanted to do that for so long. He couldn't hold back any longer. He didn't have to tell her how he felt. He took Justin's advice and made a bold move. He was glad he did.

She felt as though the butterflies in her stomach could fly her away. Their hands were all over each other. Hers were up his shirt, her nails in those perfect, tan pecks. The scruff on his face wasn't even as rough as she thought it would be. She wrapped her legs around him and he pulled her in as tight as he could.

She started lifting his shirt and his phone rang again. They ignored it and even hit decline on the call as his lips refused to retreat from hers. He was gentle yet passionate. His hands kept a tight grip on her upper thighs and hips as he began kissing down her neck and onto her bare shoulder. Her fingers raked through his hair; her legs squeezed tighter. His hands slid under her rear, squeezing her cheeks. She had never felt like this for anyone before. She felt as though her body was on fire from within.

His phone rang again and he hit decline.

Oh, the things this man could do with his tongue. *He had licked many beaters in his life* is what she was thinking. This wasn't just lust, this was more. This was pent-up feelings from both him and her. Those feelings were rushing out like a flood causing a mudslide. Maybe waiting to show their feelings was a good thing. It allowed this heat to boil over.

His phone rang again.

"Damn it!" He looked at it this time.

"It's my mom again." He set the phone down.

"Maybe you should answer."

He sighed. "I'm sorry." He picked it up.

"No, don't be. Maybe something's wrong."

"I'll be quick." He answered the phone, "Hey, mom. Everything okay? He paused, then his eyes got huge. "Oh! You're where?" He spun around and looked at Marina with a worried look on his face. The timer went off for the pies so Marina hopped off the counter and took them out of the oven.

"Ok, Mom. Thanks for letting me know. Sorry that I couldn't

answer, I was, um...baking. Yes, ma'am, see you soon." He ended the call.

"Shit!" He darted around the kitchen, cleaning up.

She jumped in to help, "Everything okay?"

"My parents decided to come early. They're less than twenty minutes out."

"And they're staying with you?"

"Yeah..." He sighed again with a groan. "I'm so sorry."

"It's okay," she assured him.

"We made a mess." He grabbed a dishcloth from the drawer and ran it under the faucet then wiped down the counter while she put ingredients away and put trash in the trash can.

"I can get this, really."

"I don't mind helping. After all, I helped make the mess."

"Thank you."

"For what?"

"Everything." He tossed the cloth into the sink and attacked her with a passionate kiss that bent her slightly backward. It felt as though he was about to suck her face off. She loved it though; it gave her a good tingle up her spine.

This man was like a thrill ride at an amusement park; a good kind of scary feeling, the anxiety, then the excitement and butter-flies making her want to scream, then the excitement of wanting to do it all over again.

Did they want his parents to walk in on this? This would be how they first meet her: her hair now messy, half her makeup smeared off. She put her hands on his chest and gently pushed him back.

"We can't. They'll be here any minute. I should go before we make dinner with them tomorrow really awkward." She headed to the front door with him behind her. "I'm not really presentable." She put her boots on.

"You're always presentable but yeah, you're right. I guess I could use a minute myself to um...calm down," he looked down at himself and pulled his shirt down over his zipper.

She bit her lip and smiled. "Just text me what time you want me over here tomorrow. Have a good evening with your parents."

"Will do, thanks. Drive carefully."

She headed to her car and hollered back, "Don't forget to take the chocolate pie out of the freezer in the morning and put it in the fridge."

"Yes, ma'am!" He leaned on the doorframe with his arms crossed.

She found herself smiling a guilty smile all the way home, the best part of the evening replaying on repeat in her head. When she got home, she rushed to bed, feeling like a kid on Christmas Eve, so excited for Christmas morning. She couldn't wait to see him again the next afternoon.

CHAPTER 27

Thanksgiving Day

S he lay awake for what seemed like most of the night, unable to stop thinking about their kitchen scandals. He really did feel the same way about her as she did for him. It had become obvious that he had felt that way the entire time. She was in disbelief that any of it actually happened. It wasn't just a dream, was it? It couldn't be. She didn't want to forget a single second, a single detail. She would get the butterflies all over again just thinking about it. She would eventually need to fall asleep so she didn't have raccoon eyes when meeting his parents.

She managed to get a few hours of sleep in. She woke herself up having a dream about him, not that she was complaining at all. It was Thanksgiving morning and she had a hot cup of coffee in her hands, a cozy set of pjs, and a blanket on the couch with a book. She had been debating on what to wear. She should've asked for a suggestion last night but her mind was elsewhere. Maybe texting him would be best in case he was preoccupied with his parents, that way he could answer when it was convenient for him.

She wrote, "Good morning, I hate to bother you, but I was wondering what to wear today."

He replied quickly, as if he was waiting to hear from her, "It doesn't matter what you wear because you're beautiful in everything. For the record, you're never a bother. I was hoping to hear from you soon. Seriously though, we aren't dressing up. Dad and I are wearing button-up shirts and mom is wearing a nice sweater and jeans. I think mom wants to start cooking in about two hours if you wanted to come around then. And, yes, I remembered the chocolate pie."

She laughed and replied, "I'll be there within 2 hours. I'd love to help out in the kitchen. Can't wait to see you."

He texted back a heart emoji.

She ate a light breakfast and showered then took a stroll through her closet. She decided on a different pair of black leggings and a pale aqua sweater with her tall heeled black boots. She straightened her hair then put some curls in it, applied her makeup, and packed a small clutch with essentials.

She stopped briefly at the flower shop and bought a fall-inspired centerpiece to take. She was taught to never come to an event empty-handed. Luckily they were open.

The whole drive there she was worried about what his parents would think of her. If they didn't care for her, how would Sawyer react to it? She took some deep breaths when she pulled into the drive and took a quick peek at herself in her visor mirror. She gathered the centerpiece and her clutch and slowly made her way to the front door. Should she just walk in or knock? She didn't want his parents thinking she was rude. Just as she raised a fist to knock, Sawyer opened the door.

He wore an excited grin.

"Hi." She quickly lowered her arm.

"Hey." He bit his lip. She loved it when he did that. "Come on in." He stood to the side then shut the door when she entered.

"I wasn't sure if I should knock so I'm glad you opened the door."

"You never have to knock." He took the centerpiece from her. "This is beautiful."

"Thanks, I thought so too. I didn't want to come empty-handed."

"What are you talking about? You brought stuff and we baked the pies."

"Well, you and I know that." She was starting to unzip her boots when he stopped her.

"Don't take 'em off, please."

She stood up. "Why not? I don't want to dirty up your floor."

"You won't but I wouldn't care. They look so hot on you. You look beautiful." He leaned in and kissed her, a good one too.

His dad came around the corner from the kitchen and set his whiskey glass on the coffee table. "Well, hello there." He smiled and walked toward them and her lips pulled away from Sawyer's.

She shyly cleared her throat and said, "Hello."

"This must be Marina. Just as beautiful as Sawyer described. I'm Tom." He reached a hand out.

She accepted the gesture, shaking his hand. "Aww, you're sweet. It's a pleasure."

"Well, Mom's in the kitchen if you wanna come with me." Sawyer took her by the hand, leading her to the kitchen as if she had never been there. His dad followed after scooping up his glass of sloshing whiskey.

His mom shut the sink faucet off and dried her hands as they entered the kitchen. She too was all smiles as she greeted with, "Oh, hello! You must be Marina."

"Yes, ma'am." Marina smiled back, approaching her.

"I'm Caroline." She gave Marina a hug. "It's so wonderful to finally meet you."

Marina replied, "Likewise," wondering what she meant by finally. Marina tilted her head at Sawyer with a wrinkle between her brows. He clenched his lips together and raised his brows. It didn't seem as though he wanted his parents to mention he's been going on and on about her for months. She smiled and elbowed his arm.

"Marina brought a centerpiece for the table." Sawyer placed it on the countertop, changing the subject.

"Oh, that's lovely!" Caroline smelled the flowers in it. "How wonderful of you, Dear. Sawyer, put this over on the table. Right in the center. So, Marina...how long have you and my son been dating?" Caroline went back to chopping chives.

Marina was surprised by the question and had no idea how to answer.

"Uh..." She looked at Sawyer who looked just as confused.

"Oh, honey, you can't fool me. I'm his mother. A mother knows these things. I know my son hasn't ever talked about or looked at a woman the way he does you."

Marina's eyebrows raised and her jaw relaxed enough for her mouth to drop open.

"Mom!" Sawyer gave her a 'just stop' look. She was embarrassing him.

"Actually, I guess maybe...Sawyer, you didn't tell them we started dating?"

"I thought I'd bring it up today." He shrugged. "About a week, Mom, officially."

"Just now?" Caroline asked with doubt.

"Yes ma'am." After a pause Marina stepped over to the sink and rolled up her sleeves. She washed her hands, looking at Sawyer. Sawyer put his hand on Caroline's shoulder and gave her a kiss on the head. "Oh, Mom. I love you."

"I love you too, son. I apologize, I thought you two were an item. I mean, the way Sawyer has talked for so long."

"It's okay, Mom. It's my fault for the confusion. As you know, she works for me, but we became good friends, then eventually we couldn't fight those feelings we had for each other anymore." He looked at Marina.

"Absolutely," she agreed.

"Well, it's settled then. My son has a lady." Caroline hugged Sawyer. He tried not to laugh so Marina turned away to hide her grin.

"I brought stuff to make bruschetta."

"Oh? You must have brought it last night. I remember seeing the stuff in the fridge."

Caroline looked around for it.

"Yes, ma'am, I did."

"Okay, well if you'd like to make that, I will start peeling potatoes. Would you boys like to make yourselves useful and go ahead and set the table?"

"Of course." Sawyer got glass plates down from the cabinet behind Marina and Tom took silverware from the drawer. As they were setting the table, Tom spoke low to Sawyer so as to not get Caroline into the conversation.

"So, are you serious about this girl?"

"Yeah, Dad."

"More so than the last?"

Sawyer looked up at Tom. "Absolutely. Ya know, I wasn't even looking for a relationship. I hired her because she knew horses and volunteered working with them, but also because she was breathtakingly beautiful. She was sweet. The more I was around her the more I couldn't stop thinking about her."

"Well, that's probably because it's been a while since you've been interested in a lady." Tom sat at the table.

"Nah, it's because I'm attracted to her in every way. The way she talks, walks, dances, how she's so caring and strong. She was in a bad relationship and I knew she wasn't ready for another yet. It didn't take me long to know she's the one. She was there at the rescue center the one day out of the quarter year that I go out there. It wasn't her normal volunteer day either. Our eyes connected that day. We've been there for each other since. Her smile was an illusion of scars left on her heart. I didn't want to push too hard for a romance because I didn't wanna push her away. I think she thought I wasn't ready either after having my heart broken and I didn't expect to be. She made me forget about my previous relationship. I didn't want her to think that after all these months I wasn't interested, so last week I made a move and kissed her. I just couldn't hold back anymore." He leaned his palms on the table edge.

"I understand completely. Sounds like it was bound to happen, you two being an item. It's exciting, I'm excited for you. I hope she doesn't break your heart. You don't need that again."

"No, I don't. Thanks, Dad. I can't see her ever doing that. We went from boss and employee to friends, then really good friends...of course, flirting a bit the entire time and now I hope what we've started just gets stronger."

"I hope so too, son. You deserve it." He patted Sawyer on the back.

"I appreciate it." He gave his dad a pat in return.

"It's so sweet when they bond. They had a nice time doing chores together this morning." Caroline tossed potatoes in a pot.

"Aww. I'm sure they miss that. Didn't they used to do that stuff together back home?" Marina chopped tomatoes.

"They did. They've always gotten along so well; as a father and son should."

"Sawyer never has me work a holiday, even though I wouldn't mind, but he told me that today he was looking forward to doing chores with his dad."

"Oh, that's so sweet." Carline placed her hand upon her heart.

"Tom seems great."

"He is. We've been together thirty-five years. Can you believe it?"

"That's amazing. I want a love like that." Marina looked up at Sawyer, who was in the dining room pulling out a chair to sit across from Tom.

Caroline paused with a potato in her hand. "You know I see the way you two look at each other. It reminds me so much of Tom and I at a young age."

"Really?" Marina turned to her.

"Absolutely. Honey, I think you've done found your love like that." She smiled and winked at Marina.

Marina couldn't contain her smile. "I sure hope so."

"Is there any doubt in your mind about how you feel about him?"

Marina shook her head no while staring softly at Sawyer. "Absolutely not."

"Well, then you do everything in your power to hang on to him. He's a wonderful man. I may be biased since I'm his mother but I truly believe in the whole world's eyes that he is the best out there."

"I don't think you're being biased at all. I completely agree with you. I never imagined there would be such a perfect man. He has a perfect soul and personality. He treats me perfectly, and I apologize but look at him...he's perfect on the outside too." Marina let out a deep breath.

Caroline looked at her with admiration. "I think you both have found your soulmate."

"Yes ma'am." Marina smiled proudly.

"Uh oh, they're smiling and gossiping in there." Tom took a sip of his golden whiskey after swirling it around in his glass.

"I'm not worried." Sawyer smiled at Marina, then got up and walked around behind her, wrapping his big strong arms around her. She put the knife down and turned around, hugging him and staring up into those ice-blue eyes.

Caroline looked excitedly at Tom, then scooted around the counter to join Tom at the table. Together, they held hands and watched their son look into the eyes of his soulmate. Sawyer kissed Marina, more gently than he did the night before, his hand upon the side of her face.

"Just look at them. He truly is happy," Caroline whispered to Tom. He squeezed her hand in agreement.

A few moments passed before Sawyer's lips slowly retreated. He swept her hair from her face. Tom cleared his throat. Sawyer looked up at his parents, who were staring at them.

"Sorry." Sawyer realized his passion for Marina had taken over the room.

"Oh, don't apologize. You two were the only people in your little world." Caroline giggled.

Marina patted Sawyer's chest. "I better get back to cooking."

"Yeah, yeah. I just can't help it." He stole another kiss before leaving the kitchen. Her face expressed tenderness. He got the Bluetooth speaker from his bedroom and put it on the countertop and plugged it in. He said, "We have a tradition when cooking for holidays."

"Oh, boy, here we go." Tom laughed.

Marina's interest was piqued.

Sawyer told the speaker to play *Thought You Should Know* by Morgan Wallen. Sawyer took Caroline by the hand and danced with her, singing along. Marina thought this was the sweetest thing in the world. She was impressed by the way Sawyer showed his love for his mom. Tom came over, asking Marina for a dance. She accepted. The potatoes kept boiling while they all danced. What fun they were!

His parents were humble and relaxed. Marina didn't expect that. She had found out they were very well off so her expectations were that of less humble or that they may think their son was out of her league, which is what she had thought for months. She didn't mean to judge them before meeting them, just nervous not knowing what to expect. She didn't know why she was nervous about meeting them, they were as amazing as Sawyer was. They raised one amazing son, whom she had fallen hard for.

The music played on as the cooking continued and they all danced around and snacked on bruschetta. Tom took the turkey out of the oven and Caroline drained the juice to make gravy. They set the turkey over on the table and took over the side dishes that were ready.

"Well, Son, you do the honors this year. You're the host." Tom handed the carving knife to Sawyer.

"Thanks, Dad."

"Oh, honey, we're not super religious but for the holidays we usually say a few words. Would you like to start then we'll each say something."

"Sure. Thanks."

They all sat at the big rustic table that Sawyer himself built.

She cleared her throat and began, "Today, and every day, we're thankful for this food provided for us and the wonderful company we keep. Thank you all for inviting me and making me feel comfortable when I started out the day so incredibly nervous. There are treasures every day in simple things. I have so much to be thankful for. Mainly, I'm thankful for you, Sawyer."

He smiled dearly.

"Aww, I'll go next." Caroline placed her hands together. "Thanks for the food, the company, and for this wonderful gal that has brought a sparkle back to our son's eyes and a beat back to his heart."

Sawyer looked over at Marina with a crooked smile. Marina smiled shyly.

"Thank you for the invite, Son. Thanks for introducing us to this wonderful young lady. Thanks for the food and our health. It's great to spend the holiday all together as a family." Tom nodded, passing the turn on to Sawyer.

"Thank you all for joining and for the fun we all have together. Thanks for the food, our health, and the life we live. I feel most thankful for Marina, who has changed the way I feel toward love and everyday life. I feel hopeful and excited about the future. I'm thankful we met that day." There was a sweet pause of appreciation before Sawyer started carving the turkey. Dishes were passed and laughs had. Great food and great conversations.

Everyone was stuffed.

"I think I need to wait to have pie." Marina helped Caroline gather plates and take them to the kitchen.

"Oh, sweetie, I can get these." Caroline dropped them into the sink.

"I don't mind helping, really."

"That's so sweet of you."

Sawyer and Tom brought food platters to the kitchen.

After all was taken care of, they sat around the living room watching the last quarter of the football game.

"Pie and drinks?" Sawyer got up off the couch.

"Sure," everyone agreed.

He nodded in the direction of the kitchen for Marina to come along.

"I'll help you." She followed him and as soon as they got into the kitchen, he grabbed her by the waist and gently put her up against the wall. His tongue was everywhere in her mouth. Again, the things he could do with that tongue amazed her. Her hands started at his upper chest and were sliding down, she pulled him closer by the belt loops on his jeans. He intertwined his fingers with hers and held her hands above her head on the wall. She was melting. She felt like she could slide all the way down the wall like butter. He made her knees feel weak. He was so sensual and gentle but she loved that he could be a little aggressive in a passionate way. It made her go into submissive mode. She didn't want to take charge; she liked him being in control.

"Did you kids forget where the pies are?" Tom hollered from the living room.

"Y'all need help in there?" Caroline hollered then giggled.

"Nah, we're good. Thanks though," Sawyer hollered back, still pinning Marina against the wall.

Marina giggled as Sawyer kissed down her neck. "We really should get the pies."

"I don't need pie, I have dessert right here." His grin turned sly.

She didn't want it to stop either, not in the slightest. She put a finger up to his lips as he leaned in to kiss her again. "How about you make me a strong drink while I take the pies in."

"Okay, I can do that." He sighed.

CHAPTER 28

Bar Shift

I t was a chilly Saturday evening. Leaves rustled across the dimly
lit parking lot as Marina made her way from her car to the bar
entrance. She donned her fitted black leather jacket. It paired well
with her distressed jeans. Some regulars recognized her, even
without Sawyer at her side. They shouted her name when she
entered. She was pleasantly surprised. She strapped on a little
black serving apron and hugged Gladys.

"Hey, you're just in time!" Bob pushed the double swinging
doors to the kitchen.

"Y'all about to get busy?" she asked just as a biker gang came
through the front doors.

"Oh boy." Marina took a deep breath and placed a pen behind
her ear. She took a notepad off the bar and met the bikers at their
tables. She stayed organized in her order-taking. Bob stayed busy
pouring beer and placing it on the bar top with its corresponding
ticket; that was his system for such busy nights. Gladys was flying
pizzas on each hand in the air, kicking the swinging doors with
her foot.

"How's everyone treating ya?" Gladys put an order into the
computer as Marina washed sloshed beer off her hands.

"Actually, that group is fun. Great guys. Polite too."

"Yeah, they're pretty great. Always a respectful group. Not sure why most people look down on bikers. They're usually the best kind at the bar."

"I guess you don't have to worry about hiring a bouncer for Saturday nights," Marina joked.

"You're not kiddin'. I wouldn't wanna mess with these guys."

"This is the safest place you can be tonight." Bob laughed.

"I bet," Marina agreed. The gang played the jukebox loud. Marina hadn't hustled that much in a long time but she enjoyed it. She was smiling all night. The gang made her laugh and tipped her really well. Gladys waited on the rest of the bar with Bob, which wasn't much but she stayed busy making pizzas. Bob was happy to just be pouring all night and not have to be running back and forth from floor to bar.

"She's a good sport! Keep her around!" One of the bikers hollered on their way out the door.

"Glad to hear it." Bob waved. Marina helped clean up, taking dishes to the kitchen and sweeping. Gladys ran the dishes through the dishwasher as Bob cleaned behind the bar and squeaked the glasses dry with a cloth, polishing each before stacking them.

"You thinkin' you wanna keep coming in Saturday nights?" Bob wiped the bar top down.

"Yeah, I do. This was a good group y'all had in here tonight."

"It's the usual Saturday crew. Well, some Saturdays. Never a problem with those guys.

"Yeah, they were cool. They tipped really well too. I kinda feel guilty for accepting it."

"Nah, you earned that, girl. No screw ups tonight, you hustled, you made sure they were taken care of... you earned it. We appreciate you busting your rear tonight. You did us proud." Bob gave her a pat on the back.

"Aww, thanks, Bob. Can I help y'all do anything else? I can take the trash out." The last of the customers left.

"Well, if you want to that would be great. Just be careful and take your phone with you."

"Yes, sir." She gathered trash and headed for the door just as Sawyer walked in. His hat was tipped low and he was chewing on a toothpick.

"Hey!" Marina was surprised to see him there.

"Hey, how was your night?"

"It went smoothly, thanks."

Sawyer took the large bag of trash from her. "I'll take it out."

"Thanks, I'll walk with you."

They walked out to the side of the building and Sawyer tossed the trash into the dumpster.

"I need to get a better light hung out here. I don't like the thought of you out here in the dark alone."

"I'll be okay. That's so sweet of you to worry about me though." They turned back to go back in.

"Of course I worry. I didn't come up here sooner because I didn't want you to think I was hovering or being controlling or anything. I just wanted to make sure you leave safely."

"I wouldn't have thought that. It's sweet you came to make sure I survived my first night." She looked up at his eyes, which were just a glimmer under that hat. He opened the door for her and placed his hand on the small of her back as she entered.

"You have more to do?" he asked as they neared the bar. She scooched a chair in as she walked by it.

"I'm not sure but I'll ask." Marina took her apron off and stuffed it under the bar on a shelf.

She didn't get a chance to ask as Gladys came out and gave Sawyer a hug. "Y'all crazy kids get on outta here. We're about to scoot out too. Thanks again, sweetie."

"No, thank you." Marina gave her a hug as Gladys mouthed "Keep her" to Sawyer.

He nodded and winked and took 2 bottles of beer from Bob when he extended them across the bar.

"Y'all have a good night." Sawyer wrapped an arm around Marina and left out the doors and into the night.

CHAPTER 29

Tailgate Trouble

The crisp breeze blew Marina's hair to the side and she had to pull it out of her face.

"Have time for a beer before going home? Maybe a nightcap?" Sawyer handed her one of the beer bottles that Bob had handed him on their way out.

"Sure. Yeah, of course." She looked at the label.

"I know you don't like beer but I remembered you saying you like Ciderboys hard cider."

"Wow, you listen too! I gotta keep you around," she teased as she took a sip.

He chuckled as he took a sip. He flopped his tailgate down and leaned against it with his backside. She lifted herself onto the tailgate backwards.

"You gonna sit with me?"

He smiled and adjusted his hat then lifted himself onto the tailgate right next to her.

"Cheers." He tapped his bottle against hers.

"So...how was your night?"

"It went really well, thanks."

"That was a big crowd, wasn't it?"

"Yeah. There had to have been more than two dozen bikers in

addition to all the regulars. I guess that seems like more when they all come in at once."

"Anybody give you a hard time? Do I need to jack any jaws?"

She almost spit her mouthful out. She wiped her mouth with the back of her hand. "Nope. All is good. It's like riding a bike, serving. Just different place and different computer system."

"Glad it all went smoothly."

"Thanks, me too. What did you do this evening?"

"Chores. Then I watched tv for a bit and talked with my buddy about Smokie's progress. I grabbed a bite to eat then came up here to check on you."

"You're sweet."

"Nah, I just care about you." He inched closer. She stared at those heated, intensified pools of desire.

Gladys and Bob exited the bar and locked the door. That caught Marina's attention but not Sawyer's until they hollered goodnight. They both waved and said goodnight in return.

Sawyer sat his beer up on the side edge of the truck bed then leaned back on the palms of his hands as Gladys and Bob drove out of the parking lot.

Marina liked to be alone with him. He was exciting. She found herself still feeling a bit nervous around him too. She took a drink then looked over at him. He was looking right at her under the brim of his hat. The sleeves of his teal long-sleeved Henley were pushed up halfway to his elbows. That color was perfect on him.

"Your jacket warm enough? Mine is inside the truck if you'd like it."

"I'm okay, thanks."

He just nodded.

She stared up at the moon. "It looks full tonight, doesn't it?"

"It sure does. It's bright. You know, this probably sounds corny but you make me feel as high as the moon."

She smiled and tilted her head. "Do I?"

"You do. That moon has magical powers. It controls the tides and gravitational pull, among other things. The same way you control me, that pull that gravitates us to each other. Just naturally a beautiful thing."

"I'm not sure if I should tell you how amazingly sweet that was or if I should ask how much you've had to drink." She bit her bottom lip and wrinkled her nose.

He laughed. "I've only drunk this one."

"Ok, so that was really sweet. A little corny, but really sweet." She laughed and bumped her arm into his.

He laughed again. "Really though, there's something magnetic about you. I'm done fighting that pull too." He leaned in, her lips parted and her eyes closed. The sound of shattering glass startled them both.

"What the Hell?" Sawyer jumped off the tailgate. "Hop in the truck."

She jumped down and quickly got in the truck but was quiet to shut the door while Sawyer retrieved his handgun from the center console.

"What are you doing?" she asked, sliding down in the seat to avoid being seen.

"I'm going to check it out. Stay here and honk if you need me."

"Sawyer!" she whispered loudly. He shut the door quietly and racked a round into the chamber. He looked through a front window but didn't see anything. He went around back, both hands on the gun, bent knees, and stealthy like an FBI agent on tv.

Her eyes peered just barely out the window as she remained low in the seat. Her heart was beating quickly, not as quickly as when Sawyer was up close to her, but this was a different type of race; a nervous-scared one. She didn't want anything happening to him. Should she attempt to help? He might accidentally shoot her, not expecting her to creep up. Or she could get hurt by whoever was breaking in. She decided it was best to stay put.

The time seemed to be dragging, not knowing if he was okay. She heard a gunshot. Now her heart was really racing scared. A few minutes later Sawyer came walking calmly back out to the truck. The gun lowered and his guard down. He looked back once, got in the truck, and got his phone from the dash and called Bob.

"Did you shoot someone?" Marina whispered as he put the phone to his ear. He shook his head no as Bob answered.

"Somebody just threw a brick through a back window at the bar. We heard glass break so I went to check it out. I saw a brick inside the bar where the glass had been broken. Heard somebody running near the edge of the woods. I fired off a round to the side at the big tree beside the dumpster to scare them off. I can call the cops if you want but you'll wanna bring a piece of plywood back over here tonight and I'll help you board it up." He paused. "Yes, sir." Sawyer hung up.

"Thank God you didn't get hurt. I was so scared for you," she panicked.

He touched her face. "I'm so sorry you were scared. I didn't mean to scare you."

"I know, I was just worried about you going after someone with a gun. Who knows what could've been back there waiting for you."

"I'm okay. Everything's okay. I was more worried about your safety." He leaned his forehead against hers and she grasped his wrists as he cradled her face.

"Bob is calling the cops but they'll want me to wait for them. You okay with that? Or you can go."

"Of course, I'm staying with you."

"Okay. I don't want you working here now."

"Oh, Sawyer. I'll be fine. It's only one night a week or less. I'll walk out with Gladys and Bob if that makes you feel better."

"I'm going to go buy a camera system tomorrow morning and install it around here. I'd rather be here every Saturday night when you get out of work too."

"Oh, you don't need to do that. It's probably punk kids."

"I'd feel better about it. Nothing ever happens here and now that you work here, on your first day no-less..."

"If you would like to come up here when I get off work or even before, I'm okay with that."

"Really? You wouldn't think I was smothering you?"

"What? No! I think it's incredibly sweet you're so protective of me."

"Yeah?"

"Yeah. The cameras are probably a good idea though."

"Yeah, I worry about Gladys and Bob too. I just want you to be safe. I don't know what I'd do if something happened to you." He put a hand on her thigh and his other elbow on the console.

A cop car drove into the parking lot and they squinted in the bright headlights. The cop parked next to them and got out, adjusting his belt.

Sawyer rolled his window down. He explained all that had happened as the cop jotted down notes on his little flip notepad.

"The same thing happened tonight at the corner store. I gotta stop there after here. I'll go take a look and take a picture of the damage."

"I appreciate it." Sawyer tipped his hat.

Bob drove back in with a sheet of plywood hanging out of the bed of his truck further than the tailgate. Gladys had stayed home. They lived just up the next dirt road, opposite of Sawyer.

"I'll go help them with that real quick. You okay here?"

"Yeah, I'm good."

"Gun's in the console if you need it."

"Noted." She nodded with no intention of needing it. Sawyer pulled the plywood out of the bed of Bob's truck and carried it as Bob grabbed a nail gun out of his passenger seat.

It only took ten or fifteen minutes for them to board up the smashed window with the cop's help. They shook the officer's hand in the parking lot then each parted ways and drove out.

"He said he thinks it's just punk kids. We all took a look

around inside but nobody was in there. Got it boarded up good for now and I'll put cameras up tomorrow."

"It's so nice you help them the way you do. Good thing you were here tonight, the place would've been accessible all night."

"Yeah, just luck, I guess. Hopefully, I scared them enough to not come back or do it again to anyone else.

"Everyone is right about you, ya know?"

"What do ya mean?"

"You're a great guy, Sawyer. You're one of a kind."

"Aww, you're one of a kind too." He gave her a hug and kiss before she got out and went to her car. He made sure she was good and set before they both left for the night.

CHAPTER 30

Tough as Nails

"Hardware store after chores? We need a 4x4x8 and 3-1x6x6. Just tell them it's under my name. My card is on file. Thank you bunches," is what the barn note read.

After chores, she lightly sprayed the horses with fly spray. The flies were plentiful after a storm that went through during the night. She noticed the pasture near the gate had a small section of broken fence that Sawyer had temporarily fixed it by nailing a thin-cut piece of plywood up. It wouldn't fly for long though; Athena would try busting through it. She put Athena in a different pasture, just in case.

The storm had brought out the spunkiness in the horses. As soon as the last one was put out to pasture, they all started running around. She stood against the fence with a foot up on the bottom wooden rail, arm over the top. Legend had taken a liking to Marina. He approached the fence begging for scratchin's.

Marina grabbed a brush from the barn and entered the pasture to brush him. At the low of his mane, as she brushed his withers, he stretched his neck out and lipped the air. That always made Marina laugh. Fur flew as she brushed down his back.

The others were grazing out further so she put the brush away when she finished. The lead rope was hung up on the wall on her way out and she clunked dirt off her boots before getting into his truck. He had left the key in it so she could use it to go get the boards.

At the hardware store she loaded up what she needed and took the lumber cart to the checkout. She greeted the cashier, who seemed friendly enough at first.

"This is going on Sawyer Brandton's account, please. He said his card is on file."

The cashier stopped as she went to scan the first board. "Sawyer?"

"Yes ma'am."

The cashier just gave her a scowl then huffed before scanning. She asked for Marina's name so she could make sure she was listed on the account as a user then checked her ID. Marina noticed her name tag said Shanda and made sure to thank her by name before leaving. She loaded the boards into the truck bed and went back to the barn, where she put the boards along the wall under the lead ropes just inside the door. She made sure they were out of the way but where they could be seen right away.

"Dinner at my place tonight?" He texted her later in the morning.

"I'd love to," she answered back.

Sawyer's phone rang while he and Marina were cooking dinner. He was washing his hands in the sink so asked Marina to answer it. She sat the tomato she was about to slice on the counter and hesitated when reaching for his phone.

"It's Gabriella. Maybe you should get it."

"Not sure why the hell she'd be calling but go ahead."

Marina answered, "Hello?" She paused. "This is Marina." She paused again. "Sure, just one second."

She handed the phone to Sawyer as he finished drying his hands.

"Hello?" He paused as he stepped around the corner. Marina continued chopping veggies as if she didn't care another woman was calling him but she was curious and worried since he left the room. She tiptoed over closer to eavesdrop but he put it on speaker. *So why go around the corner*, she wondered?

"So, who's Marina?" Gabriella asked.

"Marina is my girlfriend," he answered, trying to keep his voice down. "Why are you calling me?" His voice carried a confused tone.

"My friend at the hardware store said a pretty girl came in there charging supplies to your account."

"So?"

"I wanted to know who she was."

"Why? Why is that any of your business?"

"Well, I just...I just miss you and I think that, ya know, maybe we could try again."

"Seriously? Hmm, first of all, I wasn't important enough to you then. Second, it's been a couple of years so why now? You must not want me to be happy with someone else. Third, I've found someone who has shown me what true love is. She's shown me what a real relationship should be like. I'm happier now than I have ever been, so I should say thank you, actually, for breaking my heart because I am unexpectedly in love for real this time. She mended my heart that you broke and takes really damn good care of it." There was a long pause. Sawyer's eyebrows raised as he waited for a response.

"So, you've moved on? I can't say I'm surprised. You're a great guy so you were bound to be scooped up. Every girl in town dreamt of being with you. I wish I would've come to my senses sooner. I missed out."

Sawyer shook his head in disbelief, "Gabby, I wouldn't have taken you back anyways. I do appreciate that we parted ways though, honestly thank you. Otherwise, I wouldn't be with who I'm with today. Then I would be the one missing out. I wish you the best, I really do, but please don't ever call me again." Sawyer hung up so Marina dashed back over to the counter and started wiping it down.

"I seriously can't believe her." He put his phone down on the counter, almost tossing it.

"Who was she?"

"My ex. Apparently she's come to her senses and wants me back."

"Oh!" Her eyebrows raised considerably.

"You don't have to worry, Babe. I don't want her back and I told her that. Even if I were single, it wouldn't happen. I told her I'm in love with someone better."

"That's sweet." She wrapped her arms around him and squeezed him tight. She was relieved by how he felt about her as well as not wanting his ex back.

"Wait. You said you're in love." She looked up at him.

"Yes, I did." He smiled. "I'm guessing big mouth Shanda was the cashier at the hardware store?"

Marina snickered. "That was the girl's name, yeah."

"I thought so. She told Gabby a pretty girl came in charging stuff to my account. She got nosey and wanted to know who you were."

"Wow, okay. What did you say?" She looked at him as if she didn't already know the answer as she rinsed tomato juice from her hands.

"I told her you're my girlfriend."

"You did?" Marina felt comforted knowing he would be truthful.

"Yeah, I did. Is that okay? If not, at least she thinks that."

"Absolutely, I love it." Marina took hold of his perfectly scruffy face and planted a kiss on his lips.

"I guess we haven't had that exact conversation yet...a label. I kinda thought, ya know, since we've made out and told my parents we're dating..."

"To be clear, we're exclusively together as a couple then, right?" She smirked.

"Of course. I don't wanna be with anyone else."

Marina's smile couldn't have grown any bigger and his matched it.

He flashed those pearly whites, "Shall we eat?" Sawyer reached over and grabbed the dish towel as Marina went to get a platter of food near the stove. He wrapped the towel around her waist and pulled her back to him. He leaned against the counter, her leaning into him. He kissed her so sensually. Soft and moist, sharing breath, their lips didn't leave each other. Tender yet intense. He had nothing but good intentions for her and this she knew deep down.

His hands dropped the towel and framed her face. His eyes stared into hers, setting her soul on fire. He made her breathe heavier as he reflected deep commitment with his glacier blues. She looked delicate but had been reassured. Her hands lay upon his beating chest, sliding down to the waist of his jeans. She leaned her forehead upon his chest and murmured, "Our food is going to get cold," then looked up at him as he laughed. He glided his fingers through her hair and kissed her on the forehead.

She grabbed the platter as he grabbed plates and they sat to eat together at the table.

CHAPTER 31
Wood Chopping (Axes and Ohs)

I t was a warm day for being so late in the fall. It was practically winter and eighty degrees. She was glad she wore shorts that day. She entered the barn but didn't pour coffee like usual. She had two cups at home and decided it best to stay hydrated. On the counter, like every morning, there was a barn note. Sawyer was there still though somewhere; his truck was in the drive. She flipped the note open. It read "We might get rained on today. Could be fun." This stirred her curiosity.

She rushed to do the chores and saw he was on the other side of the barn driveway near the edge of the woods. There was a stump and a stack of wood, some chopped, and a pile of logs. Sawyer was chopping wood in a white t-shirt and jeans, adjusting his white hat after a few hits. She took a couple of bottles of water from the fridge and left the horses in the barn, eager to go see him.

"Good morning. I brought you water." She handed it to him as he wiped his forearm across his forehead.

"Thanks, good morning."

"You been out here a while?"

"Not really. I should've come out sooner." He looked at the sky behind the house. She turned around to look. It was getting dark. Just beyond the house and pasture, the clouds were building and moving in their direction. Her attention focused back on him.

She couldn't resist noticing how his white shirt stuck to his sweaty skin, most of his shirt was damp and every curve of his muscles could be seen. Oh, the definition of them all. He looked so daringly hot. Thunder cracked as the distant storm clouds rolled closer quickly. She stared at him, her mouth watering as if she was looking at desserts through a bakery window. The thunder didn't seem to bother him as he kept swinging the ax up over his head and then down onto the log with such force. She was thinking there is a God after all. How else could such a creature be created? How could there be such a wonderful, generous, caring, gentle, sexy man all wrapped up in one gorgeous package? Yes, that was an elaborate description, but true. Every word of it. Who wouldn't want this man?

It couldn't be that women don't want him but rather that he didn't want them. He could have any woman he wanted on Earth or beyond. Why did he want her? She didn't understand. It seemed too good to be true. There's no way. There's no way a guy like him could be interested in her. Her expectations would be too high but he'd live up to them and she would be giving her hopes up if it didn't work out. But why should she deny herself the possibility? She had prayed for a miracle, a saving grace. Something, someone to light a spark within her and make her happy again. He did that just by being her boss, her friend, and now her boyfriend.

Hard to believe they were a couple. It didn't seem like it was reality. Taking it slow was extremely difficult but she was afraid of her heart being broken again. She felt an undeniable lustfulness toward him.

Thunder cracked again, louder, and it started raining, but he seemed to not notice. He kept chopping. The sky cut loose. Rain poured off the brim of his hat as he kept chopping still. Streams of rain ran down his bulged arm veins like a river branching. Maybe she should offer to help so he wasn't out there so long. It looked as though he didn't plan to stop. She yelled so he could hear her over the sound of the downpour. It was loud, pounding on the metal barn roof.

"Would you like help?" Now her shirt was stuck to her. It was a slightly low-cut t-shirt, fitting and lavender, her sleeves cuffed. The outline of her bra could be seen clearly. He waved her over, "If you'd like. You aren't obligated though. You'd stay drier in the house."

"I'm not made of sugar. I won't melt."

He whacked the ax into a second stump as she approached. He sat on the larger stump and grabbed her by the waist to pull her closer. "Nah, you make me melt though." He pulled her into him, positioning her between his legs. His hand was upon the side of her face, the other around the small of her back. How did he know that drives her crazy? All of it! He kissed her so passionately, almost slightly aggressively, which made her spine tingle.

She straddled him and sat tightly against his soaked body.

He took his hat off and put it onto her to shield her face from the rain.

Her hands slowly ran from his thick, broad shoulders and down his chest and to the bottom of his shirt, which she then grabbed and brought up over his head. It landed in the mud that was puddling nearby on the edge of the drive. He looked deep into her eyes and licked his bottom lip then kissed her again like he hadn't already. He took the hat off her to pull her shirt up over her head, her breasts bulging from her bra. Her shirt landed near his as he placed the hat back onto her. She dug her nails into his solid thighs. He kissed her neck and down her chest, which shot an excited chill up her back. His hair wasn't wavy anymore but she ran her fingers through it anyways, his breath almost panting upon her.

He readjusted her legs, wrapping them tighter around him and firmly pressing her against him. She felt the large bulge through his jeans. It excited her. They paid no attention to the rain, the flash flooding that was accumulating all around them. They had not a care in the world, besides each other.

The temptation had overcome them both. The everyday sexual tension had become too much to bear. She kissed his bare chest as he moved her drenched hair to the side. She grabbed his shoulders and kissed him aggressively then nibbled his earlobe. His hands were on the rear of her cut-off jean shorts as she released the button on his jeans and an unforeseen hasty bolt of lightning struck a nearby tree in the field. The crack was loud and sparks flew. They jumped up, grabbed their shirts, him taking her by the hand and, together, they ran for the house, mud sloshing behind them.

Stepping inside the front door, he said, "I'll go grab a couple of towels," as he kicked off his boots and went to his bathroom. She took her boots off, for they too were covered in red mud. She stood waiting, cold and covering her chest with crossed arms. It was a cold rain and she could feel her skin covered in goosebumps. He came out with two towels for them to dry off and wrapped one around her.

"Wow, that was intense!" She took the towel corners from him.

"Which part?" He smirked, toweling off his hair, his jeans dripping water all over the wood floor around his bare feet.

"Um, all of it."

"Yeah. That lightning was crazy. Way too close."

"Definitely a close call." She wasn't sure if he really meant the lightning or the sparks between them. "Sparks everywhere, huh?" She looked at him to see his reaction.

"They were amazing." He stepped closer to her there in the foyer. He dropped his towel and parted her lips with his tongue again.

He paused. "Give me one second. Don't go anywhere." He held up a 'wait-a-minute' finger and sprinted to the kitchen, wet footprints following. She heard a drawer open and close and he came back only a moment later with a barn note and handed it to her. She smiled and he nodded. She flipped it open. It read, "Let's finish what we started."

She looked up at him and he reached for her hand; his eyes locked on hers. She dropped the note to the floor and took his hand. She followed him hand-in-hand to his bedroom. They had both finally given in to those urges, the intense lust toward each other, and it was magnetic. She was a little nervous and looked a mess, but was ecstatic inside. She had never been so thankful for rain in all her life. There had never been such a memorable rainstorm either. Unforgettable. They stopped at the foot of the bed, her face in his hands, her arms around him.

He kissed her slowly this time, gently. Tongues caressed each other. He dropped her towel to her feet, then unbuttoned her shorts and slowly pulled down her zipper then whispered, "Is this okay?" His warm breath upon her neck sent those good chills up her back again.

She grasped his back with her fingertips and nodded. "Definitely, yes."

He slid her shorts down off her hips and she stepped out of them, remaining up on her toes. She thought it was gentleman-like of him to ask permission although not necessary, for she wanted him more than anything. She finished undoing his pants and, as she started to pull them down, he finished pulling them off for her. Forehead to forehead, he ran his fingers down her neck, onto her breast, then unfastened her bra in the back. She lowered her arms, letting it hit the floor. He kissed her neck, sucking a little, like a vampire, then down her chest and onto her breast. She arched backward, biting her bottom lip. He pulled her thong off, one leg at a time, and it drove her absolutely wild.

Her hands wandered his chest, down his chiseled abs, then his inguinal crease. That lower abdominal *V* brought out the animal in her. She took a step back and pulled his black boxer briefs down. He finished taking them off as she grabbed his backside and squeezed, pressing him against her.

As his hand warmed her neck and rain dripped from their

hair, she placed both hands on his chest and stepped to the side. He turned to face her, his back to the bed. She shoved him back onto the mattress and he cracked a sideways smile, assured she had become more relaxed and comfortable with him. She stood before him, completely bare. He admired her up and down and back up again. His blue eyes gleamed alluringly, calling to her. He had provoked a version of her he had never witnessed and he liked it.

"God, you're so sexy." He scooched backward until he was shoulder level with the plush silk pillows behind him. She looked him up and down, practically drooling at his impressive erection. Her sly grin turned into lip-biting as she wrapped her wet hair over one shoulder. She swung her hips, slowly cat-walking the few steps to the bed, then crawled to him. He squirmed with anticipation.

He liked her demand for control.

She straddled him and pressed him back against the pillows. She teased him by rubbing and grinding up against him. She was aware the foreplay wouldn't last long; they were both too eager to have each other completely. She held a possessive posture over top of him, her fingers upon his contoured, stubbled face. Her soft lips twisted with his. She nibbled his earlobe since he seemed to enjoy it the first time. Then she slid down, her tongue painting his bare, smooth, hairless chest.

His fingers tangled in her hair and he gave a gentle pull, which made her moan. He realized she has a naughty, erotic side. He tilted his head back and closed his eyes as she made her way below the *V*. His fingers still gripping her hair, he breathed heavier and faster.

He said in a low, growling tone, "Get up here."

She crawled back up and gently positioned herself upon him. He inserted himself. She gasped. You would think they would be slightly chilled from the cold rain but their body heat and adrenaline made their blood run feverish. His hands were upon her breasts, then down on her hips, and onto her backside.

She dug her fingernails into his pecks. It didn't take her long to climax, her jaw wide open, she let out a scream of ecstasy with her head tilted back, and her back arched. He sat up, holding her tight.

He flipped her over, holding himself up over her. She liked the change in control. Her fingers glided through his hair before she gave it a yank then dug her nails into his tight, round rear, pulling him as close as she could.

Skin-to-skin he thrusted repeatedly, almost in a rolling wave motion. Not too fast, not too slow. It was perfect. He was perfect. She grabbed his biceps, they were so strong. Her toes were rubbing up and down his calves, slowly, her back arching once more. Her fingers ran from his strong broad shoulders down his arms, then she grasped hold of the silk sheets as she moaned and screamed his name, climaxing again as he kissed her neck, the sheet barely covering his rear and his hair down in his face.

He ravished her deeply then moaned and laid next to her. He took a few labored breaths then she laid upon his chest, his arm around her. Her heart was pounding like horses galloping loudly, so was his.

"That! That was amazing!" He looked at her with those eyes that she gets lost in.

"Yes, it was!" She touched her forehead to make sure she wasn't sweating too badly. Her face felt flush. He swiped her hair from her eyes and covered their glistening bodies with the sheet as she strolled her fingers across the wrist of his tattooed arm that held her and fiddled with the black-banded wristband he wore every day. She found it to be so sexy.

"You know this would've happened in the rain right there on the stump if not for the lightning, right?"

She laughed. "I actually agree, it would have. This way was much more comfortable though. I think the way it happened was perfect." They lay in silence for a few minutes before Marina said, "You've shown me that not all men are the same. I've never felt this way about anyone, ever."

"Me neither. I don't want to feel this way about anyone other than you either, ever. Only you." He held her face and kissed her again. She stroked her hand up and down his chest and abdomen and he rubbed her thigh, which was crossed over his.

"We should probably shower." He stretched an arm up behind his head, resting his head on his hand.

"Together?" She looked up at him then sat up and crawled off the bed, turned facing him, and motioned for him to follow her as she walked backwards to the bathroom.

"You're teasing. I like it." He rushed to follow her. She turned the shower on and let the water get warm while he hung a towel on the hook. She stepped into the tile walk-in shower and he followed, closing the glass door behind him. Their passionate kissing helped to quickly steam the shower and fog the mirror. He turned her around, her palms and breasts pressed up against the glass door amongst the steam. He took her once more right there in the shower.

They held each other all night, tangled in the silk sheets. The way his body felt against hers—life just made sense.

She felt complete. She was no longer nervous but was still excited to be around him even after breaking the sexual tension. Even more so now that she knew what he was capable of. It's not like she had any doubts about that at all, but he exceeded her expectations in every way. He felt amazing. *All* of him. He had accepted her for who she was and that warmed her heart.

When she woke in the morning, a sunbeam shined through a crack in the curtain. She hadn't slept that sound in a long time. She thought she would have a hard time sleeping since it wasn't her own bed but something about sleeping next to him made her sleep soundly, especially after the exhausting night they had. She felt safe. She felt comfort surrounding her. She felt his caring, hospitable presence even though when she reached over as she rolled, he wasn't there. She raised herself up onto an elbow, wondering where he was. He came into the doorway, the beam of light shining across in front of him.

"Good morning." He sat on the edge of the bed. She scooched

herself closer to him. He rubbed her leg up and down so softly. He gave her a gentle kiss.

"Good morning." She shied away.

"Everything okay?" He looked worried and raised a brow.

She covered her mouth. "Yeah, of course. I'm sure I have horrible morning breath."

"It's not that bad. Do you really think I care about that?"

"Probably." Now her eyebrows were raised.

"I absolutely do not." He kissed her a good one, separating her lips with his tongue. She was instantly wanting him again. She couldn't get enough.

"I made you breakfast." He tapped her knee and stood.

"You did?"

"I did. I wanted to make sure you were awake. I'll go get it."

She had never been treated with breakfast in bed. She sat up and pulled the covers over her legs, straightening out the wrinkles. He came in with a wooden tray. There was a full breakfast displayed perfectly, complete with a peach hibiscus flower from his landscaping. A barn note was tented beside the plate.

It read, "You're the sunshine to my storm. You have the key to my heart."

An uncontrollable wide smile swept her face. "Oh Sawyer. I feel the same way. Thank you."

He kissed her forehead and walked back down the hall in his blue boxer briefs. She loved how they fit his every curve and muscle so well. Not an ounce of jiggle on that man. He came back with a tray for himself. No flower though or note on his. He sat next to her against the stack of pillows.

"This is so nice. Nobody's ever done anything like this for me before."

"Well, I hope you can get used to it." He crunched on bacon and she tilted her head to the side in confusion.

"Since you already have a key to the house and I love you being here with me, I'm asking you to move in."

"Seriously?" She was surprised and so excited.

"I'm serious. What do you say?"

"If you're sure, I'd love to."

"Oh, I'm sure. I've wanted to ask you since that night I found you crying in the barn." He stopped chewing and kissed her on closed lips. "I wanna be your home, your safe place."

"You already are." She adored him.

"I'll do chores today," he said.

"I can do—"

"No, I got it. Thank you though," he interrupted with insistence. You pack today and you probably have to work this afternoon, don't you?"

"Yeah, I do. I go in around five."

"Let me know if you want me to come up there when you get out. I worry about you."

"Of course, I'd like for you to come up there. You can anytime."

"Again, I don't wanna hover or seem possessive. I just wanna make sure you leave safely." He stabbed eggs with his fork.

"I appreciate you. So much." She used a finger to tilt his chin to look at her. "Sawyer. You're wonderful. You know that?"

"Not as wonderful as you." He rubbed his nose to hers.

"I just can't get enough of you. It will probably take me all weekend to pack."

"Let me know if I can help."

"Oh, I will."

They finished breakfast and she got dressed in her now-clean clothes. Sawyer had been up for a while and done a load of laundry. They were folded for her on the end of the bed.

"I feel like I'm in a fancy hotel." She buttoned her shorts.

He laughed as he buttoned his jeans.

"What's this?" She gasped, her hand over her mouth. "You have fingernail marks on your chest...shoulder...and on your back too! Oh my gosh, Sawyer, I'm so sorry!" She was looking at him all over.

"They're more like claw marks on my back but what are you

sorry for? I'm not." He pulled her to him, a sideways grin on his lips, and groaned in her ear.

She laughed and gently tapped his chest. They walked out and to the front door. She put her boots on; he had clunked the dry mud off them out the front door the best he could.

"I'll see you tonight around closing." He opened the door, steaming coffee cup in his other hand.

"I can't wait." She smiled and gave him a hug and kiss. Rain danced on the metal rooftop on an otherwise quiet morning. He stood in the open doorway, bare feet crossed and leaning. She waved as she got into her car. He sipped his coffee and waved back then rested his hand in his pocket, watching her leave.

CHAPTER 32

Moving In

S unday, Marina had spent all day packing. She left all of her furniture at her house. Monday morning, she brought a load of her things but left it in her car while she did chores. The barn note that morning warmed her much more than the coffee did.

It read, "I love you!"

A warmth ran through her. She felt the same for him and couldn't wait to tell him. He was all she thought about, day and night. Unfortunately for her, he was working that day. She took her boxes into the house before going home to get another load. She didn't have much, just the two loads since she wasn't bringing furniture. She would be more than happy with everything Sawyer owned. She planned to rent out her place fully furnished once she was settled.

She brought the second load over and stacked her boxes neatly in the foyer. She decided not to start unpacking because she didn't want to come across too eager or like she was trying to take over his lovely home. By the time she finished stacking the boxes from that last load, Sawyer pulled into the driveway. He didn't waste any time getting up to the house. He opened the front door as she was approaching in the foyer. He didn't even kick his boots off, just scooped her up, lifting her feet off the floor and kissing her, her arms wrapped tightly around his neck.

"God, I missed you," he whispered in her ear.

"Not as much as I missed you. I got your barn note this morning."

"I was hoping you did." He hung his hat. "But I still wanted to say it directly to you." He held her face against his hand. "I love you, Marina."

She pressed her hand against his stubble as she replied, "I love you too, Sawyer."

"I love that you're here when I get home."

"I love it too." She nuzzled into his neck. "I got so busy today I forgot to have a plan for dinner. I'm so sorry."

"Hey, love..." He took her by the shoulders and looked down into her eyes. "Please don't feel you need to apologize for stuff like that. It's really no big deal. We'll figure out what to have together. Okay?"

"Okay."

"How about the café in town where we have lunch sometimes? I can call it in and go pick it up."

"Sure. That sounds great. I'll take a panini this time."

He nodded. "Wanna unpack some of your stuff tonight?"

"Sure, I can if you're okay with that."

"My home is now your home. Of course, I'm okay with that."

"I did leave my dresser behind; I couldn't get it in my car."

"We can go get it on the way to get the food if you wanna go with me. Or we can get it tomorrow after work."

"Let's go ahead and go get it now. That way I can get unpacked throughout the week."

"Perfect. Oh, um...I'm thinking of doing a bonfire here Saturday night. You cool with that?"

"Sawyer, it's your house."

"Nah, it's our house now."

"I'm okay with it." She smiled a sweet smile.

"Saturday morning we'll go to the store to get some food and stuff for grilling out."

"Sounds good. I'm excited."

"Me too. Do you have to work Saturday though?"

"I don't, no. Not for a few weeks. The bikers are on a ride downstate."

"Perfect. I would've rescheduled the bonfire if you had to work. I wanna show you off to my friends." He winked and slapped her rear. She giggled, not expecting that.

The end of the week came quickly. They relaxed at home with pizza and cuddling for a movie Friday night. They went to the grocery store. He thought she looked so cute in her yellow sundress and wedge sandals, carrying a shopping basket. He grabbed one as well while brushing hair off his shoulder, then walked next to her gathering food they would need for grilling out. After visiting the meat counter, he decided they needed a cart, so he went back up front to trade the basket for one.

"Marina? Hey, girl! I thought that was you." A young lady Marina had been friends with years ago approached her.

"Melanie! Hi, how are you?"

"Great, great. Last time I saw you was, what? Last year?"

"I believe it was, yeah."

"You look so much happier...or something."

"Oh yeah?"

"Yeah, you get your hair color changed?'

"Ah, nope."

"Well, you're just glowing!"

"Am I?"

"What's changed since last year? You're just beaming." Melanie's fake boujee concern made Marina wanna roll her eyes. Her boujeeness was one reason they aren't friends anymore.

"Well, I'm in love. Deeply. In fact, I've just moved in with him."

"Aww, that's great, Hun. Good for you. I thought you and Derrick already lived together?"

"I'm not with Derrick anymore; I haven't been for a couple months now."

Sawyer approached them with the cart, leaning on it.

"Incoming. Hot guy behind you. Looks like he just stepped out of a magazine. I think he's looking at me." Melanie twirled her hair and smacked her lipstick.

Marina looked over her shoulder and saw Sawyer. She couldn't contain her smile.

"Hey, Baby. Wanna throw that stuff in the cart?"

Melanie's eyes grew large and her jaw dropped.

"Who's this?" Sawyer reached a hand out. Melanie slowly shook his hand, in complete shock.

"Sawyer, dear, this is Melanie."

"Hi, nice to meet you. Marina and I go way back as friends."

Marina refrained from rolling her eyes.

"It's a pleasure, ma'am." Sawyer helped Marina unload her basket into the cart.

"Well, it was nice running into you. Take care." Marina politely tried to escape. She took the cart by the front and turned it away in the opposite direction.

"We'll have to get together sometime," Melanie waved. Marina just smiled a coy smile. Marina and Sawyer kept shopping.

"It doesn't seem like you were too thrilled to run into her," Sawyer noticed.

"Well, yeah."

"I'm confused." Sawyer picked up a bag of apples and put them in the cart.

"We were friends when we were seniors, 'til she stole my boyfriend. We haven't spoken since."

"Ugh, sorry."

"Oh, it's ok. If he could be stolen, I didn't mean that much to him anyways."

"True. You don't ever have to worry about that with me though. I hope you know that."

"You're too good of a guy to do something like that. You're

polite but you would put a chick in her place if you had to. Right?"

"Absolutely, Baby." He kissed her a peck.

"I have to admit though, she was so excited to see 'a hot guy from a magazine coming toward us'." Marina used quotation fingers.

"She said that?" His brows raised and a sideways smirk appeared.

"Yeah, then she was appalled to see you were with me. She probably wants a repeat of stealing my boyfriend."

"Well, she can want all she wants but it would never happen. She's not even attractive honestly," he whispered with a shrug.

"Good, because I don't ever want to share you with anyone."

Marina wrapped her arm up with his. They finished shopping and were checking out at the register when Marina heard whispering and chattering. She turned to see a couple of young girls rubbernecking around a chip rack, looking at Sawyer. He seemed oblivious to their envious jabber as he swiped his card. The audacity of the women in this town astonished her.

Marina flashed a crooked smirk at them as she slid a hand possessively into his back pocket as he grabbed the bags. She wanted to ensure her claim on him was implied. She had never experienced a more thrilling trip to a grocery store in her life. She was intrigued by the amount of attention he gets when he's in public. Almost like a damn celebrity. She was proud to call him hers. Not just because it was obvious that everyone else thinks he's so attractive and dreamy but because she knows how good of a man he is. She knows how lucky she is to have him. The lack of attention he shows other females makes him even more desirable.

CHAPTER 33

Bonfire

S awyer made sure the grill was all cleaned up while Marina prepped a few side dishes for their bonfire cookout. He peeked into the window at her but she didn't notice. She was chopping cilantro, carefully sliding it off the knife with her fingers while he adored her from afar. He dumped bags of ice into a large cooler out on the back patio and stocked it with drinks, then came inside and took a couple bottles of whiskey out of the liquor cabinet in the dining room.

"You want me to get out the glasses?" she asked.

"Nah, I bought solo cups, baby! Whoo!"

He went out the back door and she laughed. She loved that he made her laugh. He really was the whole package.

She stepped out back. "You need any help out here?"

"I'm beyond help. See, I fell, real hard...for you. There's no way I want help with that. I fell right where I wanna be." He set the stack of red solo cups on the picnic table and dipped her for a smooch.

"Oh, Sawyer, you're just too much." She tapped his chest.

"So, the guests should be coming soon. I think everything is set out here. I'll start cooking the meat after most people get here. I'll go get a fire started up now so it can get hot.

"Sounds good. Everything in there is ready too."

"Wanna hang out with me while I start the fire?" He crouched down next to the pit.

"Always." She sat in a fold-out chair near the firepit. Her leg crossed over the other, the sun shining on her golden honey hair. Her sundress slid and gathered up high on her thighs as he lit the fire then sat in a chair right next to her.

He noticed her hiked skirt high right away. His eyes started at her legs and made their way up to her eyes. She put a finger to his chin. "Uh, nope. You best behave, mister. Our guests will be coming any minute." He leaned back, slouched in the chair, and let out a deep exhale.

"Let it build up and save it for later, Cowboy."

"You best pull that skirt down then." He winked.

"Is it really bothering you?" She hiked it up just a little more, almost revealing her panties along her hip.

"You better stop teasing," he murmured.

"Or what?" She turned up her nose in the other direction playfully.

"Or I'm gonna just attack you right here. Giddy up, baby." He stood quickly, grabbed the arms of her chair and bent down, planting a kiss on her peach shimmery lips.

She laughed. She more than invited that kiss, parting his lips with her tongue, and sat forward, grabbing hold of his white t-shirt with both hands and pulling him to her. She spread her legs apart, inviting him to lean in closer. He folded to his knees and rested his arms in her lap, his hands gliding up and down her outer thighs as their soft kisses turned harsher and heated.

He placed a hand on the back of her head, holding her in place while his other hand slipped up her inner thigh and under her skirt. She took his hat off and dropped it to the ground. Her suggestive behavior had prompted a naughty occurrence. She couldn't help it.

He was showing her he wanted her and she thought that was the most attractive thing in the world. Their scandalous play was recklessly hot. Their guests could arrive any time. The thought of being caught in the act by his friends drove the adrenaline rush into overdrive. They were mostly strangers to her; some she had met and some she hadn't yet. A man has a one-track mind once he gets going but when it came to him, she was the same way.

His fingertips reached her panty line. Should she stop him? She didn't want to. She peeled her lips away to look around and listen. She couldn't hear anyone approaching, just the sound of his purposefully messy kisses down her neck and the crackle of the fire. His finger entered the edge of her panties and strolled lower in the front slowly, tickling her groin. She held her breath, looking him in his eyes.

"Did you hear that?" she asked, pulling her skirt down.

"Hear what?" He flopped her skirt up over his head, about to titillate her, but a car door shut and he hastened to his feet.

"Damn it." He grabbed his hat off the ground and gave his leg a slap with it before putting it back on. He faced the fire and adjusted the front of his jeans. She stood and adjusted her dress and pulled up the shoulder strap that had fallen.

"That was close," Marina whispered as a couple entered the backyard.

"You're naughty," he sniggered, straightening his baseball cap. She smiled mischievously.

"Hey, Chris." Sawyer patted Chris's shoulder then put a hand on Marina's lower back.

"Marina, this is Chris. He's the drummer in our band. He owns Smokie."

"Oh, yeah, I remember you from the bar. Great to see you again." She shook his hand.

"I forgot y'all have met before." Sawyer shrugged a shoulder.

"Great to see you again, Marina. This is Stacy, my wife."

The ladies shook hands and exchanged smiles. Marina went on to greet Gladys and Bob, who brought boxes of booze bottles. She took a small one from Gladys as they neared the picnic table. Sawyer helped Bob put beer in the cooler.

"I was wondering why you didn't buy beer at the store today," Marina noted with a chuckle.

"I don't ask anyone to bring anything but these two always bring the booze." Sawyer patted Gladys and Bob on the shoulders from in between them. The rest of the band came, Trevor brought his girlfriend, Trina. She was shy so Marina took to her right away. That's the type Marina was most comfortable being around. She felt awkward around the snooty popular types, but these ladies weren't that way. Trina was used to being around Sawyer since Trevor played keyboard in the band. She would sit up at the bar sometimes when they played but she hadn't been there any of the times Marina had been.

The ladies helped Marina bring out the side dishes from the kitchen. Sawyer was firing up the grill and kept admiring Marina from time to time. Justin came alone and had already popped a beer open by the time he parked in the driveway. He walked up to the patio, beer in one hand and the other in his pocket.

"Wondered if you were comin'." Sawyer fist bumped him before cracking open a beer.

"Of course I was comin'. I wouldn't wanna miss out on seeing that hot girlfriend of yours. Where is she anyways?"

Justin rubbernecked around Trevor and Trina, looking for Marina.

"Dude, you're not hitting on my girlfriend. Don't make me have to gouge your eyes out, bro." He snapped shut the grill tongs in his hand and then pointed them at Justin as a playful warning. They both laughed.

"Hey, guys. So uh, Sawyer. You must be serious about her." Chris joined the guys in conversation and brought some meat over to throw on the grill. Trevor and Bob joined.

"I am. I really am. I don't recall any time I've been happier. She's amazing, everything about her. We get along perfectly, have similar interests, like the same foods for the most part, same music and beliefs..." He paused. "I'm in love, y'all."

"What? You said you'd never get serious after your last serious relationship because you couldn't fully trust someone enough...I specifically recall you saying that," Justin pointed out. Chris interrupted, agreeing he recalled that conversation too.

"I know, guys. I remember. Marina changed everything. Being with her is validation that true love does exist. I seriously wasn't looking for a relationship or anything, y'all know that. She came along and I don't know, it's beautiful and terrifying to feel like this about someone because I'm just afraid to lose her."

"Wow. You've got it bad, dude." Chris helped flip some burgers.

"That's what I told him," Justin agreed. "He sounds like a damn greeting card."

"She seems to reciprocate those feelings too," Bob added. "That girl is crazy about you."

"I'm happy for you, Sawyer. She seems really nice." Trevor handed BBQ sauce to him.

"Thank you. She's the one."

The guys congratulated him for finding happiness in the form of a cute tan blonde walking over to the picnic table with a fruit bowl in her hands.

"Hey, Sawyer, don't screw it up." Justin elbowed him.

"I definitely don't plan to." Sawyer smiled, gleaming with allure.

The guys all saw the way Sawyer looked at Marina—complete worship.

"I hope you look at her that way forever." Bob smiled as he popped a top.

"I can't imagine ever not," Sawyer assured. "She captivated me the very first second I laid eyes on her."

"So, Marina, Gladys here told me you and Sawyer met at the horse rescue," Trina mentioned.

"We did. It wasn't my normal volunteer day and he said it wasn't a normal scheduled day for him to be there either. We met by chance that morning and it changed the course of my life. He's a badass with a heart of pure gold. Being with him has been liberating." Marina sat at the picnic table and popped a grape in her mouth as she looked over at him.

"He has a good moral compass, that one," Gladys confirmed.

"He's an authentic guy. Hard to come by these days. You better hold onto him." Stacy swirled her red wine cooler around in the bottle.

"I like the authenticity. That rugged desirable man brings me bliss. He makes me feel like I'm on top of the world."

"I remember when Trev and I first got together. Things are still great, don't get me wrong, he's just been a little lax on things lately." Trina shifted herself on the picnic table bench seat.

"Lax? Care to be less vague?" Stacy chimed in.

"Ya know, like not opening my car door anymore or not cooking with me, just expecting me to do it all. Little things."

"If they bother you, Trina, you should tell him. Sometimes guys just don't use their correct head," Marina encouraged.

"I guess I should. I just don't want to make a fuss over silly things. I guess they might lead to bigger things if I don't say something though, huh?" Trina questioned, picking a grape out of the bowl.

"Mmhmm," the girls all agreed.

"Honey, I don't wanna open up old wounds, but Sawyer mentioned you were in a rough relationship before him." Gladys placed a large bamboo spoon into the pasta salad.

"I was. I wasn't looking to start another relationship but as one fell apart this one started blossoming. Neither of us were ready at first, to be more than friends. I mean, obviously, the attraction was there, but emotionally I was dealing with a lot. He was so patient and comforting. He was someone I could rely on and talk to. Eventually, we couldn't contain our feelings anymore, nor did we want to," Marina explained.

The guys plated up some of the meat off the grill and brought it over to the table. They brought the smokey BBQ aroma with them. The table was large enough to fit everyone, another of Sawyer's builds. Dishes were passed and stories shared, laughs had.

The sun was setting in the direction the house was facing. The sky was painted with beautiful pastel colors. The coral color radiating from the sky set upon Marina's hair, passing a luster over her that caught Sawyer's eye. He stopped mid-conversation, astonished by her beauty. The world kept turning but for the two of them, it stopped. Time stood still, their fixed stares capturing everyone's attention. His eyes sparkled; his smile grew considerably bigger. She returned a sultry look. It was difficult to keep their hands to themselves.

"Sawyer, you got a speaker? Let's get some music going, shall we?" Chris opened his playlist on his phone.

It broke Sawyer's concentration. He answered but didn't take his eyes off her while doing so, "It's in the kitchen. Go for it."

Chris brought the speaker out as the ladies started cleaning up the table. Sawyer flipped on the hanging white party lights that outlined the patio area. He walked by the table and took Marina by the hand then led her to the grassy area where she put her arms up around his neck and he wrapped an arm around her waist. He pressed his hat on tighter.

The perfect song played as he held her closer.

His chin tucked, looking into her eyes as she gazed up at him. His hair mingling with hers. The other couples joined in dancing and Justin snapped pics incognito from the picnic table. *Still Goin' Down* by Morgan Wallen played as the couples danced in the low-lit nightfall, Sawyer's abs rolling, their hips in sync and his thigh between hers. His breath upon hers as they resisted a kiss. A near-perfect sensual moment between the two of them, a display of true affection.

After a few dances, with twirls and dips included, they all gathered around the fire, strumming and picking guitars, hands tapping on knees. They passed a jar of pecan moonshine around and Trev played Sawyer's acoustic guitar while Sawyer sang *Cover Me Up*, slow dancing with Marina. The other couples witnessed the love between the two of them as the orange embers crackled and floated into the air beneath the stars.

The night came to a gradual close, the two of them chatting and thanking everyone for a great gathering. They walked their friends out to the drive.

"Thanks for the invite, bro." Justin gave Sawyer a quick hug then asked him permission to give Marina one. Of course, Sawyer gave a nod and a chuckle as Justin gave Marina a hug.

"Y'all are great together. He deserves a great gal."

"Aww thank you, Justin." Marina squeezed Sawyer's arm, leaning against him.

"Y'all drive careful." Sawyer and Marina gave a wave as cars exited the driveway. Sawyer popped his tailgate down and sat her on it then sat next to her.

"This was a great night. Great people."

"Yeah, it was. They are great. Everyone around here that I'm closest to was here tonight. Well, except Jake, he couldn't make it. It was fun."

"It was. Glad I got to meet them...and see those I've already met again."

"Me too. Everyone really likes you. How could they not though?"

"Good. I like them too. Ya know, I really loved the party light touch."

"Yeah?"

"Yeah, I mean. It surprised me."

"Because I'm a guy and it's kinda romantic?"

"Yeah, I guess so. You have a romantic side, not just the hot, rugged cowboy."

"Well, I do have the office work cowboy side as well."

"You do. You have many layers and I love them all."

"Yeah? For the record, I love your layers too."

"I have layers?"

"Yeah, there's the hot cowgirl, the calm coffee-loving reader, the action-movie-loving girl who would rather eat pizza at home cuddled on the couch than go out to a nice dinner. Yeah, I love all those layers."

"I love our tailgate talks and the barn notes you leave me daily."

"I love that you're here every day now when I come home. I don't have to miss you quite as long."

"You are just the sweetest." She kissed his soft lips then he rested his chin on the top of her head. He stroked her hair and was quiet for a minute.

"When you fall tired of the stress of the world, promise you'll fall into my arms."

"Oh, Sawyer, I won't fall. You take me higher than the moon and you have me until the last star in the galaxy burns out."

They shared a slow tender kiss. He put his arm around her as she leaned against him, looking up at the stars.

"It's getting chilly. You ready to go in?" Sawyer jumped down off the tailgate.

"Permission to board your rocket?" she joked.

"I love your sense of humor too." He laughed and turned with his back to her. She hopped onto his back, arms around his shoulders and legs around his waist. They headed up the drive.

"This is the booster, by the way. Or whatever ya call it, before riding the real rocket."

"Oh really?"

"Oh yeah, Baby. I'm about to fly you over the moon. Yee-haw!"

She laughed as he carried her inside the front door and kicked it shut behind them.

CHAPTER 34

Shattered

T he morning after the bonfire they finished up chores together before Sawyer made a quick run to the store. She sipped her coffee from a white tin mug with mountains designed on it, watching out the kitchen window. She opened the window to allow the fresh morning air to flutter the curtains.

There were only a few dirty dishes from the previous evening so she chose to wash them by hand. She was drying off a whiskey glass as she entered the dining room to put it in the liquor cabinet, when it slipped from her damp fingers and hit the floor, shattering it.

Sawyer pulled into the driveway and she panicked, scrambling for the broom and dustpan, but he came in before she could begin to sweep.

She started apologizing, "I am so sorry."

"Stop!" He set the grocery bag on the table. She stiffened with the broom still vertical in her hand but told him she'd clean it up.

"You'll do no such thing. You're barefoot. You're gonna hold still."

He had his boots on still so he walked over to her, glass crunching beneath his boots, and picked her up, lowering her down several feet away from the shattered glass. He swept the glass into a pile as she sat on the end of the couch. A tear rolled out of the corner of her eye and sat at the top of her cheek. He dropped the broom when he noticed she was upset and sat next to her, his hand on her knee.

"It's just a glass, Baby. It's nothing to fret over," he explained.

"It's so sweet that you don't seem mad."

"I'm not mad, not even the slightest bit upset. Not what you're used to, huh?" He was realizing now that she had lived back home as if she had to walk on eggshells.

"Sometimes it was as if I were tiptoeing through a landmine field. He wasn't violent but still verbally abusive. I know you're not that way so I don't know why I reacted like that."

He tried to lighten the situation by joking that, "Well, now this is what you'll have to deal with," and wiped her tear away. She cracked a shy smile, not making eye contact with him. He wrapped her up in his arms and kissed her on the forehead. He finished cleaning up the broken glass while she hugged a pillow, feeling as though she could be devoured by tears because he was just so good to her.

"You deserve better than me, Sawyer."

He came around the corner from putting the broom away and knelt down on one knee in front of her, holding her hands in his. "I believe we're both good people who deserve each other. So, I thank you for miraculously coming into my life."

"Thank you for showing me what true love and compassion is supposed to feel like."

He kissed her forehead then wrapped his arms around her once more, her hands pressed against his shoulder blades and her head on his shoulder. He lovingly stroked her hair. "How about we watch tv and snuggle today?"

"Yeah?"

"Yeah. It's one of those days I don't feel like doing much of anything except holding you."

"I love that plan."

"Good." He went over to the front door to take his boots off.

"Would you rather I shut the window? It's getting chilly in here."

"Nah, it's better snuggle weather." He went into the bedroom and came back out with a big plush blanket. He settled in on the couch and she snuggled up next to him. She laid a throw pillow on his lap and rested her head upon it. He played with her hair, which she found incredibly relaxing.

"I'll never get mad at you for little things like that, just so you know. I see the heart you wear on your sleeve, I just want you to know I'll protect it."

"Oh, Sawyer, I have you now. There's nothing I should need to be protected from."

"Promise me something? That you'll always let me know if I've upset you in any way. I'd want to fix it right away. No arguments or doubt, always honest with each other. I want to know if your feelings toward me ever change."

She turned to look up at him.

"I want that too. Of course, I promise. Sawyer, you never have to worry about any of that." She sat up to face him and laid her head against his chest, his arm around her. She weaved her fingers through his hair to push it back out of his face.

"I yearn for you constantly. I want us to forever remain this way."

"Me too." She barely got the words out, she realized she was holding her breath so she attempted to breathe, but he had simply taken her breath away with his words. Completely. Literally. How could one man have so much control over her? Unintentional control. Not that it wasn't inviting, she enjoyed this type of control. It left her helpless, but she liked this feeling of falling; falling weightless with her eyes closed but like she was floating on a cloud, drifting downward safely, knowing there would be a cushion for her to land on. It was comforting to know that he was falling with her, hand-in-hand.

CHAPTER 35

Turning the Page

The rain was cold that evening and all was quiet. Sawyer was doing some paperwork out at the dining room table after he started a fire in the fireplace and Marina cuddled up on the couch with a cozy blanket. Her leggings and sweater didn't warm the cold she couldn't shake.

Sawyer sat facing the living room, her in his view. She looked so sexy in her thin-framed reading glasses. He didn't know she even wore glasses. She cracked open a book and sipped her steaming tea. He was having a difficult time concentrating on his paperwork. She was distracting without even trying. Once in a while she'd look over at him but it wasn't ever when he was staring at her. He looked cozy in his gray sweat joggers she loved him in, a white t-shirt, and barefoot. He had his feet crossed under the chair.

Every time he'd adore her from afar, he'd wiggle his feet, anxious to go snuggle with her. He watched how sometimes she'd tilt her head to the side when she'd flip pages. He loved her intellect appeal. He wasn't getting any work done but didn't want to interrupt her reading either. He tried to push through but couldn't take the temptation any longer. He slid his chair back and slapped his paper and pen down.

She finished reading that chapter as he flipped off the dining room light and walked over to her, politely taking the book out of her hands. He set it on the coffee table then he bent over toward her and carefully took her glasses off and placed them on the book.

"Those glasses look so sexy on you."

"Then why'd you take them off?" She smiled.

"I don't wanna break 'em." He bestrode upon her after pulling the blanket off and tossing it to the floor. His soft lips pressed against hers. He was, indeed, cozy. Warm too. She pulled him down on top of her and he rolled to his side, rolling her along with him. Their feet tangling together, their breaths becoming one. He held her tightly against him, his hand running up beneath her sweater, her hands up underneath his t-shirt.

Her body suddenly felt warmth, outside and within. She snuck a hand down the back of his sweatpants and squeezed his rear. That made his gentle, wet kisses even more sensual. She sat up and stripped her sweater off and it fell to the floor. His body heat was enough for both of them. Then she helped him strip his shirt off, which landed on the back of the couch. He peeled her leggings and panties off, then his sweats. He grabbed the blanket and covered them both up from the waist down. They caressed each other's soft skin, indulging in each other completely. The fire crackled; the bright glow illuminated the living room. The rain danced and poured off the metal roof.

She snuggled close, her back against his chest and her head resting on his arm. His other arm wrapped around her holding her hand, surrounding her with safety. His chin nestled in her neck. All was right with the world.

The next morning, Sawyer retrieved coffee for him and Justin at the coffee shop. He let traffic pass on the street before carrying it across to the office. He pulled the door open with his pinky finger, a folder under his arm, and propped the door open with his rear enough to get inside. He handed Justin's to him before sitting at his own desk.

"What's this?" Sawyer picked up a photo frame that wasn't previously there on his desk. It was a photo of Sawyer and Marina dancing together at the bonfire.

"Did you take this?" Sawyer asked as he sipped his coffee.

"Yes, I did. I took several pictures that night. I emailed them to you but that one was too perfect not to frame.

Sawyer smiled, staring at it. The party lights were lit up in the background and they faced each other with smiles upon their faces, so very much in love. It could've been a cover to a romance novel.

"This is great, man. Thank you."

"You're welcome. I got a few great shots of all the couples but this one of you two was beautiful."

"I agree. I'm going to forward these to her. She's going to love 'em." He took a pic of that one on his desk and sent it to her.

"So, what did you two get into last night?"

"Well, the weather was crap so we stayed in. I tried to get some paperwork done."

"Tried?"

Sawyer cleared his throat and put his fingers to his chin. "Yeah, tried." He leaned back in his chair. "So, she wears these cute reading glasses. I didn't know she even had them but she uses them to read or when on the computer and driving at night. They look adorable on her but last night she was reading on the couch. She looked so damn sexy, cuddled with a blanket in front of the fire. I gave up on the paperwork."

"So, you like, joined her for cuddling? That's cute."

"I more like gently attacked her. She never picked the book back up last night."

"Gotcha!" Justin laughed. "I'm happy for you."

"Thanks. What did you do last night?"

"Ordered a pizza and drank while watching tv. Alone."

"Nothin' wrong with that. That sounds similar to how my nights went before she moved in. I guess I better get this paperwork done." He sat back up and flipped open the folder. "You wanna have a card game night tomorrow? I'll ask the band if they wanna join."

"Yeah, sure. Tell Marina she can't be wearing her glasses around the house though. We need your head in the game."

Sawyer laughed and threw a paper wad at Justin.

CHAPTER 36

Game Night

"Hello, Dave. This is Marina. I met you when I came with Sawyer to your ranch a few months back."

"Oh yeah, the pretty little thing who works for him. I remember."

"Aww, that's sweet. Thank you."

"What can I do for you, dear?"

"I was hoping I could purchase a Friesian from you for Sawyer. I'd like to buy him one for Christmas. He doesn't know of course."

"Oh, of course. Well, I have one that I haven't had here long. He's less than a year old, young. He's pitch black too, of course."

"Perfect. Can I have you text me the details and purchase price?"

"Sure, sweety, I can do that. The thing is, he isn't ridable yet."

"Oh?"

"Well, I'm sure Sawyer can fix that with no problem. Just hasn't been ridden. I wanted to green-break it but I'm just getting too old to do that sort of work anymore. I don't ride much."

"I understand that. That won't be a problem. I've seen him train a horse from scratch in just a couple of weeks. He's a natural."

"He sure is. That's a pretty generous gift for your boss if I may be so bold."

She chuckled. "Well, it is but we're actually dating now."

"Oh, how wonderful! I had a feeling that would eventually be the case, with the way he looked at you and all here that day."

"Really?"

"Oh, yeah. I'm surprised you didn't notice."

"Me too."

"I'll go ahead and get you that info, dear."

"Thanks, I really appreciate your help."

"Anytime. That Sawyer's a great man. You hang on to him."

"Oh, I plan to. Have a wonderful day."

She was so excited. That was a lucky chance, finding exactly what she was looking for the first call she made. She had found Dave's number laying right on top of Sawyer's desk on a contact log sheet. She felt guilty for snooping, like she was invading his privacy, but didn't have to go through drawers of his office desk. It's not really snooping though, right? Not if it's going to ultimately benefit him.

She headed out to the barn for chores and the barn note read, "Game night tonight. Invite your friends."

She thought *okay, this could be fun*. She stuffed hay into the hanging bags out in the pasture and led the horses out before cleaning stalls.

As she finished chores it started to rain lightly. She clunked clay off her boots on the porch before going into the house. She called her girlfriends, inviting them over for game night, which she knew nothing of what it was to consist of.

Sawyer had stopped at the bar and got pizzas and beer to-go on his way home. She helped him carry it in from the truck as friends were arriving. Inside, Sawyer pulled a few boxes of cards out from the cabinet in the dining room and tossed them onto the table.

"This place is beautiful!" Raquel whispered to Marina in the kitchen as they mixed drinks.

"It is! He has great taste."

"Wow, nice place!" Andrea and Becka joined them in the kitchen.

"Thanks! I can't take any credit though."

"So...how's the relationship going? It's been a few weeks since I got any juicy details..." Andrea leaned her chin on her hands as she rested her elbows on the counter.

"Girls. It's been amazing! Seriously, better than amazing. This man feeds and nourishes my soul to the core. He's exciting and so romantic. He makes me hungry for life."

"Not to mention fine as hell," Becka added.

"I was just about to say that. I feel like our topic of conversation is always about how hot your man is. I'm totally okay with that, by the way. That hair!" Raquel said. They all giggled, which got his attention.

"Here come those heart-breaker eyes now," Andrea warned.

He walked over to Marina, stood close behind her and wrapped his arms around her, kissed her neck and asked what they were giggling about. They couldn't even answer, they just giggled and stared at him.

"So, what's your tattoo of?" Raquel asked, eager for him to pull the sleeve up on his t-shirt. He pulled it up and the girls ooh'ed and ahh'd over it. Raquel told him tattoos on a man's arms are sexy. Marina couldn't hold back the beaming smirk on her face. His shirt was tucked in just in one small area, which showed his jeans riding low in the front. She reached around and slapped his rear.

"Don't tempt me with our friends here. I'll drag you to the bedroom," he teased in her ear but loud enough for the girls to hear on purpose. Then he slapped her rear before joining the guys at the table. All the ladies giggled as they watched him walk away.

"You girls grab some pizza and come on over. Y'all want in on poker?"

The girls weren't keen on poker but sat around the guys watching. Sawyer and Jake were the last two alive in the game and

Jake won. These guys actually played for money too. They don't mess around. The girls decided to play their own card games at the coffee table in the living room while the guys played a second round in the dining room.

They had acquired the giggles and the guys would snicker at them. The guys would get loud too, competing at some card game the girls had never heard of. Apparently, it was one the guys made up. Then Justin got out the beer pong. The girls didn't participate but cheered them on. Sawyer wasn't usually much of a drinker so he was out of the game pretty quickly. Justin won but Chris played a good game. As their friends made their way safely home, Marina and Sawyer went around cleaning up with a trash bag.

"Your friends have a good time tonight?" he asked, tossing beer bottles into the bag.

"Yeah, they did. We all did. Thank you for letting me invite them over. It was a good night." She added a pizza box to the bag. He sat the bag down and cupped her face in his hands, "You can have your friends over anytime you want. They seem like great ladies."

"They are. Thank you. Your friends are great too."

"They're alright." He wrinkled his nose and shrugged, then laughed. "Listen. This house is now your home too. You aren't a guest, you live here. I want you to be completely comfortable here."

"You make me more comfortable than you know. I'm more comfortable here than I was at my own house. But yeah, I didn't see this as my place to invite people over."

"Well get used to it." He slapped her rear again and picked the bag back up. "We're in this together. Never doubt that."

"You don't make me doubt anything."

"Good. Hey, maybe next week the whole gang will wanna go bowling."

"That sounds fun. It's been a while."

"Yeah, for me too. That would be fun as a group."

She nodded. "Let's do it. I'm not very competitive either, nor can I bowl well at all."

"That's okay, I'm not too competitive myself. I'd rather have fun and relax. It's about spending time together."

"I didn't realize y'all drank so much tonight." She observed the slew of beer bottles and empty disposable shot glasses inside the trash bag.

"I didn't either. I'm starting to feel it now though. I don't drink like that often so I'm sure I'll regret it tomorrow. I still didn't drink nearly as much as Chris. I'm glad Trev was driving all of them home. I think he only drank one or two beers."

"I had three, which is a lot for me, and I'm feeling it. The trash is cleaned up so I say we crash."

"Yep." Sawyer dropped the two trash bags out the front door and took her by the hand. He led the way to the bedroom where clothes hit the floor and lights shut off.

He fell asleep right away, his light hair wild amongst his pillow. She watched him sleep with fixation, just a short time before her heavy eyelids caved to exhaustion. He wasn't even a snorer. She found it adorable how he would end up on his back each morning, one arm above his head and one out over the edge of the bed, one leg straight and the other up and to the side, the covers only covering the necessary central area. She wondered if he noticed things like that about her.

He absolutely did.

CHAPTER 37

Mending Fences and Dirt Road Pit Stops

S unday morning, Marina slept in. Saturday night was a long shift at the bar so Sawyer didn't want to wake her. The sun beamed through the crack in the curtains, which she had meant to fix, as she stretched before her feet hit the hardwood floor. She threw on an off-the-shoulder crop top with a calf-length ruffled split-front skirt and a pair of flip-flops and poured coffee into a thermos mug before going out to see what Sawyer was up to.

It was unusually warm for December.

He could hear her approaching in the circled driveway from the sound of her shoes. Oh, Lord. He was in jeans and boots, work gloves, and his black cowboy hat. Shirtless. Valorous. His tan skin glistened with sweat.

"Good mornin', beautiful," he greeted before turning to look at her. He wiped the sweat off his brow with his tattooed arm as he stood from a crouching and hammering position at the fence. He brushed the dirt off the knee of his distressed jeans.

"Good morning, sexy," she flirted.

He was holding a nail between his teeth. "Well don't you look purdy?" He lifted the front of his hat enough for her to see those eyes of his. He was an open book but there was mystery in those eyes, especially just under the brim of that hat.

"Aww, you're sweet." She batted her eyes and ruffled her skirt. Around him, her femininity flourished. The sun beat down on her, adding a tint of pink to her face and shoulders.

"Can I hug you bein' all sweaty?" He spit the nail out, tossed the hammer to the ground, and stepped up to her.

"Always." They wrapped their arms around each other, her still holding her thermos in one hand. She lifted to her toes and kissed him. She could taste the sweat on his lips.

"You could give a girl a heart attack lookin' like this out here, you know that?"

He laughed. "Oh yeah? All dirty and sweaty?"

"Oh, you have no idea." She kissed him again.

A truck with a horse trailer attached pulled into the drive, all the way up to the barn.

"Who's this?" she inquired, trying to see through the tinted truck windows.

"Oh, that's Chris. He's here to pick up Smokie." He took his gloves off and tossed them down by the hammer.

"Aww, I'll miss Smokie."

"Yeah, he's a good one." Sawyer took her by the hand and met Chris out by the barn.

"My boy ready?" Chris shook Sawyer's hand and then said, "Ma'am" to Marina.

"I believe he is. He's done really well. I think you got yourself a good horse here."

"I'm glad to hear it. I appreciate you working with him, man, I really do. I know I can trust him after you've trained him."

"He had his moments but he's really come a long way." Sawyer chuckled and itched his nose with the back of his hand. He opened Smokie's stall and put the halter on him then snapped on the lead rope and handed it to Chris. Marina scratched Smokie's forehead and tousled his forelock.

"Thanks for letting me work with him." Sawyer gave Smokie a good pat on the neck.

"No, thank you! I appreciate your help."

"Anytime."

They all walked out of the barn and Chris loaded Smokie up into the trailer smoothly.

"I see an improvement already." Chris laughed as he got in the truck. He waved back to Marina and Sawyer as the dust clouded behind the trailer.

"I told my mom I'd give her a call back this morning. Would you like help with the fence first?"

"Nah, Darlin', thank you though. You go on ahead and give her a call." He put his work gloves back on and stuck a nail between his teeth after she gave him a kiss. He slapped her rear as she went to walk away. She sat on the porch sipping her coffee while making her phone call, watching him work in all his masculinity.

"Hey, Sweetie. What are you up to this morning?" Marina's mom, Aliza answered.

"Not much so far. The horse Sawyer was training just got picked up and I'm just watching him mend a fence."

"Everything going well? He treating you good?"

"Oh, Mom...nobody else on Earth could treat me better."

"Oh, I'm so glad to hear that. I worry about you."

"You don't have to worry anymore, Mom. He's my gallant protector. He's so empathetic and understanding. I could go on and on about all the things he is. I never thought I could love someone as much as I love him. He's a strong yet soft unmatchable soul. I can't wait for you to meet him."

"I'm excited to meet him. You haven't even shown me a picture of him yet, you know. I wish you'd share these things with me."

"Well, I didn't want to jinx the relationship by bragging too early."

"Oh, I know you've shown your girlfriends pics, you had to have had by now."

"They've actually met him, back when he was just my boss. Seems like just yesterday."

"Your sister told me she met him and she said he's total eye candy."

"Mom!" Marina giggled, "Well she isn't wrong. I'll forward you a few pics real quick right now. I should've sooner, I'm sorry. Did I tell you that he's in a band? Very talented too. He sings to me sometimes; his voice is heavenly. There's no better sound in the world."

"I love that you've found love and you're happy..." She paused as she received the pics Marina sent, "Oh, sweet Lord, Marina!"

Marina giggled.

"Good for you, honey! No wonder you're over the moon! Oh, I'm so happy for you."

"Thanks, Mom."

"Your sister wasn't exaggerating."

Marina laughed. "I'm not even going to ask what she said."

"Oh, good because I don't think I should repeat it to you."

They both laughed as Sawyer went into the barn and came back out with two bottles of water. He chugged one in a few gulps then poured the other over himself after taking his hat off. Marina caught it on video as her mom was on speakerphone. She sent the video to her mom, then mass-texted it to her sister and girlfriends. Marina sat with her elbow on her knee and her chin in her hand, watching him.

"I feel like I'm watching a naughty movie right now," Aliza admitted. "I'm having a major hot flash."

"I'm so lucky. He really is the sweetest guy on Earth though. Everything about him I just love. His exterior is the bonus, definitely one to brag about. You should come to visit soon, Mom. You can stay here. I'm sure it's been a while since you went horseback riding and I miss you."

"I miss you too. It has actually been a while since I rode a horse. It would be nice if your sister would visit too."

"Absolutely. You two should come to visit together. Please!"

"Well, you check with Sawyer on when a good time would be and I'll kidnap your workaholic sister if I have to."

"Deal. I can't wait to spend time with you both, and for you to meet Sawyer, of course."

"I can't wait either. Now you go get asking him, okay?"

Sawyer came up to the porch and sat next to her on the steps. "Ask me what?"

"Oh, hello!" Aliza hollered.

"Hello, ma'am."

"Aww, I want to say thank you for taking such good care of my little girl."

"You're welcome. She takes good care of me too."

"Mom and sis are wanting to come for a visit soon so she wanted me to discuss timing with you."

"I don't wanna intrude."

"Oh never, you'd never be intruding. You're welcome anytime. I can't wait to meet you."

"Feeling is mutual, Hun, so you two talk it over and let me know."

"Will do, Mom. Love you."

"Love you too, Sweetie."

Marina hung up.

"It would be great to have your mom here. All three of you ladies. Y'all need that time together, it's important." He put his hand on her thigh.

"Probably should try to get them here right after Christmas."

"Sounds good. I'm gonna need to take a horse up to my parent's place at Christmas time. Probably the week before Christmas and I want you to come with me. It'll just be for a few days."

"I'd love to. Our first road trip together."

"It'll be fun."

"Doing anything and going anywhere with you is fun. So, we'll get to have Christmas morning here together?"

"Absolutely. Just me and you, Baby." He gave her a sweet kiss.

"Sounds perfect." She smiled sweetly.

"Can I take you to dinner tonight?"

"You want to take me to dinner?"

"Yeah, I do."

"Okay...where to?"

"Where you wanna go? Somewhere nice."

"Um...I'm not sure. I can't say I've been anywhere really nice around here."

"Seriously?"

"Yeah, I didn't get out much."

"He never took you out on a nice dinner date?"

"No..." She shook her head shamefully.

He tipped her chin up. "Well I'm taking you out to show you off. It's a high heels night." He raised his brows twice quickly.

"Oooh heels? Okay, yeah. Anywhere you choose."

"I can't wait to see you all dressed up. I better go take a shower. Lunch here?"

"Sure. I'll go make something while you shower."

"Great, thanks. What you wanna do today, before dinner?"

"Maybe we should start planning our Christmas trip to Tennessee?"

"Okay, yeah we can do that." He stood up and took her by the hand to help her up.

She put on music in the kitchen as she made lunch. When he got out of the shower, he threw pants on and was toweling his hair. He stood around the doorway watching her dance from across the room. As much as he wanted to join, he decided to just watch. The way she moved, carefree and ambrosial, her dress flowed with her motions. He couldn't help but wear a smile. Not wanting to fluster her, he waited for the song to end before clearing his throat and entering the kitchen.

His torso still dewy from his shower, he came up behind her, wrapping his arms around her and resting his chin on her shoulder.

"You hungry?" she asked, turning to him.

"Always. Oh, you meant for food!" He laughed.

"Yes, I meant for food. But when it comes to you, I'm always hungry too." She kissed his soft lips and tousled his wet hair playfully.

After lunch, they called his parents and figured out dates and details. That time of year was approaching quickly.

"Do you normally decorate the house?" She asked as she took their plates to the kitchen from the dining room table.

"Well, I usually put up a tree but don't decorate it. I like having a real pine tree in the house. I do have white lights I can hang on the house outside."

"Could we?" she asked excitedly, her hands folded in front of her chin.

"Of course. We can do whatever you want."

"I'd like that."

"I can go out and do it now. We have time."

"Sure! Want my help?"

"Actually, I have indoor lights too if you wanna put those up inside. Then we'll go get a tree tomorrow."

"Perfect."

Sawyer got up into the attic and handed her down a tote of white lights and another of realistic wreaths. She put up white lights in the living room around the fireplace and the main doorway to the dining room. She took out a large, beautiful wreath and hung it on the front door. He put lights up at the roof's edge along the front of the house and barn and hung the exterior wreaths. She hung garland along the fireplace mantle then took advantage of Sawyer still being outside occupied so she could pick the dress she would wear to dinner.

He came inside and got his clothes out, but let her get ready first. She chose a black strapless cocktail dress. The fabric was soft and stretchy and the top was shaped fittingly so the skirt flowed outward. She put some loose curls in her hair and refreshed her makeup. She colored her lips with a light, soft, shimmery pink. She felt excited to be going out with him, really going out as in a fancy dinner. She had never been that spoiled. She slid on little black stiletto suede mule heels and exhaled a deep breath before opening the bathroom door to see Sawyer all dressed up already. He had been so patient waiting for her to get herself ready.

His jaw dropped a little as he was folding up a sleeve on his white dress shirt—a tightly fitted dress shirt, which he had left the top two buttons undone on. He had on gray dress pants that were snug on his thighs and rear and gray HEYDUDE shoes. No cowboy hat. He pulled off the city boy look very well.

"Wow! You look incredible!" He finally got the words out as he rubbed his chin stubble, staring at her.

"You look dapper yourself." She walked over to him and helped him roll up his sleeve and button it at mid-forearm. She looked up at him, her wide eyes batting long eyelashes, he was staring right into her eyes.

"I don't know if I want to take you out or take that dress back off you right now." His voice was deep, almost a whisper. She got that spine tingle when he talked to her that way.

"I think you should take me out then come home and take this dress off."

"Yes, ma'am." He scooped an arm around her and pulled her in for a passionate kiss.

She about gave in right then and there.

Downtown by the ocean docks, the boardwalk was embellished with holiday décor. The restaurant played classical style holiday music, which she wasn't used to. Even the waiters wore dress clothes.

She stood a little taller that night walking in on his arm.

They sat at a window table and the outside deck was lit up with white Christmas lights. There was an immense, densely decorated Christmas tree in the center of the restaurant, a centerpiece and candles on their table. He pulled her chair out for her and they ordered drinks first.

The meal was exquisite, dessert too. The conversation came easy to them, they always found things to talk about. He was never distracted by anything or anyone, just fully attentive to her. After a second drink and the check paid, they left arm-in-arm. It was a short walk along the lit boardwalk back to the truck but along the way she thanked him.

"Thank you, Sawyer, for a lovely evening."

"You deserve it. It was time I took you out for a fancy night. I feel bad I hadn't done it before now."

"Why? You know I don't need fancy things. I'm a simple girl. Once in a while though...this was really nice."

"I wanna lay the world at your feet."

"But all I need is you." She smiled.

"That's another thing I love about you." He stopped walking and looked her in the eyes. They were still on the boardwalk, the white lights strung from light post to light post, building to building, shining brightly amongst the night sky. The waves couldn't be seen from there but could be heard.

"Marina, I love you." He held her hand in one of his own and placed the other along the side of her face. "I have loved you since forever ago."

"I love you too, Sawyer." She reached up for a kiss, her hands upon his chest. His hand against her face remained but the other traveled to her waist as he parted her lips with his tongue. He kissed her passionately, intensely, right there on the boardwalk.

"I have an idea. You up for it?" He took her by the hand. "You might wanna take your shoes off."

"Absolutely!" She would follow him to the end of the Earth.

She removed her shoes, as did he. They carried them down to the water and dropped them in the sand. He rolled his pant legs up to his knees and led her to the water's edge. The water was cold but calm. There was a slight breeze that blew their hair lightly into each other's faces as they held each other, looking into each other's eyes. They saw deep into each other's souls. It was just them, the waves, and the moon and stars.

On their drive back home from dinner, they took a shortcut down a dark, unlit road. Just the beams of headlights shined upon the red clay, lighting up the tree line on either side of the road.

The heat along the floor of the truck warmed their chilled, damp feet.

The radio was on low volume and there was a pause in the conversation.

They had driven a country mile when *Silverado for Sale* played on the radio and she turned the volume up.

It drove her crazy how Sawyer looked. He was just driving, one-handed, but that was the thing; he didn't have to be doing anything at all for her to crave him. He smelled so good too. Delicious. He looked so sexy with his arms bulging inside the sleeves of his dress shirt, begging to escape, and the black leather wristband that she found extremely appealing. She couldn't resist. She reached over, biting her lip, and squeezed his bicep. She ran her hand up his rock-hard thigh, digging her nails into him, her hand slowly inching higher and higher. He looked at her with a raised brow, a bit surprised.

"Every time I look into your eyes I get lost amongst the stars in the sky." She looked at him as he took his eyes off the road to look at her.

"You have a full moon in yours and it calls to the wolf in me."

He ran his hand up her thigh right up under her dress. Suddenly he pulled the truck over to the side of the road, got out, and ran around to open her door. He took her by the hand as she exited the truck, careful not to slip with her heels on.

"What are we doing?" She trotted alongside his quick walking pace. He was tall so she had to keep up while holding his hand. He was on a mission. He didn't answer her either. Spontaneously, out of the road's view, he pinned her backside up against a big oak tree and kissed her so roughly that she could feel drum beats in her chest. She loved his spontaneity.

He was a romantic, and an impulsive one at that. The barn notes should've given that away and, in a way, they did.

His hand was on the side of her face, the other sliding fluently up the side of her outer thigh. Then he hoisted her up. She wrapped her legs tightly around him, squeezing her thighs into his sides. Her back was against the big oak as she ran her fingers through his hair with her arms around his neck. Her hands couldn't stay in one place. She wanted to feel all of him. Her head tilted to the side and their lips locked, tongues dancing. His hands shifted to her rear, helping to hold her up but squeezing her cheeks which she thoroughly enjoyed. She fumbled to unbutton his shirt quickly. She flapped his shirt wide open, her left hand admiring his pecks while her right hand worked to unbutton his dress pants between her legs.

"I'm going to keep kissing you until my name is the only man's name you ever remember tasting." He gently bit her bottom lip, sliding his teeth off it slowly. She then pushed the front of his pants downward. He kept one hand on her rear but pulled her panties to the side with the other. The skirt of her dress hiked up to her waistline, her hips exposed.

He smoothly inserted himself, igniting pure ecstasy within her. He made her feel like her insides were on fire, yearning with an uncontrollable desire for him. Her strapless dress top provided easy access for him too. His kisses trailed down the side of her neck and down her now-exposed breasts. The sound of crickets chirping the only sound in the quiet woods that night besides him thrusting into her and her dress rubbing against the tree.

They were louder than the entire forest. She no longer felt grounded. She was afloat on cloud nine once again. He played with her wild side, there was no doubt. She needed the savage, primal, animalistic side of him. The vigorous kissing, gentle hair pulling, and he did just that as if he were reading her mind. He read her body just as well. They and only them were shined upon by a single beam of moonlight—nature's spotlight. It was as if they were where they were supposed to be at that exact moment in time.

CHAPTER 38

Galloping to Tennessee

"Mistletoe" is what the barn note read.

She stood confused for a moment before Sawyer entered the barn and pointed to the rafter above her head and dipped her backwards for a wet kiss.

"I love that you're so creative." Marina stood and took his hat off and laid it on the counter by the coffee pot. She reached her arms through his to place her hands upon his strong shoulder blades. His fingers raked through her wavy hair as his lips locked with hers.

"You almost packed?" he asked, his hands sliding down her arms and onto her waist.

"I am. You?"

"Yes, ma'am. We'll stop and pick up my parent's horse from Dave's on our way out."

"How's she doing on her training?"

"Great! Yeah, I've been out to Dave's just four or five times to work with her the last two weeks but she's good to go. She must have been worked with before. Super easy. She put on the weight she needed and she's looking great." He put his hat back on.

"That's wonderful. Your parents are going to love her. What's her name?"

"Not sure she even has one. Dave doesn't have it on the paper-work. You can name her when we pick her up if you want."

"Really? You don't think your parents would want to?"

"I don't think they'd care." He shrugged then threw a bale of hay into the horse trailer.

"If a name comes to mind before we get her up there to your parents, I'll run it by them. Sound good?"

"Sounds good, Babe. That's considerate of you." He kissed her forehead as he adjusted his hat on his head.

"If your bags are ready, I'll go load them up."

"They're by the front door." She straightened the collar on his teal plaid button-up shirt.

"I've already filled the troughs and cleaned the stalls. They just need hay put in their bags and put out to pasture if you don't mind starting. I'll get the truck loaded then come back out to help ya finish."

"Sure, Babe." She patted his chest and took the feed bags from the hook near the feed room. He loaded all their luggage into the truck while she filled feed bags and hung them in the pastures. She had started walking the horses out by the time Sawyer came out to help. It was a chilly morning; the cold front was there to stay for a while. Marina wore calf-high boots over her skinny jeans and a sweater.

"The cold weather came just in time to prepare us for moun-tain weather, didn't it?" She took Sawyer's hand as they walked to the truck after locking the barn.

"It sure did. It even got cold inside the house last night." He opened her truck door.

"Yeah, it did. I found warmth against you though." She kissed him as she got in.

"Did I mention I like it cold at night inside?" He shut her door and got in on the driver's side. He shivered as he started the truck.

"Well good because I love snuggling with you." She held his hand on the console.

"Oh, I love it too. Anytime, not just when it's cold." He drove around the full-circle driveway, it was easier with hauling the trailer. The empty metal trailer thumped as it rolled over bumps in the drive then onto the dirt road.

When they got to Dave's ranch, Sawyer led Marina to the barn where the Belgian was. Dave brought the horse out of her stall and handed the lead rope to Sawyer.

"Luna," Marina said.

Sawyer wrinkled a brow. "Huh?"

"Her name. It should be Luna. She has a white moon down her forehead. White speckles like stars or snowflakes on her croup too."

"I think that's a perfect name, Darlin'."

"Yeah, it's a good one." Dave zipped his jacket.

"Think you parents will like it?"

"I think so. Feel free to run it by them when we get there if you'd rather."

Sawyer shook Dave's hand and spoke in almost a whisper. Marina didn't hear what was said as she was opening the trailer door. Sawyer loaded the horse easily and they were off to Tennessee.

They jammed to music, singing along, Sawyer drumming on the steering wheel on the upbeat songs. Marina asked to stop a third time to use the restroom quickly. She thought it was sweet that he didn't get frustrated with needing to stop again.

Between the stops they made, not being able to drive as fast as normal with hauling the trailer, it took just shy of nine hours to get to the mountains. Upon entering his parents' drive, Marina commented on how lovely his parents' estate was. They too had an impressive barn and their house was just as beautiful, although slightly smaller and a different style than Sawyer's.

His parents came out to greet them in the drive, and gave them both hugs. Tom said, "You know, son, y'all can ride our horses. You didn't have to bring your own."

Sawyer looked at Marina and smiled then walked to the back of the trailer.

"You didn't have anyone to take care of them while you're gone?" Caroline asked, wrapping her sweater tighter in the front.

"Chris is taking care of mine." They heard hooves on the metal ramp then Sawyer walked around toward them with the Belgian.

"Oh, my goodness!" Caroline put her hands to her face. "I don't remember seeing this one at your place."

"Mama..." He handed Caroline the lead rope. "She's for you both. Merry Christmas."

"What?" Tom and Caroline both asked, completely surprised.

"You had to retire your other from sleigh rides. Y'all can't be disappointing those kids now."

"Oh, Sawyer," Tom shook his head then gave Sawyer a big, manly hug.

"She's from Marina and I both. We picked her up on our way this morning but I've been working with her over at Dave's."

"Oh, thank you both so much. She's stunning." Caroline gave them both a hug as well.

"Marina came up with a name as soon as she saw her this morning but she'd rather let you name her."

"What was the name, sweetie?"

"Luna, because of the moon shape on her forehead. But if you—"

"No. Luna it is! I love it. It's perfect," Caroline interrupted.

"She'll work out perfectly for that sleigh. In fact, I think you two should be the first to try it out," Tom said.

"I think I'll take y'all up on that. Maybe tomorrow since it's about to get dark. I'm sure Luna would like to settle in for the night and calm her muscles after that trailer ride." Sawyer patted Luna on her side as she let out a huff of breath, fogging the frigid air.

"Let's go show Luna her stall. She can meet her new friends in there." Tom and Sawyer walked Luna to the barn as Marina and

Caroline unloaded the truck. They took a few bags in but Sawyer insisted he get the last, it was heavy.

"You know, Sawyer called me a few days ago. He was already planning to take you on a sleigh ride but I was wondering how when he knew I retired my old draft."

"Uh oh! He almost blew the surprise," Marina laughed.

"I bet you he caught himself on that one." Caroline laughed. "Oh, I'm so glad y'all came up to stay a few days. It's so wonderful to see you again. My Sawyer is just head over heels in love with you. You know that? The way he talks about you just warms my heart."

"I feel the same way about him, I assure you. Your son is absolutely perfect."

"Well, he was a little peeler when he was little." Caroline laughed.

"Really? I wouldn't have thought that."

"He was. He was a strong-willed little boy. Once he was given more responsibility, and we got him into 4-H and eventually football, he straightened up. He was always polite with manners but he did what he wanted and when he had something in his little blonde curly head it was impossible to change his mind. Bless his heart."

"And look at him now. Y'all raised a great man with a big heart."

"Thank you, honey. That means so much."

The guys came inside and took their boots off.

"Where's your Christmas tree, Ma?"

"I thought maybe you and I could go chop one tomorrow," Tom said.

"Yeah, sure."

"I have a small tote of decorations we can all decorate the tree with when y'all return with it," Caroline said excitedly.

"Sounds good, Mom."

"So, I've made hot cocoa the good ol' fashioned way if y'all would like some. It's in the kitchen on the stove."

"Sounds great, Caroline. Thank you."

Their home smelled of cinnamon. Marina loved the aroma of cinnamon around Christmas time.

"I thought maybe in the morning after breakfast we could bake some cookies. I have a famous recipe that's been passed down from generations. It's very special to me." Caroline loved to bake.

"I'd love to bake with you," Marina expressed enthusiasm.

"It's like a secret recipe," Tom mentioned.

"Yeah, she makes people leave the room when she adds a secret ingredient." Sawyer laughed and Caroline swatted his arm. He scowled playfully at her.

"Seriously?" Marina thought he was being comical.

"Seriously." Tom nodded.

"Noted." Marina smirked.

The next morning Caroline had breakfast ready by the time everyone else woke up. They all ate together at the table then the guys cleaned up the kitchen before heading out to do chores. The ladies gathered ingredients for cookies and Caroline got down her recipe box, which was tucked away in the back of the baking cabinet, then handed Marina an apron.

Ingredients were mixed for two different kinds of cookies; traditional sugar and her special gingerbread and molasses cookies. Marina started stirring the sugar cookie dough together while Caroline got her big mixer out. The guys came in and washed their hands and Sawyer told the speaker to play *Talkin' Tennessee* as he came up behind Marina, helping her stir the dough.

"I might not need that mixer. I've got muscles here now," Marina joked. There was more dancing involved than stirring. Caroline thought it was adorable. Marina ate raw cookie dough from his finger.

"If you two keep this up I'm going to have to leave the kitchen," Caroline teased.

"If I sit her up on this countertop, Mama, that's your cue to leave." Sawyer laughed.

"Sawyer, shame on you. Not in your parents' house," Marina warned playfully.

"I have a feeling that wouldn't stop him," Tom joined in conversation from the dining room table.

"See, Dad understands. He's a romantic opportunist too."

"Oh, for goodness sake." Caroline slapped Sawyer with a hand towel. "You go on now."

"I really should help bake. You and I both know what's gonna happen if you stay in this kitchen." Marina softly pushed his chest away.

He poured a glass of tea and joined his dad at the table.

"Maybe we should get those decorations down and go chop a tree. Let the ladies bake and gossip." Tom stood from the table. He and Sawyer put on their boots and coats and left out the front door.

"I truly believe you two have a timeless love. I can tell" Caroline smiled at Marina.

"I like that description. It sure feels that way. I know it always will," Marina agreed.

"That's why I'm not kicking you out of the kitchen when I add this secret ingredient."

"Really? Are you sure? Because I don't mind?"

"I'm positive. I've never given this recipe out to anyone before, but I want you to have it." Caroline wrote it down for Marina.

"Oh, my goodness, Caroline, I feel so honored." Marina gave her a hug, almost tearing up.

"Oh, sweetie, don't you make me cry now. I told Tom on our drive home from Sawyer's place at Thanksgiving time that I was going to do this. I just knew you'd be with Sawyer for the long haul. We're so happy he found you."

"That means the world to me. You both have been so welcoming and accepting."

"Well, what's not to like? You're wonderful."

"I love y'all already. I hope you know that." Marina put her hand on Caroline's shoulder.

"We love you too." She smiled sweetly at Marina.

They put the pans of cookies in the oven.

"Did you two put up a tree?" Caroline asked, putting the potholders on the counter.

"We did. We went to a Christmas tree lot and picked one out. Down there ya can't just go chop one, they have to be shipped in from up north. It was nice though, going to pick one out together. Sawyer was so funny, he had to make sure the tree was absolutely perfect. We put white lights on it when we set it up in the living room. Just simple white lights. It looks beautiful."

"No decorations? I'm not judging, I'm sure it looks wonderful, but I do have so many of Sawyer's from when he was a kid. He can take some if he wants to."

"Aww, that's sweet. You can ask him." Marina washed the counter off with a clean dishcloth. "Is it supposed to snow today?"

"It is this evening."

"I've never had a snowy Christmas before but I picture Christmas with snow."

"It sure makes it more special."

"More magical, I guess. As kids we are taught Christmas stories which include snow at Christmas time."

"That's true. We've had a few years without snow on Christmas day and it just doesn't seem the same."

The guys came through the front door as Caroline took cookies out of the oven.

"You want it inside, Mom?"

"Oh, yes, dear, please. I'll get the stand out." She went to a back room and brought out the stand as the guys carried it in. They put it in the stand and took their boots and coats off.

"It's beautiful." Marina stood looking at it.

Sawyer hung his coat up near the door and stood behind her with his arms around her tight.

"Sawyer picked a good one. It's huge." Tom hung his coat next to Sawyer's.

"He sure did. It's perfect," Caroline agreed. She placed a tote full of lights and decorations near the tree.

"Would you want to take some of these home with you?" she asked Sawyer.

"Aww, nah, Ma. You should keep them."

"Well, we'll hang them on this tree then." She started handing them to him but he set them down on the floor and went to the kitchen.

"He upset?" Marina asked but he came right back in with a handful of cookies, one in his mouth.

"What?" he asked while chewing as everyone stared at him.

Caroline laughed. "You just couldn't wait for them to cool down, could you?"

"The aroma hooked and reeled me in. I couldn't help it."

The ladies giggled.

"Okay, now I'm ready to help."

"All that wood chopping made you hungry?" Marina asked, flirting.

He smiled a crooked smile, knowing exactly what she was referring to, and whispered in her ear, "Want me to go find a stump?"

She busted out with uncontrollable laughter, then covered her mouth.

He laughed and handed her one of the cookies in his hand.

"I'm not going to ask," Tom said, shaking his head.

"Okay, thanks." Sawyer rubbed his chin scruff.

Marina turned to Sawyer, tongue in cheek, smirking.

"It only took about three whacks with the ax for Sawyer to chop that tree anyways."

Sawyer refrained from laughing.

"Should we get something to eat first before doing the tree? I feel like we should save the decorating for later with hot cocoa and popcorn, maybe a Christmas movie," Marina suggested.

"I think that's a great idea!" Caroline put the tote near the tree and put the lid back on.

"Maybe it'll be snowing by then," Sawyer added.

"I hope so!" She side-hugged him as they followed Caroline to the kitchen.

After they ate a late lunch, Sawyer and Marina went out to the barn so he could show her the sled they would hook Luna up to the following day.

Tom was watching a football game, kicked back in his recliner, and Caroline had just left for the store.

The sled was actually a carriage that looked more like a sleigh. It was white and silver with a large wreath on the front. There were three bench seats, a front to steer the horses and two back seats for passengers. Sawyer got in the sleigh and nodded for her to join. She slid over next to him and he put his arm around her, stealing kisses like they were two teenagers on a date to the movie theater.

He whispered sweet nothin's in her ear as he took her scarf off to kiss her neck.

"You know what I don't like about winter?" he asked.

"What's that?" She was enjoying his affection.

"The fact that more layers of clothing makes you less accessible."

She laughed at his sexy humor. He took his coat off and laid it in the seat on the other side of her. With a deep voice and his forehead against hers, taking her coat off her, he said, "Lay back."

She laid back and positioned his coat under her head.

"I might get cold..." She batted her eyes.

"I'll keep you warm." He straddled over her, holding himself up, careful to not put his weight on her. He reached up under her sweater and she felt his jeans get tighter in the front.

"You're so naughty," she whispered in his ear, her spine tingling yet again.

"I can't help it. You do that to me."

"You want to risk one of your parents finding us like this?"

"With our clothes on? Nah! We'll risk it with our clothes off."

"Are you serious?" Marina giggled.

"Oh, I'm serious." He sat up and unbuttoned his jeans. "Might as well make our first sleigh *ride* memorable."

Their body heat fought off the chill, clouds of warm breath rising above them.

They were just beginning to dress when headlights reflected in the barn windows. It was getting dark. They hustled to finish getting dressed, laughing at their escapades. They combed each other's hair with their fingers then walked back to the house hand-in-hand, ready for tree decorating.

As they entered the house and removed their coats and boots, Caroline started passing out hot cocoa cups that were displayed just so on a bamboo tray with a large bowl of popcorn.

"So, were you two out in the cold the entire time I was gone?"

"Uh, yeah. Checking out the sleigh and hanging with the horses." Sawyer ate a handful of popcorn but Marina nearly choked on hers.

"Aren't y'all cold? I can turn the fireplace on." Caroline cupped her hands around her cocoa mug.

"Nah, I'm good. You, Babe?"

"Oh, actually I'm good too." Marina ate a handful of popcorn to avoid being questioned further. She opened the tote and carefully and took out heirlooms from holidays past.

"You missed a whole quarter of the game, Son." Tom dimmed the lights so the lights on the tree would shine brighter but not so dim that they couldn't see details of Sawyer's childhood ornaments.

"Sorry, Dad." Sawyer patted Tom on the shoulder.

"This is from Tom and I." Caroline handed a small giftbox to Sawyer. "It's for both of you."

He opened it, Marina looking over his arm.

"This is nice, Mom and Dad. Thank you."

"It's beautiful," Marina took an ornament out of the box. It was a horseshoe with a picture of the two of them inside the center. There were words on the horseshoe that read "Our first Christmas together" and the year.

"This is really sweet, thank you." Marina gave Caroline a hug.

"I believe you got your wish, sweetie." Caroline pointed to the window which the tree stood in front of. It was snowing. Sawyer turned off the porch light so they could see the white flakes fall.

"Oh, my goodness!" Marina hugged Sawyer as they watched the snow from the window.

"Wanna grab your coat? We'll step outside."

"Yes!" She excitedly snatched her coat off the hook and slid her tall black-heeled boots back on. Sawyer took her arm in his as she stepped down off the porch. She held out a hand to catch flakes as they collected in their hair. The snowfall was quickly becoming heavier.

After only a few minutes, Marina said, "I'm ready to go back in, it's too cold." Marina turned to go to the house so Sawyer took her by the arm again to ensure she didn't slip. "It's so pretty but I'd rather watch it from inside."

"Me too." He laughed.

They finished decorating the tree, adding their new ornament to the front.

"Don't let us forget to take this with us when we leave." Marina chose the perfect spot to hang it.

"Oh, don't worry, I won't. You'll need it to hang on your tree." Caroline set the camera timer for a family photo in front of the tree. The picture turned out priceless.

The next morning, after the guys finished chores and the ladies made breakfast, cookies were packaged up and the sleigh was prepped for sleigh rides in town. Luna was loaded into Sawyer's trailer and Tom hauled the sleigh, on wheels, with his own truck. Marina and Sawyer met Tom and Caroline in town behind a local grocery store to hook Luna up to the sleigh.

The grocery store was handing out free hot cocoa to locals and there were carolers, the street light poles decorated with wreaths, lights, and bows. The snow continued to fall generously from the blue-gray sky. The mountain line in the distance could barely be seen from the street due to the snowfall.

Tom and Caroline gave sleigh rides to the locals while Sawyer and Marina handed out hot cocoa and candy canes up at the store front. Fluffy snow outlined the sidewalks and the snowfall was filling in tracks in the street. Pine trees were dusted in white. Holiday music played from the store and children were aglow. It was a long day out in the cold and the sun was setting early this time of year. As a navy sky settled in, the locals' headlights faded into the evening.

"Wanna go for a sleigh ride before going back to the house?" Sawyer wrapped his arms around Marina, sharing his body heat.

"I would love that."

He held her close to him as they walked out to the street. Luna was patiently waiting. Sawyer helped Marina up into the sleigh then climbed in as Tom handed him the reigns.

"Thanks, Dad."

"You bet. There's a blanket there on the seat."

Tom and Caroline enjoyed wrapping their cold hands around cups of hot cocoa while Sawyer took Marina on a star-twinkling tour of the little town.

She snuggled up close to him, taking in the scenery, the blanket wrapped around the two of them.

"It's clear enough to see the stars. They're bright tonight." She rested her head against his arm, looking up at the dark sky.

"That means it's going to be really cold out tonight."

"Perfect snuggle weather." She looked up at him and he smiled.

"I'm looking forward to snuggling with you in front of the fireplace with that big fleece blanket that's your favorite."

"That sounds like the perfect end to the evening."

"Almost."

"Almost?"

"Falling asleep with you laying on my chest is the perfect end to the evening."

"You're such a romantic. I love it."

"Good because I won't change."

"Good, I don't want you to." She hugged him tighter.

The night fell silent as the heavy snowfall deadened any sounds except the crunch of the snow beneath the sleigh wheels, the rhythmic clop of hooves, and the tiny jingle bells on Luna's harness.

"Luna was wonderful today." Marina admired Luna's beauty, the snowflakes falling upon her back and mane.

"She did really well. I'm proud of her. You looked to be enjoying yourself today."

"I did. Thank you for this experience. The snow, the mountains, spending time with your parents, both sleigh rides with you...all of it."

"I wouldn't want to enjoy this with anyone else." He kissed her tenderly, his bare hand against her chilled face. He pointed out a few of his favorite places around the town before heading back to load up. Their night ended with that snuggle in front of the fireplace before nestling in each other's arms. Thankful for the simple things, knowing that happiness lies with them.

CHAPTER 39

Our First Christmas

O n their road trip back south, they hadn't made it far off
the mountains when they came across an SUV that was
stuck on the side of the road. It looked to just be stuck in deep
plowed-to-the-shoulder snow but the tire was also flat.

"Uh oh, somebody got stuck," Sawyer said, slowing down.
The unplowed road was filled in with fresh snowfall.

"Looks like an elderly man."

Sawyer pulled up slowly behind the vehicle and told Marina
to stay inside the truck and keep the doors locked. She followed
his instruction as he left the truck running and stepped out,
zipping up his coat and adjusting his black hat. Marina couldn't
hear what was said but Sawyer helped the old man get a spare tire
from the trunk. Sawyer rolled it around to the passenger side as
the old man hauled a tool kit. Sawyer changed the tire then
walked back to the truck for a chain. He attached one end to his
truck then the other to the SUV. Sawyer got in the truck and the
old man got in his SUV. Sawyer pulled the SUV out of the snow-
bank and back onto the road.

"They've been out here almost an hour. Nobody driving by
offered to help. Can you believe that?" Sawyer got back out and
shook the old man's hand. The couple came over to Marina's side

so Marina rolled her window down, snow falling into the car and onto her seat. Sawyer loaded the tools back into their SUV for them.

"Thank you both for stopping to help. We understand how scary the world can be. You have a brave and generous man," the old lady said.

"Of course, and thank you, he really is wonderful." Marina shook their hands.

"I'm not as young as I used to be. It's nice to know there are still kind people in the world," the old man said, putting his arm around his wife as they waved and walked back to their vehicle. They thanked Sawyer again before Sawyer got into the truck.

"I'll make sure they get going okay before we leave." He rubbed his hands together then put them to his mouth, blowing warm air into them. He held his hands up to the heating vents on the dash, his hat, hair and shoulders of his coat dusted with snow.

"This weather is horrible. How much further did they have to drive?"

"He said they're less than fifteen minutes from home. I'll just follow them 'til they turn off."

"Good idea. I'm glad you stopped to help them. They sure appreciated it too."

"They would've frozen out here. They only have an eighth of a tank of gas left."

"They're lucky we were driving through. They didn't have a phone?"

"No, he said he's been against them but he plans to buy one now."

"I'm proud to be with such a wonderful man." She smiled at him and took his hand, holding it on the center console.

"Aww, thanks, baby."

They returned home just before dark with the empty trailer. It was cold but not cold enough to snow. They hauled their bags in and she asked, "Are you unhooking the trailer?"

"Nah, I'll do it tomorrow."

"Do we have plans for tomorrow? It's Christmas Eve."

"Besides hitting the store in the morning and going to pick up your gift, I don't have plans for us. You?"

"Just waiting for your gift to arrive."

"I guess we both waited 'til last minute, didn't we?" He laughed.

"Not really...I mean I bought yours, it just isn't here yet."

"Interesting. I did the same." He was speculating in his head. They laughed and shrugged.

"So maybe you should go to town around lunch-time? Maybe pick us up some lunch from the café too?"

"I'm guessing that's when my gift should be arriving?" he asked.

"Maybe." She shrugged.

"Deal. Bed early? I'm whooped." He hung his hat up. They were thrilled to be back in their own bed that night.

The next morning, he was up early and had just finished making breakfast when she got up. They did chores then unpacked from their vacation after they ate. She had a text come through on her phone that she didn't open in front of Sawyer.

"Was that yours or mine?" he asked, washing dishes.

"Mine. It's a delivery update on your gift."

"You need me to go?" He smirked.

"Um..." She opened the text but not near him. "Yeah, in a few minutes if you don't mind."

"Okay." He grinned.

He washed and dried his hands then gave her a hug and kiss before pulling his boots on. He pulled his jeans down over his boots and grabbed his coat.

"Oh, you still have the trailer hooked up to your truck," she reminded him.

"It's okay, I'll unhook it when I get back. I don't have far to go."

Somehow, Chris had left Dave's and passed Sawyer on the way without either of them noticing. Chris arrived at the house with the Friesian stallion that Marina bought for Sawyer. She met him out at the barn to help unload quickly.

"Thank you, Chris, so much for helping me out."

"No problem. He's going to love this. He's wanted one for a long time. Not sure why he doesn't already have one, honestly."

"Well, I'm glad he doesn't because I had no other ideas."

"I imagine he's a hard guy to buy for."

"Yeah, he is."

"Although he'd love anything that came from you."

"I think he would too. He's a sweet guy like that." She smiled and shook Chris's hand. He left quickly so he could be gone before Sawyer got back.

It wasn't fifteen minutes and Marina received a text from Sawyer asking if it was safe to return home yet.

She replied with a quick "Yes" as she led the young stallion out to pasture. She put him in the furthest out in hopes that Sawyer wouldn't see him when he returned. Sawyer texted her to stay in the house and he'd come inside after he stashed her gift.

She was getting nervous about him being out there a while when he finally came inside and kicked his boots off, "Since tomorrow is Christmas, I say we do gifts before chores. The horses can wait. It's not supposed to get real cold tonight either." He hung his coat and hat up and rustled his hair around with his hand.

"Perfect," she agreed but was worried about how chores would work that night. She didn't want Chris to have to bring the stallion on Christmas but she hadn't planned to not be able to go out to do evening chores either. Her surprise might just be ruined.

She couldn't leave the stallion out all night, could she? He did have hay and water out there. It wasn't supposed to get really cold either. It might be her only option.

Luckily, she had put all the horses in the front pastures so he wouldn't bother with the last...unless he saw the stallion out there. She would have to distract the horse from the back side of the pasture then try to beat Sawyer back to the house.

Sawyer didn't go into work that day but worked for an hour or so on his computer in his office. They did a workout together afterwards. Oh, how she loved to watch his muscles flex and the sweat bead up on his skin. She tried to keep him busy inside so he was less apt to see his gift.

Little did she know he was doing the same.

"I probably better shower." He pulled his damp tank top off and flung it to the floor by the laundry room. She followed behind him, flinging her tank top off too. He turned around when hers hit the floor and bit his bottom lip. She walked into his arms, he kept walking backwards, bear hugging her, then he tossed her up over his shoulder and spanked her bottom.

He carried her to the shower where the steam rolled out from under the door.

They ate dinner after cooking together and darkness fell upon the night. The breeze blew strong that evening, they could hear it begging at the windows. Sawyer went out to do chores, instructing Marina kindly to stay inside so not to ruin her surprise, but she quietly snuck out the French doors and around to the backside of the last pasture. She clicked for the stallion, who quickly approached the fence. She petted him as he grazed. When she saw the barn light go off, she ran for the house. She entered the French doors and ran her fingers through her hair. The wind had tangled it pretty good. She tried to hide the fact that she was fairly out of breath when he came in and took his boots and coat off, then entered the kitchen where she had started plating up cookies.

"I thought maybe we could watch a Christmas movie and eat some cookies that your mom sent back with us."

"That sounds great. I've been thinking about those cookies half the day, ever since I worked up an appetite in the shower." He winked and opened the fridge to pour a glass of milk. She got her cuddling blanket out and took the cookies to the couch. He sat next to her, snuggling while they watched a movie. By the time the movie was over, she had fallen asleep against him, his arm around her. He got up, careful not to tip her over. He put an arm under her legs and one behind her back and carried her to the bed.

Christmas morning when she woke up, she rolled over to see him on his elbow, resting his head in his hand, just watching her.

"Merry Christmas, Marina."

"Merry Christmas, Sawyer." She pulled his shoulder, bringing him down to kiss her. "You're my gift, you know that?"

"Mmm, no. You're mine." He kissed her passionately then whipped the covers back and got out of bed. His black boxer briefs fit so snuggly she couldn't help but watch him walk to the other side of the room. He pulled a pair of jeans off a hanger in the closet and balanced on one leg to put them on.

"I know what I want for breakfast." She sat up, holding the sheet to her chest.

"What's that?" he asked before looking up at her and seeing her devilish smile.

He laughed. "As much as I want you for breakfast too, I'm just so excited to give you your gift. You're getting yours first by the way. We'll uh...eat breakfast later, if that's okay."

"Of course, it's ok. I must say I'm really surprised though... you must be really excited for this gift exchange." She got out of bed and got dressed. "I'm actually excited to give you your gift too."

"I guess we need to go out to the barn then, I can't really bring yours in the house." He put his boots on at the front door. She followed and slipped on shoes. The sun was shining bright across the property, making the trees glow with an orange hue. It was chilly but there was no real need for a coat. He opened the barn door then stood behind her and covered her eyes with his hands, "Go on ahead inside. I'll guide you."

She walked forward slowly, completely trusting his guidance. When they reached the last stall he asked, "Are you ready?"

"Yes!"

"Keep them closed for a second." He opened the stall door then said, "You can open your eyes now."

She opened her pretty eyes and squealed with excitement, "Oh my goodness! Oh, Sawyer! Thank you!" She flung herself onto him and planted a kiss on his lips.

"Merry Christmas, Baby."

"She's beautiful!" Marina petted her new horse, the young Gypsy Vanner she had loved back at Dave's ranch.

"You know I bought her that day. As soon as we left Dave's I transferred the money to him.

"Did you really?"

"I sure did. I've worked with her too when I went to work with Luna. She needs more work but she'll be ready for you to ride in a couple months. She's gotten big fast and you're petite so you won't have to wait long. It'll give y'all time to bond."

"She's perfect! Absolutely perfect. Sawyer I've never received such a generous gift. You have no idea how much it means to me that you did this. You're amazing."

"Aww, nah, Baby, you are. You deserve her. You're going to look beautiful on her too."

Marina loved on the foal for a bit longer before closing the stall.

"Yours is outside." She took him by the hand and they walked side-by-side out to the last pasture.

"Go ahead and whistle. I can't whistle as loudly as you can."

He hesitated, confused with a wrinkled brow, but let out a loud whistle. The stallion came running. Sawyer covered his face with his hands and slid them down to his chin.

"You've got to be kidding me! Marina, you didn't!"

"I did."

He jumped the fence to greet the horse, whose nostrils were flared as it let out a whuffled breath. Marina leaned onto the fence, thrilled with his reaction. He was not expecting this extravagant of a gift.

"Is this why you insisted on working at the bar?" he asked.

She nodded yes, her lips pressed together.

"Where did you get him?"

"Dave. Chris brought him here yesterday, must be while you were gone getting my gypsy. I hope you don't mind; I got their phone numbers from your office desk."

"Baby, I don't have anything to hide. I don't mind at all. I'm just...I can't believe you did this." He rushed over and grabbed her face, kissing her above the fence rail.

"I feel bad he had to stay out all night. I knew you didn't want me in the barn."

"How did I not see him last night?"

"I kinda snuck out the back door and to the back pasture to keep him occupied until you turned off the barn light."

"That's why you were short of breath?"

"You noticed?"

"I notice everything about you." He winked and patted the horse on the neck. He climbed back over the fence and embraced her like a soldier who had been overseas finally getting to hug his lady.

"Looks like in a couple of months we'll both be riding new horses." He smiled ear to ear. "You know I don't expect stuff like this, right?"

"I know. Neither do I. You've been everything to me though. I knew of only one thing you've been wanting so I was determined to make it happen."

"You're an amazing woman." He kissed her on the top of the head.

"You're an amazing man. I was convinced such a wonderful man didn't exist until meeting you. Being with you has been the best time of my life. I can't imagine going a day without you."

"I don't plan on you ever having to." He held her hand while walking back to the barn to start chores. "Just so you know, Marina, I seriously have nothing to hide. You're welcome to have access to my computer, phone, paperwork or whatever. I have no secrets; I won't ever have secrets to hide from you. I want you to know you can trust me completely."

"Oh, I do. I trust you completely already. You've given me no reason not to. I don't have anything to hide either. I already have the perfect man. I know there's no one out there better than you."

"I'm lucky enough to have snagged me the perfect woman. I might have kinda stole her heart away from a less deserving man who was less than a man."

"You absolutely did and I am beyond thankful."

"Me too." He grabbed a bale of hay with one hand, carrying it as if it weighed only twenty pounds.

They finished chores then both stood along the fence watching the new manes flying behind the galloping muscles. Hooves pounded the ground as they ran alongside each other, a fence separating them.

"You going to name him Pegasus?" she asked.

"You remembered the Equine Fantasy conversation."

"Yeah."

"I think he needs a sexier name; Pegasus is mythical like a fantasy but he's graceful like a dancer. You see how he prances? I'm thinking Tango."

"I like that!"

"Yeah?"

"Yeah. That is a sexy name. I mean look at the long wavy mane, how he stands with his head stretched high. He does prance like he's dancing."

"Tango it is. So have you thought of a name for your southern belle?"

"Well, since she's a southern belle, maybe I should call her Dixie."

"I like it. It suits her. She seems fun and has a polite demeanor."

"So, do they need long ridiculous names to be registered? Most do, I know racehorses have weird names."

Sawyer chuckled. "You can if you want. Get creative."

"Dixieland Delight. I'll just call her Dixie."

"That's cute. She does resemble a sundae in color. That's what that name reminds me of. Vanilla, caramel and hot fudge."

"I guess it does," she agreed, laughing.

"I'll just call him Tango. Damn we have some fine lookin' horses." He slapped her rear with his hat and made her laugh. "Got me a fine lookin' woman too. What do say we get some breakfast now?"

"Actual breakfast or...?" She was being serious, not knowing which he meant per their previous conversation. He didn't answer with words, but chuckled as she walked beside him to the house.

He took his boots off and hung his hat then went straight to the fridge as she removed her shoes. He turned on the speaker on the counter then started getting out breakfast food to cook. She joined him, getting a pan from out of the cabinet and placing it on the stove burner, but he instructed not to turn it on yet.

He told the speaker to play *She Likes It* and sang along, singing to her. He took her by the hips. He was about to do that dirty dancing thing that he does so well. She loved it too. She has her very own Magic Mike right at home but she doesn't have to share him with anyone else. Sure enough, there it came. The dirty dancing in the kitchen.

He loved it when she'd bite her bottom lip, it made him slip his tongue into her mouth. It drove him crazy, like his grinding drove her crazy.

An instant hot flash came over her. She felt a spontaneous combustion flare up inside her body every time he did this. She wanted to subside into his dominant control, one of her hands up on his shoulder, the other all over him. He had one hand on her rear and the other on the side of her neck and face. He'd sneak a sexy kiss here and there, a subtle suck on her neck. Their foreheads would touch, sharing breath in such close space. He'd roll those perfect abs, his thigh between hers or hers between his.

He didn't wait til the song was finished, he sat her up on the countertop and spread her legs. He stood between them and pulled her to him, wrapping her legs around his rear. She hooked her ankles together. It was déjà vu from Thanksgiving. Hopefully, without interruption this time. She shoved him back and hopped down. Their clothes started peeling off, one article at a time, until they were completely naked, right there in the kitchen. Breakfast would have to wait; he was too driven. He had a one-track mind and she wasn't about to derail him. He swiped plates and ingredients to the side with his arm, some crashing to the floor. He sat her back up on the countertop and she wrapped around him again. They lusted after each other like it was the first time.

After making passionate, aggressive love, they dressed and cleaned up the kitchen before cooking breakfast together. By this time, it was already noon but they didn't care.

Cloud cover dimmed the natural lighting throughout the house, which made the Christmas lights glow brighter. It wasn't cold enough outside to feel like Christmas and they sat out on the porch together for a while, spent time with the new horses, then went for a ride on Foxtrot together bareback.

She sat in front of him, his arms around her, his face against the side of hers often, his thighs squeezing against hers. This was Heaven. T-shirt and jean weather in December, riding a horse with the man of her dreams after making love. They had exchanged the best gifts that morning. She hadn't had a Christmas this special ever. Neither had he. Life just couldn't get any better. She leaned back against him, surrendering herself to the peace she found with him. They flowed together like a brook flows through a mossy forest.

Immersed in true love, they both were, she looked up at him and said, "You're the wildflower to my meadow."

He smiled and replied, "You're the flame to my fire," in that deep sexy voice. He does that purposely to get a rise out of her. Her wide eyes bright, he touched her lips with his thumb before kissing her. They were in that mushy stage where they gushed over each other constantly. Neither of them wanted that to end though and were determined to never let it.

On their way back, he dismounted Foxtrot and picked her a wildflower. There wasn't much blooming that time of year, but the first bloom he saw, he thought it would look better with her holding it.

"The wildflower to your meadow, my love." He handed it to her and she smiled, accepting it from him. She leaned down to give him a kiss. She kept her eyes on him as he walked alongside Foxtrot's striding neck. He'd look back at her sometimes and their eyes would lock.

They made dinner together, a picnic ham and all the fixings. The holiday centerpiece on the dining room table held a candle inside a lantern decorated with pinecones. After dinner they did chores then he laid a thick blanket in the back of his truck. They laid on their backs, starting up at the stars. She snuggled up to him. His snug white waffle hoodie felt cozy. She used his bicep as a pillow. The white lights strung around the house and the barn were beautiful and crickets could be heard in the distance.

"I have another gift for you."

"What? Another? You really didn't need to do that, Sawyer."

"I wanted to. It might seem corny but since we like to gaze at the stars together, I had a star named after you." He pointed to the sky and pulled out a small constellation map from his pocket and handed it to her.

"You did? Oh, my goodness. What a perfect idea. That's the sweetest thing." She laid a hand upon his face and kissed him tenderly. "You know, my star needs a match. We need to name one next to it after you now."

"We can do that. We burn brighter together."

"We certainly do." She got comfortable on his arm again. "I can't think of a better way to spend Christmas. It was absolutely perfect."

"I agree. It was perfect because we spent it together. I love nights under the stars with you. I see them differently since meeting you, ya know that?" His soul danced by her eyes' instruction. Her kisses kept it dancing like it was the only soul on the dancefloor. The moon unveiled the beauty of the dark sky, the stars a blanket laid upon their wild southern hearts.

CHAPTER 40

Mom & Sis

The Friday morning barn note read, "Good morning, beautiful. I'll be home before your family arrives."

She drank her coffee as she did chores. Legend followed along beside her, sniffing at the mug she carried. This horse had become her puppy dog; they had formed a strong bond which remained even after Marina gained Dixie. Dixie was almost rideable; she had grown tall rapidly. She too followed Marina along but was easily distracted, whether it be by feed or by butterflies. She liked to run and Marina loved to watch her. Her long mane and tail flowed with the wind. She was stunning.

Dixie and Legend got along well. Dixie was still very young and Legend was a gentle, calm horse. Marina had bought toy balls for the horses and Dixie was hilarious, flopping it and kicking it around the pasture. After grooming, Marina went to town to grocery shop, but Sawyer called to ask her to lunch. They went to the deli café. She received a text from her mom while at lunch saying they should arrive around four o'clock that afternoon so she went to the store while Sawyer went back to work. She put away groceries at home, swept the floor, and read a few chapters of a book after putting brownies in the oven until Sawyer got home.

It was about 3:30pm.

He came in the front door and took his boots off, hung up his hat, and gave her a kiss as she sat comfortably on the couch with her feet up. That was his routine as soon as he would get home every day.

"Think I have time for a quick shower? Justin and I worked out at work before leaving."

"You worked out at work?"

"I know, it sounds stupid and I should've been here helping you, but he showed me some complicated workout on his social media and we challenged each other."

"Wow, y'all must have been bored."

"More like we lost track of time." He shrugged.

"Yeah, go ahead and shower. Mom said around four and if she's driving it'll be at least that."

"Cool, I'll hustle. It smells awesome in here, by the way." He darted for the bedroom but stopped and came back out to ask, "Should I shave?" He ran a hand over his facial scruff.

"Baby, you look handsome no matter what. They aren't going to care."

"That's a yes then." He darted back to the bedroom. She heard the bathroom door shut and the shower turn on. He opened the door and hollered out, "Would you mind grabbing my folded clothes on top of the dryer for me?"

"Sure. I'll lay them on the bed," she hollered back as she stood from the couch, laughing at his silliness. Her phone dinged. She picked up her phone from the coffee table. It was her mom saying they were about to pull in within five minutes. The timer went off in the kitchen to take the brownies out of the oven so she rushed to shut the oven off. She grabbed a pot holder from the drawer to take the pan out. She checked with a toothpick to make sure they were done then got a glass of water. She brought her water glass into the living room and put it down on the end-table as her mom and sister arrived. She went out to help bring their bags in.

They embraced each other, and exchanged "I missed yous".

"Where's that strapping man of yours? I could use his muscles for my bag, it's heavy." Her mom opened the trunk.

"He's in the shower. He just got home from work."

"I see."

"Shit, I forgot his clothes!" Marina muttered to herself as she just about dropped her mom's bag.

"What's that, dear?"

"Oh...nothing."

Savannah got her bag out of the back seat and they each carried a bag in.

"This place is gorgeous!" Her mom looked all around as she entered.

"Wow, he definitely has nice taste," Savannah agreed.

"He does, for sure," Marina leaned her mom's heavy suitcase up against the wall.

The bathroom door opened and Sawyer came out toweling his hair wearing only a white towel. It was wrapped snug and above the knee enough for his lower vastus muscles to show and of course riding low on his hips. Both Aliza and Savannah's jaws dropped.

"I'm guessing Savannah drove." He held onto his towel to ensure it stayed put.

Savannah giggled and nodded.

"I forgot your clothes, I'm so sorry." Marina wrinkled her nose and started to head in the direction of the laundry room but Sawyer said, "It's okay, babe. I'll go get them. Excuse me, ladies." He trekked dewy footprints through the living room on his way to the dryer. The ladies looked at Marina with huge eyes and raised brows. Marina just smiled and shrugged her shoulders.

Sawyer got dressed in the laundry room and came back out. His usual style jeans never disappointed. He finished pulling his blue t-shirt down over his torso as he entered the room, making those blue eyes light up.

"Oh, dear God." Aliza turned her face back over her shoulder and muttered to herself. He reached out a hand to shake Aliza's and when she took his hand he pulled her in for a hug.

"It's a pleasure to meet you finally."

"Oh! You too!" Aliza blushed.

"Savannah, nice to see you again." He gave her a hug as well.

"You're a hugger, huh?" She laughed. "It's nice to see you again too. Not just as my sister's boss this time!"

He smiled, flashing those perfect white teeth.

"Oh my," Aliza muttered but quickly realized he had heard her. "You have the most handsome smile."

"Thank you, ma'am. I see where Marina got her good looks. You're all beautiful ladies."

They shyly thanked him.

"While y'all are here this is considered y'all's house too, so don't be shy. Help yourselves to whatever. Make yourselves comfortable."

"Thank you, Sawyer, that's very kind. Marina, honey, I sure could use a glass of ice water."

"Sure, Mom. Come, I'll show you around, starting with the kitchen."

Savannah followed.

"You ladies have any more bags out in the car?" Sawyer hollered from the living room.

"We got them, Babe."

"Sorry I didn't come out to help."

"In a towel?" Marina smiled.

"Point taken." He went back into the bedroom.

Aliza leaned forward against the kitchen counter toward Marina and whispered, "Pictures don't do him justice!"

Savannah elbowed her mom's arm.

"There's nothin' like the real thing." Marina winked as she gave her mom a glass of water. "I'll show you the rest of the house."

"You should post a sign on the front door that says 'viewer discretion advised," Savannah joked.

"Yeah, he's not a big fan of clothes." Marina laughed. "And personally, I'm okay with that."

The ladies all laughed on their way down the hall.

"Anybody hungry? I actually hadn't planned dinner yet. I wasn't sure what y'all would want."

"No, not yet," Savannah said and Aliza agreed.

"Wanna go for a ride before dinner then?" Marina asked.

"Sure, why not?" Aliza took a drink of her water.

Marina showed them the rest of the house, including the master bed and bath once Sawyer came back out. The ladies came back through to the living room to get their shoes at the front door. Sawyer was sitting on the couch, slouched and his legs wide apart, his arm up on the couch arm.

"We're going to take the horses out if that's okay." Marina leaned over him for a kiss.

"Yeah, absolutely. I'll help y'all saddle up."

"Thanks, Babe." Marina grabbed her jacket as he slid on a pair of flip-flops and opened the door, letting the ladies out first.

"I can't wait for y'all to see the foal Sawyer got me for Christmas. She's absolutely perfect."

"I can't wait either. Your description of her over text sounded beautiful." Savanna pulled her hoodie on over her head.

"I didn't want to spoil the surprise by texting a picture."

"The young stallion Marina bought me is a sexy beast." Sawyer took her hand as they all walked to the barn.

"That he is." She smiled proudly.

Sawyer slid the big barn door open, letting the ladies enter first.

"Oh, wow!" Aliza looked around, admiring the impressive equine living quarters. "These horses sure have it made."

"Thanks, I appreciate that." Sawyer led Legend out and handed him off to Marina.

"Your home is just lovely, Sawyer. You have immaculate taste. It's like this whole place is out of a magazine," Aliza complimented as she petted Athena.

"Thank you, ma'am. Marina said the same thing. I designed it and my dad and I built most of it ourselves. I'm not a decorator so I thought a clean, simple look would do for now. Mom gave me tips. Marina is welcome to add her touch to it if she wants." He looked at Marina and smiled as he took a saddle off the rack. He flopped it onto Legend and Marina strapped and cinched it while he saddled Foxtrot.

"I think it's perfect the way it is." Marina smiled back.

Athena pawed at her stall door.

"Hold your horses." Sawyer grabbed her halter after tightening Foxtrot's saddle. Marina haltered him and handed him over to Savannah.

"Marina said you grew up having horses?" Sawyer asked Aliza. "I did."

"Athena's more for an experienced rider but she usually behaves herself just fine. She just gets a little moody around the boys."

"Don't we all?" Aliza joked.

Sawyer laughed and flopped Athena's saddle onto her. The girls all just watched him as he cinched the strap tight, his arm muscles flexing.

Aliza took Athena by the halter and followed the others out of the barn. Sawyer brushed his hands together and nodded forward toward the pasture. "The new additions are out there. Let me hang with these three while y'all go check 'em out."

Marina took her mom and sis out into the pasture. Dixie came galloping right over from under a big live oak tree with hanging moss, her mane and tail flowing like a slow-motion movie.

"Oh wow!" Savannah was astonished at the foal's beauty, "How old is she?"

"Maybe six or seven months, I think. A couple more months and she'll be ready to ride. I'm so excited. Sawyer's been working with her already with putting a blanket on her back and halter on just to get her used to it."

"She's huge for being that young," Aliza petted down Dixie's neck.

"She really is. She'll be a good fifteen hands. She's a Gypsy Vanner, so a small draft."

"I just love her showy long mane." Aliza brushed her fingers through it.

"I'm liking the hock 'n hoof fluff," Savannah mentioned.

"I know, she's already got a fun personality too." Marina hugged Dixie, who was sweet enough to appear to hug her back.

"That's spellbinding beauty, right there," Sawyer hollered from back at the gate.

"Definitely. You chose the perfect gift," Aliza agreed.

"Yeah, thanks, the horse is pretty too." He grinned a wide one.

"Is he always like that? Like...the compliments and flirting?" Savannah asked.

"He is. Has been since I met him." Marina smiled, looking at him.

"That's so sweet. Where's the other horse?" Aliza looked around for Sawyer's new horse.

"Actually, I don't know. Sawyer! Where is he?"

Sawyer whistled loudly and Tango came running from the field and around the outside of the pasture. He had jumped the fence.

"Ah, shit!" Sawyer went into the barn to fetch a halter and brought it out to put on him.

"Boy, what am I gonna do with you?" He looped the halter around the horse's ears. The ladies all walked up to the horse just outside of the gate, locking the gate behind them as they exited the pasture.

"He's a black beauty," Savannah touched Tango's face. He was tall; the tallest horse there but one of the youngest. They petted and admired Tango with his long wavy mane for a few minutes as Marina admired how handsome Sawyer looked next to him. So sexy.

"That's the second time he's jumped the fence that I know of.

I'll put him in the barn for now while you ladies ride. I don't want him to follow y'all."

"You could join us," Savannah offered.

"Nah, you ladies go on ahead and have some girl time. Thanks though."

"We'll be back in a bit. Love you." Marina gave him a kiss before loading up onto Legend. It was always so hard to just give him one little kiss without wanting more of him.

"Love you too. Be careful," he said, his hand on her thigh.

"I'm not the one riding Athena," she joked.

Her mom laughed and replied, "I've got this."

"Y'all think about dinner while you're out. I'll either cook or take y'all out."

"Deal." Marina clicked for Legend to start walking.

Once they got beyond the pasture and into the field, they rode next to each other. The sound of leather crinkling with each step.

"Maybe we should let him cook," Marina pondered.

"Why's that?" Savannah asked.

"One night I got home from shopping with Becka and he was cooking in the kitchen. He was wearing a chef's apron."

There was a pause, "Okay?" Savannah was waiting for her to finish the sentence.

"Just. The apron. Seriously bare assed."

"Oh, good lord!" Aliza could barely contain herself.

"He knows how to spice things up doesn't he?" Savannah laughed.

Marina told them about the spontaneous night in the woods on their drive home from dinner and their kitchen rendezvous.

"What does this man put in his food? Because I need some!" Savannah bantered. "It's always pertaining to food."

"Not always. There wasn't food when he was wood chopping." Marina went on to tell them about that stormy steamy day but not in specific detail of course, out of respect for her mother.

"You should see him in the pool." Marina acted as though she was melting off the horse.

"We need to come back for a summer visit," Savannah said. They all laughed.

Tails swatted as the ladies chatted.

"Yesterday we had a picnic out in the yard. We laid on our backs on the blanket looking up at the sky, watching the clouds morph into different shapes as they rolled by. Sometimes we sit on the tailgate and chat. We end up laying back looking at the stars."

"Oh, that's so sweet." Aliza was happy that her daughter was finally happy again, more so than she had ever been before.

"Ya know, I needed that wakeup call. I needed that push toward finally realizing I deserved better and I needed to focus on myself. I'm not sure it would've happened, not any time soon anyway, if Sawyer hadn't come along. He showed me how I ought to be treated and gave me something to look forward to everyday. Even as I was just working for him, not knowing if he'd be home that morning when I went to work. I found it disappointing when days would go by without getting a quick chance to see him. He helped me let go of my heaviness so I could rediscover myself again. I needed her back and I needed Sawyer to see the real me. He would listen without judgment to my drama. He would offer advice only if I asked for it. He was consoling; a good listener. He tried making me feel better when I was feeling down and gave me my confidence back. He made me believe in true love again, just when I was giving up on love altogether."

"You seem to reciprocate his positive energy. He's bringing back the Marina we used to know and I can't tell you how happy I am for you," Savannah added.

"Thanks, he really is. He's consistent, always loving, not just when he wants something. I didn't realize how manipulative the asshole was until being around Sawyer for a while. Sawyer makes me feel free. I don't aim to tame him either; there's no roping the wind." She paused. "He's actually gained a distinguished status in the community. I have no idea how I hadn't come across him before I did."

"Probably because you were rarely allowed to leave the house," Savannah pointed out.

"True…" Marina snickered and shrugged. "Sawyer doesn't go many places either. His office is right across from my favorite coffee shop even. Hey, tonight is Friday!"

"Yeah?" Aliza was wondering what her point was.

"We usually go to this little dive bar on Friday nights. Sawyer and his band play and they have the best brick oven pizza…y'all wanna go?"

"Mmm you know how I feel about bars," Aliza was unsure.

"This place can convince you to see at least this one differently. I work there some Saturdays too. Sawyer is friends with the owners, they let the band play there and Sawyer kindly helps them out with everything from handyman stuff to whatever. Anyways, I like the environment, the people, the regulars that I was shy toward at first. I was never a bar person either. Sawyer asks me to sing with him sometimes. He's got me to open up a bit in public, believe it or not. We have a good time there. What do y'all say?"

"Sure, why not?" Savannah agreed enthusiastically.

Aliza paused before answering, "Okay, we'll try it out."

"Y'all want pizza there?"

"Of course," Savannah answered quickly. They went on to talk about Aliza's nearing retirement and what she planned to do with having extra time on her hands. They also talked about Savannah's new job as a vet practice manager and how excited she was to finally have a workplace where she felt she belonged.

Sawyer was brushing Dixie's mane in the pasture when the ladies returned, "How was the ride?"

"Relaxing," Aliza answered as she brought Athena to a halt. She climbed down but twisted her ankle upon landing and let out an, "Ouch!"

"Mom, you okay?" Marina climbed down off of Legend to check on her. Savannah jumped down off of Foxtrot. All three horses stayed there; they knew not to take off. Sawyer came out the gate and closed it behind him.

He hustled over to Aliza, "What happened?"

"Oh, I just stepped down wrong, I think I twisted my ankle a little. I'm fine."

"Well, you shouldn't walk on it." Sawyer scooped her up and carried her to the house. Marina and Savannah stayed with the horses to take tack off them. Sawyer sat Aliza on the couch and got an ice pack out of the freezer and handed it to her. He put the footrest up on the couch so she could elevate her ankle.

"You're such a gentleman, a strong one too, but you don't have to make a fuss."

"Sure, I do."He smiled and stood at the front door. "You need anything before I go help the ladies?"

"No, Hun, I'm good now. Thank you."

"Of course." He went out to help and put the saddles back on the saddle racks and the girls hung up halters and led the horses to pasture.

"Is Mom okay?" Savannah asked Sawyer.

"Yeah, she just needs to elevate and ice it for a bit."

"We were hoping to go to Backcountry tonight. She might not be up for it now," Marina mentioned.

"Yeah? Pizza and music?" Sawyer asked.

"Yeah. You gonna play for us?" Savannah asked.

"Sure. I'll give the guys a holler."

"Yay!" Marina got excited and clapped her hands.

"But you're singing with me too. At least one song."

"Deal," Marina agreed.

After icing her ankle for a little while, Aliza and the girls all got around to go to the bar. Sawyer politely and patiently let the girls all get around in the master bed and bathroom before he went in to change clothes.

"You ladies look beautiful." They thanked him and moved to the living room. He intentionally passed Marina in the doorway to sneak in a kiss and a butt grab. They sat on the couch chatting while waiting for him. He didn't take long.

He'd put on sexy distressed bootcut jeans and a clean blue t-shirt, his black cowboy hat, and cologne. He came out with his guitar case in hand. His guitar was in the bedroom because he played and sang for Marina in bed the night before. All the ladies smiled when he came out.

"Oh my! That shirt sure brings out those eyes!" Aliza pointed out.

He smiled big and tipped his hat. "Thank you, ma'am," he replied in a deep voice.

Savannah squeezed Marina's leg and gave her a look.

"My man is looking smokin' hot!" Marina stood and grabbed her purse off the end-table before giving him a smooch.

"Not as hot as you, Baby." He pulled her in for another kiss. A good kiss this time.

She wore a pretty blue country sundress with little white flowers on it and ruffled shoulder straps with her white lace wedge sandals. The other ladies wore sundresses as well.

When they arrived at the bar, they were greeted in their usual celebratory way. Sawyer introduced the ladies to Bob and Gladys then to his band buddies. The ladies grabbed a table right in front of the stage and Bob made their drinks. Sawyer made sure they were set before joining the guys on stage, drink in one hand and guitar case in the other.

"I can't wait to hear this." Savannah smirked.

"He's really good. They're all talented musicians. Sawyer's so passionate about music and it shows," Marina convinced. "But he's really good at everything." She winked.

"He's the singer?" Aliza asked, swirling her straw around in her drink, cautious to try it since she wasn't a drinker.

"Yes, ma'am. His voice is smooth as butter too. "

"Oh, that's right, you told me over the phone he sings to you."

"He does. I'm telling y'all, this man is perfect in every way." Marina crossed one leg over the other and straightened her skirt.

"You don't have to try to convince anyone of that. It's pretty obvious," Savannah admitted. "His band buddies aren't bad looking either."

"Yeah, they're good guys. All spoken for actually."

Aliza took a cautious sip of her drink finally.

"Can you believe mom is drinking?" Marina asked Savannah.

"I know, right!" Savannah laughed.

"Haha, girls. You both know I won't drink the whole thing. I'd be dancing too if it weren't for my ankle."

"I don't ever get up to dance when he's here playing. I suppose I'm always just staring at his every move instead." Marina laughed. "Y'all ought to see the way he dances with me in the kitchen though." The ladies giggled.

Sawyer tapped the microphone and it got everyone's attention, "Hey, y'all we have some new ladies in the house tonight, Marina's sweet mama, Aliza, and her charming sister, Savannah. Let's give them a warm welcome." Everyone clapped. "Now let's play some music!" Sawyer tapped his heel a few times on the stage floor then they began to play. They began the evening with a slow number, sitting on the stool, *Silverado for Sale* by Morgan Wallen, with great acoustics.

A patron told him his woman left angry last night so he needed to hear something in particular and Sawyer loved the song the guy requested; *F150-50* by Morgan Wallen. The way Sawyer moved to the music, his knee bouncing to the beat, he played so smoothly, his voice tranquil.

The ladies soaked it all in.

He'd look at Marina often, those bright blue eyes matched her dress that evening and pierced straight to her heart. He nodded for her to come up between songs. He already had an extra stool waiting for her right beside him. Their legs touched as they shared the microphone that he sat closer to her. He wasn't ashamed of public affection, which seemed nice. They stared into each other's eyes for most of the song, *Another you, Another Me* by Brady Seals and Marina sang harmony. She then sang *Gunpowder and Lead* while standing and dedicated it to her ex, which Sawyer found hilarious. Everyone clapped for them as the song ended and he stood up off his stool and kissed her, his guitar still on his lap.

She stepped off the stage and joined the ladies and he watched her walk all the way back to the table then took a minute to take a drink.

"That was lovely! You two are wonderful together." Aliza hugged Marina.

"It was great!" Savannah cheered.

"Thanks! I have so much fun with him. He lets me sit in on and even join in their practice sessions too."

"You just light right up when he's in the same room. Even when you just talk about him," Aliza noticed.

"It's hard not to."

He then dedicated one to *his* ex, called *Hope That's True* by none other than Morgan Wallen. That was a fun one, pretty much pointing out all the ways his ex wasn't compatible with him.

The band played *Good Time* by Niko Moon, his shoulders moving to the beat, tapping his hip, and *Country Stuff* by Walker Hayes and Jake Owen; Jake sang the duet with Sawyer. They had the crowd laughing.

"This is great!" Savannah was enjoying the band, everyone was.

He propped his guitar up against the stool and stood, sipping his whiskey, which he then set on his stool with his black hat. He tousled his hair then cued Trev on keyboard and adjusted the microphone to a better standing height. The first few notes got Marina excited, she loved this song. *I Wrote the Book* began, and Marina was excited to see him perform it. It was one of her favorite songs.

He was amazing and would give the ladies a smoldering look. He had everyone on their feet. Both hands were on the horizontal microphone, his black wrist band barely sliding on his arm. His thighs were just about ripping through his jeans as he stood with his feet shoulder width apart. All the ladies in the joint were begging for more and he gave it to them. Toward the end of the song, he lifted his shirt and threw in an ab roll for the ladies while raking his hair then jerked his shirt back down. They all made some noise which made him laugh.

He ended with that as their finale, he couldn't think of a better way to end the night for the band. He put his guitar in the case and joined the ladies for pizza.

"You rocked that song! Your stage presence is spot on." Marina grabbed hold of his thigh. "My sexy beast."

He laughed and thanked her. "Thanks, ladies. I thought I'd stir things up a bit. I saved that song for tonight."

"Glad you did! You killed it!" Savannah laughed and Aliza nodded.

"Another round?" Gladys asked as she approached the table.

"Ladies?" Sawyer asked.

"I think we're good. I'll take a Pepsi though, please." Marina smiled as Gladys patted her shoulder.

"Same. Thanks," Sawyer smiled.

"You two go together like bread and peanut butter. Smooth and creamy," Aliza said.

He laughed. "I think so too." He put his arm around Marina and pulled her over onto his lap, "I'm glad y'all wanted to come up here tonight. I was hoping y'all would want to."

"It's part of getting to know you but we're having a great time," Aliza said. "I didn't realize how well my daughter could sing."

"She's been blessed in so many ways. I'm the luckiest man alive. My prayers were answered when she was sent to me." He kissed Marina on the lips, just a polite smooch, not to offend. "She's that song you can't get out of your head. The melody to my music. Her lyrics are addicting." He looked at her with such steamy allure.

They enjoyed the pizza and had a great evening, chatting and storytelling. They all went home tired and got settled in for bed.

CHAPTER 41

Fireworks

T he day was New Year's Eve and the barn note read "Sparks are gonna fly." This sparked her curiosity without a doubt.

Sawyer worked that day to wrap up a few projects so he could take off New Year's Day. He returned home late that afternoon and apologized for the time it took for him to complete his tasks. There was no need for him to apologize; she did the chores and housework which she was, of course, capable of doing on her own and did the evening chores before getting ready for dinner. He hadn't yet told her where they were going but did inform her it wasn't a lavish establishment. She had slipped into distressed skinny jeans and a white lace halter top. She packed a light-weight cardigan sweater in her purse. He stuck with jeans and a t-shirt.

"So where are we going?" she asked as he held up her jacket for her to put on.

"A little diner I used to go to often. It's been a while since I've stopped in there. Great food."

"Sounds great." She grabbed her purse off the end-table closest to the front door.

The diner was a silver airstream like in the movies. Cute and charming. It wasn't very busy inside upon arrival but quickly began to pick up. A second waitress left in a rush, leaving only one to wait on the incoming crowd. Sawyer and Marina had ordered in time. Their meal came out to them in a timely manner and was great but soon after, the waitress was completely overwhelmed. A late dinner rush came in after dark and the poor woman was almost in tears trying to keep up. Marina and Sawyer looked at each other, feeling pity for the waitress. Sawyer nodded his head at Marina. They stood up from their bar stools and took their own dishes to the kitchen. Sawyer grabbed a bus tub from the back and started bussing tables with a cloth hanging out of his back pocket to wipe tables with while Marina snatched a notepad and pen off the counter top and started taking orders. The waitress was confused and eventually made her way over to Marina.

"What are you doing?" She asked in a polite but nervous tone.

"We thought we'd help you out. I'm a server at a bar that he plays music at."

"Y'all don't need to do this."

"We can't just sit and watch you be in the weeds. We got you." Marina winked at her.

"Y'all are so sweet. Thank you."

All three of them hustled for a couple hours, they helped run food as well.

"I was planning to get out on time to watch the fireworks with my kids at the river but it doesn't look like that's going to happen," the waitress said, carrying dishes to the back.

"Go ahead and go," Sawyer told her.

"I can't just leave."

"Sure you can, we can hold the fort down til you come back."

Marina realized Sawyer's barn note that morning was referring to watching fireworks and he derailed their plans to help this woman out. It was so incredibly sweet. Such a generous man he was.

"Are you sure?"

"Absolutely. They'll be starting soon so you go on ahead."

"I'll be back real soon. I owe you two big time."

"Nah, just glad we could help out. Take your time."

"The world needs more folks like y'all." She took her apron off, tossed it on the counter, and darted out the door.

"You're such a good man, Sawyer. I love you." Marina pecked his scruffy cheek as she passed him in the kitchen doorway.

The place cleared out pretty quickly once the fireworks started. They lit up the sky through the glass windows and Sawyer flopped the cloth on the nearest table, taking Marina by the hand as they stepped out the front door. He held her against his chest, his arms around her and her hands on his arms in front of her as they faced the decorated night sky. The firework display was beautiful.

"I'm glad we still got to see the fireworks. I had packed a blanket in the truck for us to go to the park after dinner to sit and watch." He sounded a bit disappointed.

"Oh, that's ok. That does sound lovely, but we helped someone out and still got to watch the fireworks together, so I'm happy."

"Thank you for being understanding. Although, I'm sure we were both thinking of jumping up to help. Happy New Year, Baby." He kissed her when she looked up at him.

"You're such a considerate man. I'm proud to call you mine. Happy New Year." She turned around and kissed him passionately, the grand finale exploding in the sky behind her as the clock struck midnight. They watched the end of the display then returned inside to run the dishes. They put all the tips they earned into a tip jar near the register, and it wasn't a small amount when all was said and done. Sawyer threw a generous tip in as well after covering their bill. The waitress returned to find the dishes running and the dining room cleaned. She hugged them both, thanking them for their kindness.

They left quickly before she could notice the tip jar.

"I enjoyed doing this with you tonight." She held his hand in the truck.

"Me too. The fireworks were nice but I've got my own fire-cracker right here next to me."

She laughed and nodded.

"What do ya say we go to the park and use that blanket in the back of the truck to light our own fireworks?" He grinned a devilish grin that she just couldn't say no to.

CHAPTER 42

Permission

S awyer wasn't in bed when Marina woke up. She got dressed and poured coffee, slipped on her cowgirl boots, and walked out to the barn, coffee mug in her hand.

He wasn't in the barn and Foxtrot was missing. She found a barn note on the counter that read, "Went for a ride. Won't be long. Needed to do some thinking".

She suddenly felt a cloud of worry pass over her. What would he need to think about? It sounded serious. Was it about them as a couple? If not, she wanted him to know he could talk to her about anything.

She finished her coffee but chores had already been done. She groomed Dixie, Tango, and Legend but Athena wasn't feeling it; she wanted to be left alone with her hay. A couple days from now would be Valentine's Day so she made herself presentable to go into town to shop for something for Sawyer. Perhaps that's what he needed time to think about.

In town, she went to three little shops in search of the perfect gift. She actually found two and decided to get them both. She stopped into the coffee shop to get two "fancy coffees" to-go.

She got home and hid his gifts then set their coffees on the kitchen counter, hoping the ice in them wouldn't melt before he got home. She saw him from the kitchen window, galloping through the field on his way home. She went outside, watching him ride so gracefully as she approached the fence closest to the barn. She leaned her backside against the fence, the sun beaming on her as he slowed Foxtrot to a trot then to a walk as he approached, metal tinging and leather squeaking.

"Mornin', my love." He tipped his hat and dismounted.

"Morning. There's an iced coffee waiting for you in the kitchen."

"Perfect. You go into town already?"

"I did."

"Okay, let me turn him out and I'll be right in." He gave her a kiss and walked Foxtrot to the barn doors to remove the tack.

She went back up to the house and started drinking her coffee.

He came in through the garage door and kicked his boots off then washed his hands at the kitchen sink. He was drying them with the towel when he noticed an index card poking out of the cabinet above. He squinted, reading the text on it. He pulled it out and it was addressed to Marina from Caroline; it was his mom's secret cookie recipe. He looked over at her but she was swirling her coffee, not paying attention, so he quickly tucked it back into the cabinet crack.

"You have a nice ride?"

"I did, thanks. I'm sorry I didn't wait for you to get up. I was kind of on a mission"

"You don't have to apologize, Babe. You can ride whenever you want. You can also talk to me whenever about anything, I hope you know that."

"I know, Baby, I appreciate it. This I couldn't talk to you about though. I was out there doin' some thinkin', actually I needed to ask up above an important question and...you'll never believe this..."

"What?" She leaned her elbows onto the counter, coffee between her hands. He took a drink of his and wiped the condensation from his hands onto his jeans.

"I found another rose bush out there."

"Really? Where?"

"Near the old train tracks behind the property."

"That's crazy. You think they're originating from there?"

"No, I don't. It was the only one out there." He smiled, then gave her a kiss from across the counter. "Thanks for the fancy coffee."

"You're welcome. I hope you got the answer you were looking for."

"I do believe I did." He handed her a single long-stem red rose he pulled from the back of his jeans, which had been hidden under his shirt. Emotions poured through her as she hugged him tightly.

CHAPTER 43

V-Day

There was a note for Marina on Valentine's morning. It sat upon her silk pillow when she awoke. It read, "I love you. Will you be my Valentine?" She thought it was absolutely precious.

A smile commenced upon her face as she rolled over toward him. He was laying on his side, facing her, in just his boxer briefs, propped up on his elbow.

"Good morning," he whispered.

"Good morning, and yes, I will be your Valentine. I wouldn't be anyone else's."

"I was hoping you'd say yes." He wrapped his arm around her and pulled her closer to him. She loved his sense of humor.

"I love you, Sawyer."

"I love you too, Baby." He leaned to her, his lips pressed against hers.

"What are we doing today?" she asked.

"What do you want to do today?"

"Well, I bought you a little something. It's nothing much but when I saw it I just had to get it for you." She sat up and faced him.

"You didn't have to do that."

"I know. I wanted to." She reached over into the nightstand and pulled out a box.

"I should be giving you your gift first." He sat up.

"Why?"

"It's the gentlemanly thing to do."

"Oh stop. Just stay here and let me give you yours first."

"If that's what you want, I'll respect that."

She handed him a small wooden box and he opened it. Inside was a wooden guitar-shaped box which held guitar pics inside. They had writing on them which reminded her of candy hearts. One read "I pick you" another said "Love" and the other said "my heartbeat" with a music note. The outside of the guitar box had his name and a music note custom engraved on it. On the bottom of the box it read "Love, your Marina".

He smiled, "I love this."

"You do?"

"Yes, I do. This is perfect. Very thoughtful." He held her face as he kissed her lovingly.

"It's not too sappy?"

"Never. In fact..." He went to another room then came back in quickly. He handed her a small wrapped gift then sat back down on the bed. She opened the gift excitedly, pulling off the red and silver metallic paper. It was a square wooden box, slightly larger than the shaped one she'd given him. There were two fitted puzzle pieces on top, one with each of their names. Inside the box, on top of the shredded red gift paper were a dozen wooden hearts with words on them.

She looked surprised reading them one-by-one. "This is a sex game!"

He laughed at her reaction. "It is!"

"Well, that's definitely not sappy!" She laughed. "Although, the adorable box and hearts look to be. It's just...the words."

"I can't wait to try it out."

"We actually had similar ideas with the wooden boxes, so that's adorable."

"Oh, I do actually have another gift for you too but it'll have to wait 'til we do chores." He got up off the bed.

"Same." She smiled a sneaky smile.

"Did you really?" He stopped in the doorway.

"I did."

"Well, then you deserve breakfast in bed. Don't move, I'll bring it to you when it's ready."

He slapped the doorframe with his hand and darted for the kitchen. Again, making her laugh. He came back only a few seconds later with a white box.

"What's that?" she asked.

"Breakfast."

"Breakfast?" She sat up against the headboard.

"The bakery was actually open this morning."

"What? How long have you been up? I hope you didn't go in just your underwear." She framed one side of her face with her hand.

"Over an hour. Luckily, you slept 'til I got back and stripped my clothes back off." He sat next to her and opened the box.

"Oh, my goodness." She sniggered as she took a donut out of the box. He was so endearing.

He took a huge bite of donut and crumbs fell onto the bed. "Whoops. Oh well, I'll have to wash the sheets later anyways."

"Why?" She knew it wasn't laundry day.

"It'll be necessary after we play that sex game." He swallowed as she laughed then he kissed her neck with a moan like he was trying to bite her. "By the way, you stole something of mine," he whispered in her ear.

Her laughter fell silent. "I'm sorry?"

"You heard me." He looked her in the eyes, inches from her face.

She was taken aback. "Sawyer, I'd never steal from you!" She felt appalled and almost offended briefly.

"It's okay. I don't want it back." He took a bite of donut.

"What did I steal from you?" She wore a serious look upon her growingly upset face, her brows narrowed.

He calmly put his hand on the side of her neck and tilted his head to the side. "My heart."

"Oh, Sawyer." Relief washed through her.

He flashed his pretty white teeth after he swallowed and kissed her.

"I didn't mean to freak you out." He tried to fight his laughter but failed.

"Well, you did."

"Oh, Baby..." He wrapped his arms around her, her face against his chest. He stroked her honey hair. She could listen to his heart beat all day.

"How about this? How about we get dressed and do chores, exchange the other gifts, then we'll shower and I'll take you to lunch. We can do whatever you want to do 'til I take you to dinner, then I have dessert plans for this evening."

"Dessert plans?"

"Yeah, it's my last surprise for Valentine's Day."

"You've really thought this all out."

"I have, for a while now."

"Is that what you needed ride time to think about?"

"Partially."

"Okay, so lunch and dinner out, huh?"

"My Valentine doesn't need to be cookin' on Valentine's Day."

"I've never had such a fuss thrown over me for Valentine's Day before."

"Oh, Baby, you haven't seen anything yet." His feet hit the floor and he stood, holding a hand out for her to take hold of.

Out in the barn there was a new mountain bike for Marina parked in the walkway in front of the stalls.

"Seriously?" She practically skipped toward it.

"I noticed you didn't have one when you moved all your stuff in."

"I love it! Can we ride today?"

"Absolutely!"

"Thank you!" She planted a kiss on his lips then ran off. She brought her gift for him out from the feed room where she had hid it. It was a hammock.

"This is awesome! I've been thinking about getting one."

"I thought we could hang it out by the pool or patio."

"We'll do that today. Wanna lay in it with me?"

"Of course, there's a stand for it too."

"Perfect. This is great, Baby. Thank you."

"I can't wait to lay with you in it." She bear-hugged him and lifted his hat slightly to kiss him as she lifted to her toes.

They went to lunch at the little café they enjoy in town. She talked him into ordering extra from the café to take home for dinner so they could stay in the rest of the day. When they returned home, they went for that bike ride, down then back up the red clay road, with the light breeze in their hair and the smiles upon their faces. It just doesn't get better than that. They set up the hammock out in the grass out back, near the pool.

"Think it's too much in the sun right here?" he asked.

"Maybe we should move it under the edge of the trees," she suggested.

"I like that idea." He had no trouble moving the entire thing himself. There were a few trees planted in a line separating the back yard from the pastures. The horses could still be seen through the trees but it felt more private. The sweet tea olives and Japanese magnolias in the tree line were blooming amongst the azalea bushes and a big live oak with sphagnum hanging moss. It was the only one on the property besides one in the last pasture and the ones down the trail. He got in the hammock and held it still for her to sit on then laid back and put his feet up. She laid close next to him, her head on his bicep.

He reached a foot down to rock them since the breeze wasn't strong enough. White clouds rolled over through the blue sky as they relaxed. Birds chirped and wings flapped. Leaves rustled softly above them.

"Spring is in the air early this year." He took in all the blooms.

"It is! Everything is blooming so beautifully. I love when the trees start turning bright green."

"Me too." He looked over at her and smiled. "I'm so deeply in love with you." He touched the side of her face delicately.

"I couldn't be more in love."

Their fingers locked together.

"Ya know, not long ago I saw you as, I guess sort of like Japanese pottery."

"What?" She was confused at his comment.

"You were once broken but not shattered, still fragile, but were put back together, gold mended and something that was already beautiful, became more beautiful and priceless."

"Well, you mended me, Sawyer. You turned me into something better. You bring the magic out in me because you have magic in your soul."

Here he thought he'd be brilliant with his poetry but she had that knack too.

"You loved me in my broken pieces while I was putting myself back together, you gave me the strength to save myself but I didn't have to."

"Well, it's my job to light fire to your darkness and calm your stormy seas."

"I'm so glad you did."

He wrapped both arms around her, holding her tight.

Darkness fell upon the evening. It was getting cooler outside, the sky was clear, and the stars were bright. He told Marina he could bring the horses in himself and she should stay inside. While she was showering, he rushed through chores out at the barn, along with doing a little extra. She saw it as the perfect opportunity to doll herself up a bit and put on lingerie; a black and red corset set. She tied a black silk bathrobe on over it and she darkened her eyes a bit with a smokey flare. She had time to put a few curls in her hair and slipped black heels on.

He texted her saying he only needed twenty minutes before she could come out to the barn so she waited twenty before walking out. The barn was lit up outside with white lights that he never took down after Christmas for this exact reason. She entered the barn and her jaw dropped. He had strung white lights up all over in the barn rafters and the loft. The strumming of an acoustic guitar began, the notes drifting through the barn as the smile upon her face grew.

She removed her heels and carried them up the ladder to the loft. He was sitting on straw bales that he'd pushed together and covered with a quilted blanket, strumming his guitar while singing to her. The song was unfamiliar. She listened to the words as she slid her heels on and sat next to him quietly, keeping her robe closed tightly. She faced him at the edge of the makeshift straw-built bed, becoming lost in those blue eyes as he sang a song that he wrote just for her.

"I'm Proud to Call You Mine"
Verse 1:
My world stopped spinning,
When I saw your smiling face.
My heart raced at a galloping pace,
That hot summer day.
You stole my heart right from the start.
You're all I've ever dreamed of.
I knew you had my heart.
Verse 2:
I fell hard and fast for you.
You lit a fire within me,
That keeps on burning.
Watching clouds roll by,
Weathering storms with you.
You're the sunshine to my storm,

After those sparks flew.
Chorus:
I want you by my side,
The wind in our hair,
The smell of rain on the dirt road,
As tires stir dust in the air.
When darkness begins to fall,
The stars and moon know it all.
Dancin' with you all night,
I'm proud to call you mine.
Verse 3:
I love to hold you in my arms,
Holding you against me tight.
Making love to you all night,
All seems right with the world.
Yeah, we were meant to be.
You make me feel alive,
Aww with the way you look at me.
Chorus:
I want you by my side,
The wind in our hair,
The smell of rain on the dirt road,
As tires stir dust in the air.
When darkness begins to fall,
The stars and moon know it all.
Dancin' with you all night,
I'm proud to call you mine.
Outro:
With you, I've found my forever,
And I'll love you more each day.
You're the rhythm to my rhyme,
And my heart will never stray.

Next to the bale bed there was a small wooden folding stand holding champagne and chocolate covered strawberries. There were potted hyacinths of all color varieties sitting around the straw bales. Those were her favorite and they smelled amazing.

"Sawyer, this is amazing. I love the song, it's beautiful." She was completely taken by surprise.

He propped his guitar against the bales and took her by both hands. "Now that I have you up here, I guess I'm a little nervous."

"Why?" She could feel her hands getting clammy and acquired a slight nervous tremble.

"Because I had a whole speech planned and memorized but don't remember much of it now. I'm going to just say what I need to say from the heart."

"It will be perfect." She encouraged nervously with restless butterflies in her stomach.

He looked deep into her eyes and took a deep breath.

"From the very first moment we met, there was an undeniable attraction. Physical, of course, but the more I got to know you the more I wanted to take care of your wild and carefree heart. I wanted to see inside your loyal soul. You were and have been all I think about since that summer day. I don't know why it took us so long to find each other, but the universe made sure it happened. I couldn't be more thankful. You have shown me a love that I didn't know existed. I can't imagine my life without you. I know whatever life throws at us will be overcome with grace and companionship. You're everything I've been searching for. I had given up on true love at one point but here you came, showing me what life and love is really about. Love is easy with you. It comes naturally. I've always known you were the one. We didn't meet by accident, you know. This was written in the stars for us. We fit perfectly together in every way. You're the melody to my music after all. From the bottom of my heart and with my entire soul, I love you more than life itself." He nodded over at a barn note that was perfectly positioned next to the filled champagne glasses after he had just served his gold heart to her on a silver platter.

She looked over and picked up the note as he knelt onto one knee. She flipped it open slowly, exhaling. It read "Marina, love... will you marry me?"

The note fell to the floor amongst stray straw stalks as she looked back at him. He pulled a ring from his back pocket. It was stunning and the perfect size for her dainty fingers; the diamond not small but not uncomfortably large. He knew she didn't like showy jewelry.

"Yes! Yes, Sawyer, absolutely I'll marry you!"

He stood. "Yeah? You'll marry me? He slipped her ring onto her finger.

"Yes!"

"Yee Haw!" he shouted as he embraced her, lifting her feet off the floor as he spun her around. Her feet had barely touched the floor again before he kissed her passionately.

"Oh, Sawyer..." She had no other words.

He wiped a happy tear from her cheek, careful not to smudge her makeup.

"The words were perfect. I feel the exact same about you. I've waited my entire life for you. You're absolutely extraordinary."

"We make one hell of a couple, don't we?"

"We sure do. We always will."

They sat on the blanket atop of the straw bales and enjoyed the strawberries and champagne, feeding them to one another.

"So, let's see this surprise you have for me." He set his flute down and turned to her, his elbows on his knees with his hands folded together. She placed hers down and stood before him. She wasn't sure why she felt as nervous as she did on that wild stormy day, maybe the pressure of a ring being placed on her finger. She untied her robe and slid it down off her shoulders, letting it fall to the floor. His lips parted and he was speechless.

Her breasts were pushed high and almost busting out of the top, the corset framing her shape. He motioned for her to spin around, his eyes widening at the sight of her black thong. Her round bottom he found irresistible.

"My God, you're stunning." He stood and stared into her eyes and trailed a single finger down her cleavage. "Miss Marina, I do believe you should crawl up onto that blanket."

She did exactly that. She crawled onto the blanket then rolled over onto her back, her shoulders against a stack of throw pillows as he kicked off his shoes. He slowly took her heels off then lifted his t-shirt and held the front of it in his teeth, his abs and one peck exposed, before he unbuckled his belt and slowly pulled it out of the loops of his jeans. He snapped it at the ground like a whip then tossed it to the side.

He removed his shirt and threw it to the floor with force. He was driving her crazy. Next came unbuttoning his jeans, then those came off. In just his black boxer briefs, he leaned one knee on the blanket, then the other. He got on all fours and slowly crawled up to her, stopping half way up her legs. She slid down the pillow a little toward him, her heart racing.

He pulled her thong down with his teeth, it slid off one foot that she held up, then the other. He dropped it onto the blanket next to them. She felt her spine tingle, loving that he did that to her. He kissed the top of her foot, leading slow kisses up her leg, his hand and lips going up her thigh. Her fingers ran through his hair and she held her breath as he reached her groin.

As she arched her back, he kissed her lower stomach. Without removing her corset, his kisses skipped up to her overflowing breasts, his hand running up her thigh onto her hip. She touched his face ever so softly; he barely felt her touch. He looked up at her with mystery and lust in his eyes as though he saw her soul.

He inched up further and melted his lips into hers, kissing her like an animal. The taste of chocolate upon his tongue, her hands on his back, pulling him down closer to her, feeling down his sides and hips then harshly grabbing his rear, it all served to heighten and overwhelm her already-fraying senses.

Her thumbs dug under the edge of his briefs at the waist, pulling them down over his muscular glutes. He took them off the rest of the way. Her legs against his hips, her toes rubbing his calves. He kissed from her neck down her chest and reached behind her, untying her corset. He pulled it off and let it fall to the floor, exposing her breasts to the cool air. Her curled hair flowed above her on the pillows.

"I want you completely bare beneath me," he whispered warm breath upon her neck. She melted, complying with his domination. His body felt so warm against hers. Tender caresses and silky-smooth kisses. He knew the secrets she desired without her having to tell him, he found them on his own. Perhaps they shared the same passionate secrets.

The aroma of hay would never awaken her senses the same way after this.

His thumb passed over her lips and down her chin as he bowed up over her. Any qualms she previously had about her body were whisked away by his sincere touch. They took the night slowly, letting their lust for one another linger. He was a balance of gentleman and savage, everything to be desired. She was enjoying the beauty of being in the present. She wanted it to last forever, to be in his warm, strong arms, held tight, forever.

He made her feel safe and alive.

They let their bodies do the talking that night.

They lie there together, wrapped in each other's arms and warmth under a blanket in the loft...until the morning light.

Acknowledgments

No matter what chaos and stress gets thrown at my life, I know I have writing and reading to bring me hope and joy. Once the inspiration is sparked, the rest of the writing flows. I wish to share my way of thinking and creativity with readers so they can find hope from the fictitious reality they may become lost in. Thank you, readers!

I would like to thank my closest friends for being an inspiration for the supporting characters in this series. I'd also like to thank one of those close friends, who is a fellow author, for her process guidance in getting my first novel over the finish line.

A shout-out to the musical artists that are mentioned in this series, you're much appreciated. The song titles mentioned are personal favorites as well. I encourage readers to listen to the songs mentioned within the book to gain a better feel for the need to mention them.

Thank you to Russian model Konstantin Kamynin for being the perfect vision of "Sawyer".

Much Love, Marina Skye

About the Author

Marina Skye is from the country in a small southern town. She's a beach girl at heart but loves being around horses and volunteers with a local equine rescue center. As a romantic, this is where her inspiration for the book series bloomed. When she isn't writing, she's working one of several jobs and raising her two boys. She hopes her sons will grow to be respectful gentlemen just like the character in this series.

 facebook.com/MarinaSkyeNovels

 instagram.com/Marina_Skye23

www.ingramcontent.com/pod-product-compliance
Lightning Source LLC
Chambersburg PA
CBHW030524120726
47904CB00005B/1617